SPY

Spy

America's First Double Agent,
Dr. Edward Bancroft

An Historical Novel by

ARTHUR MULLIN

Capra Press / 1987

To Leinie,
with love.

⧼⧽

Copyright ©1987 by Arthur Mullin.
ALL RIGHTS RESERVED.
PRINTED IN THE UNITED STATES OF AMERICA.

Cover design by Mary Schlesinger.
Jacket photograph of author by Hal Boucher.
Design and typography by Jim Cook
SANTA BARBARA, CALIFORNIA

LIBRARY OF CONGRESS CATALOGING IN PUBLICATION DATA
Mullin, Arthur, 1917
Spy: America's first double agent.
1. Bancroft, Edward, 1744-1821—Fiction.
2. United States—History—Revolution, 1775-1783—Fiction.
I. Title.
PS3563.U3984S6   1987   813'.54   87-11695

ISBN 0-88496-268-7

Published by
CAPRA PRESS
Post Office Box 2068
Santa Barbara, California 93120

Spy

CHAPTER I

L ATE ONE EVENING in May, 1776, a light appeared at the intersection of Tower Street and St. Martin's Lane in London. It was a strange sight at such a late hour, and as it moved along with a bobbing motion, the rats nosing and fighting in the refuse-strewn streets retreated to the black alleyways until it passed. At this hour and until dawn, London belonged to the rats, to the scavengers and street thieves, all of them enemies to light.

The brightness moved up the street, a torch carried by a ragged boy guiding the bearers of a sedan chair past the refuse piles in the street. The boy might have been eight or sixteen—a slum child, starved and shrunken, with dark, matted hair that dangled far below his rag of a jacket. Walking beside the leading bearer of the chair, he peered first in the direction they were moving, then, swinging his torch around in a hissing arc, he glanced back at the darkness that stalked close behind the chair, and finally, furtively, he peered into each black alleyway, as if in each one he expected to discover the danger his torch was to guard against.

In spite of his nervousness, he could not give his entire attention to his duties. He was much too interested in the rats. He had a pocketful of stones, and whenever his torch forced the reluctant withdrawal of one of the fat, grey rodents half as big as a hare, he took a stone from his pocket and hurled it. When he heard a soft thump and a squeak, he grinned and bared his broken teeth

Several times the leading bearer warned the boy, ordering him to stay closer to the chair, but the urchin could not resist menacing the creatures by brandishing his torch at them. Finally, the sight of one of them, huge and ponderous, proved too great a temptation. The boy sped for the alleyway toward which his prey was headed.

Just as he reached it and began to lower his torch to burn the rat's hide, the leading bearer stumbled on some refuse, cursed, and cried for light; as the boy turned in alarmed obedience, a hand reached out and seized his torch; a club smashed down on his head, stretching him senseless on the cobblestones.

The band of thieves struck, but not before the bearers had seen the felling of their torch urchin and had slipped out of their harness to prepare for the coming attack. They were strong and Irish and had weathered such attacks before; as a further precaution, one of them begain bellowing for the watch at the top of his voice.

They seized the poles that supported the chair and already were wielding them like oversized quarterstaves.

Although stones and bottles and pieces of wood hurtled against the chair and the bearers, they stood fast, thrusting out at their shadowy opponents with such vigor and skill that several of the thieves already lay moaning in the street.

The passenger in the sedan chair emerged at this moment. He had been roused from a pleasant nap when the bearers tumbled the chair to the street; through the window he had watched the struggle until he saw the forward bearer knocked to his knees by a blow from behind. With a single push, he raised the top of the chair and threw open the door. He charged headlong into the back of the man who had felled the bearer. The man struck the cobblestones hard and lay motionless. The passenger turned to look back at the other bearer and ducked as a large stick whistled over his head. He groped for a weapon; seizing a heavy club which had been dropped by the man he had felled, he flailed about him with such fury that momentarily he forced the attackers back.

The band of thieves regrouped and slowly closed in around this unexpected menace. The bearers watched in astonishment and noticed that the darkness offered no difficulty to their passenger who seemed to see as well as if it had been midday. When one of the thieves tried to leap in on him beneath the arc of his club, he lowered his club and caught the man's head with the full force of his blow. There was a sound like a melon smashed onto a rock. Blood spurted from the man's mouth and ears even before his head struck the stones of the street. Another of the thieves slipped in the blood of his fallen companion and cried out in pain as his leg twisted beneath him.

At the sight of this second mishap, the thieves halted their attack and darted back into the shadows as silently as they had come.

"Four to one," the passenger called out with a laugh of triumph, "and our loss but half a man. Let's find him."

The passenger and the leading bearer hurried to the other side of the street. The torchboy lay where he had fallen. The huge Irish bearer picked him up gently and carried him back to the chair.

"Put him inside," the passenger directed. "I'll walk alongside. Stop at the first tavern we find open. I want to take a look at him."

They had not traveled more than two or three blocks before they came to a brightly lighted tavern. The proprietor began to protest when one bearer carried the boy inside, but seeing the look on the passenger's face and hearing the terse commands that followed one upon the other, he obediently brought more candles, hot water and clean rags. Soon the boy's head was washed and covered with a tight, neat bandage.

"Gor, sir," exclaimed the bearer, "you couldn't ha' done that better if ye were a surgeon."

"Which I am," the passenger said with a smile. "He'll be all right. I daresay he's had many a crack like this and never before a bandage to go with it."

The bearer picked up the urchin and following the directions of the tall man placed him carefully inside the chair. The passenger handed him some money.

"I've only a few streets to go. Here's what I owe you and a bit more for the boy."

"Thank'ee, your lordship. If I may say it, your lordship's a fine man in a fight."

"You may say it," the passenger said, smiling. "It's a compliment I like to hear. Good night."

"Good night, sir."

The bearers stood together, watching their passenger walk away into the darkness. As they slipped into their harness again, the leading bearer called back over his shoulder:

"A rum one, eh, Gesh?"

"Aye. Glad he was with us and not agin' us."

Several minutes later, the passenger knocked loudly at the door of a large house on Montagu Street. As he waited, he dabbed at his forehead with his kerchief. The door opened at last, and a servant peered out over the guard-chain.

"What—" the man gasped in astonishment. "Why, you're all blood, sir."

"A small cut, that's all, Richards. The foolish man who gave it to me will be carved up tomorrow by the apprentice surgeons."

He stepped inside, and as Richards closed the door again and bolted it carefully, Dr. Edward Bancroft walked upstairs and knocked on a door beneath which light was showing.

As he entered the room, the light of the candles on his face made him glow with an animal vitality. His recent exertions had heightened his complexion, and the drops of blood that had fallen onto his jacket and his ruffles glowed like rubies in shadow.

"Good evening, Olivia," he said with a nod.

His wife was sitting at a small table, a deck of cards arranged like waiting soldiers for a new game of patience. Patience was her only pastime. Edward knew that she would play on until the hours just before dawn. Then, feeling herself beginning to nod, she would hurriedly climb into bed and fall asleep. They had shared a bedroom during the first year of their marriage, but after that, Edward had decided that they would sleep in separate rooms. Several times during that first year, he had awakened to find her bent over her table, going on with her interminable games of patience.

"Edward," she gasped, her long fingers white against her cheek, "whatever has happened? You look as if—"

"Nothing to worry about, my dear. It looks worse than it is."

As she stared at him, her eyes gradually narrowed with suspicion; her lips became a thin line of accusation.

"A gambling house brawl, I expect," she said with a sniff, turning back to her game.

"No," he replied coldly, "it was not that. My chair was attacked by a band of street thieves. There was quite a battle. Our torchboy was knocked senseless by one of the brutes."

Olivia kept her fingers tightly clenched. Now, as Edward explained what had happened, tears suddenly filled her eyes and her fingers opened and closed spasmodically.

"I'm sorry I spoke as I did," she remarked.

"It's not your fault, my dear; after all, your father and your brothers led you to expect only the worst from men. At least you're never unprepared. However, I did not come in to discuss tonight's excitement. I am going to your bankers tomorrow. This is an excellent time for me to buy a larger interest in Sam Wharton's firm. I wanted you to know about it, so you will not be confused by such a large withdrawal."

"I see. Do it, by all means, if you think it is wise."

"Good night, my dear," Edward said as he rose to his feet.

Olivia stared after him, and when he had closed the door, she let her head rest on her clasped hands, while soundlessly, tears coursed down her cheeks.

The next morning, after visiting Olivia's bankers, Edward hurried to Sam Wharton's office. As soon as he had settled himself comfortably, he took a paper from his pocket and dropped it on Sam's desk.

"Here's a draft for three thousand more, Sam," he announced with a smile. "We should find some good shares for this."

Wharton picked up the paper with polite fingers and incredulous eyes.

"Three thousand? Damnation, Edward, we'll run it up to twenty."

"So far, Sam, you haven't done too well by me, considering I'm your partner."

"I know. I can't be lucky every time, Edward. Everyone was caught in that last mess. Old Gilderstein lost everything, and you know how clever he was supposed to be. He's not even in business anymore—the sheriff's men took him to court this morning. At least that hasn't happened to us."

"Gilderstein's trouble was that he never knew anyone except jobbers. When he did get in trouble, there was no one he could call on to help him. What's the newest speculation?"

"Massachusetts shares. They're to be sold tomorrow. Then next week, they're bringing out shares for another Ohio Company."

Edward looked at his friend in surprise. He shook his head slowly and then reached for the paper, which Sam moved away just in time.

"Ohio Company?" Edward asked incredulously. "Again? After what the court told you when the first one collapsed?"

"This is different, Edward. A completely new corporation. New officers and new capital. The man we have to lead the shareholders is a close friend of Germaine's. There won't be any investigation of this one."

Edward lit his pipe before answering Sam's last remark.

"Won't you ever learn, Sam? Suppose we buy into this company and something goes wrong with it? Who will be culled from the list of shareholders and called by the examiners to testify? None other than the notorious Sam Wharton, whose name is still spit out with rage by the people who were defrauded in the original Ohio Company. This time things might not go so easily for you. Walpole might not feel able to give you his support again. If he shouldn't, you'd be spending a long time in Newgate after the judge finished with you."

"Notorious is a harsh word, Edward," Sam murmured ruefully, "and Newgate is a horrible one."

Then, passing his hand swiftly across his face, his eyes twinkled and he smiled broadly at Edward, as if, in the gesture itself, he had found comfort and a solution to his difficulties.

"I've already considered the possibility of an investigation. I'm not personally buying any of these new shares. As you say, if my name appeared, I might be investigated and unjustly thrown in jail, just because I'm Sam Wharton. I thought we might buy the shares in . . . well . . . in your name."

"My name? Oh, no. No, you don't, Sam," Edward declared. "I'm not going to be mixed up in anything like that. The minute you start selling our shares, they'll all be in my name and everyone at the 'Change will know that. If people start dumping after our sales, I'll get the blame for the disaster. Remember, Sam, I'm not one of the unsuspecting public."

"All right," Sam sighed, "if you don't want the shares in your name, and if they can't be in mine, whose will they be in? We should buy them, and we'll have to put them in someone's name."

"What about someone in your office? Someone not known to your competitors."

"Hmm." Wharton scratched his cheek and pondered.

While Sam was musing, Edward walked over to the window and stared out into the street.

It was a lovely May morning, but he knew it would soon be uncomfortably hot in the city. He felt suddenly pleased when he remembered that he had accepted Thomas Walpole's invitation to spend the weekend at Carshalton, the Walpole estate. It was a pleasant drive out of the city, for the road to Carshalton was not as rough as some.

An hour or two and he would be in the peaceful quiet of the countryside. London always seemed more crowded during the hot weather. People grew noisier and more irritable; their faces and their necks and their clothes were damp with perspiration from the coming of spring until the end of summer.

"I know!" The voice of his partner startled him.

Edward turned around and stared at Sam.

"It's simple, Edward. Peabody, that little man in the office. He's been with me a long time. Many people know his face, but I never knew one who could remember his name. We'll buy them in his name. He's not the type you'd think of as an investor."

"It might work, Sam," Edward nodded. "I should think he'd be remembered by one of Meyer's men who's been here for interest payments, but, as you say, they'd probably not suspect him of being an investor."

"Of course they won't. It's a perfect solution."

"Very well, use him. By the way, I must have a return on this money fairly soon. My debts are beginning to mount up."

"You should give up vingt-et-un and try cockfighting, Edward. It doesn't cost as much, and it's more sport."

"For you, perhaps, but I don't fancy it myself. Gambling may be more expensive, but it's more exciting, too. The other night there was a single spot between me and a thousand pounds, and that didn't show up until the last card had been turned."

"Too bad, too bad," Wharton sympathized. "Sometimes, Edward, I thank God that I never acquired this lust for gambling. So many people suffer from it today. They play for such tremendous stakes—that's what frightens me. Whole estates, whole fortunes, rents for the next fifty years—all gambled away on a single card. I couldn't stand playing for stakes like that. My nerves would give way."

"I don't think so. Your experience on the 'Change would be invaluable to you," Edward laughed. "I wager that the more you played, the steadier your nerves would become. I find mine do. Nothing bothers me now."

"I'm glad it's done you some good," Wharton chuckled, rising to his feet and slipping Edward's draft into his desk, "though it seems a most expensive method of improving one's character. I'll invest this as soon as I can and try to have some return on it for you before too long. We have to move more slowly now; the government's still watching us. It's not like the days before the Ohio Company when we could buy and sell and not care who was looking."

"I'll stop in and see you after next week, when I return from the country."

"You're going to Carlshalton?"

"Yes."

"Give my respects to Mr. Walpole. You might ask him if he knows how close a check they're keeping on me. That would give us some indication of how far we can tempt fate."

That afternoon Edward left for Carshalton. After Olivia had bidden him an expressionless farewell from her patience table, Edward climbed into the coach and settled himself as comfortably as he could against the cushions.

Throngs of hawkers and beggars filled the streets, and tradesmen's carts kept blocking the passage of the coach. He could hear his coachman's voice as it cursed and thundered at the laggards who slowed their progress.

Suddenly he noticed a girl's face in the crowd. She had a basket of apples on her arm and stood at the side of the street, selling them to the passersby. As his coach drew alongside her, she looked up, straight into his eyes. Just then, a peddler's cart rattled its way between them.

Ordering the coachman to halt, Edward opened the door of the coach and called out: "You there, girl. How much for your apples?"

She moved next to the coach, but merely stared at him and gave no answer. Edward reddened when he heard the coachman repeat his question.

"A crown enough?" Edward asked brusquely.

"That's more than enough, m'lord," she answered in a soft, surprised voice.

As he reached down to give her the coin, she held the basket up between her hands. The artlessly perfect line of her figure stopped his breath. His original impulse fortified, he smiled and held back the door.

"Get in. I'll take you wherever you live and pay for the apples as well."

She laughed, then sprang into the coach with the ease of a boy. The coachman cracked his whip over the backs of the horses and they started forward. Straightening her dress with suddenly nervous fingers, she sat tense and erect in the seat, as if determined to quell any doubt that a lady was riding past.

Edward was amused as he watched her swift attempt at composure. The faded calico dress she wore was shorter than fashion decreed, but infinitely more attractive.

"What is your name?"

"Ellen, Ellen Vaughn," she answered quietly. "What is m'lord's name?"

Her question was so unexpected that Edward started, then laughed.

"My name is Edward Bancroft," he replied. "I meant what I said to you— that I would take you wherever you lived—but perhaps you'd better tell me where that is, in case we are going in the wrong direction."

"I wondered when you would ask that," she smiled. "We are going in the wrong direction. I live above the Golden Anchor, on Vesey Street, near the Serpentine, but you needn't take me there. You've paid me so generously for my apples that I can go back by chair."

"You'd better not do that. Chairmen are weak-minded creatures and extremely susceptible to pretty girls. No telling if you'd get home or not."

"Don't worry about that, m'lord. I know how to take care of men. I have to, living over a tavern."

"I suppose you do," Edward nodded. Leaning back in the seat, he called up the address to the coachman. When he gazed back at the girl again, she was staring out over the crowds in the street. Her long black hair shone in the sunlight.

"Do you like London?" he asked.

"Very much, m'lord, though, of course, it's difficult at times. Since my father was put in prison, I've been alone, and I've had to learn to cope. 'Out of this nettle, danger,' you know."

Edward turned and stared at the girl. "What did you say?"

"I said, 'Out of this nettle, danger,' m'lord."

"Can you finish that?"

"Of course, m'lord. 'We pluck this flower, safety.' "

"Well, I'm damned. Forgive my curiosity, but why was your father put in prison?"

"Debts, m'lord. He believed a vicar was entitled to live as comfortably as his parishioners. So we lived very comfortably, for quite a few years, until his debts became too great. That's when he was put in debtors' prison. He died there last year. He was a good man, my father. He raised me after my mother died and taught me himself, everything he could, like Shakespeare and Greek and even a little Hebrew."

"But why are you selling apples? You could certainly find a post with a family."

"I know, m'lord. I suppose I could. But I'm young, and living like this is much more exciting than being a servant to spoiled children."

Edward laughed and reached down for an apple, which he began to eat. "Damme, you're quite a girl. You're pretty ... "

He paused, and as his eyes moved over her, taking in her face, her body, her breasts so clearly outlined by the thin dress, she blushed and stared out of the coach.

"No, you're not pretty, you're beautiful. You're bright, and you like a challenge, just as I do. How much of London have you seen?"

"Quite a bit, m'lord. I haven't seen all of it, but there's lots I've seen that people like yourself wouldn't dream existed. Bedlam, for instance, with all those poor, mad people screaming their heads off day and night. And the thieves' auctions at Shoreditch. Sometimes I go as far away as Vauxhall; I like to watch the masquerades there."

"I shouldn't think you'd risk the robbers and the thieves."

"I'm as ugly a woman as you can imagine when I go there," she laughed. "I'm certain your lordship wouldn't stop your carriage for me then. I wear a dirty, floppy rag of a dress and blacken my teeth. I must look quite disgusting. No one has ever spoken to me, let alone bothered me. Once I met a highwayman on the way there, but he wasn't like most of them. Fine speaking and courteous he was, too. He gave me a shilling and said, 'Don't be afraid, Grandam. Take this shilling for yourself. It's just come from the purse of a pretty lady. She was on her way to Vauxhall too, but now you'll have the admission price and she won't.' No, m'lord, I don't have any trouble—I'm much too ugly."

Edward smiled at the girl's ingenuity. He felt even more grateful to the happy impulse which had led him to offer her a ride home.

"There will be a masquerade at Vauxhall next Tuesday," he said. "How would you like to go with me as the pretty girl you are, rather than that crone you have pretended to be?"

Her eyes sparkled for a moment. The sudden quickening of her breath and the soft flush on her cheeks told him that he had struck a vulnerable spot. Then, a curtain of doubt dulled her eyes. She looked at him warily.

"I've nothing to wear, m'lord. I should like to go, but if I went with you, I'd not be properly dressed. I wouldn't like that—I'd feel uncomfortable. All the ladies would look down their noses at me, and at you, for having brought a girl who didn't have a proper dress to wear."

"Don't worry about the dress," Edward exclaimed. "I'll take care of that. The important thing is, would you like to come?"

"Oh, yes, m'lord. My father used to tell me about the gay times there. I've dreamed of going to Vauxhall; I've even dreamed of going as a lady, too, though not often. I'd love to go with you, m'Lord."

"Fine. Then it's settled," Edward said. "I'll have the dress sent around to you before Tuesday." He reached in his wallet and pulled out some notes. "Meanwhile, this will buy whatever else you may need."

Just then the coach stopped. Looking outside, Edward saw the signboard of the Golden Anchor. He climbed out of the coach and helped the girl to the street.

"I must hurry on, but I shall be back on Tuesday. I'll have the dress sent before then; if it doesn't fit, take it back to the dressmaker and have her fix it for you. I shall call for you at seven."

"I shall be waiting, m'lord," she promised. "I hope you'll be pleased."

"I shall be, I know. You'll be so pretty you'll make all the women uneasy. Good-bye, Ellen."

"Good-bye, m'lord."

She turned and ran up the steps beside the tavern, pausing at the top to wave to him.

Before leaving for the country, Edward ordered the coachman to stop at Mrs. Whipple's.

Mrs. Whipple had been clothing the fashionable world for so many years that no request from a customer was too strange for her to fulfill. After Edward had given her his somewhat indefinite ideas about size and fabrics, she smiled, pulled several bolts of fabrics from the shelves behind her, and sent them to the workrooms in the rear of the shop.

"She'll need more than just the dresses," Edward suggested.

"Never mind about that, Dr. Bancroft," Mrs. Whipple laughed. "I know exactly what she'll need, and I'll send one of my girls over to her to see that everything is perfect."

"I'm sure it will be," Edward said with a smile. "Send the bill to my club."

He nodded good-bye and strode out to his coach. "To Carshalton," he called.

The private road that led to Carshalton was one of the most beautiful in England. The house had been built centuries before, and the forests and woods had been maintained in their original state, with only special plantings ordered by the master of the house wherever he felt them necessary. As a result, once the well-traveled public road had been left behind, the long drive to the house was a superb example of nature's munificence and man's care.

Elm and hickory and oak towered in the air, their trunks thick with age, their lower branches trimmed just high enough for the coaches to pass beneath. Animals abounded in the woods; twice on the way to the main house,

Edward's coach surprised deer crossing the road. Pheasants and partridge promised excellent shooting in the months to come.

Carshalton had been built in the 1500s. It had been remodeled several times since then, but the later members of the family had always respected the wishes of the first Sir Robert Walpole who had built the original house; they had left the general plan as he had conceived it.

There was a long, three-storied central section, with a wing on each side. Behind the house were the formal gardens, the pride of every Walpole lady for the past two hundred years. The gardeners at Carshalton were of the same family that had first laid out the trees and shrubs, and their skill was proverbial in the county.

As his coach halted, Edward noted with pleasure how perfectly displayed the house was this May afternoon. He had arrived just as the sun was casting long, red-gold rays against the ivied walls and through the tall mullioned windows; Carshalton glowed with welcome.

As Edward descended from the carriage, Thomas Walpole's man appeared at his side and gathered up his luggage.

"Good afternoon, Dr. Bancroft. Mr. Walpole is in the library. He asks that you join him there when you are ready, sir."

"Fine, Grimms. I'll clean up a bit first. Where am I to stay?"

"In the east wing, sir. Your usual room. Please follow me."

Bancroft finished his bath quickly and walked downstairs. As he entered the library, he saw Thomas Walpole standing at one of the windows, the sunlight mantling him with a soft, golden radiance. He was looking out over the park, watching the deer as they browsed and wandered along the fence.

"Hello, Thomas," Edward called, striding across the polished floor.

Walpole turned and peered toward the door. "Oh, Edward. Welcome. Delighted to see you."

He moved toward Bancroft, his hand outstretched in greeting.

Thomas Walpole was a short man with a tendency toward fat. His neck was already creeping down over his collar, and the lace at his throat could no longer conceal the jowls which grew heavier month by month. Although his mother frequently told him that a little discreet exercise might lessen his weight, he detested exercise of any kind, even walking; the flabby bulk of his fingers attested to his success in avoiding it.

His eyes were a deep brown, almost black, and set so deeply that his thick eyebrows arched over them like balconies. He walked clumsily, shifting his bulk from one foot to the other with a little hopping motion which made him look absurd and deformed. It was this characteristic which had earned him the sobriquet of the Toad on the Exchange.

In complete contrast to his rather forbidding appearance was his smile. It was sudden and bright and so unexpected that because of it people dismissed their first opinion of him, so completely were they deceived by the honesty and good humor his smile seemed to typify. Their generous impulse was unfortunate; Thomas had long since learned to combine the charm of his smile with the lessons taught him at the gaming table to forge an equivocal career as a member of the Exchange.

He had been a great disappointment to his mother. He was the last of a long line of famous statesmen, yet he exhibited none of the ability in government or politics which had so distinguished his family. Although he was regularly elected to Parliament as the representative for Carshalton and the district which surrounded it, he found political activity prosaic and uninteresting.

Until he was twenty-five, Walpole had spent most of his time at the gaming tables, winning occasionally, but losing more often, until his debts reached such proportions that his mother forbade him to play any longer. This he had resented bitterly, as he felt it the right and duty of the eldest son to live and act as he pleased, to gamble if he wished, without hindrance from the female members of his family. His mother, however, was not merely a female member of the household. She had complete control of the family money, and Thomas soon realized the stupidity of contesting her in such an unequal struggle.

Rather than make an enemy of her son by denying him what seemed his only interest, Mrs. Walpole had bought a partnership for him in one of the oldest firms of the Royal Exchange. She admitted to herself that stock and share speculation was a form of gambling that interested even her. Thomas's wide circle of acquaintances, his invaluable connections in the government, and his predisposition toward gambling on almost any chance made him a spectacular member of the Exchange, if not always its most successful one.

Soon after Edward arrived in London, he had been introduced to Walpole by Paul Wentworth, whose plantation Edward had managed in Surinam. He and Thomas had become close friends. Edward had seen in him the answer to his need for a sponsor in London society, since Wentworth was so often absent on the Continent. In Edward, with his knowledge of America, where he had been born, and South America where he had worked for several years, Walpole discerned a man who might prove invaluable to him, a man whose character was so similar to his own that he sensed it could be most rewarding to make him his friend. Since the night they had been introduced, they had a wary respect for each other, even though each realized that the other was completely selfish and would not hesitate to sacrifice his friend if the stakes were high enough.

The combination of the two men had been unusually successful. Bancroft had an uncanny ability of discovering news from the Colonies before it became known to anyone else, while Walpole, through his connections in Parliament and government offices, frequently knew of coming shifts in policy weeks before they officially occurred.

In their Exchange operations, Edward had learned far better than Walpole the merit of taking a quick profit and selling out before any sudden depreciation. Walpole could be extremely, even foolishly, stubborn about such matters, as he well demonstrated in the affair of the Walpole Grant.

He had formed a corporation, assisted by Edward, and had obtained the king's charter on lands along the Ohio River, in the North American Colonies. The scheme had promised huge success; the corporation's shares climbed higher and higher, and all seemed to augur enormous profits when suddenly the members of the corporation were called up before the king's ministers. Explanations were demanded concerning the overissuance of shares, and when these proved unsatisfactory, the charter was revoked.

Almost a month before this happened, Edward had resigned his office in the corporation and had sold all his shares. For this, Walpole had never forgiven him, because Edward's sale of his shares left the greatest number in Walpole's name, and it was he whom the ministers questioned. Only the eminence of his family name had saved him from a public trial. Shortly after, Edward had given up his partnership in Walpole's firm to become a partner of Sam Wharton.

More concerned with his personal pocket than his family pride, Thomas Walpole had gradually renewed his friendship with Edward and recently had bought a small interest in Wharton's firm, as if to indicate that he had forgiven Edward's desertion in the Walpole Grant affair. Together, they discussed every new colonial enterprise, most of which originated in London, and decided how much of the firm's money it would be wise to risk.

"I was just looking out at the park," Walpole commented as they walked back to the tall window. "The deer are feeding so close to the house that you feel they'd come in if you opened the window. It's such a beautiful day that, of all people, I am tempted to take a short walk. Would you care to go with me?"

"I'd be delighted. London was hot and sticky today."

"Good. Mother will not be down for another hour, so we should have time enough."

They walked outside, down the long steps, and started across the lawn. The park was indeed beautiful. The colors of every growing thing seemed miraculously softened by the twilight. Only the occasional call of a bird, or the rustle of a deer grazing disturbed the quiet. Their feet made a soft, whispering sound as they walked over the clipped grass and they were both too content to speak for a long time.

"This reminds me a little of Westfield, that village in the Colonies where I was born," Edward said at last. "From what I still remember, there were only a few houses—rough, crude, frontier houses—but all of them surrounded by unbelievably tall trees. As a little boy, I found it much like church, standing or lying down under those trees, but how much better, to my young mind, than the church I had to attend twice each Sunday."

"I daresay you wouldn't find as much peace in the Colonies now as you knew then."

"I suppose not. What is the latest news in Parliament?"

"The Americans are sending a man to France shortly. A Mr. Deane. He's to try to arrange a treaty between France and the Colonies. Apparently, the leaders in Philadelphia realize that they must have outside support quickly or their rebellion will be snuffed out before it is even underway."

"I've heard that they are desperately short of materiel. In fact, they are short of everything they need for fighting—guns, cannon, uniforms, ships, even soldiers," Edward concluded with a grimace.

"They don't lack for talk. We receive information on all their meetings in Philadelphia. I have never read so many bad speeches. Everyone seems determined to have his say before the English doctor arrives and pronounces the obvious diagnosis: that the revolution is stillborn."

"I don't quite understand why they should choose this man Deane. Why didn't they send someone like Franklin?"

"He's too busy in Philadelphia," Walpole laughed, "or so we are told. I believe he's a member of every committee they have appointed and chairman of most of them, too."

"No word that I've had from the Colonies has mentioned Deane. Who is he?"

"A merchant, from Connecticut. A contributor, too. He has a good deal of money, and he has been so liberal with it that they probably felt they had to give him something to do. Franklin must have told them that the work in Paris would be simple. No one knows better than he how much Vergennes hates us and how much he would do to separate our Colonies from us."

"With a foreign minister like Vergennes," Edward said with a smile, "the work in Paris shouldn't be difficult, even for a novice. Do you think Vergennes will be able to convince Spain that she should help the Colonies?"

"I don't think so, and no one I've talked with, whose opinion I respect, thinks so either. Spain is waiting for France to fight us. She doesn't want to commit herself, which is a wise decision. If we should go to war, she would be in an excellent position, especially if it proved, as it probably would, a long and costly war. She could regain some of the power she has lost, if both England and France were too engaged to hinder her."

When the two returned to the house, they were greeted by an edict from Mrs. Walpole, who was just walking toward the drawing room. "Come in here, you two. You're late, and I want tea and conversation with someone besides myself."

Mrs. Walpole was almost eighty. She was small, wrinkled, and bitter-tongued, as Edward well knew through his long acquaintance with her. The only concession she made to her age was the cane which she was now rapping imperiously on the floor as she led the way to the drawing room and tea. This heavy, gold-handled cane had been presented to her husband as a gift from the villagers. Before her husband died, she had been fond of saying that it was perhaps the only family possession which had not been exacted as tribute or extorted by fraud. Although she was proud of the name she bore, she was about that, as about all things, realistic.

The old lady settled herself behind an enormous tea service and beckoned regally to Edward, whom she placed on her left, close to her good ear. Two mouselike servant girls, in crisp, starched uniforms, nervously awaited the commands of their unpredictable mistress.

"I'm sorry we are late, Mother," Walpole apologized, "but it was so lovely outside that we decided to take a walk."

"Since you made that enormous physical effort, Thomas, I forgive you," the old lady replied. Then, leaning toward Edward, she said, "Tell me about London, Dr. Bancroft."

"It's still the same hot, dirty place," he began.

Mrs. Walpole made a gesture of impatience with the biscuit in her hand, and he hurried on.

"I had one experience, however, a few nights ago that might interest you. I was returning from Rathebone's after a masquerade."

"And a little gambling?" Mrs. Walpole asked acidly.

"Just a little," he admitted with a smile. "It was a very dark night, and my coach was suddenly halted on a lonely stretch of road. A highwayman flung open the door and demanded my money. Before I could move or say a word, several hands reached out from the darkness and seized the fellow. When I looked out, I saw a half-dozen men busily beating the robber into insensibility. I watched until they had finished and then their leader came over to me. He bowed and said, 'Sir, I hope you haven't been too inconvenienced by this rogue. Rathebone's wishes you a safe journey.' "

"Extraordinary!" Thomas exclaimed.

Mrs. Walpole puffed her cheeks out and reached for another biscuit.

"It was. It so amazed me that I queried the leader. He informed me that most of the resorts now maintain such squads of men who patrol the road back to London. If trouble arises, as it did with me, they catch the robber, beat him to death, and sell his body to the surgeons the next morning. Robberies had become so frequent that they were obliged to furnish some sort of protection to their patrons."

Mrs. Walpole nodded furiously at Edward's last remark and then shooed the gaping servant girls out of the room.

"Shocking, shocking," she exclaimed after they had disappeared, "but what else can we expect with a German on our throne?"

"Now, Mother," Thomas protested, "don't start on His Majesty again. Edward has already heard your views on that subject."

"Humph," Mrs. Walpole snorted, squinting at her son.

"If both of you—and more like you—would listen to what I say, we wouldn't be forced to endure that creature squatting on our throne. What's happened to the English, I ask? Aren't we good enough to have a king of our own? Do we have to borrow these dreadful Germans to be our monarchs? It's no wonder our colonists no longer respect us."

Since neither Thomas nor Edward would add fuel to her fury by making any comment, she subsided and contented herself by chuntering about the weakening character of Englishmen.

AFTER A RELAXING DAY of reading and leisurely conversation, Edward and Thomas went the next evening to Lord Camden's for supper. Their host's estate was not a long drive from Carshalton, but Thomas started early; first, because he was not one to be late for supper, and second, because he knew the wisdom of remaining in the good graces of Lord Camden.

Before his elevation to the peerage, Lord Camden had been an eminent jurist. He had been lord chancellor of England and presently occupied an important place in the meetings which plotted the future course of the kingdom.

Edward had never met Camden, so on the way to Camden Hall, Walpole endeavoured to give him his impression of that famous man.

"You will find him, Edward, a charming and gracious host. He's a little deaf, but it is the deafness sometimes cultivated by men in high positions. He's not at all deaf on the hunt, or at least he wasn't last year. He will discuss politics, religion, or what you will, but never one word concerning the Colonies. I must warn you, in that connection, never to mention the governing of the Colonies to him. He believes Lord North's policy has been eminently fair and just.

"I have not told him that you are the same man who once wrote a book defending certain of the actions of the colonists.Otherwise, you would not be accompanying me tonight. He knows you, so far as I can tell, to be a doctor and the author of an important book on the history and medicine of Surinam. He also knows you as a friend of mine and a colonist who, though born in the Colonies, prefers England to the birthplace that is his by chance. I believe you will like the man, if you have an opportunity to talk with him. I might say that he is especially interested in Dr. Franklin, whom he regards as a genius without a country.

"And then there is Lady Camden, a voluble, but otherwise charming lady. She knows you as Olivia's husband. She was well acquainted with the Trents when they lived near here. Only the other day she said to me that she was afraid Olivia bore an unfortunate resemblance to her late mother, for whom, she added, life had been nothing but one long, tired feeling."

As if embarassed to have blundered into personal affairs which Edward never discussed with him, Walpole fell silent and said nothing further until they arrived at Camden Hall.

Alighting from their coach, the men went inside the great mansion and were received by their host and hostess. They soon found many acquaintances among the score of people who had been invited for supper.

Edward found himself seated between Lady Downes and the Marchioness of Ridgely. Lady Downes he had never met before, and while she was talking to the dinner partner on her right, Edward found an opportunity to observe her carefully. He had heard of her frequently in London; she was a woman who attracted gossip as easily as she attracted men. Noticing the animated fashion in which she abandoned herself, conversationally, to her other dinner partner, and dwelling with undisputed pleasure on the reverse side of her well-molded charms, Edward sighed a little in envy of Lord Downes.

"I understand, Dr. Bancroft," Lady Downes said, turning in her chair, "that you are an American and that you have lived for several years in the savage wilderness of Surinam."

"The last is true, Lady Downes," Edward replied swiftly, "but as for the first, I am an Englishman, who has spent a small part of his life in the Colonies."

"I see. But weren't you born in the Colonies?"

"Yes, in Massachusetts. However, I have lived in England long enough, I believe, to be regarded as a loyal subject of His Majesty."

"I remember hearing that you worked at one time for the famous Dr. Franklin, before he returned to the Colonies. Certainly that was not work performed for His Majesty?"

"No, it was not, at least not directly. I had hoped, through my efforts, to persuade Dr. Franklin that the Colonies would be wiser to settle their differences with their mother country in an amicable way, without resorting to the extremity of rebellion. I am not yet without hope, for I believe that Dr. Franklin feels as I do. As much as any Englishman, he desires a speedy and peaceful settlement."

"I have met Dr. Franklin; my father knew him well and admired him for his genius," Lady Downes admitted. "He also admired him, as I do, for being one of the most innocent-appearing men in the world, while at the same time, one of the world's wiliest diplomats. But tell me, Doctor, do you think our difficulties with the Colonies will continue?"

"I do not know the answer to that, Lady Downes. I wish I did. I can only say that England will not be censured by history for the incendiarism of a few Colonial rioters."

While Edward was talking with Lady Downes, he suddenly became conscious of an angry, red face which kept appearing and reappearing over the lady's shoulder.

Almost at the same moment that he realized he was monopolizing the charming lady's attention, he recognized the angry face. It belonged to Baron Quarles, an influential member of the Privy Council and a man whose friendship and assistance he might someday need.

He decided it would be wise to forgo further pleasure in his dinner partner's conversation and during the next few moments was so noncommittal in his replies that finally Lady Downes turned to her right almost in despair.

To Edward's relief, he saw an expression of sudden friendliness on the baron's face. He was also relieved that he would not have to commit himself further in a discussion of the Colonies. Lady Downes was too close to the highest officials in the government to risk having an incautious remark of his repeated in the wrong ears.

Late that night, Edward and Walpole returned to Carshalton and stopped in the library for a final glass of port. Although Edward had to make an early start for London the next morning, he had noticed that Thomas was eager to discuss something with him.

"I heard a rumor tonight that should interest both of us," Walpole began, as soon as they were comfortably settled. "Mr. Silas Deane has just arrived in Paris. He is alone, cannot speak a word of French, and according to reports received today by the foreign ministry, he has credits amounting to more than two million livres."

"Very interesting," Edward agreed, "but I don't quite see the connection with us."

"As soon as I heard this, I had the idea," Walpole continued, "that you would be the ideal person to help Mr. Deane, this merchant turned diplomat, out of all the difficulties in which he is already mired."

"I help him?" Edward asked in astonishment. "Whatever for?"

"Because he has two million livres, Edward. That is the best reason of all, although there are others. Look—you are an American, since you were born in the Colonies; you are so well known to Franklin that you have his confidence; you speak French; you are acquainted with many influential people in the British government. What more could poor Deane be praying for at this moment?"

"It does have possibilities," Edward said, smiling. "I suppose you want me to leave for France at once, before someone else seizes the chance to help him."

"Yes, the sooner the better. After you have met Deane and surveyed the situation there, write me. When you have worked your way into his confidence, you will be bound to hear valuable information. This information will have considerable influence on the rise or fall of shares on the Exchange. That is the real reason for your going to France. The moment you obtain anything important, let Sam Wharton know by special courier. It makes no difference what the news is, whether it's favorable to us or to the Colonies. All we are interested in doing is selling our shares before they fall or buying Colonial shares before they rise. A disaster, or the outcome of a major battle— with either of those, you could buy your own Carshalton."

Edward felt excitement rise in him as Walpole unfolded his plan. The past few years had lacked that sense of adventure which had so colored his early life. He was bored with his existence in London and as weary of Olivia's card games as he was of her complaints. This adventurous journey to France beckoned him with an irresistible attraction.

"I think we understand the situation," Walpole said, rising to his feet. "I don't want to keep you up too late, in view of your early departure tomorrow. Keep in close touch, Edward, and don't forget to use a special courier for really important news. If we don't have the information before anyone else, we might as well not have it at all."

Soon after they took leave of each other, Edward was stretched out in bed, his hands clasped behind his head, his thoughts as far away as Paris. The sudden joy he had felt in the library had not deserted him. It kept him awake, surging through him and quickening his pulse, so that it was nearly dawn before he fell asleep.

CHAPTER II

A S SOON AS HE RETURNED home the next morning, Edward went into his study. There was a packet of mail on his desk which he picked up at once. Flicking through the letters, he came upon one which puzzled him. Sitting down at his desk, he broke open the seals and spread the letter out before him. As he looked at the signature, his eyes narrowed and then all at once, he burst out laughing. Settling down in his chair, a broad smile on his face, he began to read:

Most Honored Sir,

I have been advised by certain members of the Convention presently meeting in Philadelphia that I should arrange to see you in order to discuss certain matters of interest to you and of importance to the welfare of my country. Dr. Franklin has urged upon me the wisdom of a speedy meeting with you, and it is for that purpose that I now write.

I should be grateful if you could arrange to visit me in Paris at your earliest convenience, since I am, for obvious reasons, unable to journey to London.

Trusting that you will look favorably upon this request, I am,

Dear Sir, Your Most Humble Servant,
Silas Deane

Hotel du Grand Villars
June 1, 1776

Edward sat at his desk for more than an hour, puzzling out not only the import of Deane's letter, but also the curious timing of its arrival, only a day after he and Walpole had been discussing the man.

Superstition was a matter that he had always left to women and to gullible creatures like the natives in Surinam. He did not believe in magic or spells or incantations and regarded them of a piece with witches and goblins. Still, he knew what people called luck or chance had profoundly influenced the lives and careers of some of his friends, and he admitted a healthy respect for that phenomenon called coincidence. Sometimes, it didn't seem to be coincidence at all, but rather the working out of a larger plan, the design and import of which its participants only vaguely comprehended.

The more he considered Deane's letter, the more perplexed Edward became. Now there were two aspects to the situation, where before there had been only one.

Walpole had wanted him to go to Deane, get information from him, and send it back to England; Deane wanted him to come to Paris, very probably to give him information about England which Deane could then send back to America.

As he sat in his study, considering every aspect of this new situation, Edward perceived, faintly at first, and then as clearly as if written on the desk in front of him, the logical course to follow. He grew excited when he saw it, for he sensed that his life was going to change completely. Before this, there had always been an impelling necessity to use friends and acquaintances to further his career. Now, all that was finished. Through his own cleverness, he would be able to obtain not only wealth, but also that position of influence he deserved.

He realized that spying was a dangerous occupation. Many others had tried it before him, but he doubted whether any of them had been given such a perfect combination of circumstances. He would be able to spy for the British upon the Americans, and for the Americans upon the British, and have enthusiastic support in the high councils of both sides.

With sudden resolve, he pulled a large brass tray toward him. Setting fire to one edge of the letter, he watched it burn until only ashes were left. Then, carefully, he crushed the ashes until the tray contained only a fine gray powder.

It seemed to Edward as he looked at the powder that he had now set himself completely free. He was alone now, quite alone. His own talent and his own brain would be his only trustworthy resources in the dangerous times to come.

If he succeeded, he would be powerful, rich, and highly respected. If he failed—there was no need to think of failure.

Pushing back the tray, Edward took out a sheet of paper and wrote to Walpole:

> My dear Thomas,
>> Going soon to Paris to see Mr. Deane. I am confident that he will be grateful for my offer of assistance.
>> I shall communicate with you immediately upon my return. Meanwhile, the monies which we discussed should be deposited with Wharton.
>
> —Edward

At seven o'clock on Tuesday evening, Edward's coach drew up before the door of the Golden Anchor. A completely transformed Ellen stepped into the coach, and as Edward turned to look at her on the seat beside him, he felt himself already repaid for the expense of the dress which Mrs. Whipple had made.

Ellen's dress was of heavy, rustling gold brocade, the color of which accentuated the freshness of her complexion and emphasized the blackness of her long hair. It was cut low in front and displayed a tantalizing amount of bosom. The dress molded her figure as far down as the waist, where it began to sweep out in graceful flares.

She was wearing long gloves, and as Edward studied her, he noticed that she was holding a small, black silk mask. He sensed with what desperation she was awaiting his judgment of her appearance: the mask trembled in her hands like a leaf in the breeze. He reached out and took one of her hands in his.

"You look almost too lovely to risk in that mob at Vauxhall," he said.

There was a sparkle in her eyes as she turned toward him, but she replied swiftly, as if to conceal her emotion. "You are too kind, m'lord. I'm certain I'll cut a sorry figure, compared to the other ladies."

"Nonsense. I wager you will have the other ladies fussing with their faces in public. A higher compliment than that you could not be paid."

"I hope you're right, m'lord. I do want to make you proud of me. I can't believe that I'm really going to Vauxhall."

"Look outside," Edward laughed. "Perhaps that will convince you."

They had approached close to the gardens, and as Ellen turned to look out the window, the coach stopped.

The road was blocked by a great congestion of people and carriages. Many were waiting beside the entrance to the gardens, watching the quality as they arrived in their coaches.

Mr. Geoffrey, the proprietor of Vauxhall Gardens, stood in front of this group of spectators, stretching out his arms from time to time and pushing the people back from the street so that carriages could make their way inside. He bowed to the occupants of each carriage and swept his hat to the ground whenever a particularly favored patron arrived. He had already acquired three or four imitators, as he did every night, boys from the streets of London who so perfectly imitated his every gesture and word that the guests of Vauxhall regarded them as a kind of Greek chorus behind the wide figure of the proprietor.

Mr. Geoffrey was well acquainted with Edward, so when he and Ellen passed through the gate, the proprietor made a deep bow. Ellen laughed and pressed her hands against her breast. Her color was high, and she looked so eager and excited that Edward wondered, as he watched her, how she would react to so much excitement in a single night.

They descended from the coach and went inside the pavilion, mingling with the gay, noisy crowd that had come to enjoy the masquerade. As Edward's gaze passed over the throng of people, he nodded to those acquaintances he recognized, and frowned at the men he knew were nodding to him only because he was escorting a remarkably beautiful woman.

Ellen had adjusted her mask, and it only served to intensify her attractiveness by adding an air of mystery to her youthful grace. She had recovered from the anxiety she had felt in the coach and was now gazing at the crowd with all the aplomb of a duchess.

The music began again, and as Edward started to lead Ellen to the dance floor, she whispered in desperation, "But I can't, m'lord. I don't know any polite dances."

"Nonsense, Ellen," he whispered back to her, as he bowed low in a figure of the minuet, "all dances are polite if they're danced by beautiful people. Watch the other ladies and do what they do."

Before the evening was much further advanced, Ellen had watched and learned enough to feel confident in the dance. She had fine coordination, in addition to her natural grace, and Edward soon found himself besieged by unspoken requests from the eyes of his friends who were watching him.

He asked her if she was tired, and when she denied it hotly, he decided to present her to an acquaintance whose sole ability he knew to be dancing. He wanted to look in on the gaming, but it would not be wise to chance Ellen to one of his more predatory friends. Also, he had a strong desire to see how she looked when dancing with another man.

Edward had decided to choose the duke of Lauregais, whom he had seen earlier and whom he trusted completely. Henri de Lauregais was well known to London society. A foppish little Frenchman, he was the possessor of a large fortune and an infallible taste for those niceties of living which were so important in the lives of ladies of the beau monde.

Edward whispered a few words to Ellen to tell her something about the duke and shortly after stopped in front of Henri, who was waiting with respectful impatience.

"Good evening, Henri. Ellen, may I present the duke of Lauregais? Monsieur le Duc, Miss Vaughan."

"Charmed, mademoiselle. You are much too lovely to dance all evening with only one man. You will permit me, Doctor?"

Edward watched them as they moved through the complicated figures of the dance. Ellen was breathtaking, he had to admit, and she seemed quite capable of following her partner, who was, whatever else the London wags said of him, a fine dancer. When they had disappeared, Edward turned and walked to the rear of the pavilion.

The gaming rooms were filled; Edward sensed the eager attention of the players at the various tables.

Luck was, as always, her mercurial self, now tempting, now aloof. Moving to a table of vingt-et-un, Edward stopped for a moment to watch. He was not as fond of vingt-et-un as he was of roulette, but it was an interesting game and sometimes rewarding.

He did not recognize any of the players; the one who seemed to be losing most was a young blond boy who was obviously suffering from eagerness to continue the play and thus recoup his losses. He straightened his wig with an impatient gesture and in a hoarse voice demanded that the dealer get on with the game.

The dealer was uncertain as to the amount of credit that could be allowed the youth. He had stopped dealing just as Edward arrived and was looking about anxiously for the proprietor. Seeing him at the roulette table, he sent a servant to fetch him.

All this time, the boy was growing more and more nervous; as the minutes slipped past and his chances of recouping his losses diminished, he became more and more distraught.

At last, the proprietor came over to the table, recognized the boy with a glance, and bowed to him, wishing him good fortune. Play resumed at once after this unspoken signal. Edward watched the next deal with interest.

The boy drew a ten, the dealer another ten. Pushing his entire stack of chips to the center of the table, the boy leaned back with a sudden brash confidence. The dealer covered the bet without a change of expression, and dealt the next cards. Carefully, the boy turned his card up slightly, peered at it, then put it down again on the table, his face shining with relief and anticipation.

"Enough," he called out, his voice suddenly strong in the hushed atmosphere around the table. The dealer kept his eyes on the table; very slowly, he drew the top card from the pile and placed it, without looking at it, on his ten.

The boy scratched some figures on a piece of paper and threw it on the center of the table. It was for seven hundred pounds. The dealer looked at the amount, then matched it with chips from the large stack on the table in front of him. The boy flipped over his card with one finger—the ace of clubs. Twenty-one, with the ace of clubs and the ten of hearts. Twenty-one, which would almost pay, in this single game, for all his losses. The dealer smiled, and turning over his card, revealed the ace of spades. Paired with the ten of the same suit, it won the game.

The boy looked incredulously at the dealer's cards and then gave a bellow of rage and frustration. Rising in his chair, he reached across the table, seized the cards, and hurled them at the astonished dealer. A murmur of protest rose from the spectators as well as the dealer. Mortified and aware that he had violated the code which gentlemen gamblers professed, the boy rushed from the room.

Edward watched the gambling for a while longer, sat down for a few turns of the roulette wheel, and after he had lost ten pounds or so, walked back into the ballroom.

Ellen and the duke of Lauregais were nowhere to be seen.

While Edward was standing on one side of the ballroom, scanning the crowd for a sign of Ellen or her partner, he heard a familiar voice.

"Good evening, Dr. Bancroft. You look as though you had lost someone."

Turning, he saw Lady Downes standing next to him, an amused smile playing over her lips, her eyes bright behind the tiny mask she wore.

"Good evening, Lady Downes," Edward replied, bowing, "you are quite correct. I am looking for someone, though without success."

"I am piqued, Doctor, that you should recognize me so easily."

"Your mask may conceal a few of your beautiful features," Edward laughed, "but you must blind your admirers before they can mistake you for another."

"For that long, though pretty compliment, Doctor, I shall allow you to take me to supper."

"I should be delighted, m'lady."

When they had found a suitable table, Lady Downes turned to Edward with a look of curiosity. "I did not know you attended masquerades, Doctor. I don't believe I have seen you here before."

"I come now and then," Edward replied. "I am rarely so fortunate to have such a lovely supper companion."

"That is not entirely true, Doctor, if you will permit my saying so. I chanced to see your arrival this evening. That astonishingly lovely girl whom I don't believe I have met is much prettier than I. Ah, there she is now."

Edward shifted slightly in his chair and glanced down the line of tables. Ellen and the duke were just sitting down, and from Henri's animated expression, Edward gathered that he was well pleased with his companion. It required an amazing girl to come to Vauxhall for the first time, learn the minuet, and fascinate a French duke all in a single evening.

Lady Downes broke in upon his thoughts. "You needn't sit there mourning, Doctor. That is hardly a compliment to me, however beautiful the woman may be."

A waiter brought supper to them and made Edward's reply unnecessary. Lady Downes was right, he admitted, he was becoming too engrossed in this girl; he could not afford to annoy his supper partner.

Throughout supper they conversed of politics, gambling, and statesmen. Edward became more and more interested in Lady Downes. As they talked in that rapid, far-ranging way which people with many common interests do, he perceived how sharp a mind was hidden behind that worldly facade. She was exceedingly well read and had traveled widely. Whatever the subject of conversation—books, fashions, foods, country seats, and systems of government—she spoke well and succinctly on each. She was one of those rare people who really saw what she looked at and could remember it afterwards.

After they finished dinner, they rose and went into the ballroom, but before they could dance, Lord Downes appeared at his wife's side. He was bluff, ruddy enough to slice, and obviously perturbed by a bad session at the gaming table.

"How do you do, Dr. Bancroft? You were fortunate you left the gambling. I should have, too. You've at least spent an enjoyable evening."

Edward agreed and took his leave of Lady Downes.

Several moments later, Henri and Ellen stopped beside him at the edge of the dance floor.

"Doctor," warbled Henri, his cheeks red under the powder and his eyes shining, "she is a lovely dancer. Truly, I envy you."

"The duke is too kind," Ellen broke in. "He showed me how to do everything."

"Not at all, my dear girl. If I had your youth and your figure, I should be the most beautiful dancer in all England, and France as well. Since I have not, it pleases me to compliment you and thus conceal my own failings."

Edward interrupted to announce that he and Ellen must leave. She looked at him a moment and nodded. After they had said good-bye to the duke, who vowed to go to the gaming tables and lose an enormous sum of money in order to forget his grief, they walked outside to wait until their coach appeared.

At the door of the Golden Anchor Edward said goodbye to Ellen.

"I should like to see you again," he said to her quietly. "There is to be an excellent play at the Haymarket. Would you like to go?"

"I'd love to, m'lord, you know that. I hope you have not been disappointed in me tonight."

"No, indeed," Edward replied emphatically. "I knew you would be the loveliest woman at Vauxhall tonight, and you were. I believe I've gained a rival in the duke."

"I hope you're not serious, m'lord," Ellen replied quickly. "That funny little man could never be a rival of yours."

"I'm delighted to hear it," Edward laughed. "I shall sleep better tonight knowing that."

She looked at him suddenly with a reproachful look. Impulsively, he reached out and took her hand in his.

"I didn't mean to hurt your feelings, my dear. I was joking."

"I know. I know perfectly well. But all this has been so lovely, so unbelievable, that I can't help feeling it's all just sport on your part, something you're doing to pass the time."

"It isn't that, believe me. However, let's not become serious, after such a splendid evening together. Good night. I'll call for you the day after tomorrow at seven."

She stood perfectly still for a moment, then, a slight smile appearing on her lips, she turned and ran inside.

The coachman was startled by the exuberance of Edward's command. "Home, Henry, and be quick."

The coach started off, rumbling and rocking down the cobbled road. Although Edward was bounced about in the back, he hummed and smiled in the darkness. Tonight's experiment had been more successful than he had dared hope. With a little planning, this girl could be invaluable.

During the next few weeks, Edward took Ellen from one affair to another in London. The theater, Vauxhall, Raneleigh, a musical evening at a small club, and a large reception which was given as a masquerade. This last affair had almost proved the undoing of Edward's careful plans. He did not wish them to be announced as Dr. and Mrs. Bancroft, for there were undoubtedly many friends of Olivia's present who would be more than confused when they tried to reconcile Olivia's pale hair and tired droop with Ellen's raven hair and beautiful figure. As a compromise, he decided to use the name of Paul Wentworth, the man whose plantation he had managed for several years in Surinam. Because it was a masquerade, Edward ran little risk of detection, since he was about Paul's height. If Paul ever learned of it, he would understand, Edward felt, for he had probably done the same thing himself.

Soon after Edward and Ellen had joined the guests in the main ballroom, Edward felt a tap on his shoulder. Turning, he stared for a moment at the man beside him, then broke into a laugh.

"Paul," Edward exclaimed, "I'm delighted to see you."

"Good evening, Edward," Paul laughed, "Would you mind presenting me to my wife?"

Ellen was so embarrassed that a bright flush crept swiftly from her neck to her hair. She bowed to Paul wordlessly, in order not to add to her confusion.

"I am charmed, m'lady," Paul said. "I should allow Dr. Bancroft to select all my wives." Turning to Edward, Paul remarked, "I have not seen you much this last year. Working hard?"

"I keep busy."

"I see. We must have a talk someday. I should like to hear more about your activities. I feel more remote from you here in London than when you were in Surinam."

"I know what you mean," Edward agreed. "Perhaps we could meet next week, at my club or yours, and have dinner."

"Splendid. Now I must say good-bye. My wife is waiting. She is extremely curious to learn what my other wife looks like."

After he had gone, Edward turned toward Ellen, the corners of his mouth turned up in a smile.

"An odd situation, my dear, wasn't it? I compliment you on your poise. Well, such misfortunes will happen."

"I would like to meet his wife," Ellen said unexpectedly.

"Whatever for?"

"Oh, curiosity, I suppose. Or perhaps just a woman's fancy," she replied slowly. "It must be a shock to be dancing and then hear yourself announced at the door. Besides, I wonder if she's pretty."

"Knowing Paul, I should say she would be extremely pretty," Edward replied. "Very pretty, very reserved, and rather thin. Would you have guessed he was a Colonist, too?"

"No. Did you know him there?"

"I met him only after I came to London. When I landed in Surinam, after I ran away to sea, his brother asked me if I would like to manage Paul's plantation. I thought it a good idea, so I did, for five years. All that time, Paul and I never met. He was too busy to come to Surinam, always working at something for the government."

"But I thought you said he was a Colonist?"

"He is. Part of his family still lives in New Hampshire, one of the colonies near Massachusetts. He has spent so much of his life here, however, and done so much of his work here that he is like me, an Englishman who happened to be born outside of England. We don't dress or act or even think like Colonists anymore."

Shortly after taking Ellen home, Edward settled himself comfortably in his study and began thinking back over the week which he had spent with Ellen. Now that it was time for him to leave for France, he realized that he would have to come to a decision about her.

Edward had never been in love, nor had he allowed himself to become too attached to the few women he had known intimately. Every time he heard that simple, apparently inevitable question, 'Do you love me?' he knew it was the beginning of the end of the affair. And every time he answered, 'Of course I do,' he knew he didn't and so did she. Love demanded more of him than he had ever been willing to give. Perhaps this was the result of those early, lonely years in Surinam, where he had learned by necessity to rechannel his sexual drive into other activities. Whatever the reason, he had long ago resolved to keep women on the periphery of his life; there was too much he had to do, too much to achieve.

His marriage was another matter, quite another matter, he reflected ruefully, suddenly thinking of Olivia. To Olivia, and to that crafty, wealthy, but monumentally dull family of hers, he had brought, he knew, a worldliness they had never known, an intimation of power and influence that extended far beyond their mills, a vicarious acquaintance with eminence as represented by Franklin and the Walpoles. He had kept his part of the bargain, he mused; but then, he had to admit, so had Olivia. She had provided money, and with it the social framework and position which he had needed.

The thought of leaving Ellen depressed him. She had proved such an interesting surprise that for several days he had been considering the possibility of taking her with him to France. How she might react to such an offer, he didn't know. He doubted that she would hesitate for long at the idea of leaving the Golden Anchor, but placing herself totally in his hands and journeying to France could be a bit frightening. She was adventurous and responsive, he knew; nevertheless, the prospect of life in a strange country, and communication made all but impossible by a foreign language, might be too much of a change.

If she stayed in England, Edward realized, he would lose her completely. One evening alone at Vauxhall, in the dress she had worn there, and she would never be alone again. London was filled with hundreds of prowling squires with wife-jaded appetites.

I'm damned if I'll leave her here, he thought, and instantly felt better. If he were to be foolish, he decided, he could hardly choose a more desirable creature for his foolishness. He had believed that his life with Olivia had destroyed any desires he had left, but he had forgotten that he was still comparatively young. As he thought back to that first night when he had taken Ellen to Vauxhall, he felt a warm glow spread through him at the thought that they might soon leave for France together.

Late the next evening, after the theater, he accompanied Ellen upstairs to her rooms. Taking his arm at the top of the stairs, she led him through the unfamiliar hall to her sitting room, where the candles she lighted dispelled the darkness. It was clean, though sparsely furnished; neatly stacked beside a bookshelf in one corner of the room were the large boxes in which her clothes had come from Mrs. Whipple's.

Ellen seated herself beside Edward, and for a long moment, neither of them spoke.

"This is good-bye," she said suddenly, in a flat, emotionless voice, "isn't it?"

"I must leave for France the day after tomorrow," he admitted. "I don't know when I shall return."

"I was afraid of this. I knew it would come, of course, but I had so hoped it wouldn't, at least not for a long time."

"Tell me, Ellen, have I been unkind?"

"What do you mean?" she asked, her forehead wrinkling in surprise. "How could you have been unkind to me, when you have given me so much?"

"That is exactly what I mean," Edward replied. "When I go to France, what will you do? How will you feel then, living on here above the tavern, with all your lovely dreams in those boxes? Was it unkind of me to buy them for you, to take you to Raneleigh and the other places?"

"No," she said, "it wasn't. It may seem so during the next few months, while I accustom myself to not seeing you. But it wasn't unkind. Someday I'll remember it as the strangest but the most beautiful time of my life. I'll always be grateful to you. Aren't we grateful to people who leave us happy memories?"

Edward stood up and walked over to the window. He looked down at the darkened street and watched his horses moving their heads restlessly, as if they were holding conversation with passing ghosts. A sound made him turn, Ellen had risen from her chair and was standing next to the wall, her arms pressed tightly against her sides, as she tried to stifle her sobs. Quickly, he crossed the room and gathered her in his arms. He bent his head down and pressed his lips hard against her soft mouth. She was warm and fragrant; as her body trembled with delight and desire, Edward felt his blood surging through him with an ardor he had forgotten.

"I can't leave you here," he whispered to her. "Will you come with me to France?"

Tearing herself out of his arms, she ran toward the window, trying desperately to regain her breath. Edward stood behind her, his arms about her waist, and suddenly buried his face in her curls.

"No, no," she said pleadingly. "You must go, m'lord—now."

He turned her around slowly and took her face in his hands. Leaning down, he kissed her tenderly and felt her lips grow warm under his caress. She turned her face aside and whispered softly, "I'll go with you to France, m'lord, if you wish."

Edward felt a fierce delight rush through him. He began to embrace her again, but she pushed him away. She walked swiftly over to his hat, picked it up, and held it out to him, smiling.

"You must go, m'lord, you really must this time."

At the door, Edward kissed her good night. He wanted to savor the full enjoyment of this changed Ellen, so he gave his mind and his body time enough to cool before saying anything.

"Will you be ready to leave the day after tomorrow?"

"Of course I will," she said. Stretching up, she kissed him lightly on the cheek and whispered, "Good night, Edward."

"That's better," he laughed. "Good night."

Two days later, at an hour when Dover was dark and sleeping, a coach rumbled noisily onto the wharf and stopped beside the mail packet to France. A man and a woman alighted, boarded the ship, and disappeared below. Several minutes afterward, the man reappeared on deck and stood at the rail, watching the last-minute preparations.

An officer of the ship approached him and bowed slightly. "We are almost ready to sail, sir. I'll have to ask you to go below as soon as we cast off. This promises to be a bad crossing."

"Quite right," Edward murmured. "I shall go below presently. Good night."

As the officer moved on to warn the other passengers, Edward stared out again at the invisible city. He could feel the ship lean as the waters of the channel surged beneath her. The night was black, and a brisk breeze was blowing from the east. The faint cry of the watch echoed toward him, and he could hear in the distance the sound of oars as they splashed against the dark waters. He watched for some time, sniffing the strange smells of the sea and listening to the unfamiliar sounds of the waterfront.

When preparations had been completed and the mooring lines were being hauled onto the ship, Edward walked toward the ladder which led to his cabin. Before descending, he watched the sailors move over the decks, performing their duties with that systematic confusion that so bewilders those who dwell on land.

The ship turned out toward the channel, and suddenly England lay behind, a brooding island in a dark world.

Such a leave-taking, for however long or short a time, always occasioned the same poignant feeling of regret in Edward. He felt his security desert him, the security one builds on habit. Tonight, it was more sad than usual, for there was no moon overhead and no stars to serve as guides into the unknown. Yet, as he turned to go below, his eye caught a glimpse of the channel. It was a black, unfriendly thing, tossing and cold, but beyond it, toward the south where France lay, there was a faint glow in the sky. It seemed as if he were leaving the darkness to go into the light, and he went happily down to his cabin, as if he had received an omen.

Edward opened the door of his cabin softly. Ellen was standing beside a basin at the other side of the cabin. She had just finished bathing, and as she looked at Edward, the towel in her hand slipped to the floor.

She had as perfect a figure as he had imagined; straight and slender, with a full, high bosom and long, shapely legs. Her long black hair fell like a soft mist over her shoulders.

Drawing in her breath suddenly, Ellen leaned down and blew out the candles. In a moment she was in his arms, her lips next to his ear.

"Hurry," she said in a fierce whisper. Then twisting out of his arms, she slipped away and into bed.

Hurry! No, he thought, that's the wrong way.

Use the waves, go with the gentle rocking of the ship.

Very gently, very slowly, show her how much she's loved, prove to her she's wanted for herself. Tonight can determine so much of the future. If you hurry, you'll spoil everything, and you'll never get it back again. Take your time, bring her to that pitch when she must have you or die. Slowly, very, very slowly.

As he slid between the sheets, he could feel her trembling. His hands moved over her body; suddenly, she pressed herself against him, her arms around him, the whole beautiful length of her tight against him.

The first trembling had stopped, but a different kind of trembling had taken its place.

Slowly he caressed her—her breasts, her nipples, her flanks. He consumed her, bit by bit, place by place, her smooth sides, her haunches, her thighs. He kissed her ears with his tongue and with it roused her nipples as he caressed her breasts.

She was in a welter of feeling, pressing herself to him, stroking him and rubbing him until he felt himself stiffening.

Slowly, he kept telling himself. Don't move, don't do anything until she lets you know she can't wait another moment.

It happened—all at once she was even tighter against him, her lips raining kisses on him. "Now," she gasped. "Now, Edward. I can't bear it. I can't wait. I want you inside me. I want to feel you filling me up."

He reached down, separated her legs, and caressed her sex. She was soaking wet, and as he touched her, the lips opened and his fingers moved softly up and down on her clitoris.

"Oh, God. Edward. Now. Take me now. I can't stand it."

He shifted his body and covered hers. He was hard, as hard as he could ever remember. Slowly, he pressed into her and suddenly, as she cried out, he was inside her, sliding up further and further. Very slowly he brought her into rhythm with him. Her breath mounted, and there was a moan in her throat, a rasping sound that increased as her body heaved faster and faster.

Excited, he increased his rhythm and they strained into each other. Suddenly his fingers tightened around her, and with a loud cry he surged into her. She cried out and fell back onto the pillows, half-fainting.

As she lay beside him, both of them trying to catch their breath, she turned to him and slowly moved her hand down his cheek.

"Edward, my darling, my lover—that was incredible. I can still feel you inside me. Bless you, love. I'm happy I waited. I so wanted it to be like this."

Her hand moved down his side and began caressing him. Edward felt himself stiffening again. As he grew larger and larger, he rolled her over onto her stomach and raising her hips slightly, he slid into her, his hands around her breasts.

"Oh," she moaned, "oh, yes."

As she abandoned herself to his movements, her sex tightening on him, Edward felt himself caught by the surprising strength of that pressure, caught and squeezed until his seed burst out of him again and he cried out, half in ecstasy and half in pain. A moment later she came, and he felt her flow over him.

Very quietly, she began to sob.

"It's nothing," she murmured. "I'm just tired and happy—most of all, happy to think I've pleased you."

He cradled her head on his arm and kissed her softly. "You did much more than please me," he whispered. "You let me know how much I pleased you."

CHAPTER III

T HE NEXT MORNING was cool and clear when Edward and Ellen came out on deck. A verdant France loomed up in front of the ship. Seagulls wheeled and cried overhead, and before long they began to pass small fishing smacks headed for grounds farther down the channel. A larger vessel passed close on their port side; the two captains, each holding a large speaking trumpet, traded news by bellowing at each other until the captain of the mail packet leaned against the rail, exhausted, his face bright red from his exertions.

Calais came in sight about nine o'clock. It looked, from the ship's rail, like another Dover, its Gallic quality emphasized chiefly by a gray patina of age on the ancient houses which lined the waterfront.

The voices of the market women, bickering with their customers, were carried by the soft morning wind to the ears of the passengers lining the rail of the packet.

As soon as they had disembarked, Edward engaged space in a coach which was leaving for Paris. There were three other passengers, two ladies and a gentleman who had appropriated a window seat for himself. One of the women was about seventy and the other some twenty years her junior. The elder, attired in brilliant blue silk, settled herself determinedly in one corner of the rear seat and peered out into the street.

"Are you comfortable, Madame?" her companion said as she sat down beside her. "Is there anything I can obtain for you? A pillow? Cognac? A journal?"

"Enough, Therese!" the old woman bellowed. "You're worse than a nagging wife with these questions of yours. I'm comfortable as I am. Find something to do and be still."

"Very well, Madame. I was only trying to be helpful. I remember how often you have told me ... "

"*Pardieu!* Be still! Read your journal and be silent."

The old woman glared at her companion, who sniffed audibly, stifled a reproach, and finally buried her nose in the journal, which she commenced to read half aloud.

Edward had not felt well since shortly after breakfast on board ship. He had had a dish of eggs and sausage; even while eating it, he had felt that the sausage was bad. As the coach moved from Calais toward Amiens he became even more certain that there had been something very wrong with the sausage.

Ellen watched him anxiously. She grew alarmed the farther they progressed, for she could see that his eyes were inflamed and that perspiration kept gathering on his forehead, in spite of his attempts to wipe it away while she was not watching.

"What is it, darling?" she asked finally. "You don't look well at all."

"I'm all right," Edward grunted. "I don't feel too well, to be truthful, but I believe a night's rest in Amiens will cure me. I haven't felt right since breakfast."

"Poor Edward," she sympathized, patting his hand. "I do hope you'll feel better."

The trip to Amiens seemed interminable to Edward. His head had begun to ache and throb; every few minutes he was forced to mop his forehead and wipe away the drops of perspiration that gathered there. His stomach pained him, and spasms of nausea and dizziness cramped him without warning, leaving him weak and listless. When they finally arrived at Amiens, he had just enough strength left to climb out of the coach and, supported by Ellen, make his way into the inn and upstairs to his room, where he fell on his bed and lost consciousness.

Ellen was trying to explain to the proprietor of the inn, whose English was almost entirely monosyllabic, what she needed for Edward, when the old lady in the coach passed behind her.

"Hold on, young lady," the old woman interrupted. "Don't waste your breath on him. He's only nodding when he thinks he should. He hardly understands a word you're telling him. What's the matter? Is it that man of yours?"

"Yes, it is," Ellen said in a rush. "He's sick, and I don't know what I should do for him. I can't speak French, and—"

"That's enough, my dear. I understand. Where is he now?"

Ellen led her upstairs without pausing to answer. The old lady climbed carefully up the stairs after her, wheezing and mumbling to herself. After she had taken one look at Edward, she sent Ellen downstairs for her companion Therese and told her to order some hot water, mustard, and a large basin.

"This won't be pleasant, my dear," she said to Ellen. "I'm too old to care, and you might as well become accustomed to it now. Your gentleman has been poisoned by something, and there's only one sure cure for that—vomiting. Make him get rid of everything he has on his stomach, and start him off fresh—feed him whatever he wants."

"I just want him to get better," Ellen said quickly. "Are you certain that's what it is?"

"Absolutely. My husband used to be like this sometimes, before he began having gout. I saw hundreds like him in Paris once, when the city water was polluted. When you start doing the right thing for them, they're well within an hour. Weak, to be sure, but with no more fever. He'll be quite all right in another day."

"I'm so relieved. He must be in Paris, you see, very soon. He told me he had an important meeting."

The companion arrived, followed by a servant who carried a large basin and a pitcher of steaming hot water. The old lady assembled the mustard and water and basin carefully beside the bed and then dismissed the servants in a torrent of French. Ellen saw Therese look anxiously toward the bed before she hurried out.

For more than an hour the old lady sat beside the bed, administering the foul-smelling mixture to a barely conscious Edward. She was so relentless in forcing the liquid down his throat that Ellen was more than once tempted to beg her to stop. But soon the good effects of the treatment began to show.

Edward had gone to sleep. The constant vomiting, although it weakened him and left him absolutely limp, had driven the fever out of him.

At length the old lady seemed satisfied. She perched like an owl on the edge of her chair, surveying Edward with her hands on her knees and her eyes bright with triumph.

"You see, young lady," she declared, turning toward Ellen, "he's better. I knew he would be."

"He is better," Ellen agreed. She moved to the edge of the bed and stood there quietly, looking down at him.

"I am so grateful to you, Madame," she said at last, tearing her eyes away from Edward's face. "I don't know what I would have done. I couldn't seem to make the proprietor understand anything, even though he acted as if he did understand."

The old lady laughed. "I know," she chuckled, "only we French can be like that. It is a form of courtesy; we bow and nod our heads as though we understand each word perfectly, while all the time we may not know one word that is spoken. I have known this man many years—I stop here often. He is kind, but he loves to pretend he knows the English tongue better than he does."

They were silent for a few moments, both of them watching the sleeping man.

The old lady gestured to a chair beside her. "Come here and sit down," she ordered. "You will tire yourself. He is sleeping now, and you should rest. I want to know who you are. I am going to Paris myself. I have a large house there, but empty now that all my children are grown. It is sometimes lonely. All my relatives are shocked by me or afraid of me. They never come to see me, except on my saint's day. Where will you stay?"

"I don't know that, Madame. Edward—Dr. Bancroft—told me that we would stay at an inn until he was able to find a house he liked."

"A sensible man. However, if he is a man of affairs, you will soon find yourself bored to death living in an inn. I hope you will come to see me if this happens."

"I should like to very much, Madame . . . "

"My name is Clothilde de Treymes, and my house is at Number 7 Rue St. Honore. I hope you will visit me even before your life at the inn becomes boring. What is your name?"

"Ellen, Madame, Ellen Vaughn."

"What do you plan to do in Paris?"

"Truly, I don't know very much about that. Edward has told me only that he wanted me to take charge of his house and entertain his guests."

"Amazing," the old lady exclaimed. "I didn't know any Englishman gave that much consideration to courtesy and good living. He doesn't seem like the ordinary, meaty type at that. How long have you known him?"

Ellen could not conceal a blush as she replied. "Only two weeks, Madame."

Mme. de Treymes leaned back in her chair and began to laugh. Soon the tears rolled down her cheeks while her shoulders quivered like the branches of a tree in a storm.

She recovered her breath finally and reached over to pat Ellen's hand.

"Marvelous! Formidable! Ah, how I would love to be so young again! But no, I would not go through it a second time. Do you like him so far?"

"Oh, yes, Madame. He is the most generous and thoughtful man I ever knew."

"Enough, enough." Madame raised her hand. "Spare me, child. I'm certain he is, if you say so. Be sure you keep him like that; most men start that way, but few of them so continue."

They talked through most of the night, though occasionally Ellen dozed. Once she awoke to see Therese standing beside her mistress, who was busily working on some embroidery.

Therese was pleading with her to go to bed, but the old lady glared at the suggestion and waved her imperiously out of the room. When Ellen awoke again, she stood and walked over to the window. Through the shutters she saw that dawn had begun to brighten the sky.

Edward moved restlessly in the bed. While the two women watched, his eyes opened and searched the room until he saw Ellen. "Food," he said with a faint smile, "food for a starving man. Hello, Ellen. Where is that old harridan who treated me so shamefully?"

"Right here, you wretch," Madame snapped, leaning forward in her chair and peering at him. "That shameful treatment you speak of was what cured you. I'm not a believer in powders and herbs. Something strong—like mustard and hot water—that's what makes a man well again."

She rose and went to the door. Stepping out into the corridor, she bellowed, "Therese." They could hear the quick shuffle of Therese's feet as she hurried to serve her mistress. After a few moments' conversation, Madame reentered the room.

"Food will be here at once, Dr. Bancroft, so I shall leave you. Don't be too active for a few days. It will take time for you to recover your strength."

"I hope I shall have the opportunity of seeing you again, Madame," Edward said, managing to raise himself up on one elbow. "I should like to thank you properly for your kindness."

"Don't bother about that," Madame replied, her eyes twinkling. "I feel well repaid already. Few women my age can say that they have made such a strong man weak. Good-bye, Doctor."

Ellen went to the door to say good-bye, and as Madame walked out into the hallway, she said to Ellen in a low voice, "Don't forget where I live, Number 7, Rue St. Honore. I want you to come and see me."

"I shall, Madame. Thank you so much for all your help. If you hadn't been here ... "

"Bah," the old lady erupted. "I enjoyed myself, and he doesn't seem any the worse for my treatment. Good-bye, my dear."

She turned and walked quickly down the dark hallway. Ellen stood looking after her until she had started down the stairs. Closing the door softly, she walked back to Edward's bed. "Do you really feel better?" she asked.

"Much better. I'll be all right as soon as I have something to eat. Who was she? Did you find out?"

"Her name is Clothilde de Treymes. She wants me to come and see her after we're settled."

There was a knock on the door and a servant entered, followed by Therese. Therese seized upon this occasion to display her efficiency; it was an almost desperate effort to recover the prestige her mistress had demolished. The servant was completely baffled by the conflicting orders Therese flung at him; he stood in the middle of the room, the large breakfast tray gripped in his hands, and kicked a small stool, first toward the left side of the bed, then back toward the right while Therese, her brow furrowed deeply, deliberated on the merits of Edward's eating from his left side or his right.

Edward and Ellen watched the two in silent enjoyment; it was almost a pantomime. At last the right side was selected, and, with a sigh, the man pushed the stool beside the bed and set the tray down upon it. The two of them left, Therese chuntering in angry French, the servant calmly ignoring her.

After they had gone, Edward turned to inspect the tray. It was a tremendous breakfast of porridge, an omelette, and a large pitcher of tea. There was also a small glass of calvados which he seized and drained at a gulp.

"I know I can never convince you," he smiled, "but this calvados will do me more good than everything else on the tray."

Ellen smiled back at him without speaking and watched him finish his breakfast. He ate as if he had not seen food for weeks and soon the dishes were empty and the pitcher of tea drained. Sinking back against his pillows, he sighed. "That's better. What about you, darling? No breakfast?"

"I'll have something before long, but I'm not hungry now. I'd rather watch you. Do you think you should go on to Paris today? Wouldn't it be wiser to stay another day, until you feel stronger?"

"No, I'm strong enough now. I must get to Paris. I'll be able to rest more comfortably there, in any case, and it will be much more pleasant for you. The coach leaves at seven, so we had better hurry."

"You're sure you want to go?"

"Of course, my dear. The air will be good for me. What kind of day is it?"

Ellen rose and walked across the room to the window.

Opening the shutters, she looked out and all at once pulled open the curtain. Sunlight, radiant, early morning sunlight, transformed the room, filling it with cheer.

"It's heavenly," she breathed, "a beautiful morning. The sun is just coming up, and all the roofs are wet. They shine like silver."

"Then it's a perfect day for traveling," Edward declared. "Why don't you go downstairs and have some breakfast? I'll get up and dress and be ready shortly."

After Edward had settled the bill, they climbed into the coach. Madame de Treymes and Therese had just settled themselves. They were soon all talking together, and as they moved closer to Paris, Madame's vivacious commentary on the countryside, the French peasants, and life in Paris kept them all so amused that they were within the city gates before they realized it.

The Hotel Gravelot, which Edward had selected as his headquarters until he could find a suitable house, was situated on a quiet street not too far from Silas Deane's residence.

Edward immediately engaged a tutor to teach Ellen French. The next morning, after promising to take her to the theater that evening, he left the inn and went to meet Silas Deane.

Deane's young secretary started when Edward gave his name. He led him immediately to an inner office where he presented him to a corpulent man sitting behind a desk.

"Good morning, Dr. Bancroft, I am delighted to meet you."

Silas Deane made a jerky bow, which Edward returned.

They sat down, facing each other, and began their conversation with those stilted pleasantries traditional at first meetings.

Deane was a man of medium height, built like a bull, with heavy shoulders and a deep chest. His legs were short and in his badly fitted breaches seemed like thick pieces of cordwood. A strand of dull, brown hair strayed out from under his loose wig and as they talked, Deane kept pushing at it nervously. The skin of his face was tight and freckled from long acquaintance with the sun, and his hands gestured incessantly when he spoke.

Before he left London, Edward had investigated and discovered that Deane had married a wealthy woman in Connecticut; during the past few years he had achieved an excellent reputation through his ability to soothe the more fiery delegates to the American Continental Congress. He had been selected as chairman of several important committees, and his work on them was reported to be efficient if not inspired.

"As you may have heard, Dr. Bancroft," Deane said, "I have just arrived from America."

"Yes, Mr. Deane, I heard that news in London, even before your letter came to me."

"I wrote you as soon as I arrived," Deane continued, "on the advice of Dr. Franklin, who has great admiration for you. He told me before I left that I should get in touch with you. He said you were a man who knew many people in England and could advise me about the actions of the British Parliament. I need such a man, Doctor. I must obtain all the information I can regarding English moves and policies. That is why I asked you to come to see me."

"I understand," Edward said, nodding. "You want information about England's activities while you woo France, to put it briefly."

Deane looked at him for a moment, the expression on his face changing from anxiety and uncertainty to pleased approval. "I see Dr. Franklin was correct," Deane said with a laugh. "He told me that you were clever enough to read my mind, which is just what you have finished doing. I could not express better than that my true purpose here in France."

Deane stood up and walked over to Edward. Standing just in front of him, he clasped his hands behind his back.

"My mission here is to arrange a treaty between my country and France. In order to do this, I must know at all times what the English are thinking and planning. I would like to have you work with me, Doctor, securing that information."

Deane turned and paced toward the center of the large room, his fingers flicking nervously at the lace on his cuffs.

"I am a poor diplomat, Doctor. I had little to do with public affairs until two years ago, and nothing to do with diplomacy until two weeks ago. I am in an unfortunate position here in France, because I am unable to speak the language of the nation to which I am accredited. Mr. Vergennes has already requested me to call on him. Perhaps, with your prescience, you can tell what that gentleman will discuss with me."

"I am not a seer, Mr. Deane," Edward laughed. "However, I have dealt with the French often, so I would say that M. Vergennes will certainly discuss three matters with you. First, he will express every admiration for you; then, he will utter many fine sentiments approving the Colonists and their spirit of independence; and last, he will tell you, quite confidentially, how much he hates England and how he will do all in his power to assist the Colonies against her."

Deane frowned. "Lovely talk, but empty, Doctor, empty. We need more than expressions of admiration and goodwill from the French. We need uniforms, guns, cannon, and ships. And we need them desperately."

"France wants to help the Colonies, Mr. Deane; don't forget that. As long as she feels the Colonies have a chance to make increasing trouble for England, France will do everything possible to help them. At the same time, she must preserve outward neutrality in the dispute."

Deane picked up a pouch of tobacco on his desk and after offering it to Edward, commenced to fill his pipe. As he tamped the tobacco into the bowl of his pipe, Deane looked at Edward for a long minute.

It was not an impolite stare, but rather the frank scrutiny of a man about to make an important decision.

After he had lighted his pipe, he puffed at it for a moment and then leaned forward over his desk with an air of decision.

"We need a confidential agent in England, Dr. Bancroft. A man who will be able to obtain such information for us as would be at the disposal of Privy Councillors, king's ministers, and other high officials. Naturally, this agent could not be connected with us in any official capacity. Actually, he would hold the position of a special commissioner, responsible only to me. The salary would be 200 pounds per annum, and once our independence is won, he would receive a pension from our government amounting to the same figure. The Continental Congress, through one of its committees, has authorized me to make this offer to you, Doctor. I hope for myself, as well as for my country, that you will accept. I realize that the salary is extremely low for work of this kind, but at the same time, it is perhaps unnecessary for me to point out that in similar circumstances, men have amassed sizeable fortunes through a discreet use of the information they obtained."

Edward did not answer for several minutes, yet his mind had been made up since he had first received Deane's letter. This offer fitted in perfectly with his plans, but he was surprised that Deane should make that last statement. Perhaps it was Yankee mercantilism showing through the diplomat's coat.

Deane continued to puff on his pipe while Edward deliberated; clouds of smoke rose over his head and floated along the beams of the ceiling.

"I will accept your offer, Mr. Deane," Edward said finally, rising to his feet and looking down at Deane. "I shall do whatever I can to assist you. There is, however, one stipulation which I must make. I have many interests, both in England and here on the Continent. It will be necessary for me to travel back and forth from time to time to take care of them. I do not believe that they will interfere with my work for you. I must, nevertheless, feel free to take care of such situations if they arise."

"I am delighted that you accept, Doctor," Deane said, rising and extending his hand. "I understand perfectly your concern over your own affairs. I have a similar concern, although I must cross an ocean and not a channel to get to mine."

Deane led Edward to a large map that had been placed on the wall. It was a map of the Atlantic Ocean, showing the Continent, England, and the Colonies. He pointed to England, then traced a line with his thumbnail across the sea to Boston.

"This sea route is our major anxiety," he said. "Over it, British troops, armaments, and supplies are flowing to Boston and also, though to a lesser extent, to New York and Virginia. We must know everything we can about this shipping lane—the ships that travel it, the cargoes they carry, their arrivals and departures—and especially, we must know in advance of any large concentration of ships in the English harbors. When war comes, as it must, we will have to conduct a sea campaign. We are a young country, poor, and almost friendless. Naturally, we cannot challenge the English navy. We *can* prey on merchant shipping, however. Our ships are fast and our captains brave and experienced."

Deane's voice had grown hoarse, almost strident.

Edward could imagine these same words echoing through the assembly rooms in Philadelphia.

"But that is the future," Deane said wryly. "It is the present that worries me. I shall need your assistance during the next few days in preparing my campaign to win the support of the French. What sort of a man is Vergennes?"

"Shrewd, calculating, and as cold as death," Edward replied. "I regret to say he is not fond of me. He holds me responsible for certain speculations against French securities."

"I've heard about some of your speculations," Deane said with a smile. "I trust, now that you are one of us, you will warn us before you start another squeezing operation. I was caught very close to the middle of that last one— the Ohio Company—and I've been suffering for it ever since."

"You're luckier than you may realize, Mr. Deane," Edward chuckled. "Actually, there were three 'squeezing operations,' as you call them. You'll have a special advance warning before the next one, I promise you."

They resumed their seats again, and Deane's face grew suddenly tired and serious.

"I'm not sure what to do, Doctor, when I see Vergennes. Would you believe it? How does one act? What does one say?"

"First impressions are more critical in diplomacy, Mr. Deane, than they are in any other meeting. Above all else, be natural. That would be my counsel. The French are in the throes of a cult of simplicity, and anyone coming to court who has that quality will be well received. As to what Vergennes will expect of you—who knows? I can only say that Vergennes is a shrewd man who conducts the foreign affairs of France to suit first his own, and then his king's beliefs. He wants to support America, and I am sure that he will do everything in his power to assist you, since it means that at the same time he will be weakening England."

Deane nodded his understanding.

"The man you must avoid, as I must, is the British ambassador, Lord Stormont. He knows you're here, of course, and he knows why. He will do everything he can to interfere with you and to bring your work to nothing. He will use the journals and the court circular to give Paris news of your activities; he will hire and bribe persons close to the court to whisper scandal and calumny about you; he will set agents on your trail who, if the situation requires it, may try to do you injury, so long as there is no danger of detection."

"Your Stormont sounds like a fine fellow."

"Actually, he is," Edward replied, to Deane's surprise. "He's an eminently capable and personally attractive man. He has done fine work for England wherever he has been. People frequently question the morality of his methods, but that is a rather simplistic viewpoint. Whenever he sets his hand to something, it is to win. That is his only object. With such a person as Stormont, it is foolish to apply the usual rules of conduct."

"It would be wiser, I judge, to avoid him, rather than challenge him."

"Much wiser," Edward agreed. "You mentioned that you were concerned because you could not speak French. That presents no problem, really. All the people at court speak English."

There was a knock on the door, and at Deane's call, the secretary entered.

"Dr. Bancroft, may I present my secretary, Mr. Edward Carmichael, of Maryland."

Bancroft stretched out his hand, and Carmichael seized it in an artless, overly hearty grip.

Carmichael was exquisitely dressed in the latest fashion. He was an emptily handsome youth, blond and large-boned, his face so bland and open that it looked as if it had never been lived in. His eyes were a faint gray and created an instant impression, in those meeting him for the first time, that no serious matter ever crossed his young mind, unless by pure chance.

"I beg pardon for interrupting you, sir," Carmichael said, "but you must be at Versailles shortly."

Deane muttered and pulled out his watch, a heavy gold one, whose protest soon after leaving the warm fastness of Deane's pocket was a wonderfully sweet series of chimes tolling the hour.

"Thank heaven you remembered," Deane exclaimed. "Is the coach ready?"

"It's waiting outside."

"Fine. Would you care to come along, Doctor? The ride to Versailles should be enjoyable."

On the way, Deane talked chiefly about Carmichael. "He's a nice enough young man, I suppose," Deane began, somewhat perplexed, "but he enjoys the strangest people. I've seen him at a dinner, surrounded by people of his own class. He's charming then, a graceful dancer and a fair conversationalist.

"But he loves to drink, and whenever he's been drinking, he moves from one dreadful spot to another, lower and lower, until finally, when I'm summoned to get him out of trouble or pay his bill because he's wasted all his money, he's invariably in the lowest den in town, standing there like a blond god, surrounded by the greatest crowd of admiring panderers and murderers and cutpurses you've ever seen. Why no harm has come to him I shall never know.

"I brought him here with me at the request of his uncle who is an important member of the Continental Congress. I'm beginning to understand why he didn't want him in Maryland any longer."

While Deane met with Vergennes, Edward walked about the gardens of the palace. He was watching the swans in the little lake when he heard, "Dr. Bancroft! What a pleasant surprise!"

Startled, he turned and saw the Countess de Grere standing behind him.

"Madame!" he exclaimed. Moving swiftly to her side, he bowed and kissed her hand with an enthusiasm that brought an additional sparkle to her bright eyes. "An even more pleasant surprise for me. I have not seen you since Carshalton, last summer. How is M. le Comte?"

"For an old man, he is well, thank you. What are you doing at Versailles?"

"Waiting," Edward replied with a smile. "I came out for the ride, and a chance to walk around these beautiful grounds again."

"I can understand that easily," she nodded. "Did Mrs. Bancroft come with you?"

"No, she didn't. She is in London."

"I might as well be honest with you, Doctor," she laughed, "Madame de Treymes is an old friend of mine. When may I meet your Ellen?"

"How foolish it is to try to conceal anything from a lady-in-waiting," Edward sighed. "Whenever you like, Madame."

"Come and see me. I am at home on Wednesday afternoons. Perhaps I shall hear of a house that might suit you."

Edward watched her disappear down the long avenue of trees. An unexpected meeting, he told himself, but a fortunate one. The Countess de Grere wielded considerable influence. If she and Madame de Treymes both sponsored Ellen, there would be no question of Ellen's acceptance in Paris. What a long way we have come, he thought with a smile, from that street corner and that basket of apples.

Deane's first words to him as they left Versailles came as a question: "Do you know a Mr. Beaumarchais?"

Edward leaned back against the seat and laughed. Poor Deane! His first day at the French court and he had to encounter Beaumarchais.

"Yes, Mr. Deane," he replied, smiling at the puzzled expression on his companion's face, "I do know Beaumarchais. I hope you will forgive my laughter, but Beaumarchais has always been the terror of newcomers to the court. You must discount his strange manners and his personal idiosyncracies. There is a very capable individual hidden beneath that deceiving exterior. He is a brilliant man, one of Vergennes's most trusted friends. He is also a rake, a roisterer, and the most famous playwright in France today. As long as you are in Paris, you will hear his name; and as long as you deal with Vergennes, you must take him into consideration, for it is well known that he decides nothing before Vergennes wrangles about it with Beaumarchais."

Deane nodded his understanding.

"Beaumarchais," Edward continued, "is most enthusiastic toward the cause of the Colonists. I believe he will do all he can to help you, but he will do it in the manner he likes best, which is always the most dramatic he can invent."

"I gathered something of this from what was discussed today," Deane said. "Vergennes informed me that Beaumarchais has just founded a new company in Paris—Hortalez and Company—whose principal business will be to supply us with French arms and materiel. The company, entirely subsidized by the French government, will be controlled by Beaumarchais. From it we will be permitted to buy whatever we need."

"It's an interesting scheme."

"Yes, very. A damned clever one, too," Deane continued, "because now the British can't complain that we are receiving aid from the French government, since these supplies will come from a private company."

The coach drew up before the Hotel du Grand Villars, and Deane got out. "Keep the carriage, Doctor. Could you come to see me sometime tomorrow morning? We might plan for future discussions with Mr. Vergennes."

"I should be glad to. Goodbye, Mr. Deane."

In a few minutes, Edward was hurrying upstairs to Ellen.

"Darling," she cried as he strode into the room, "I'm so glad you're back."

She ran to him and flung her arms around his neck. Her joy and vitality were infectious. Sweeping her up in his arms, he whirled her around, kissing her eyes and her mouth until, laughing, she begged him to stop.

"Would you still like to go to the theater tonight?" she asked. "I've been thinking of little else all day, except for these flowers. I know I won't understand what's being said, but I'll try. My French is better! I thanked the lady who sold me the flowers, in French."

That night, as they were seating themselves in their box at the theater, a lackey entered and handed Edward a note. It was from the Countess de Grere, requesting him and Ellen to join her in her box.

They entered the countess's box just before the play began. There was hardly time for a quick introduction and a rapid rearranging of chairs, before the curtains were drawn apart and the play, Moliere's *Tartu*ffe, began.

Ellen stared fixedly at the stage, her attention so intently focused on the action of the play that Edward had an opportunity to converse quietly with the countess, next to whom he had been seated.

"A beautiful girl, Doctor. I congratulate you. A little insecure, still, but she interests me. I would like to help polish this Diana."

"I would be very grateful for your assistance, Madame."

"Bring her around, as I told you. It will be an interesting venture for me, although with beauty like that there is not much that needs be done."

Once back at the hotel, Ellen slipped into her nightgown rapidly and slid into bed, murmuring a soft complaint against the cold sheets.

He moved into the bed and pushed the covers down to look at her. His hands tugged at her nightgown, and she shifted her body so he could take it off.

My God, how beautiful, he thought, as he caressed her breasts and leaned down to tongue her nipples which were already erect. She was lying on her back, her eyes closed, smiling a little. The candlelight cast shadows on the whole length of her, outlining her hips and her long, smooth legs.

As he kissed her, her breasts, her sides, her arms, then buried his face in her middle, she reached down and curled her fingers around him. He looked up at her and smiled.

"With that little hand you can make me do just what you want, can't you?"

"I can try, and I do. I love to touch you. You seem to like it; you're not slow to respond. Look at you now!"

"We talk too much." He spread her legs apart and buried his face between them, while his hands caressed the soft skin of her thighs. His tongue moved lightly up and down her sex.

"No, Edward. No. Darling, that's too much. Please."

"Oh, yes." He leaned closer and slowly tongued the wet lips of her sex.

"God, that's heaven. Don't listen to me. Don't stop."

Her hips thrust spasmodically up and down, ever stronger; her hands pressed his head closer to her.

"Inside me, darling. I want to feel you inside me. Hurry! Oh, God, hurry! I want you inside me. Fill me up with you."

She murmured incoherently as he moved upon her, slipping deep inside her, deeper than ever before. She began moving with great thrusts of her body, swallowing him up inside her. Now her sex tightened on him, and his pleasure surged. Again and again he thrust deep inside her until suddenly he came in a long burst that brought a cry to his throat. Her sex was still tight around him, as if she couldn't bear to let him go. Suddenly her arms tightened around him, pressed him even closer to her, and her moan reverberated in the room.

"Oh, God," she sighed. "I can't stand it. You drive me wild—absolutely wild. When I come, I'm drained, totally drained. My darling, what you do to me."

Just before he fell asleep, his head cradled against Ellen's breast, he thought of Olivia and her games of patience. A wry smile crossed his face as he remembered how Olivia had always felt like a long, damp piece of crockery.

DURING THE NEXT WEEKS, Edward consulted almost daily with Silas Deane. He gained Deane's complete confidence and became acquainted with those who visited him frequently—Beaumarchais, Dubourg, Geradot, and Chaumont, all ardent partisans of the Colonies' cause. The last two men were prominent in the commercial life of Paris, men of vast personal fortunes who found the American cause almost as exciting as the profit they garnered while assisting the Colonies.

Through the assistance of the Countess de Grere, Edward found a small but charming house not too far from Deane's hotel. Ellen had been so enchanted with it from the moment she saw it that Edward had leased it immediately. In less than a week, the furnishing had been completed and they had invited a small group of people for supper.

Considering the brief time that Ellen had been in Paris, Edward was astonished by her progress. Her speech and manners had been so smoothed and polished by the assiduous countess that Ellen already seemed at ease in any gathering. Several times Edward had come home unexpectedly to discover her in front of the long mirror in her bedroom, practicing low, graceful curtsies with the mirror as her judge. Although she laughed when he discovered her, the practice continued. However perfunctory might be the compliments which were paid her, Edward was pleased to hear them, for he realized how much time she dedicated to becoming the woman he wanted her to be.

One day he came to visit Deane and found the older man awaiting him eagerly.

"I'm glad you're here, Doctor. I've had news this morning that something is stirring in London. If you think it wise, perhaps it would be well for you to check on it."

"What was the news?"

"I was told that there will soon be an effort made in Parliament to settle the differences with the Colonies. The British intend to promise us everything short of independence. Vergennes seems worried, because such a maneuver might make the king loathe to help us further. Vergennes wants the rumor, if it is that, disproved. If that is impossible, he wants to find out who is spreading it, and for what purpose."

"I have an idea who it might be," Edward replied, watching Deane and speaking very slowly.

Deane's eyes brightened, and he leaned toward Edward with a sudden eagerness.

"I'm glad you do," he sighed gratefully. "That's what I told Vergennes. I told him I knew a man who could give me the answer to his question. I think it might be wise if you went to England, just to find out what is going on. As soon as you return, I'll send a report to Vergennes."

Deane looked so relieved by this solution to his problem that Edward could hardly resist a smile. "I shall leave at once," he said. "By the way, Mr. Deane, are you still wary of my speculations?"

"I don't trust them any more than I did before," Deane replied, "unless I hear about them before they happen. Why do you ask?"

"The month I plan to spend in England will be an excellent time to capitalize on this information we have been discussing."

Deane was silent for a few moments; his hand flicked restlessly across his forehead. He pulled out his wallet and handed a paper from it to Edward.

"There's a bill of exchange for a thousand pounds, Doctor. I just received it from Bordeaux. As you know, I am in a rather delicate position, being unable to speculate in my own name. It might cause unpleasant gossip in Philadelphia."

"I shall invest it for you, Mr. Deane. I would not like to seem too optimistic, but the return should be more than satisfactory."

Edward told Ellen about his forthcoming trip to England as soon as he reached his house. It was not for some time that he was able to persuade her that she would do him a greater service to stay in Paris than to return to London with him.

"How long will you be gone, Edward?"

"I'm not exactly sure, my dear. I should be back by the first of September or thereabouts."

"September first? Oh, Edward, that's ages away!"

"I have some important work to do, darling. It's work that can't be rushed. It will require patience, and most of all, time."

As he packed, Edward noticed that Ellen looked more and more dispirited. "Don't worry, darling," he said. "It isn't as if I were leaving you all alone in a strange city. The servants will take good care of you. Mr. Deane would welcome an invitation to dinner. Both Madame de Treymes and the countess are anxious for you to call on them. And you have your French lessons, too— by the time I return, you'll speak French better than I."

"It's just that I know how much I'll miss you, Edward. I know that's selfish, but I can't help myself."

He stopped his packing and took her in his arms. "It won't be as long as it now seems, darling. Someday, when I have finished what I've planned to do here and in London, I won't have to leave you."

"I wonder how long men have been saying that to women," she laughed, looking up at him. "Do you suppose they said the same thing when they lived in caves?"

Edward smiled. "I wouldn't be surprised," he said, walking back to his luggage. "It's a natural feeling for men to have. It pursues most men all their lives—this vision of tranquility. It's the reason they're so preoccupied in their working lives. They think that once they have security, they can relax and never hurry again."

"I hope you're able to change, when the time comes," Ellen said suddenly. "So many men don't."

"I will," Edward replied. "What a serious discussion this has become."

"I like it," Ellen confessed. "It tells me things about you I hadn't known before."

CHAPTER IV

WHEN HE REACHED London a few days later, Edward hurried to Sam Wharton's office near the Exchange.

"Thank God, it's you!" Wharton exclaimed. "Everything's in a mess! I don't know which way to turn with you off in Paris. Every day it gets worse instead of better. What's the latest news from the Colonies?"

"There wasn't anything of interest when I left," Edward answered, "at least not from the Colonies. But there was news from the court. That's what I want to talk to you about. Also, we have a new customer."

He opened his wallet, took out Deane's bill of exchange, and placed it on the desk.

"With the compliments of Mr. Silas Deane, who wants a share of our schemes," Edward laughed.

"Good, good," Wharton nodded, picking up the draft, "the more there are like Deane, the happier I'll be. If only you and Thomas could get more English customers from the right families, I'd never have to worry about investigations. What does the honorable gentleman from the Colonies expect from this?"

"Miracles, of course," Edward replied. "He has heard some rather exaggerated stories about our speculations, and he wants to find out if we really do lay golden eggs, as people claim."

"We do," Wharton chortled, "but the gold is not always pure."

"I think we should give him a nice profit on this," Edward said, "a few hundred pounds perhaps. That way we will have a good customer, and I will have an ardent supporter in Paris if I should need one."

"Two hundred pounds, Edward?" Sam asked in a hushed voice. "You're not beginning to believe that story about the golden eggs yourself, are you?"

"No, Sam, don't worry. There's a reason. Contrary to what is said in London, there is a great deal of money in America. The people over there keep it well hidden, however. If we build up our reputation with Silas Deane, he'll bring in enough customers to pay for these two hundred pounds twenty times over."

"What is this news from the French court?"

"Peace rumors, Sam. Deane has had word that England is going to try for peace without granting independence. Deane's orders are to hold out for independence and anything else be damned."

"That means Colonial shares will fall."

"Yes, and fall hard as soon as Deane turns down the English offer."

"We'd better be prepared then," Sam grunted. "I'll convert everything we have in Colonial shares to governments. How do you stand with the Americans?"

"Very well. Everything went more smoothly than I had dared hope. Deane trusts me so completely that I handle all the shipping data for him. He's even given me a key to his lockbox, so nothing comes into the office that I don't read."

"Edward, you're the damnedest man I ever knew. How can you always seem so honest?"

"That's a rather harsh judgment, Sam. I'm too tactful to mention your less than legal maneuvers."

Wharton grinned. "We make a fine pair. Just the same, you go on making friends with all the best people, and I'll go on using their money to make us rich."

Wharton sighed and pointed to an intricate design on his desk top. "That's my crest, Edward. When I quit, I'm going to endow a library and be made a lord, so all my descendents will praise me as a man of virtue and a lover of truth. I've often thought that I would like just 'A Pillar of Strength in a Corruptible Age' engraved on my tombstone. Wouldn't that make old

Tannenbaum furious?" Wharton leaned back in his chair and bellowed with laughter.

Edward was still smiling as he walked out of Sam's office and made his way down Threadneedle Street. Sam was a strange man, he thought, the last he would have suspected of being whimsical. Edward had to laugh again when he thought of the picture Sam had called up: Old Tannenbaum, the wiliest broker in London, wearing his ubiquitous black bowler and his double spectacles, crouching down to read the inscription on Sam's tomb.

As he approached the heavy stone mass of the government buildings, Edward's mood changed to fit his forthcoming meeting with William Eden.

Shortly after he had met Deane and determined the extent of his influence with the Americans, Edward had decided to see Eden the next time he came to London. It was the other half of his plan, the plan he had envisaged when he first received Deane's letter. The initial half of the plan was already in operation—he had been welcomed by the representative for the Colonies and given a position with them to work against the British. Now he must see Eden and attempt to secure the same kind of position working for the British against the Americans.

Edward did not come to the interview unprepared. He had met Eden several times in London. He knew from what Walpole had told him that Eden was already considering him, because he was a Colonist by birth, as a possible agent for the English. Walpole had added that Eden had been forced to give up the idea because of the king's displeasure. His Majesty had heard of Edward's activities on the Royal Exchange and had a violent dislike for all speculators.

The secretary in Eden's office was polite but firm. "Mr. Eden is not here, Dr. Bancroft. He's in the country, and we don't expect him until next week. Perhaps if you could tell me something of your business with him, I might be able to send a note along with the dispatches this afternoon."

"I have obtained information which I have been informed Mr. Eden would like to receive," Edward replied. "I am not at liberty to disclose its nature. Could you send a note saying that I have some interesting papers for him from Paris?"

The secretary blinked at him, then went into an adjoining office. In a moment he was back and asked Edward to follow him. Edward was led into a large sunny office where, behind an enormous desk, sat William Eden.

Eden was in his forties, but his duties and responsibilities were so great that he had aged prematurely. His face was heavily lined, and his shoulders were curved from bending over his desk for long hours. He was rated an extremely clever man, the only one of the king's ministers who had the courage and the ability to handle the British Secret Service.

He had been a protégé of Lord Suffolk and had been put in charge of the secret service when Suffolk fell ill. At that time, both the French and the Spanish secret services were vastly superior to the English; so superior, in fact, that the phrase 'as clever as a British spy' was a term of opprobrium. Eden had made immediate and startling changes in the service, though not without enormous opposition. He had ruthlessly weeded out the older, more conservative element and had installed his own aggressive young men. The result was a service that was the envy and despair of the other nations of Europe. No opportunity was neglected to gain men for the service, once Eden was convinced of their usefulness and their enterprise.

"Good morning, Dr. Bancroft. Glad to see you. Still speculating, Doctor?"

"Only modestly, Mr. Eden."

"What is this information you have? I hope it isn't idle gossip about Deane. I've already had four or five such reports from my agents."

"I doubt if you have a copy of Mr. Deane's instructions from the Continental Congress," Edward replied quietly.

Eden straightened up in his chair. "No, I don't have. And His Majesty has been making my life miserable the last few weeks because of it. Do you have it with you?"

"It is in my luggage. I can bring it here easily, if you feel it would interest you."

"Everything interests me, Doctor. Especially matters concerning the Colonies. That is a very delicate problem just now. Not our most important problem, but—delicate. The more we can find out about the intentions of these Colonists, the easier it will be for Parliament to act. How long are you to be in England, Doctor?"

"About a month. I have business to take care of, and then I expect to return to Paris."

"How much does Deane pay you?" Eden's question snapped in the air like the crack of a whip, but Edward had been expecting it and was not caught unprepared.

"Three hundred pounds a year and a pension for life of the same amount."

"We can do much better than that, Doctor," Eden said disdainfully. "Before

I go further into that, let me revert to the matter of Deane's instructions. For a copy of these, I will pay 500 pounds, as soon as the paper has been delivered to me. Naturally, you realize that there must be as little delay as possible."

"I'll have it here this afternoon," Edward said as he rose to his feet.

Eden nodded. "Good. I shall be waiting for it."

Edward returned in a few hours, the paper in his pocket. As Eden read, he betrayed no sign of excitement, except that his nostrils quivered slightly. He was like a hound on the hunt, Edward thought as he watched him, sniffing the air for the scent of his quarry.

"Fine. Excellent," Eden breathed. "This, Doctor, is exactly what I need to convince the king how desperately America is trying to win France to her support."

Edward, thinking of Beaumarchais's Hortalez and Company, smiled inwardly.

"I want to have a talk with you, Doctor," Eden said, laying the paper gently on his desk. "Could you come in again, toward the end of the month?"

"Certainly," Edward replied.

"Very well, then." Eden stood up. "Here is the five hundred pounds. And with it, I should like to make a request. Please be extremely careful not to allow your name to be associated with any speculations. I know better than to tell you to avoid them completely." He laughed humorlessly and then continued. "His Majesty is still angry with you for that Ohio scandal. If you and I are to reach an agreement, you cannot have any connection with speculation. Otherwise, His Majesty's disapproval will nullify your value to me."

"I understand," Edward said with a nod. "I shall do all I can to raise His Majesty's opinion of me."

The date set for Edward to return to the office was the twenty-fourth of August. He spent the next weeks working with Wharton, consolidating their interests and putting all their capital into Governments, to catch the first rise at the news of the Colonists' turndown of the British offer.

When his business affairs had been arranged to his satisfaction, Edward left London to spend several days at Carshalton.

The first evening, Walpole and Edward talked for hours. When Edward had finished telling the news from Paris, Walpole showed him a copy of the British proposals that were to be made to Deane. Sir Thomas Dent had been selected to discuss them with Deane, Walpole told him, and had left for France only the day before. Edward felt a great relief when he heard this. His work with Wharton had not been for nothing; they would be ready to capitalize on the news of Deane's refusal, which, he calculated, would become public knowledge on Friday.

The proposals were much as he had imagined them: full of sentiment, the majesty of Britain and the rewards of the British system, but containing no reference whatsoever to independence, only a vague and unspecific promise that the grievances of the Colonists concerning taxation would be reviewed.

The sentiment in Parliament, Walpole explained to him, was bitter against the Americans. They had a few influential supporters, but the majority of the members felt that the Colonists were being misguided by adventurers who envisaged more profit in the fortunes of war than in the misfortunes of peace.

A few nights later, after dinner, one of the guests, Lord Mansfield, drew Edward aside. "Doctor," he began as solemnly as if he were expounding the doctrine of Original Sin, "I have recently seen Eden, who gave me a message for you. He asked me to say, if I saw you, that he was delighted with the care you have exercised in not becoming involved in any speculation. I might also add that the information you gave him has been extremely useful. The effect of it was remarkable: His Majesty spoke almost civilly to Mr. Eden during the last audience."

Mansfield raised a fat hand to his lips and belched softly.

"You see, for some time the king has believed that our agents in France are either disloyal or incompetent. As soon as your information was presented—without mention of your name, of course—he admitted that there might be one or two honest rogues in the group. From George the Third, that is as high a compliment as one could expect."

They had walked into the Carshalton gallery while talking, and Mansfield broke off his conversation to admire one of the paintings.

"Lovely thing," he chuntered. "Eh—where was I? Oh, yes. Eden has discussed with me the possibility of your working for him. As his superior in the foreign office, I am quite in favor of such an arrangement. I am certain such collaboration will prove profitable to us both."

Edward bowed but could think of no suitable reply. He was too amazed for speech. To think that this grumpy old lord—whose wig was usually tipped back to reveal his bald head, whose clothes hung on him like window drapes, whose rage against London prices was notorious—was Eden's superior, was incredible. It was fantastic that a man so quick and cunning as Eden should be led by this ponderous creature.

While Edward pretended to inspect a painting, he felt himself the object of close scrutiny. He turned just in time to see Lord Mansfield watching him, his eyes direct and piercing. The strength of that gaze vanished almost the second Edward turned around, and Mansfield appeared as he had before, weak, doddering, almost senile.

That fleeting glimpse warned Edward that Mansfield was a man to be watched. Like an animal sensing danger, he had a sudden impulse to run for cover.

The morning after his conversation with Mansfield, Edward left Carshalton and returned to London. He gave Wharton the information he had obtained, and they sold their Colonial holdings that same day.

In the middle of the week, London buzzed with rumors of an English vessel that had been seized by an American privateer miles off the coast. One of the passengers had been an agent for the Ohio Company. All the notes and specie which he had been carrying had been taken from him.

In their place, his captors had sent a message to the governors of the Ohio company in London, thanking them for their industriousness and the aid which they had furnished the Colonists.

This was the first occasion of American privateers being reckless enough to invade the home waters of England. It brought the rebellion home to England for the first time. A year before, the battle of Breed's Hill had occurred at Boston. To the English, it meant no more than another minor Colonial dispute. Centuries of rule over other peoples had established an appreciation of the curative power of time, a realization that the events of a single year do not make a Colonial policy.

The English had learned, many of them with shame, that Hessian mercenaries had been sent to fight against the Colonists. They had followed, but with increasing indifference, the speeches in Parliament concerning the Colonial rebellion. This new affront in British waters would create a different feeling in England, Edward realized at once. Although he could not help feeling an intense admiration for the courage of these American privateers, he was certain such recklessness could not long continue, with all the ships available to England for searching and scouring the seas. There was, nevertheless, a daring in this action, a courage and fortitude which strangely exhilarated him.

"Mr. Eden is expecting you, sir. Please follow me."

Edward followed the secretary into the same office where he had first met Eden. He noted with some surprise that Lord Mansfield was also there.

"Hallo, Bancroft," Mansfield called out. "Thought I'd come down and see you. Eden advised me that you were stopping by. I wanted to be in on the discussion."

Eden sat quietly in his chair as the two men exchanged greetings, watching Edward with his sly eyes and making little marks on his blotter with a long, pointed quill.

When the two had seated themselves, Eden shifted upwards in his chair. From his questions, from the very tone in which they were put, Edward realized that Eden was in full charge. Mansfield was there only to watch. Although he remembered vividly his impression of the keen brain behind Mansfield's pudding-like exterior, Edward knew that operating a secret service required not only a man who was both clever and ruthless, but one who could devote all his energies to the problem of infiltrating his men into the courts and ministries of Europe. Mansfield could probably still do it, Edward felt, but he seemed pleased to have Eden doing the work. Spying was a young man's game—the old felt the strain too quickly.

Eden showed his brilliance when he spoke. He had a dry, incisive manner that scorned polite phrases and leaped to the essentials of the matter under discussion. The more he talked and discussed his office and its work, the more amazed Edward became. He learned that there were whole troops of special British agents scattered all over the world—in the Colonies, in the Continental Congress itself, in banks and counting houses, in taverns and clubs, in the government offices, and in the fashionable salons of every European country.

Eden carefully avoided all names in his discussion; in Paris alone, he told Edward, there were more than seventy paid agents working for his service.

"I will not bother you with their names, Doctor," Eden said, smiling, "most of them would mean nothing to you. Since you have accepted this position with us, and since you have already provided us with certain valuable information, I shall now tell you what I tell everyone who joins us. It is the same thing that Lord Mansfield told me, when I first began working here. We shall treat you well—in your case, to be specific, we will pay you 400 pounds per annum, and as soon as the rebellion has been put down, we shall pay you a similar amount as a pension. We demand complete loyalty from you. If we find we are not receiving that, we will be forced to consider you an embarrassment and a danger to our service. We do not hesitate to rid ourselves of such dangers, completely. I trust you understand."

Edward nodded. There was no possibility of misunderstanding.

"Now," Eden continued, "I would like to have you meet the man under whom you will work in Paris."

Eden rose from his desk and walked to a small door on the far side of the room. Opening it, he peered in, greeted someone, and mumbled words which Edward could not make out. Edward kept his eyes on the doorway, watching the man who was just entering the room. He recognized the walk, but it was not until the man had come halfway across the room that Edward rose to his feet in sudden amazement.

"Paul!" he called out, oblivious to Eden's halfsmile.

"Hello, Edward," Paul Wentworth replied. "I'm delighted to see you."

There are times when, among strangers, one courts danger and takes risks one would never dream of attempting in the presence of friends and acquaintances. Yet let a familiar face appear, let a friend call out, and this sudden access of derring-do falters, then ebbs away. So it was now with Edward. He grasped Paul's hand, shook it heartily, and uttered the usual pleasantries while inwardly he fought for mastery over his emotions, over his breath, over his heart which he could feel beating rapidly. As he regained control, he began to savor this moment of danger; with a smile, he deliberately seated himself first.

Eden continued to outline the information that he desired. "I want you to tell us everything you discover about the progress of the American treaty with France. This is by far the most important news to us at all times. If Spain or any other foreign court should become involved with the Americans, we must know about that at once. The matter of ships and supplies destined for the Americans is also important, for with advance information, we should be able to intercept all supply ships and set traps for their privateers."

"I realize," Eden continued, after shifting himself about in his chair, "that this may seem a rather large undertaking for one man. It is. However, you, Doctor, are in a position to find out these things. If we can anticipate their moves and forestall their intrigues with other nations, the Americans will have no hope of succeeding in their rebellion. On the other hand, if we make no effort to hinder and obstruct their agents and their operations, there is every possibility that we will lose our American Colonies, despite our power and our greater military establishment."

"And despite the soothing words from Admiral Howe," Mansfield added with a snort.

"Deane is in an especially advantageous position," Eden continued, "working as he is with Beaumarchais and Vergennes. As you must realize, Doctor, those two are the bitterest enemies England has, except possibly for that noisy man Adams. The French hate us and will do everything they can, short of war, to undermine our prestige and raise their own."

"Do you wish to add anything to what I have said, Lord Mansfield?" Eden asked, turning deferentially toward the older man.

"Only one thing, Mr. Eden," Mansfield replied. "Dr. Bancroft will undoubtedly hear much about the privateers, these same pirates that all London is trembling over today. I want all that information; it is of vital importance to our navy. When you hear anything in this regard, communicate at once with Mr. Wentworth, and he will, in turn, advise me."

"I shall do that, Lord Mansfield, as soon as I learn something definite."

"One last word, Doctor," Eden interrupted. "You mentioned that you had access to all Deane's private papers. Perhaps you would do well to make copies of every paper that arrives from the Continental Congress. In that way, we will not run the risk of presuming a paper is of no importance when it may actually be encoded. It is vital, as I am sure you understand, that you never be suspected of copying these papers. From time to time, unless they directly concern the treaty with France, it may be wiser to let them slip by, if you do not have an opportunity to copy them in perfect safety. If they should concern the treaty, however, they *must* be copied—whatever the risk."

"I understand."

"Very good. Now Lord Mansfield and I will leave you. Wentworth, you can discuss with Dr. Bancroft the means of transmitting his information. Good day, Doctor. I know you will prove a valuable member of our group."

Wentworth, with the aid of a large map of Paris, went over the details of transmitting information. He pointed to a spot in the center of the Jardin des Tuileries.

"You may remember, Edward, a grove of trees here in the center of the gardens. On the north side, about fifty paces from a large basin where the children are so fond of playing, there is an old plane tree with a twisted trunk. In the trunk, at the base, there is a hole. I will instruct my messenger to stop there every day. You can leave your messages to me there at whatever time you please. He will get them and bring them back to me. From now on, in our correspondence, you will be Dr. Edwards or George Chalmers and I shall be Cartling. Is that clear so far?"

"Yes, very clear."

"It will be wiser for us not to acknowledge each other in public, save where we cannot possibly avoid it. The less connection you have with me, the more trusting the Americans will be toward you. They are already aware of my position in Paris because of Vergennes, who automatically warns each newcomer to the court against me. However, they believe me merely one of the English agents in Paris."

"Why does Vergennes dislike you so?"

"It is an old and very long story, Edward. Once he and I were great friends. For some reason I am not able to fathom, he suspected me of informing Choiseul about his relationship with Mme. Testa. It was Choiseul's influence that prevented him from gaining a higher position in the government for so long. He will continue to blame me for this, I suspect, as long as he lives.

"However, all that was a long time ago. Let's stay with the present. This is where I live in Paris. If you ever need to see me on pressing business, come to the house and in through the side door. Only in emergencies, however. Above all, don't come in the front. It's impossible to tell who might be visiting me. When he comes to France, as we expect him to shortly, it might even be Franklin. Naturally, a meeting between you two there, in my house, would leave you highly suspect if something should go amiss at the American headquarters. Franklin, of all people, is the last we can allow to suspect your true position. Apparently, he is very fond of you. That is excellent, and you must make yourself so valuable to him that he cannot bear the thought of losing you. Then, unless irrefutable proof can be furnished, he will always be on your side. A more valuable friend you could not have."

"I realize that."

"Do you have any questions?"

"No, none at all. It has all been extremely clear."

"Very well. When do you plan to return to France?"

"In the next few days. I have several things still to do, but they should all be finished by tomorrow night at the latest. I might possibly leave the next morning."

"To our work together in Paris, then," Paul said, rising to his feet.

As Edward left the ministry and walked toward Wharton's office, he thought back to the interview he had just concluded. There had been a great deal said and implied which he did not yet fully understand. One thing was terribly clear to him, however. The game he had decided to play was one which would tolerate no false moves. The first wrong move he made would be his finish; he realized that very clearly from what Eden had told him. Still, he assured himself, they were not all so clever as they would have him feel they were. Eden had not tried to obtain any more information from him, although he had a great deal more. There were papers in his luggage at the club which were just as valuable as Deane's instructions. A sudden impulse of caution warned him against overconfidence. These are clever men, it told him, not fools; much of their power lies in their ability to conceal their cleverness.

On Friday there was a great commotion in Wharton's office when Edward arrived. Clerks were running back and forth with papers clutched in their hands and a frenzied look in their eyes. Above the noise and confusion, Wharton's voice, like the call of a mating moose, echoed wildly through the office. Opening Sam's door, Edward saw his partner pacing wildly about the room while in the chair before his desk sat a little man completely unperturbed. Sam looked up when Edward entered the room and paused in his wandering long enough to splutter an explanation.

"This—this is Peabody, Edward. This miserable object. He used to work for me, but when I am through with him, he'll be looking for work with someone else! Not that they'll take him! I'll tell every broker in London—I'll even tell old Tannenbaum—what he's done to me today. He'll never get a job. He'll have to become a grave robber or a scavenger, or maybe he can go with the Hessians . . . ." He broke off his explanation to glare again at Peabody, who sat quietly.

"I thought you had a spark of intelligence in that tiny skull, you little worm. How wrong I was! How could you have been so damned stupid? Eh? How *could* you?" Sam turned back to Edward again.

"It happened this morning. Panic selling everywhere. The Massachusetts shares were doing just what we expected. They were so far down that the bank, when it decided to stabilize the market, could hardly find them. The bank began to buy, just as we thought it would, and the market steadied. The Massachusetts shares rose a few points, just as you had thought. But then! This . . . this maggot! What did he do? Did he buy, as I told him to? No! He waited, he, Peabody, the great speculator—he waited! And what happened? Just what any fool would know. The shares kept on rising, and when he finally did buy, half the profit was gone. We're twenty thousand to the good, instead of forty. So look at him closely, Edward. That runt who wouldn't make a good meal for a dancing bear cost us twenty thousand pounds today. Get out of here, you bedbug! You're through!

Peabody rose to his full height of five foot three and glared across the desk at Wharton. His chest heaved, and the sparse hair on his head quivered with fury.

"I'll go, Wharton, you stinking old buzzard," he screamed, "but before I get out, I want to tell you something. You never told me when to buy those shares back. If I'd waited for word from you, the firm would never have bought them. You're a windbag, that's all! You're too weak to make up your own mind, what there is of it. Everyone in the firm has to do your thinking for you, as well as your work. If you think I mind leaving this rat hole, come around to Rothschild's and see how unhappy I am there!"

Wharton stared at the bantam for a moment, too amazed to move. His mouth dropped open, and he shook his head slowly, as if he couldn't believe what he heard. His hand reached out to his desk for support and fell on a large ledger. By instinct, his fingers closed around the heavy book, and he raised it over his head. Peabody saw the ledger and fled. The book crashed against the wall just as he went through the door. Wharton slumped back in his chair, exhausted.

"Well, Sam, at least you won't have to tell me that bad news again. It could be worse. We did make something."

"Yes, Edward," Sam sighed, "but how little! Think what we had right in our hands before that pygmy made such a mess!"

"Never mind. This is only the first of its kind. There'll be others, lots of others. I have to return to France tomorrow, and I want to take Deane's money back with me."

"All right," Sam replied. He sat up in his chair suddenly, as if he were grateful for something new to occupy his mind and take the place of the loathsome Peabody. "I'll send it round to your club. Two hundred pounds profit?"

"Yes."

"When do you expect to be back?"

"I don't know. I'll have to spend a great deal of time in Paris from now on, I imagine."

"Well, don't wait too long. Things become very dull around here when you're away."

Edward smiled with pleasure. This was as close to a compliment as Sam's gruffness would allow him to make.

Edward walked back slowly to his club. He took a roundabout way through the park, for the weather was beautiful and something in the air reminded him of Ellen, whom he would see in only several days' time. The thought of his return to Paris became so overpowering that he could not resist stopping at his jeweler's to find something that might please Ellen. He finally selected a round emerald brooch and was assured that it would be engraved and delivered that afternoon.

Early the next morning, Edward arrived in Dover and began searching the waterfront for a boat to carry him to Calais before the scheduled trip of the packet. He was eager to return to France and did not wish to waste even an hour's time. One of the innkeepers he questioned in his search recommended a Captain Joseph Hynson to him. Hynson, the innkeeper said, was a good sailor, drunk or sober, who made his living taking passengers across the channel. He did not know where Edward could find him, but he suggested a tour of the taverns that lined the waterfront. The Sailor's Rest, he said, would be the most likely place.

Edward found the Sailor's Rest with no difficulty; as he stepped inside, the noise of the quarrel which he had first heard some distance away became deafening. He noticed a spindly, unshaven man at the rear of the tavern swaying from side to side as he shook his fist beneath the jutting, fiercely red nose of a man twice his size.

"You can't say that to Joe Hynson, you fat porpoise! Take it back, before I make pie out of you."

The big man was not as drunk as Hynson, but he was drunk enough to be eager for a fight! "No scupper rat can say that to me. I'm a man what's served on the ships of His Brittanic Majesty. I'll ram that loose talk right back down that scraggly neck of yours! Porpoise, am I? Why..."

The big man lunged at Hynson who darted away, but not quite swiftly enough. His coat sleeve dangled from the other's fingers. Hynson seemed surprised, as if he had not expected his challenge to be accepted. He trotted toward the watching proprietor.

"Landlord," he exclaimed in a quavering voice, "this man is too drunk to fight. Sober him up, so I can start working him over."

The big fellow lumbered up beside Hynson. His arm curved out as if he was about to seize an unwary chicken by the neck, but Hynson dodged behind a table.

"Sober him up, landlord, I say, and I'll leave him in strips, big as he is."

"Stay away from me," the big man bellowed as the proprietor put a placating hand on his shoulder.

Brawls were common enough in the Sailor's Rest, but the proprietor, although he enjoyed a good fight, preferred to watch one in the ring rather than in his own tavern. Something always got broken, and there was rarely money to pay for it. He swung the small, weighted club he had been hiding behind his back. It caught the big man just behind the ear. Falling forward onto one of the tables, he rolled off and lay on the floor, glassy-eyed, his tongue moistening his lips weakly and his fingers scratching helplessly at the rough boards. Hynson looked down at him in triumph.

"See what happens, you ugly baboon, when you fool with old Joe Hynson," he crowed. "There's always trouble. Beached like a whale, ain't he?"

Edward smiled as he heard Hynson's words, but a sudden glance at the proprietor made him move swiftly to Hynson's side. "Don't worry about Captain Hynson, proprietor," he said. "He and I are going for a walk. He won't give you any more trouble."

The proprietor sighed and let his club fall to his side. Bancroft took a coin out of his pocket and tossed it on the table. "This is for what he owes you. Give the other man a drink when he wakes up."

Before he had time to protest, Hynson found himself in the street, his arm in Edward's tight grasp.

"Stop complaining, man," Edward told him. "That club was ready to tickle your head when I dragged you out of there. You're luckier than the other fellow."

"It's a good thing for him he never swung at me," Hynson blustered. "I'd have stretched him out flatter than the floor. Who are you, mate? What do you want with me?"

"I want to get to France," Edward explained. "Right now. I was told you had a boat, and if you were sober enough, you might be able to find the way to Calais."

"Who said that? I'd like to put my hands on him. I'm never too drunk to sail. Everyone in Dover knows that. What's it worth to you, if I take you to Calais?"

"A guinea," Edward answered. "And that would be too much, if I weren't in a hurry."

"I can't take you all that way just for a guinea," Hynson complained. "It ain't right. I always get three, at least. I have to come back all alone, all alone across that stinkin' channel. Three guineas."

"You're a robber, Hynson. Two guineas, and that's all."

"All right, all right. Don't be angry. I'll cut my price for you because you kept that club off my head. Two guineas it is."

Hynson weaved down Wharf Street, past the Admiralty docks and the main piers almost to the end of the waterfront. He turned off into a small, decrepit pier, the planks of which were loose and rotting. Clambering down a swaying ladder with sudden familiarity, he dropped onto his boat. Edward followed close behind him and after he had completed the perilous descent, gazed at the craft with open doubt.

"Never you mind, mate," Hynson declared with some heat when he saw the expression on Edward's face. "She's better than she looks. She beats most of 'em in this harbor. Never think she's got a tapered hull, would you? Well, she has. When sail's on her, she flits across the channel like a water bug, she does. With luck and a good wind, we'll be in Calais harbor while the sun's still high."

Once they had cleared the harbor and started for France, the little boat performed just as her skipper had promised she would. She whipped over the water and responded instantly to the slightest pressure of Hynson's hand on the tiller. Edward had been put to work early; he was holding fast to the lines of the mainsheet. Hynson soon finished his work forward and, sitting down beside Edward, took the ropes from his hands.

"How long have you had the boat?" Edward asked.

"Not too long. Three months, maybe. I won her from a fellow who thought he was clever with the dice. Mad he was, too, losin' her. I wouldn't give her up now, not for twice what I won from him. She's the fastest little boat in Dover. She lies so close to the water that the patrol boats never see her, not unless they run smack dab on top of her."

The little craft began to pitch as the channel grew rougher, and for the remainder of the voyage, Edward was busy doing the small tasks which Hynson assigned him.

He did not mind being used by Hynson in this way. He was surprised at first by his own passivity in taking orders from this shrunken, bleary-eyed man. Watching Hynson, however, Edward became more and more aware of the man's ability, and he understood his own willingness to obey him. Hynson's manner had changed completely, and the authority which he assumed seemed quite natural.

When he had made the boat fast to the pier at Calais, Hynson turned to Edward.

"Sorry it was a bit rough out there," Hynson said to him. "I want to thank you, before you go, for taking my part at the Sailor's Rest. If you ever want to cross the channel quick like this, look me up and I'll be glad to take you. When I'm in Calais, you can find me up the street here. There's a little place called the Cafe des Anglais; a woman named Perret runs it. She'll know where I am, if you don't find me there."

As Edward walked toward the Paris coach, he glanced at the time, three o'clock—and yet he had left Dover only a few hours before. To confirm the doubt in his mind, he peered up at the clock tower in the center of Calais. Three o'clock. He looked back at his watch thoughtfully. Hynson might prove more valuable to him than he had realized. At night, that little boat could be an excellent method for transporting messages and papers without the scrutiny of the French and British patrols. At any hour it would be the quickest way to carry the news.

CHAPTER V

D ARLING," Ellen cried when she saw Edward the next afternoon, "you're back."

He caught her up in his arms and whirled her around. "I am indeed," he laughed, "back with my love. You're more beautiful than ever."

While they sat together in the library, he told her what had taken place in London. She listened quietly as she watched the changing expression on his face when he spoke of Walpole and Sam Wharton and Peabody. He did not mention his meeting with Eden or Wentworth.

"What has happened here, while I've been away?" he asked.

"I can show you far better than I can tell you," she said, beginning to rise. But before she had time to stand up, Edward reached into his pocket and pulled out a small box which he placed in her lap. She looked down at it curiously for a moment, then started to unwrap it, her fingers clumsy with sudden nervousness.

"A surprise?" she asked. "How sweet of you, Edward."

She opened the little box and her eyes widened. An ecstatic "Oh!" escaped from her lips as she took the emerald brooch from its box. "It's beautiful, darling."

"I thought you'd like it."

"I love it," she laughed at him. "It's much prettier than the one the countess de Grere wears. She'll be jealous when she sees it."

She looked down at the brooch and as she turned it over, she saw the engraving on the back "Ellen from Edward." Her eyes filling with sudden tears, she put her arms around him and began to kiss his eyes, his cheeks, his mouth.

Her warmth and the fragrance of the scent she used intoxicated him. He pressed her against him and felt her eager response. Lord, he thought to himself, how could I have stayed away so long?

They stood up at last, still trembling, and walked through the house together. She proudly pointed out all the changes that had been made during his absence.

"I haven't been as extravagant as it looks, Edward. I did spend all the money you gave me, but not any more than that. Do you like it?"

"Yes, very much," he answered. "I think you've done superbly well."

"The countess has been very kind to me," she went on. "She has helped me and told me about many things I never would have heard of: people selling privately, and little shops where the prices aren't as high as they are in the most fashionable shops."

At dinner that night, Ellen told him all the latest gossip from the salons of Paris. The countess's salon was one of the most famous in Paris and usually provided exciting news. She told him all she could remember hearing about the Americans since his departure.

"Mr. Deane's waistcoats are attracting more attention, I think, than his political efforts," she began. "Would you believe this, Edward? I saw him one day at the countess's—he was wearing a waistcoat of blue silk, embroidered with bright red and yellow flowers. The moment he entered the room, conversation became impossible. Everyone fell silent—they couldn't help themselves—and stared. Finally, the countess broke the spell: 'Mr. Deane, your waistcoat belongs with the wonders at Versailles. I am honored by its unveiling here this afternoon.'"

"Was Carmichael with Deane?" Edward asked.

"Yes, he goes everywhere with him. I must say, he's not very discreet; his eyes always seem to be flitting from bodice to bodice."

"Carmichael is harmless, my dear. He's just very young. In time he may make a satisfactory official. At the present, he is learning and, we hope, profiting from his mistakes. But still he suffers from a childish desire to be friendly with everyone he meets."

"I saw your friend the duc de Lauregais several times while you were away."

"Really? How is he?"

"Fine. Just as charming as he was the night we met him at the masquerade. He asked particularly for you. I think he was disappointed you were in London."

"I'll make a point of seeing him," Edward said. "Perhaps we could have him here for dinner some night, if he hasn't gone back to London."

"That would be splendid. Now that you're here, we can have lots of people. What about Mr. Deane and Madame de Treymes?"

"Of course," Edward nodded. "Would you enjoy entertaining?"

"You know I would, darling." Her eyes sparkled at the thought.

"Let me warn you about one thing: don't ever invite Silas Deane and Paul Wentworth on the same evening. They're not on very good terms."

"Oh, I see. I didn't realize that. Is it something I should know about?"

"Paul is completely English, and thus completely against everything Deane stands for, politically. They not only don't like each other, but if they were here together, they'd fight all evening long and spoil your dinner completely. Perhaps it would be wiser if you'd let me know first whom you'd like to invite; in that way we could avoid any confrontations."

The next morning Edward hurried to the Hotel du Grand Villars to see Deane.

"Dr. Bancroft! You returned! Good, good," Deane thundered as he pumped Edward's hand. His stomach, which had grown larger in compliment to the excellent French food, quivered as he laughed, and the embroidered horse and carriage on his waistcoat moved restlessly.

"What's the news from England? I suppose you know I had a visitor?"

"Sir Thomas Dent? Yes, I heard that while I was in London. They were rather upset when he returned."

"Upset? Well, why not? Let them be upset. If they don't want to grant us independence, then they're the ones who are throwing peace out the window. They expect the Colonies will be forced back to the forgiving bosom of

Mother England, don't they? Well, they're wrong, as you and I know. Mother England—humbug!"

Deane picked up a quill and scowled at it blackly. Edward felt this was as good a moment as any for his news. He reached into his pocket and pulled out the packet Wharton had prepared for Deane.

"This may make you feel a bit better, Mr. Deane. It wasn't as much as I'd like it to be, but at least it's more than you gave me."

Deane opened the paper and after counting the money quickly, whistled softly.

"That's wonderful," he exclaimed. "You had this money only a short time. I am most indebted to you."

"Not at all." Edward shook his head. "I'm glad you're pleased. It may make some of this other news less depressing. What is the word from the court?"

"Much the same," Deane shrugged. "Vergennes has been growing somewhat cooler lately. I suspect the absence of good news from America has much to do with his aloofness. We are still able to ship goods, but our original loan is fast disappearing. I'm not certain that we'll be able to raise another. His Majesty is growing less enthusiastic about sending ships to America."

"That sounds like Stormont's work."

"It is. He has spoken several times to Vergennes about breaches of neutrality. Vergennes has had to proceed with much more caution than he showed when I first arrived. Fortunately, he despises Stormont. Every time he has difficulty with the king, he blames his troubles on the British ambassador."

Deane sighed and rubbed his hand over his face.

"The government in England today confuses me, Doctor. How could a country as experienced as England believe the ridiculous lies that Howe sends back from America? To him, a minor skirmish, in which the British capture four supply wagons, translates itself into a major victory. And Stormont, too— any chance to complain about the Americans becomes a major protest against the methods of the French foreign minister. How can they let such people handle their affairs?"

Edward smiled, then rose and walked to the map on the wall. Moving his hand across the whole expanse of the map, he explained, "British public servants are in every part of the world. For you to understand how England can allow Howe and Stormont to act and speak as they do, you must understand the English philosophy of ruling. They never rule for the present day, Mr. Deane, always for the future. For example, why do they worry more about France than their own Colonies?"

"I don't understand that at all," Deane said with a grunt.

"France is at peace," Edward continued. "Her trade is growing, and her influence is again spreading all over Europe. The English worry most about this because it challenges their authority where they are most sensitive—on the continent of Europe. They are trying to contain this new France. They would like to establish a balance between France and Russia. The weight of England would then give supremacy to whichever side she decided to support. Peace in Europe, with this balance in effect, would afford England all the time she needed to subdue her rebellious colonists. Does that make it clearer for you?"

"A little, but not much," Deane admitted.

"Look at it this way, then. If France helps the American Colonies gain independence, England will suffer, not only from loss of power, but from loss of prestige, which is more enduring. In addition to having her own colonies in the West Indies, France would then have the favored position in trade with the new nation. Should that nation grow in power and strength, as she certainly will, the balance of power which England has so long maintained in Europe would no longer be valid. A new balance would have to be effected, to take into account the geographical position and the sympathies of the new nation. Those sympathies would be for France. Do you see now, Mr. Deane, why England feels it more important to keep France occupied in Europe than to put down what she considers only an irritating rebellion?"

"Yes, I can see that, Doctor. You're speaking about the future, though. What I'm interested in is today. What can we do in America, even if all this is true?"

"Fight, Mr. Deane, fight hard and keep up our courage. As far as we are concerned, here in Paris, the best thing we can do is to keep the French on our side—to keep them enthusiastic and eager to help us in any way they can. We need every bit of help we can get. England is the most serious enemy we will ever face. No effort we make to gain our liberty can be too great. We must win our freedom."

Edward sat down and wiped his forehead. He had talked more than was wise, but the words had sprung to his lips almost without thought. He had never discussed with anyone what he had just told Deane. When his book on the Colonies had been published, he thought that he had extinguished any emotional partiality to the land of his birth. Apparently a good deal of his loyalty still remained. Something about the look of the Colonies on the map had stirred him, as if suddenly he saw them for the first time as they really were—angry, unsure, but full of courage and promise.

His usual discretion had been swallowed up. It was almost as if his grandfather, the old sea captain, had been speaking through him to Deane. He would have to be more careful; too much was at stake for him to speak so openly.

When he looked up, he noticed that Deane was watching him with a gaze of admiration and wonder.

"Doctor," Deane said, "you should never have gone to England. You should have stayed where you were born—in Massachusetts. Lord, how they need men like you there now! To tell the colonists what you've just told me. To stir them up and excite them the way you did me.

"Men like Franklin and Adams are sorely overworked—they are so few. We need men, articulate men, to go to the people and tell them these things. The people in the Colonies are confused, Doctor. Most of them think they want independence, but they're lukewarm about it. They need to be aroused. They need someone to set their blood boiling again. Breed's Hill is almost forgotten, and Sam Adams has been heard a thousand times, so he's becoming tame. Ah, well. That's no way to talk. I'm discouraged enough here in Paris, without worrying about what's happening in the Colonies. Did you find out anything else that I might put in this report to the Congress?"

"No. After Dent returned from his unsuccessful mission to you, there was a rumor about that the king would soon publish a proclamation concerning the Americans. The text of the proclamation was still most indefinite when I left; all I could learn was that the king became furious when you refused his terms. He said he was finished with any idea of reconciliation."

"If he would say that in a royal proclamation," Deane said, "I would be delighted. That is exactly what we need to make the issue clear, not only at home, but here as well. We would no longer be merely rebellious subjects then. We would be Americans, all of us, and proud of it."

During the next few weeks, Edward left many messages in the plane tree that Wentworth had designated to him on the map in London. Although he realized the childishness of it, he found this to be an exciting part of his work for the British. The information he provided seemed dull, chiefly concerned with names and figures, though occasionally he passed along more exciting news about the privateers. However, the relaying of the information tested his ingenuity, and he enjoyed overcoming the inherent difficulties.

Because of the proximity of a playground to the plane tree, Edward had acquired an understanding of the nearby children, their methods of play and their particular ability at concealment. Several times what must have been animal instinct prompted him to walk past the tree just when he had been ready to insert a message. Once, five feet beyond the tree, he had stumbled over a little boy lying concealed in the grass, who eyed him with hostility and ordered him not to disclose his hiding place to the others in the game.

He had learned as well the habits and the characteristics of the attendants in the Tuileries—he could have informed their superiors not only of the hours when they walked about, but how they walked and who was careful about picking up litter and who was not.

There was also a great relief in these visits to the gardens. Deane was despondent at this time, for events in the Colonies were going badly; every day it seemed that support for the Colonies in France grew weaker. George the Third's proclamation had been published. Its contents were harsher and more arbitrary than Edward had imagined: all colonists in America were regarded as rebels, save for those who had previously declared their allegiance to the king; Colonial sailors were to be impressed whenever discovered by His Majesty's navy; and most disastrous of all, all Colonial ports were ordered closed.

American ports closed! This news was calamitous, for it meant no more French cargoes could sail to the New Continent without danger of confiscation. Such an order would be difficult to enforce, but it had the desired effect of weakening French support of the Colonies. King Louis reluctantly ordered that no ships be sent, in order that no irremediable difficulties might arise between France and England. Some of the king's reluctance to issue this order arose because of Stormont's insistent protests over breaches of neutrality. Stormont annoyed King Louis as much as he annoyed Vergennes and the Americans.

The French were still the only people in Europe who wanted the Colonies to gain their freedom. Their attempt at persuading Spain to join them in giving aid to America had failed. Spain refused to commit herself beyond lending a small amount of money; the private opinion of the Spanish ambassador as expressed to Vergennes was that Spain would never join with France to aid the Colonies unless the situation should materially change. A smashing victory of the Colonials over British forces might effect a change in their attitude, but only something as important and unbelievable as that.

One day Edward discovered a roll of paper in the bottle that was concealed in the plane tree. Taking it out, he stuffed it in his pocket, and after placing his own message inside the bottle, he put it back in its place of concealment.

The gardens were empty at that hour, and since there was still enough light for reading, he studied the message carefully. It was addressed to him and was written in the simple code which he and Wentworth used. It came from Lord Mansfield and thanked him for the information he had sent regarding the privateers. It closed:

"The capture of one privateer was effected Tuesday, thanks to the precise information you furnished. Ten of the crew were killed in the skirmish. The rest have been jailed, for an indefinite period."

The night he received that message, he spent a long time alone in his study. Ellen came in to talk to him, but noticing the expression on his face, she left without a word and went to bed. That was a night which Edward did not soon forget.

For hours he battled with himself, pitting his determination to make his plans succeed against the guilt and remorse he had felt when he first read Mansfield's note. He went to sleep after an interminable length of time, but not before he had twice torn the hangman's noose from his own neck.

He dreamed that he was aboard an American privateer, raiding British shipping in the channel. They had just taken prisoners off a packet boat and left her blazing on the sea when a British man-of-war came up astern and quickly overhauled them. The crew prepared to repulse the British ship, although she carried twice their number of cannon. She came up so swiftly she seemed to fly out of the water. A broadside struck the privateer, tearing down the sails, toppling the masts, killing the captain, and leaving Edward in charge of the stricken ship. When the British maneuvered close alongside to cast grappling hooks, the two ships crashed against each other. The jar knocked Edward to his knees. Before he could rise, he felt the thrust of a sword in his arm. Wielding the sword was the British captain—Lord Mansfield.

Edward awoke to feel Ellen's fingers digging into his arm. "Darling, darling, wake up!" she was crying. "It's all right. Wake up!"

A dream—thank God! It had been so vivid—he could still see that sword lunging at him and feel the blade in his arm. Weakly, he lay back on the bed.

He closed his eyes gratefully as Ellen smoothed his forehead and comforted him.

"What a damnable dream," he muttered.

"I should think it must have been," she said. "You've been bellowing and shouting and cursing like a madman for nearly five minutes. You wouldn't wake up, no matter what I did. It was almost as if you had to finish it."

He went back to sleep with the touch of her hands on his forehead. When he awoke in the morning, the dream was over, but not all his memory of it. When Ellen asked him about it, he only shrugged his shoulders, trying to allay her fears.

"I'm glad you've forgotten it," she said when she saw his apparent unconcern. "I'll say no more about it."

Edward found Deane incoherent with joy that morning. It was not for several moments that he was able to stammer out his news.

"Franklin," Deane chortled, "a letter from Franklin! It just arrived. The Colonies have declared their independence. Franklin's coming to France. He doesn't know when, but he's coming."

Edward smiled back, but his mind was concentrated on this new development. Things would begin to happen as soon as Franklin arrived. He would bring news with him from America—perhaps it would be the very news he was waiting for.

Mansfield's note about the fate of the crew of the privateer had left Edward irresolute. He wondered if he was still willing to pay the price demanded in this game of spying for both sides. A single misstep or an error in judgment could cost him his freedom if not his life.

Was it worth it, to live in such peril? Was the reward equal to the risk? Yes, of course it was. Edward felt his courage return. The reward—the news he might hear from Franklin—would provide him with what he had always dreamed of—a fortune gained through his own cleverness. When this had been accomplished, he could bow out of his present work, pleading illness or some other excuse.

He had come far, but not far enough. It would be foolish to give up now when he was so close to the goal. Whatever the risk, he must carry out his plan. There was danger in it and, he had to admit, he loved danger.

As for Ellen—that part of his future could wait. Now, he told himself, now the chase was about to begin and he must be ready.

"Here's his letter," Deane said.

Edward smiled when he saw the precise handwriting which was so much in keeping with the mind of its fashioner:

My dear Deane,
    The action for which we have so long prayed and worked is done.

The Continental Congress has published to the world the intention of these Colonies to gain their independence.

I will not try to quote all that the document sets forth, but shall bring a copy of it with me when I come to France. It is enough for me to say that many concessions had to be made to timidity. We—Jefferson, Adams, and I, with some assistance from Livingston—were able to fashion a document which should call forth assistance and support from our European friends.

The English will be furious when they read it. I have said to my friends here that from this day forward we must work together. If we do not, we shall certainly all hang separately.

The committee is disturbed at hearing so little news from you. Your last dispatches which mentioned the cooling of relations between ourselves and the French filled them with gloom. I regret that Vergennes insists on using Beaumarchais. Dubourg is far the better man for this business. The fact that he is an intimate friend of mine is the least of his qualifications—he is a loyal friend to America, a prominent and respected man, while Beaumarchais is an idler and a stage tripper whose only real qualification seems to be a suspiciously intimate connection with the king's household.

My work here is nearly concluded. Something unexpected may well arise to prove me wrong in this assumption, but I am too tired to foresee such a possibility.

If you should be suffering from the same discouragement which I have known so well these last months, remember that you are fortunate to be in such a beautiful country as France. The French are a kind and reasonable people, the only true friends America has in Europe.

Kindly give my good wishes to such of my friends as you may see. I hope to journey to France in the near future, and I look forward to seeing you and my good friend, Dr. Bancroft.

Franklin

After he had helped Deane compose a suitable reply to Franklin's letter, Edward departed and hurried to Paul Wentworth's house. His knock at the side door was answered by Sylvestre, Wentworth's Negro servant, who ushered him into a small book-lined study. Edward had just sat down when Paul Wentworth entered.

"Good morning, Edward. Glad to see you."

"Good morning, Paul. I thought it wise to come as soon as I could. Things have been stirring this morning—we received a letter from Franklin. He says the Colonies have declared their independence."

"Yes, I heard that," Wentworth nodded.

Edward felt a sudden annoyance pass over him, as if he had been cheated of the surprise he expected his news to create.

"Also, Dr. Franklin is coming to France, as soon as he can finish his work in Philadelphia."

"That is news—bad news," Wentworth exclaimed. "If he comes to France, he is bound to upset our plans. He will make this struggle for French assistance a personal campaign—and he's a very dangerous antagonist, as I know all too well. I remember what he did in London, just before he fled to America."

"You mean after the trial in the Cockpit Tavern?"

"Yes. That was what changed Franklin. Until then he had not really hated us, because we always gave him an opportunity to express himself in journals and at public meetings. After that trial, he was a different man. He seemed to feel that war was inevitable; and before he left, as you remember, his speeches, at least the few he was able to make, prophesied the coming struggle with the Colonies. Did the letter say anything else?"

"Only that he doesn't trust Beaumarchais. He'd prefer to have his friend Dubourg handle things."

"I shouldn't wonder," Wentworth laughed. "Beaumarchais has almost as much of the actor in him as Franklin. Franklin realizes that if there are two heroes in the play, the audience will soon grow bored. That's why he wants Dubourg, who's a perfect foil for him."

"It will be interesting to see the meeting between Franklin and Beaumarchais," Edward said.

"Yes, very. I'm glad you brought this news to me, Edward. I shall send it to Eden at once, with a reference as to its source. Let me know if any word is received about the date of Franklin's arrival. We must be prepared to act even before he sets foot on shore."

Almost a month after Franklin's letter arrived, Edward and Ellen received an invitation to a ball at the home of the Marquis de Rochefort. It was to be the most brilliant social event of the season, and Paris prepared for it with anticipation.

Ellen was ecstatic from the moment Edward told her that they were going. She worried through her clothes, and after a brief search, sighed that she had nothing appropriate to wear for such an occasion. Edward, amused and pleased by her excitement, sent her to Mme. Fremand, the most elegant dressmaker in Paris.

A few days later, a large box arrived from Mme. Fremand's, and Ellen rushed upstairs with it. In a few moments, she was downstairs again, standing before him in the gown she was to wear to the ball. It was beautifully fashioned of white and gold tulle, with delicate gold flowers embroidered on it. Ellen looked at him without speaking, her eyes pleading for his approval.

He rose and put his arms around her.

"I am fast becoming a prophet," he laughed, holding her at arms length and surveying her. "Once before, I prophesied that you would take the masquerade at Vauxhall by storm. Now, I will say the same thing of the ball at the Rocheforts. You are so lovely in that. I hate to share you with anyone else."

She smiled with pleasure. Without another word, she slipped out of his arms and hurried upstairs to put the dress away.

On the night of the ball, the carriages waiting to stop before the Rochefort house lined the streets for nearly a mile. The line moved slowly, and as they waited, Edward noticed the handkerchief in Ellen's hand was becoming more and more wrinkled and crushed. Leaning over, he patted her hand softly.

"Don't fret, my dear. We shall be there shortly. There is really lots of time—these affairs continue all night and on into the morning."

She returned his smile, but her attention soon reverted to the carriages in front of them while her handkerchief suffered further agony. Finally, they arrived and walked up the great stone staircase to join the throng of guests which had filled the house.

Troops of servants wove a pattern about the guests, bringing chairs and offering food and wine, like soldiers performing an intricate drill. Music filled the air, and from every side echoed the excited voices of friends chattering and calling greetings to each other.

The Marquis de Rochefort and his wife were kindly, completely unpretentious people who, by a combination of ancestry and wealth, were one of the most prominent families of France. Edward noticed that the graciousness with which the Marquise greeted Ellen had created a new Ellen. No longer was she nervous or uncertain. The color had returned to her cheeks, and as Edward walked down the great drawing room beside her, he was conscious of her new radiance and proud of the attention she commanded.

There were many friends of theirs at the ball that night, and Ellen danced almost continuously. Compliments were showered on Edward, and he could not help remembering his early life with Olivia, those few first months of marriage before they had withdrawn from the social life of London. In those days there had been no compliments—only the unspoken sympathy of his close friends.

WEEKS PASSED BY with no further word from Franklin, no change in the political situation, and no ships leaving France for America. Suddenly, as if a fuse had reached a barrel of gunpowder, the quiet vanished.

Paris exploded with the news of Franklin's arrival almost at the same moment that a special messenger from Thomas Morris, the American agent in Nantes, rode up to the door of Deane's hotel. The young man, tired and rumpled from his journey, rushed in and asked for Mr. Deane.

Deane turned from his conversation with Edward when the messenger burst into his rooms. "I'm Deane. What is it?"

"A message, sir, from Mr. Morris at Nantes. He said to tell you first that Dr. Franklin has arrived at Auray."

Deane let out a loud whoop of joy, and his jubilation caught like fire on dry grass. Carmichael bounded in presently, bearing a bottle of cognac.

Glasses were filled and toasts drunk to the long-awaited Franklin, while Deane crouched on the edge of his chair, squinting over Morris's message.

"He says Franklin wrote him after he landed. First Franklin's going to Nantes—then he's coming here. The ship he came on—the Reprisal—took two prizes off the coast. The report is that Franklin spotted both of them. Carmichael!"

"Yes, sir?"

"Carmichael, go out to the Hotel d'Entrague. See if you can get enough lodgings there for Dr. Franklin and me. There's not enough room here. I'll have to stay close to him, at first anyway, until we've talked ourselves out. Tell them that Franklin will want privacy, but at the same time he'll want to be able to chat with the people on the street. A corner room would be best, with lots of windows. And check on the food—make sure it's good. He doesn't care much about that, but I do."

Edward chuckled at Deane's remark. For weeks, everyone who knew Deane had watched him with some distress. The commissioner had acquired a habit of stalking around his rooms like a man possessed. His face had shown new lines, and his stomach had shrunk.

His waistcoats now hung limp and wrinkled over the ghost of a paunch.

"Doctor," Deane cried as soon as Carmichael had left, "I won't be able to bear it. I know I won't."

"What do you mean?" Edward asked curiously.

"Well—Franklin. Here he is in France, at last, and I have only the briefest note from him, which doesn't tell me when to expect him. It's more than a man should have to bear."

"I wouldn't worry too much, Mr. Deane," Edward said to soothe him. "As soon as Dr. Franklin reaches Nantes, I feel sure that you will have further word from him."

"Perhaps you're right, Doctor. I'm too excited, I know," Deane muttered. Edward's comment did not provide him with the comfort he needed, however, for he paced about the room like a tiger in a cage.

Stopping before his desk, he picked up the letter, opened it, and handed an enclosure to Edward.

"Franklin's note which I didn't repeat aloud," he said.

Edward opened the note and read:

"Dear Deane,

"From the little I have heard and seen in France since my arrival, I note among the people a certain disinclination toward interference with England's colonial affairs. Such a sentiment does not augur well for the support we hope to obtain."

"How does he know that?" Deane asked, almost angrily. "Sometimes he's too clever. He hadn't been in France a day, I wager, when he wrote that. Yet he put his finger on the one thing that's made my work here so difficult. The French can't afford to help us, if it means open trouble with England. And Franklin senses that in some seacoast village. What will he think when he gets to Paris, I wonder?"

"I doubt whether he'll be much surprised by what he finds out," Edward replied. "Remember, Mr. Deane, the situation is not quite as black as you make out. After all, there is Hortalez and Company. No nation concerned only with peace could invent or carry on such a device as that."

He paused and smiled at Deane's perturbed face.

"Dr. Franklin is known to the world as a philosopher and a scientist. As either of these, he would be in great demand in many circles here in Paris. He is also a charming, cultivated person. Knowing the French, Mr. Deane, don't you think that Franklin can make a successful personal crusade here?"

"You may be quite right, Doctor. But it is one thing to be admitted to people's houses, to be asked to dinners and entertainments, while it is quite a different matter to pry money from the French government to support a rebellion that no one is sure will succeed. The best fortune we have had lately is the large number of people who have left France to join our army. Once they are enrolled, more people in France will interest themselves in the success of our cause, because their sons and husbands and fathers will be fighting for us."

Although for two weeks nothing more was heard directly from Franklin, news of his arrival in France had spread over all Paris. Wherever he went, Edward heard the name Franklin. It was like a slogan and appeared in the conversation of people in cafes, in salons, on boulevards, in churches, and in banks. It was even scrawled on the sides of several of the Government buildings and also the British Embassy.

Lord Stormont protested vigorously to the court. This constant iteration of the name Franklin, he claimed, was not at all spontaneous, but rather a clever campaign instituted by the rebels to build up Franklin's popularity and at the same time that of the Colonies. He was so insistent that Vergennes was forced to take certain measures of repression.

The police of Paris were ordered to interrupt all conversations in the cafes which included the name of Franklin. This order was posted on large placards in every principal meeting place and on every thoroughfare in Paris. Since the police frequently interrupted people who were discussing only the theater or the health of their aunts with the admonition that they were not allowed to use the name Franklin, Stormont's request boomeranged, as Vergennes knew it would, and mention of Franklin came even more often into most conversations.

A few days before Christmas, a messenger arrived from Versailles and inquired for Deane.

"Dr. Franklin's compliments, sir. He is at the Auberge de la Belle Image at Versailles. He sends you greetings and the message that he will be in Paris tomorrow morning."

"Maybe so," Deane thundered, "but I shall be in Versailles tonight.

Doctor, we finally have our wish. He's here. Let's all lunch together tomorrow."

CHAPTER VI

DEANE HURRIED TOWARD Versailles, impatient with every delay the coach encountered on the bumpy, crowded road. The messenger returned with him and was wise enough to sit quietly in his little forward seat and venture no conversation with the American. Deane sat tensely, his eyes staring at the floor of the coach.

From time to time he leaned forward a trifle, as if the shifting of his still not inconsiderable bulk might force the coach more quickly over the potholes in the road, through congested stretches, and around toll gates.

"How does he look?" Deane asked suddenly, as if he could no longer endure alone the painfully slow progress the coach was making.

"Very fine, Monsieur," the messenger replied. "I saw him only for an instant, when he was giving me the message for you. He is older than I had imagined, but he looked very strong. He wears strange clothes, though. A fur hat—they say he arrived in it—and no wig. Eyeglasses which make him seem like a wise monkey, meaning no disrespect, sir."

"I know what you mean," Deane laughed. "I haven't seen him for a long time, but I remember those glasses well."

The carriage finally pulled up before Franklin's inn. Deane leaped out and strode through the small crowd which had gathered around the entrance.

"Where's Dr. Franklin?" he asked the proprietor.

"Right here," a voice answered from the top of the stairs.

Glancing up, Deane saw Franklin standing at the head of the stairs, his wool comforter wrapped around him, his glasses balanced perilously on the tip of his nose, and his hair standing up in unruly fashion.

"Stop staring, Silas. I know I'm not pretty anymore," Franklin laughed. "Come up. I've been expecting you."

Deane bounded up the stairs, as if the sight of Franklin had renewed his strength. He pumped Franklin's hand up and down and stammered out his pleasure at seeing his old friend again. Franklin led him down the hall to his little sitting room.

As they entered, a thin man with a singularly small head and pointed features rose to his feet.

"Silas," Franklin said, "this is Mr. Arthur Lee, of Virginia. I don't believe you have met him."

"No, I have not had that honor," Deane replied.

He moved toward Lee and taking his hand, pressed it warmly. The muscles in his arm seemed to contract suddenly, and he released Mr. Lee's hand as quickly as he had grasped it. The touch of those cold, unresponding fingers reminded Deane of the bleak winter they were now enduring.

"Mr. Lee met me at Nantes," Franklin explained. "As I believe you know, he has been appointed by the Congress as a commissioner to France, like ourselves. I wrote him before I left America, asking him to meet me when I arrived at Nantes. He was good enough to do so, and we have talked a great deal since then about the assistance we hope to be able to give you."

"I need all the assistance I can obtain," Deane replied. Uncomfortable under the unblinking gaze of Mr. Lee's eyes, which had not left his face since the men were first introduced, Deane changed the subject abruptly. "How was your trip?"

"Fine, delightful," Franklin replied jubilantly. "I suppose you've heard about the prizes we captured off the coast?"

"Yes, I have. I also heard you were the one who sighted them."

"A deliberate falsehood, my dear Silas, even if a great compliment. I shall not deny publicly such flattering misinformation, but you may as well know the truth: I was below in my cabin almost the entire voyage. One of the prizes was sighted by my grandson William. I brought him along with me to cheer my life here in France—also his brother, Benjamin Franklin Bache. William saw the vessel just as we were nearing the coast. I didn't see it until the excitement brought me out on deck. Then, there it was."

"Don't deny the story, Doctor. It has made an even greater hero of you in Paris."

"This adulation," Franklin said, frowning, "is pleasing to an old man, I must admit, especially to one as vain as myself. It complicates matters considerably, however, and also it interferes with my sleep. At Nantes, as Mr. Lee will tell you, I accepted a quiet little retreat which M. Gruet was kind enough to offer me. All the time I was there, it was like living in the marketplace. People came in and asked me questions and paid their respects and dandled their babies for my pleasure. I hope I may be able to live a somewhat quieter existence here in Paris."

"There is not much hope for that," Deane said, "not at the moment at least. Paris has little else on its tongue but the name of Dr. Franklin. The people admired you greatly for venturing a winter trip on a privateer, but now they adore you for capturing two prizes on the way. Gossip about you has been so frequent that Stormont, the British ambassador, has complained to Vergennes. The police have been instructed to stop conversations that mention your name."

Franklin smiled when he heard this, but his face soon became serious. "What I want most is a quiet place where I can work and think undisturbed by people like those below." He waved his hand toward the door. "Most of all, it is essential that we be able to transact our affairs in absolute privacy. Our visitors must be able to arrive and depart unobserved, if they so desire. However, we can arrange all that later. Tell me about your work, Silas. That is what interests me most."

"At the moment, I am most discouraged," Deane began, shaking his head. "At first, everyone was enthusiastic. Vergennes was positive that the king would approve all the assistance that France could give, short of occasioning war with England. That optimism has gradually changed. News from America has been either bad or dubious, and France has lost her first enthusiasm.

"Things are going too smoothly here—people are making a great deal of money, commerce is thriving, and the West Indies trade is growing larger every month. Also, the influence of the French on the Continent is extending. They are regaining their prestige in Europe, and they do not wish to risk that in a sudden war over the British Colonies."

"Surely they realize that they must settle with Britain before too long?" Franklin inquired. "A friendly America would be of enormous assistance to them in a war against England."

Deane nodded. "They realize that, I'm sure. However, they're not ready to risk an open break with England yet. So long as they can help us without their assistance becoming verifiable, they will do what they can. Yet Stormont and the British spies seem to be everywhere. We can't make a move or even offer a suggestion without Stormont knowing of it almost at the same minute."

"The British have a most efficient secret service," Franklin admitted. "I came in contact with it during my last stay in London. I had the same feeling you seem to have—I was suspicious of everybody."

"Dr. Bancroft has helped me several times in this connection," Deane said. "He has warned about several people whom he said were connected with the British. We are fortunate to have him working for us. He has given me invaluable assistance in my dealings with Vergennes and has also brought back some extremely valuable information from London."

"Bancroft is an excellent man," Franklin agreed. "He is a man of honor and high intelligence. I shall be glad to see him again. What about the privateers? Have you been able to recruit enough men for them?"

"Not yet. Nicholson has been waiting for a complete crew for nearly a month. Now that Wickes is here with the *Reprisal*, he can start raiding channel shipping along with Bielby. I suppose you heard about Bielby's successful raid last summer?"

"I heard most of the details, I believe," Franklin answered, "though I had never before heard the name Bielby. Where did he come from?"

"He's a Massachusetts man, like Dr. Bancroft. I had several interviews with him just after I arrived in Paris. I liked him so much that I sponsored him and gave him enough money to buy a corvette and hire a crew. In August, he began making raids on unescorted shipping. His second raid turned up the Ohio Company's agent who was carrying funds to London. He sent me the proceeds, after removing enough to compensate himself and his men. The amount I received was much greater than my original investment, I must confess."

Franklin's eyes twinkled. He remembered how Deane was before he left America: a shrewd trader and businessman, a merchant whose boast was that he never took unnecessary risks. This was a different Deane, and from the zest with which he had told this story, Franklin judged a happier man.

"I'm glad it came off so successfully," Franklin said. "Once we have fitted out Wilkes and Nicholson, London will have greater cause to be nervous. If we have any success at all, the insurance rates should become almost prohibitive."

"If you will forgive an interruption, Dr. Franklin," Lee said suddenly, his lips compressed, "I wonder if it is wise to be so sanguine in our estimate of the future successes of these privateers. We cannot afford to forget the British Navy."

"I never forget the British Navy, Mr. Lee," Franklin replied dryly. "But on the other hand, I don't overestimate it either. Unless they are betrayed by informers, or caught while in port, I believe our captains can outwit and outsail any British vessel. This is a time when we must be bold. We should strike when we can, and as often as we can. Success in this operation cannot but increase French assistance to us, since we will be weakening their enemy at no cost to themselves."

"Tell me about the Continental Congress, Doctor," Deane said. "What was this declaration of independence you mentioned in your letter?"

"That, Silas, makes quite a story. We had a difficult time on the committee, persuading the more timid members that it was necessary to publish such a document. We finally put it through—Jefferson, Adams, and I—with the help of Livingston, Pinckney, and a few others. The cautious members, who are always with us, thought that we went too far, that we had sacrificed every possibility of securing peace with England. Perhaps we did, but I'm glad we did. The declaration is rather simple. I'll give you a copy to read. It is an honest statement of our grievances. It should bring us many supporters, especially among the French. Sometime, Silas, I shall tell you the story of the troubles we had pushing it through the Congress."

"I gather from what you've said that it was not easy."

"Indeed not. You have no idea how many special interests delegates can have. While we were writing it, people came to see us every day, warning us that they would never vote for the declaration unless we amended it to accord with their views. I had to spend nearly twelve hours a day fending off these vultures. Frankly, I was delighted to leave Philadelphia for France. I hope that when I return to America all my rash promises will have been forgotten."

"Surely, you don't include the Virginia militia as one of those rash promises?" Lee asked quickly.

"No, Mr. Lee, that is one of the promises I shall keep," Franklin replied, his face stiffening slightly.

He turned toward Deane again.

"How did Vergennes react to the news of Washington's withdrawal from Long Island?"

"Badly, very badly. He has been too busy to see me for days now. Beaumarchais spoke valiantly in our defense, I am told. He reminded Vergennes that there never has been a war in which each side did not lose battles."

"The news will be better, I know." Franklin beat his hand on the arm of his chair, as if to emphasize his statement. "We have just started, and it's to be expected that we should make mistakes. We're not a warrior nation, but we can fight as hard as any nation when we're forced into a corner. What we need most is something to fight with. How long do they intend to delay these shipments of supplies?"

"The delay is only temporary, I know. Stormont blustered so that Vergennes was forced to placate him. Now that you're here, Stormont will have something else besides the shipments to worry him. Then perhaps Vergennes can start the supplies moving to America again. I imagine that these shipments in the French ports now are badly needed."

"They're not *badly* needed," Franklin stated bluntly, "they're *desperately* needed. Washington is trying to fight Howe with troops that have no idea how to conduct themselves. That's bad enough, but when you join to that situation a scarcity of weapons and ammunition, you can understand why we're not doing better and why we don't win battles. Somehow, we have to convince the French that unless they're willing to gamble, unless they're willing to send supplies before they expect results, America will not succeed, or at least not for a great many years. The question in my mind is—will we be able to convince the French of this?"

"With you here, I'm certain we can," Deane said confidently.

"That's flattery, Silas," Franklin smiled, "a device to which I am most susceptible, as you know."

Their conversation was interrupted by a knock on the door. Before Franklin had time to call out, the door opened and his grandchildren entered. They had just returned from playing outdoors, and their faces were pink from the cold.

"Grandfather," the smaller one cried, "can we live here? A man outside asked us if we would like to and I said we would. There's a great big park, too."

"A man asked you that?" Franklin pushed his spectacles up on his nose and walked over to the window. "What man, Benje? Can you see him?"

The little boy stood beside his grandfather, looking out at the darkening street and the park in the distance.

His blond hair was bright against the dark colors of his clothes, and his grace and youth formed a touching contrast to the old man standing next to him.

"No, I don't see him," he said at last.

Franklin's hand patted the boy's back fondly. "I'm afraid we can't stay here, Benje. We'll find another park for you to play in. What did this man look like?"

"He was a very tall man, Grandpa," Benje said suddenly, as if he detected special interest in the old man's voice. "He was dressed in blue, and he wore a great coat that had a fur collar. He asked me a lot of questions about you."

"What did you tell him, Benje?"

"Nothing. I did say that you threw your good hat away when we were on the boat and that you liked your fur hat ever so much better. I told him you hated wigs—and Englishmen."

Deane and Franklin broke out in sudden laughter.

Franklin sat down in his chair again, his eyes bright with mirth.

"What a boy you are, Benje. What else happened, William?" Franklin turned to the older boy, who had been listening carefully to Benje's story.

"Nothing more, Grandpa. Benje's told it all. I asked the man his name, but he didn't pay any attention. When I said we wouldn't talk to him unless he told us, he said his name was Cartling. He told us that he used to know you. I asked him if he was a Friend or a scientist, but he only laughed and said he had neither faith nor learning to recommend him, only perseverance. I thought that a very strange thing to say, so I didn't talk to him anymore. He talked to Benje after that.

"Benje was playing with a dog near the fountain. When I walked down there, Benje had just finished telling him that you hated Englishmen. He didn't say a word, but I know he was English himself, 'cause just after Benje said that, he walked across the park with his nose in the air."

"And he stumbled in a hole, too," Benje broke in excitedly. "It made me think of Mr. Lee when he tripped getting out of the coach and fell head first in the gutter."

"That's enough, Benje," Franklin exclaimed. "I'm glad you said nothing more to this man. William, why don't you and Benje go downstairs and see about your supper? Tell the innkeeper we'll be down shortly."

When the men came downstairs, the boys were just finishing their supper. Benje looked up at his grandfather, his eyes merry.

"Oh, what you're going to have for supper, Grandpa! We saw it in the kitchen. The cook let us lift the tops of the kettles. Can we have some tomorrow, if there's any left?"

Franklin smiled at the boy and shook his head in mock disapproval.

"I don't know what you saw, Benje, but I don't think there'll be any left, if these gentlemen are as hungry as I am. Also, your mother would scalp me if she ever found out what I've let you eat since we left home."

The innkeeper appeared from the kitchen and led the three men to a small dining room.

"This is very pleasant," Deane commented, as he looked at the freshly scrubbed little room and noticed with pleasure the clean, white tablecloth and the flickering candles. "I hope we'll be able to make you as comfortable in Paris."

"I'm sure you will, Silas."

The innkeeper placed steaming bowls of soup before them.

"Ah," Franklin grunted, after he had taken his first sip, "bouillabaise. Wonderful! If only the Friends would someday consider the merits of French cookery, I don't believe my stomach would suffer quite so much."

"Surely the eminent Dr. Franklin could not be guilty of a love for the exquisite in cookery?" Lee asked, his long teeth showing in a sudden grimace. "What consternation such news would cause to the Quakers!"

"I am glad you enjoy your little jest, Mr. Lee. It is a fact that I adore French cooking. The only cooking which I have ever discovered that approaches it is the cooking in Virginia, where the kitchen is such an important part of life. How do you find French cooking, Silas?"

"I'm fond of it. I do wish there was more meat, however." Deane looked ruefully at his waistcoat which once had stretched tight across his stomach.

Franklin, following his glance, grinned suddenly.

"I don't think you're acquainted with the best chefs, Silas. When we are settled in Paris, I shall see to it that you are fattened up."

When dinner was finished, Lee gulped his cognac and excused himself, pleading weariness. After they had heard him tramp upstairs, Deane turned to Franklin.

"Why did they send *him* to France, Doctor?"

"I know, I know, Silas," Franklin sighed. "I could do nothing about it. His brother is an extremely important member of the Congress and insisted upon the appointment. We must do the best we can. He's not a pleasant person, heaven knows, and infernally suspicious of everyone. But he's a commissioner—we must remember that, whatever our personal feelings may be. We will need his approval for many things. We will need his signature on every document we send back. We can't afford to antagonize him. We must learn, somehow, to endure him. I've had to learn—he's been with me almost three weeks now."

Deane nodded. "You're right, of course, but I dread his first meeting with Beaumarchais. It will be like throwing a torch into a barrel of powder."

"Then we must keep the torch and the gunpowder separate, Silas," Franklin said. "Although I would prefer to deal with my good friend Dubourg, I shall certainly not offend Beaumarchais, nor will I allow Lee to do so."

"When I consider how much we have to do, I confess I grow a bit discouraged," Deane sighed.

"You shouldn't feel like that," Franklin replied. "As I said, the war is just beginning. If you are discouraged, Silas, you should think of the war office in London; then you will feel better. You should see the generals who are managing British military affairs in America. Admiral Lord Howe I believe you know—he is one of the best friends we have, not merely because he underestimates the Colonists, but because he is such a bad strategist. And there are others like him, who are even worse as commanders. General Burgoyne I am not acquainted with. He was in Canada when I last heard of him, brooding over the English defeat on the Great Lakes. He'll try something early next spring. He must, or his troops will be so lazy he'll get nothing out of them."

"Are we better off than the British, so far as generals are concerned?"

"To be truthful, no," Franklin replied with a sudden frown. "Washington is the best, by far, but he's better at leading than he is at directing. He makes mistakes, and some of them have been very costly. If Lord Howe didn't like Washington and if he hadn't known he was commanding the troops on Long Island, there's no telling what catastrophe might have occurred there. Washington was caught in a trap. It was only because Howe thought he ought to be a sportsman that Washington was able to escape."

"I haven't heard the details of that battle," Deane exclaimed. "Surely we must have had scouts and informers to warn us about the movements of the British?"

"We had a few informers," Franklin replied, "but Washington's decision was a difficult one to make. He knew he would have to withdraw from Long Island if the British made a concentrated attack. He also realized the great strategic value which possession of Long Island gave to the side which held it. Perhaps he hoped that he would bluff the British long enough for him to get horses onto the island. He had no cavalry at all, and without cavalry, no reconnaissance. Hence he had no advance information of British movements, except the trickle that came in from informers. It was a dangerous position, but he held it as long as he thought wise and then withdrew. There was one bad skirmish on the twenty-seventh of August. Many men were killed, and our troops lost their confidence."

"From what you say, he was lucky to escape at all," Deane said.

"I think he was, although I admit I am not an expert in military matters. After he left Long Island and moved across to Manhattan Island, Washington faced the same problem again. Should he defend or withdraw?

"I remember clearly how strong the sentiment was in the Congress for him to defend. The members are inclined to trust more to providence than force of arms. Washington wrote to the Congress, giving a vague outline of his plans. He had decided to defend with a part of his force and to keep the remainder, the greater part, outside the city, so as to form a second line of defense.

"The British were not slow in attacking this time, and we suffered a dreadful defeat. It almost cost us the life of Washington; he was in such despair. Our troops broke under the shelling they received from the British ships in the harbor. When the British troops appeared, panic spread and there was a most dreadful rout. The officers were powerless, for the soldiers believed that all was lost; each of them tried to escape while there was still time. Washington himself tried to stop the stampeding men, but when he saw that they were beyond reason, he became almost mad himself. He spurred his horse and galloped toward the approaching British, as if believing his effort alone might halt the enemy. Fortunately, an aide was able to turn the general's horse aside before they reached the British troops."

As Franklin finished his recital of the battles, Deane shook his head despairingly.

"I find it difficult not to be pessimistic. Will it ever be any better, I wonder?

Will our men, whom we know are braver than these mercenaries the British are using, continue to run and hide?"

"Certainly it will be better," Franklin declared. "You are inclined to be a pessimist, Silas, if I may say so. You forget that these are the first battles.

"Once we have an army that has been hardened by discipline and combat, we shall run these Hessians into the sea. Then we shall come into our own. We shall have our victories. Until then, we must be able to endure defeat and preserve our faith. It is hard, I admit, but there is no other way."

"It's very late, Silas," Franklin declared as he rose to his feet. "I foresee a busy day tomorrow."

The men said good night at the head of the stairs, and Deane walked slowly down to his room at the end of the corridor. He stumbled about unhappily before he was able to find a candle. Lighting it, he was surprised to see a large picture of Charlemagne which covered most of one wall of his little room. As he undressed and prepared for bed, his eyes kept straying to the picture. Walking over to it, he studied the severe, determined face. At the bottom of the picture was inscribed the motto *Quis non audet, moritur*, "Who dares not, dies."

He crawled into his cold bed and jerked the feather quilt up to his chin. The motto kept returning to his thoughts, like a strain of music: Who dares not, dies.... Who dares not, dies....

He dared. Franklin dared. They would not fail, as long as they kept their courage.

CHAPTER VII

FTER BREAKFAST THE next morning, preparations were made for the journey to Paris. When all was ready, Franklin's grandsons could not be found. The innkeeper marshaled his help and his family to look for them, but it was nearly an hour before they were discovered. They had been conversing with one of the palace guards and had become so fascinated by the man's descriptions of the wars in which he had fought and the strange places he had visited that they had forgotten their approaching journey.

Franklin was angry at the delay, but as he listened to Benje's rapturous, if inaccurate, recounting of the guard's stories, he softened visibly. Soon after they had started out toward Paris, Franklin began telling his grandsons fantastic episodes about his trips to Canada.

As they entered Paris, the coach was forced to slow down because of the crowded streets. Franklin kept peering out of the window, as much excited by the busy life about him as were his grandsons. The sight of that fur cap bobbing beside the window attracted instant attention from the passersby, and it was not long before he was recognized.

Greetings and cries of welcome increased as the coach moved down the street. Like a magnet, the coach drew to it not only the inevitable group of small boys who, to Benje's envy, ran after it shouting and dashing back and forth in front of the horses, but also older people who had been awaiting Franklin for weeks and now, with their first glimpse of the famous man, were immediately eager for another.

Franklin kept looking out of the coach, smiling and waving his hand occasionally to return the greetings which became more and more numerous as the people in the streets heard his name repeated. A curious soldier, suddenly discovering the identity of the old man, ran over to the side of the coach and officiously took charge of its progress, as if he had assumed responsibility for the safety of the famous Dr. Franklin. He commanded people to move out of the way and waved his arm with authority, but soon a large crowd had surged onto the street in front of the coach and made further progress impossible.

Realizing that he alone could solve the dilemma, Franklin opened the door and stepped down to the street.

At this gesture, cheers broke out from the crowd, and the sudden din of noise echoed like a salvo down the street. Windows opened suddenly; the occupants of the houses stared down and smiled at the strange little man in the fur cap who was holding up his hands in a seemingly vain effort to silence the crowd.

When they were finally still, Franklin thanked them and told them of his gratitude for their warm and unexpected tribute. He spoke of his great fondness for France and his delight at finding himself in Paris, the most beautiful city in the world. That was enough; he had plucked the most sensitive strings in their hearts. The people went wild with delight.

They raised him on their shoulders and marched down the street. Franklin had been adopted by these people who loved him for his simplicity and his genius, who cherished him even more because he spurned the trappings of the aristocracy. Wherever he was intending to go in Paris, they meant to take him there in triumph on their shoulders.

Deane scrambled out of the coach as it followed along behind the crowd, but realized at once how impossible it would be to overtake Franklin. He worried for a moment whether Franklin would remember where to go, but he sighed with relief as he saw the fur cap suddenly bend down; Franklin was giving his destination to the men who carried him. At the next corner, the crowd turned and marched in the right direction.

Mopping his forehead, Deane climbed back into the coach.

It took nearly twenty minutes to reach the Hotel d'Entrague. The proprietor appeared in the doorway when he heard the noise of the approaching throng.

As soon as he saw the fur cap in the distance, a broad grin appeared on his face and he hurried down the steps to greet his famous guest. Franklin was lowered gently to the ground. He shook the hand of each man who had carried him, then hurried up the steps. On the final step he turned, and the excited throng grew quiet in a sudden hush of expectancy.

"Thank you, all of you," he shouted. "Only in Paris could such a wonderful welcome be given to me. My country thanks you, for I know that it was not me that you were cheering, but America. . . . America loves France, and I am more certain than I ever was before, after this magnificent tribute, that France loves America."

Cheering broke out again, and soon someone started a popular song of the day, a vulgar but humorous description of the English king.

Franklin laughed as he heard the words of the song. Turning about, he saw Edward standing in the hall, watching him.

"Dr. Bancroft," he called out, "how delightful to see you."

They shook hands warmly and walked toward the dining room together.

"Lee asks to be excused," Deane said as he joined them. "He has gone on in the coach to another lodging."

Franklin shook his head slightly, but made no reply.

"Deane tells me that you have been of great assistance to him here," Franklin said after they had seated themselves at the table. "I'm pleased to hear it. I knew you would be."

"That is very kind of you, Doctor," Edward replied. "I have done what I could to assist Mr. Deane, but our work has not been easy. I hope you have brought good news from America."

"I'm afraid not," Franklin shook his head. "There will be good news soon, I am sure of that. Great events are about to happen, and when they do, we shall have those happy tidings for which we all pray. Tell me, Doctor, what is the situation in England? I have been out of touch with affairs there for nearly two months. Is there any real desire for peace?"

"There is a large group in the opposition," Edward said carefully, "in favor of peace. However, Lord Chatham's influence is formidable; as you know, he has spoken definitely against freedom for America. He still envisages, as he has all his life, a string of British colonies that extends from the North Sea to the

Pacific Ocean. The idea of sacrificing that dream and allowing the Americans their independence is one he cannot endure."

"I remember Chatham well," Franklin interrupted. "He suffered quite violently, I am happy to recall, from gout."

"And still does," Edward added with a smile.

"In the government itself, Burke—though he is opposed to complete freedom—is one of America's strongest supporters. He would be in favor of at least titular independence. But ... "

Edward leaned back in his chair and sighed.

"All these viewpoints, Dr. Franklin, are influenced from month to month by the military news that reaches London. Parliament is beginning to feel that too much attention is being paid to the disturbances in the Colonies. In short, the difficulties with her Colonies are regarded as a minor and unimportant disagreement."

Franklin pushed his spectacles back on his nose and nodded his understanding.

"Should America achieve one great victory over the British forces," Edward concluded, "this feeling would vanish in an instant. It must be proved to Parliament—it cannot be told—that the fighting in the Colonies is costing her men, money, and prestige, and the longer it continues, the greater loss she will suffer. Until that victory occurs, I do not believe that there is any chance for peace."

"Who are America's best friends in England?" Franklin asked suddenly.

"In political circles," Edward answered, "Lord Shelburne and Burke. In other circles, your friend Dr. Priestley. The first two have considerable influence, especially Shelburne, if he could only maintain his ministry long enough to do America some good."

"I know what you mean about Shelburne," Franklin affirmed. "When I was in London, it always seemed that when the ministry, under Shelburne's direction, was about to make a concession to us, Shelburne would be removed and nothing further would be heard of the matter until he was again in charge."

Their conversation was interrupted by the innkeeper, who opened the door with a flourish and announced: "M. de Beaumarchais to see Dr. Franklin."

Beaumarchais paused at the threshhold and then swept into the room in the finest theatrical tradition.

He was attired in green silk, with trousers displaying his shapely legs to their best and a coat fitted snugly against his waist, perfectly tailored to show off the surprising breadth of his shoulders. His waistcoat, a nerve-strumming creation which made Silas Deane draw in his breath with envious despair, was a flaming red; sewed onto it were white silk profiles of the famous heroes of France. In his hand he carried a lace handkerchief which extended almost straight out behind him from the speed with which he crossed the room to greet the surprised Franklin. On the old doctor's face there appeared the faintest intimation of a smile of incredulity.

The contrast between the two men was astonishing—Franklin, so simply dressed in plain brown, wearing no lace or ruffles or even a wig, looked old and tired and gray, while Beaumarchais was a shining symbol of the latest in fashion and the most exquisite in tailoring, a man of delicate, cultivated tastes, but whose broad shoulders intimated the strength that so often dismayed his enemies.

"My dear Dr. Franklin," Beaumarchais cried, "I, Caron de Beaumarchais, am delighted that you have arrived safely in Paris. I heard the news not more than an hour ago, and I hurried to be the first to greet you. Am I the first?"

He looked closely at Franklin, hoping for confirmation.

"You are indeed the first, M. de Beaumarchais," Franklin said warmly. "It is very kind of you to come."

"Not at all, my dear sir. Truthfully, I wanted to be the first so that I could convince you that what Paris says about Beaumarchais is false. He is not vain; he is not a fop. He is a serious man, this Beaumarchais, with serious business to attend to; namely, helping your marvelous country—with all those lovely names—Massachusetts, Connecticut, Philadelphia—helping that country of yours achieve her independence. He will feel himself well rewarded if someday there is a Rue de Beaumarchais in your famous Philadelphia."

Franklin beamed and invited his guest to be seated. "M. de Beaumarchais," he began, "I am delighted that you have come to see me before the others, for I wanted to ask you certain questions in private about Hortalez and Company. I think it would be wise if we discussed that now, before anyone else arrives.

"I am well aware that there are few in Paris who have such a warm regard for my country as yourself. Mr. Deane has informed me that His Majesty is upset by the bad news from my country and has ordered all shipments of goods to be stopped. Is that correct?"

"Alas, yes," Beaumarchais breathed, his hands raising in despair. "It is too true. However, Doctor, that is another reason why I came early."

"Yes?" Franklin said in surprise.

"Before this order was given," Beaumarchais continued, "I, Hortalez and Company, had anticipated this difficulty. We have some fifteen ships at present in harbors of the French West Indies. They all have cargoes which I believe America will find . . . useful. All that is necessary to bring them to your ports is to transfer them to your own vessels."

Beaumarchais sat back in his chair to appreciate the effect he knew his words would create. Franklin lost his usual serenity; he took off his glasses and peered at his visitor in amazement. Deane sat woodenly in his chair, his mouth agape, his hands clasped together as if in prayer. Edward leaned forward a little, waiting breathlessly for the Frenchman to continue.

"I could trust no one with this news, Doctor. Please do not look so injured, Mr. Deane—I hardly trusted myself. I was afraid that even I might become careless and hint something about it to Vergennes. Even he does not know this secret, Doctor—it is known only to ourselves."

"I am delighted to hear this good news, M. de Beaumarchais," Franklin said. "What are these cargoes?"

"Guns, cannonballs, ammunition, food, cloth, and shoes." Beaumarchais smiled with joy when he saw Franklin wipe his eyes with sudden emotion. "Clothing—uniforms, that is—I dared not procure, for fear that I might arouse suspicion. These other articles, according to the records which I have so carefully destroyed, were to be used to subdue any possible uprising among our Negroes in the West Indies. If anyone should learn of the arrival of these goods in America, we can blame our garrison commanders in the West Indian Colonies for careless supervision of their equipment."

"The shoes, yes, and even the food," Deane said, "but what about lending a country cannon and cannonballs?"

"M. Deane, I do not concern myself with minor details. If anyone presses this point, I shall invent a suitable answer. Until then, I shall not worry."

Beaumarchais rose and bowed deeply to Franklin, who remained motionless in his chair as if he were too overcome to think of courtesy.

"I shall leave it to you, Doctor," Beaumarchais said, "to secure those cargoes from our ports. I suggest all possible speed in the matter, before His Majesty orders the ships to return."

"You need have no fear, M. de Beaumarchais," Franklin replied, suddenly springing to his feet, his face wrinkling in a broad smile. "We will have those cargoes removed as quickly as word can cross the sea. I confess that I am still a bit stunned by what you have told me. It is impossible for me to tell you how grateful I am or how grateful our country will be."

Beaumarchais pressed the old man's hand without replying and hurried out the door. Deane was the first to disturb the silence in the room.

"I'm damned if I can figure him out," he exclaimed, rubbing his hand over his face. "I hope it's all true, what he told us. It sounds incredible, but if anyone could do something like that, it would be Beaumarchais."

"I have not seen him before," Franklin answered slowly, "but I have seen other men like him, though no one just like him. He is first a playwright, Silas, and second a statesman. He delights in manipulation. He's one of those who would rather move the players on a stage than to be on the stage themselves. I fancy he would be most annoyed if he felt his public had discovered what he was really doing. He wants the result to come as a tremendous surprise."

Edward, watching Franklin as he spoke, was suddenly amused at the nearly perfect portrait the doctor had drawn of himself. Franklin was very similar to Beaumarchais, except that he had more practicality in his nature. He was an actor, too. When Franklin was forced to it, Edward knew that he was able to fill and hold the center of any stage. Yet it was an unnatural spot for him to occupy. He preferred a quieter place where he could observe and move the players about as he wished.

A few minutes later M. Dubourg was announced. He entered and peered about the room.

"*Mon ami*," he cried out when he saw Franklin.

Rushing across the room he seized his friend by the shoulders and, stretching up, kissed him on both cheeks before he could move. Franklin patted his friend gently on the back and settled him in a chair next to his own.

"I believe you know all these gentlemen?"

"Oh, yes, indeed. M. Deane, Dr. Bancroft—*bon jour,* messieurs." Twisting in his chair, he began a rapid conversation with Franklin which Edward found almost impossible to follow, so quickly did the words cascade from him. His obvious worship of Franklin and his eagerness to see that his friend should want for nothing during his stay in Paris were touching. Franklin himself was affected. From time to time, he reached out and patted his friend on the shoulder, while nodding agreement to all the suggestions of the little man.

"Yes, of course I am comfortable," Franklin said finally, chuckling over Dubourg's unrelenting concern. "Do not disturb yourself so, my friend. All is serene here. The food is excellent and our quarters, I assure you, are most satisfactory. Thus far, I have found Paris as completely delightful as you promised me it would be."

"And from what I have heard, Paris has found you equally delightful, my old friend," Dubourg exclaimed. "Did you know that your fur cap now delights the streets of Nantes? Last week I saw four of them, all worn by gentlemen who never before had the good sense to know the virtue of fur on the head during the winter months. Ribbons are out of fashion, because you wear none. It will be the same here in Paris, I know."

"I doubt that," Franklin laughed. "Paris is not interested in what one man does."

"Unless that man is you," Dubourg corrected him. "You are the latest excitement here. You will remain so for a long time. Already you are reported by thousands of tongues. Fifty people offered to show me the way to this inn when I said I had an appointment with you. Because I am your friend, I trust you will forgive my reminding you how much this can mean to the cause you serve. Think of the rage it will cause in that contemptible Stormont!"

"You are too prejudiced, my good Dubourg. Having known me so long and yet seen me so seldom, you are too charitable. The more you see of me, the more you will become convinced that I am an ordinary, unexciting person."

"That is nonsense," Dubourg fumed, "it is foolish nonsense."

"I am an old man, my friend, not one of those high-spirited bloods like Beaumarchais. I could never wear lace and ruffles with the same aplomb that he does."

"No, you are not Beaumarchais, and thank heaven for it," Dubourg exclaimed. "That man is my enemy. He has robbed me of my chance to assist you, and I shall not forgive him for it."

"Do not fret," Franklin soothed him. "If Beaumarchais has pirated the job you cherished—well, it's not the only job that needs to be done. Ask any of these gentlemen here. They'll tell you how much more there is still to do."

Franklin sat up suddenly in his chair. For several moments he was absolutely silent; the intensity of his concentration was revealed only in his eyes which stared fixedly at the heavy watch chain between his fingers.

A curtain had been dropped between his leaping, fertile brain and the distractions of people and conversation.

"I have it! I have it! Oh, curse me for a dullard!" Franklin cried, turning toward Dubourg. "Tell me, my dear friend, is it not true that you have many interests in the French West Indies?"

"Yes, that's true. I thought you knew that."

"I did, I did," Franklin shook his head from side to side, "but it was just another forgotten fact in this tired brain of mine. Do you have many ships there?"

"Quite a few," Dubourg answered, squinting in increasing bewilderment. "I believe there are twelve altogether."

"Fine! Oh, excellent." Franklin beamed at his puzzled friend. Turning to the others, he said, "You see, gentlemen? You see the connection?"

Edward nodded, and Franklin smiled at him.

"Quite right, Dr. Bancroft."

"I don't see how it can work," Deane grunted. "Too complicated."

"Of course it's complicated, Silas. I agree with you. But not hopelessly complicated. Think what it will mean to us to have those cargoes."

"We have just received word that there are supplies waiting for us in several of the West Indian harbors," Franklin explained to Dubourg. "They must be transferred to other vessels and shipped to America. Do you think your agents could arrange for this?"

"Yes, they could do that easily. We would have to plan the operation. With a list of the ships you mention and the harbors in which they are located, the planning should be simple."

"I shall obtain the list for you. How long would it take to get word to these agents? And how long would it be, do you think, before we could expect those cargoes to arrive in America?"

"The first is easier to answer than the last," Dubourg replied. "With favorable winds, which I am afraid you will not find these days on the ocean, a letter that left France within the week should arrive in Guadeloupe about the first of February. A little over a month, I should judge, taking into consideration the inevitable delays. If we allow three weeks for word to be spread and ships to be assembled at central points, and then allow two weeks for the cargoes to be transferred—those stevedores are infernally slow—the ships should arrive at American ports about the end of March."

"I see," Franklin nodded. "That would be satisfactory, so far as I know. The cargoes will be welcome whenever they arrive, but I feel that the sooner we can get them there, the sooner they will be put to use."

"Shall I write my agents then?"

"I wish you would. I will send the information concerning the names and locations of these vessels to you within the next few days. You could append your instructions to that list. Now, I have something a bit more personal to ask you: I am tired of trying to brush and clean my own clothes. Do you suppose you could find a servant for me, a man who not only knows when to keep his mouth closed, but more important, knows the right time to open it?"

"Yes, Doctor," Dubourg smiled, "I know just the man. I will see if he is available. If he is, I shall send him to you immediately."

"Good," Franklin stood up and drew a deep breath.

"You are very kind to all of us, my friend, especially to me who merits kindness least, being foul tempered and fond of cognac."

"What kind of friend would I be," Dubourg asked, his eyes twinkling, "if I did not know how to cure such common ailments? For the first, I prescribe a pretty lady. For the second, the only cure I have ever found is more cognac."

Franklin turned to the others after Dubourg had departed. "We are all tired, I know," he said, "but I'm certain that none is as tired as I, for none of you is as old. Would it be convenient, Dr. Bancroft, for you to meet us here tomorrow morning at ten?"

Edward walked directly to Wentworth's house from the meeting with Franklin. Sylvestre informed him that his master was absent, and he did not expect him to return for a few days.

Edward wrote a long note to him, describing Franklin's arrival and detailing the discussions which had taken place with Beaumarchais and Dubourg.

That night he took Ellen to a performance of *The Barber of Seville,* Beaumarchais's comedy which was playing at the Theatre des Petis Comediens.

It was one of the most popular plays of the season and the audience abandoned itself with delight to the antics of Figaro. The actor who was playing the part was so moved by this enthusiasm that be began rushing wildly about the stage to heighten the humor of his character. In one of his rushes, his coattail knocked over a candle on one of the tables.

Smoke and flame sprang up before another actor had presence of mind enough to pour a bottle of wine on the flames. Edward, realizing that the blaze was harmless and easily controlled, amused himself by watching the commotion on stage.

Ellen was delighted by the unexpected interruption. She sat spellbound in her seat, laughing at the frantic activity as wine was poured on the flames and the actors, barbers, old ladies, and dignified noblemen stamped furiously at the smoldering carpet.

After the fire had been extinguished, the play continued. Those who crowded the pit seemed to feel a sudden relief, as if they realized that the fire might have had more serious consequences, and their laughter became so loud that it was impossible to hear the speeches on the stage. Only by the postures and the gestures of the players could those seated above the pit follow the plot.

At the end of the play, Edward and Ellen managed to push their way out of the theater and found that the weather had turned extremely cold. Ellen trembled as the bitter wind blustered up the boulevard, bending the trees and menacing the wigs of the theatergoers who crowded together outside the theater. Edward managed to summon his carriage and escape the confusion in front of the theater.

"Thank you, darling," Ellen said as the light from the theater faded behind them. "That was lovely. I even enjoyed the fire."

"I thought the play extremely good," Edward replied, "but I worried a little about the fire when I first saw it. With so many people in that little place, a fire could spread panic so quickly that there would be no hope of escape."

"I hadn't thought of that," she mused. "I suppose that could happen." She shivered and held tight to his hand.

"Are you happy, Edward?" she asked unexpectedly. "I never really know, and you never say anything to let me know."

"Of course, I am," he replied. "Whatever makes you ask?"

"I don't know. Sometimes we seem so far apart. Sometimes I look at you and think to myself, What is he thinking about? How does he feel about me now? Is he happy still or is he growing bored?"

"That's silly, Ellen," he said gruffly. "If I felt that way, it would show all over me, in everything I did, in everything I said. I am happy with you. You should never doubt that."

"I know, darling. I'm sorry I said anything. It's just that as a woman, I guess, I like to be told."

THE NEXT MORNING, when Edward entered the office, he found

Franklin, Deane, and Lee sitting silently. Franklin looked up at him without a word and handed him a piece of paper.

It was a letter from Livingston at the Continental Congress in Philadelphia, dated November 20, 1776:

> I shall not endeavour to write any customary greeting, for my heart is too full of grief and there is scarce time to put this on the ship which sails tonight.
>
> Word has just reached us of the Battle of Washington Fort. Our troops were forced to relinquish their position, as we knew they would be, but calamity has a way of never telling every detail and thus confounding the carefulest plans. General Washington had advised Colonel Magow, the officer in charge of the fort, to withdraw his troops rather than fight to the end. This message was not received until after Magow had been surprised by the Hessians on the north and forced to capitulate.
>
> We lost the fort, but worst of all, we lost two thousand men as prisoners and all the considerable stores contained there, which at this crucial time are irreplaceable.
>
> This news will come to France by other messengers and, I warrant, in less truthful guise. I deemed it best that you know of it in advance.
>
> Today I am inclined toward despair; our course seems to lead us only to disaster.
>
> —Livingston"

The others were silent while Bancroft read the letter. He laid it down on Franklin's desk and waited for the old man to resume the conversation which his arrival had interrupted.

"It is most essential," Franklin said, "that we tell the truth before Stormont has an opportunity to distort it. Even though we seem to hurt our own cause by admitting this, the French will be more likely to trust our reports in the future. It is a harsh, humbling course to follow, I know—indeed, no one knows better than I, for next week I shall have to discuss this debacle with Vergennes...."

Franklin interrupted his discussion to tell Edward that Vergennes's invitation had just arrived: he would meet the doctor at Versailles on December twenty-eighth.

"However, gentlemen, this is not the worst that might have happened to us. There will be other battles, and we shall win them. The French will judge our cause and its success by the length of our faces. If our demeanor is solemn, as though we were watching a body lowered into the grave, it will be but natural for them to lose faith in us, to feel that there is no hope. We cannot go too far in the other direction, either. If we are perpetually smiling and gay in the face of adversity and defeats, we shall seem to them like children, young and ignorant."

"I feel," Franklin concluded, "that we must always exhibit a kind of tempered optimism, as if we are certain that we shall triumph in the end, although we deplore the number of men who must be killed or wounded and the amount of money that must be spent to prove this inescapable conclusion.

"As for Stormont—I feel it wiser if we adopt our own, individual attitudes toward that man. He is, from every report, a brilliant if insufferably arrogant person who holds a most responsible position at this court. We must invent ways to humiliate him, to lower his prestige until he becomes the laughing stock of Paris. Thus, what Stormont loses, England loses. How do you feel about this, Silas?"

"My only point of disagreement," Deane said thoughtfully, "is a minor one. I feel we should be a little more firm, a little more forthright in our attitude toward and in our dealings with Vergennes. After all, we are helping France achieve preeminence in Europe while she is helping us achieve our independence. I don't feel that we should adopt a subservient attitude toward the French.

"The past actions of Vergennes show him to be a very good friend of ours," Franklin objected. "I am convinced, Silas, that we must be completely honest with him. If we are always honest with him, he will trust us; and when we are able to present him with news of a victory, he will be able to sway the king and gain more tangible support for us. Lee, what do you think?"

As usual, Lee was sitting, Edward noticed, in the background, as unobtrusive as the wallpaper. Where would he fit in this divergence of viewpoint between Franklin and Deane?

"I have been listening with much interest to everything that you and Mr. Deane have said," Lee answered. "I am inclined to side with you, Dr. Franklin, with one ... "

"It's not a question of 'siding with someone,'" Franklin said angrily. "With all respect, I deplore your use of that term. We all work together here, with the same purpose and the same goal in view—namely, arranging for a treaty between France and America. We discuss, we argue, we talk ourselves nearly to death—but not for the purpose of taking sides against each other. There may be merit in what Deane has said. There may be merit in what I have said. Forgive my interruption. Pray continue, Mr. Lee."

"In one matter, I am inclined to . . . differ with you," Lee said, his face faintly flushed and his Virginia accent more pronounced than ever. "That is in the matter of being so honest about everything. If we are asked directly, then we must be, of course. If news is generally known, then we must publish the truth as we receive it. But would it not be wiser to find ways of discovering how much is known by the British and the French? Look at what the British do to secure information of this kind. I don't know whether you are acquainted with a Mr. Paul Wentworth, Doctor?"

Lee paused for a reply. Edward's hand tightened around the arm of his chair; his eyes never wavered from Franklin's face.

When Franklin shook his head, Lee continued. "He is one of the best public servants the British have. I believe he is here in Paris now, in charge of their secret service. It is said that only the devil knows how many operatives Wentworth has working for him. There are so many of them that the officials in the government offices no longer know whom they can trust. You can imagine how much information Wentworth obtains from this spy ring. If we had a similar organization, we might not have to be so honest. We would know how much bad news we would have to disclose."

Franklin nodded. "That is a very interesting idea, Mr. Lee."

Lee went on. "Why couldn't we have one? Dr. Bancroft is our first operative of that type, and a superior one, too, from what Mr. Deane has told me. But is one enough? If suspicion should fall on Dr. Bancroft, wouldn't it be wiser to have others working for us so that we were not left without any source of information? Perhaps Dr. Bancroft, as one better acquainted with the situation, could enlighten us on this subject."

The first shock which Edward had experienced when Wentworth's name was introduced into the conversation had worn off. He could now enjoy the grim humor of the situation.

"A secret service is a most difficult enterprise to establish," Edward explained. "It requires a great deal of money, unlimited patience, and most important of all, unlimited time in which to combat and overcome mistakes. Frankly, I do not believe we have enough time to establish such a service. There might be, however, a few people who could obtain information for us.

"I am one example of the many Americans in England who would be willing to do such work. Dr. Franklin, you must have many other friends in England who would be willing to serve as I am doing. There might be some who would do the work if they were paid well enough. Wouldn't it be wiser to seek out those in England and France whom we know to be our friends, those who are highly connected in the governments, and ask them to do this for us? We could arrange means by which all the information might be sent here to you, Doctor. We could read their reports and base our decisions upon them and upon what we had discovered ourselves."

"Your point is well taken, Doctor," Franklin said. "We don't have enough time, or enough money to establish a regular service. We do have friends. Silas, surely you and Mr. Lee can think of people who could secure information for us?"

"I have thought of several," Deane replied. "There are probably quite a few who would be willing."

"I, too, have thought of some," Lee broke in, "and more will probably come to mind."

Franklin smiled. "Good. I know some myself, whom I used for that very purpose when I was in England. Frequently, I was informed in advance of what to expect from the ministry. Once, during that disgraceful affair of the Hutchinson letters, I knew exactly what the outcome would be; the night before the hearing, one of my friends was at supper with that creature Wedderburn."

The color rose suddenly in Franklin's face and he puffed out his cheeks in disgust. The anger that visibly stiffened him in his chair when he recollected the trial brought the whole scene back to Edward's mind in an instant.

Franklin's trial had been the cause célèbre of London for an entire winter. The British Ministry had wished to force Franklin out of England because it believed he was obtaining too much support for the Colonial aspirations. The lever used by the ministry was a series of letters from Governor Hutchinson of Massachusetts, which warned of a potential rebellion in the Colonies. The ministry claimed that the letters—procured by theft at Franklin's instigation—had been copied and sent to high officials in the government, then published by Franklin to hasten the rupture between England and her Colonies.

Edward would never forget the scene in the Cockpit Tavern, the place chosen for the trial. Franklin had sat silent and aloof while Wedderburn, the caustic spokesman for the Privy Council, denounced him as a firebrand who was intent only on causing a war and increasing his own fortune at the expense of his countrymen's lives. Against all reason, Wedderburn branded the Hutchinson letters as forgeries, perpetrated by Franklin alone to gain money for himself. He excoriated the doctor as a highly placed criminal, while Burke and Shelburne suffered in silence, outraged by the indignities heaped upon their friend. When Wedderburn claimed that Franklin had destroyed the original letters from Hutchinson because they had shown Franklin and his friends to be a small group of malcontents attempting to foment an unwanted struggle, Franklin half rose in his place beside the fire, his face white with rage.

Before the doctor could utter a word in his own defense, Lord North, who was presiding, brusquely motioned him to silence. Franklin took his seat again, his shoulders slumped with resignation, and for the remainder of the trial appeared almost apathetic, staring into the fire and apparently hearing nothing that was said. Franklin's advocate, Dunning, after his preliminary defense, was not allowed to speak again on behalf of the man whose reputation he was trying to defend.

Wedderburn's vilification of Franklin continued for more than an hour. In the end, he proved his case to the satisfaction of the Privy Council, who sat around the largest table in the room, smiling at each fresh taunt. Yet Wedderburn proved exactly nothing. The letters predicted trouble in Massachusetts—everyone knew that. Franklin had published the letters only because he hoped to stir up trouble between the British government and the Colonists—the members of the Privy Council had agreed to this fact long before the mock trial began.

Edward remained in the tavern after the Privy Council departed, along with Priestley, Burke, Shelburne, and Franklin. Little was said, but all were saddened by the memory of the shameful manner in which Franklin had been treated, judged, and condemned by this ridiculous trial. They stood around awkwardly, these few friends left to Franklin in a hostile England, until Burke spoke. Edward remembered the majesty of that famous voice, the aura of prescience that seemed to envelop his words:

"Dr. Franklin, I speak for these gentlemen who, like myself, are your constant friends. We deplore what has happened here today. England will later deplore it. We have sacrificed our best friend in the Colonies, and today's stupidity may well cost us a continent. I know that England has estranged a loyal subject, and I feel I have lost a dear friend."

Franklin had not replied, but in moving toward the door to take his leave, solemnly and silently shook hands with each of the men present. When he'd finished with Burke, the eyes of both were wet and Burke's face quivered with an emotion too sincere to be concealed.

Franklin coughed suddenly and Edward returned with a start to the present. He shook his head slightly, as if to clear the memories of the past from his brain.

"Let us leave that for a moment," Franklin was saying. "Our present concern is with this news of the capture of Washington Fort. Shall we disclose it at once, or shall we wait, as has been suggested, for a more propitious time?"

"You might as well tell Vergennes," Deane sighed. "It seems too bad that you should have to mention such a distressing subject on your first meeting, but it's better for *you* to mention it than for Stormont to magnify it far beyond the unhappy truth. The British won't know about this, I should judge, until their transports arrive in England. They will have to land the prisoners; and that's always a long, tedious business. So we should still have at least two weeks before the news is known."

"Two weeks may be optimistic," Franklin replied. "I would not be surprised if word reached Paris before I see Vergennes."

Edward walked to Wentworth's house again that afternoon. He waited for some time in the study before Wentworth appeared and spent his time writing a note to Sam Wharton, advising him of the American defeat at Washington Fort and instructing him to buy additional government shares in anticipation of the rise which should result from the publication of the news.

"I'm sorry to keep you waiting so long, Edward," Wentworth said as he walked across the study, "but I couldn't get away Before I forget, here is something for you from Lord Mansfield. He said to be certain to give it to you the next time I saw you." Wentworth handed him a package. Opening a corner of it, Edward saw that it was a packet of bills.

"It is your salary from last August to the end of the year. I believe you will find it larger by some 500 pounds than you anticipated. When I was last in London, both Eden and Lord Mansfield told me how pleased they were with your work. This last information you secured, about the ships in the West Indies, will be particularly valuable. I believe that we will be able to

West Indies, will be particularly valuable. I believe that we will be able to intercept every one of them before they reach the Colonies. Lord Howe will welcome the supplies. He has been complaining to the Admiralty that supplies have not been reaching him. He said he could not be responsible for the discipline of the Hessians much longer if they didn't receive boots."

"I wanted to tell you about this morning's meeting with Franklin," Edward interrupted.

"Ah! That Franklin!" Wentworth exclaimed. "What a jinx he is! Every time he appears, something goes wrong. Today, one of my best men left for England, although he's infinitely more valuable to me here. He refused to stay—said if I didn't approve his transfer, he'd clear out completely. When I suggested that would be a foolish way to end his life, he came out with the truth. He said that Franklin knew him and had learned that he was working for us. He'd had one run-in with him in London, which I hadn't heard about. But tell me about the conference this morning."

"There was interesting news from the Colonies," Edward began. "Washington Fort has been captured, with two thousand prisoners and all their stores."

"Splendid! I'm delighted to hear it. That will be valuable ammunition for Stormont."

"Be certain that you cover my tracks," Edward warned. "The news is known only to the commissioners and me."

"Don't worry, Edward. It will reach Stormont by special courier from London. What else was discussed?"

"They were wondering about starting a secret service, but I argued rather convincingly against that."

"Good for you."

"They decided to use their friends to gain information, rather than try to establish a complete organization."

"Whom do they mean to use?"

"No names were mentioned. It's still rather a vague idea."

"They can probably find some excellent sources," Wentworth mused. "We must find out who these people are. Pay particular attention to that, Edward. As soon as they decide on the people they intend to use, let me know their names. It will not be difficult to provide false information for them. We can't afford to allow Franklin to have agents who are unknown to us."

"There's one other bit of information you might like to know. Arthur Lee, the new commissioner, is already cordially disliked by both Franklin and Deane. He's a vain little man, highly suspicious of everything he is told and most of the people he meets. Yet, he's not stupid at all. I feel he could be extremely dangerous. He knows a great deal more than one might suspect—in fact, he gave a rather accurate picture of you and your work in Paris."

"He did, eh? Well, perhaps I should keep an eye on Mr. Lee. If he causes trouble among the Americans, he's a valuable man. But on the other hand, I wouldn't like him to be spreading any . . . false reports."

Edward stopped at a small cafe on his way home, and after seating himself at a table in the rear of the room, he called for the proprietor.

"Good afternoon, Monsieur. I am happy to see you," the proprietor said, when he reached Edward's side.

"Thank you, M. DuMont. You will remember, perhaps, that the last time I was here you said you had a son who could, for a reasonable sum, deliver a message quickly to London."

"That is correct, Monsieur. It is my son, Claude. It is a fact that he can travel to London in less than three days. He has done it."

"Good. Is he here now?"

"Yes, Monsieur. Shall I call him?"

"Please do. And bring me some cognac."

In a few minutes the proprietor returned with the cognac. With him was a young man, about twenty-five, Edward judged, and as ugly a creature as he had seen in some time. His face was deeply pitted by smallpox scars, and his teeth were crooked and black with decay.

"I have a letter that must be delivered to London within three days. Can you deliver it?"

"Yes, Monsieur, I can," the youth answered. His eyes narrowed slightly as he added, "But it will cost you something."

"I realize that," Edward said impatiently. "I don't expect you to carry it for nothing. I will pay you two pounds."

"Two pounds, Monsieur! *Parbleu!*" he exclaimed. "That is impossible. Ten pounds at the least—my expenses will be nearly that much."

"They will be if you hire a coach for yourself," Edward retorted. "Very well, let us admit that ten pounds is too much. I will pay you four pounds, and I shall write instructions on the envelope to pay you an additional three pounds after you have delivered the letter. That should be satisfactory."

"But, Monsieur," the youth protested, "it is a difficult journey to make in three days." Edward took two notes from his wallet and laid them on the table without a word.

"However, I shall do it for M'sieu," Claude concluded, hastily taking up the notes.

When he arrived home, Edward found Mme. de Treymes in the drawing room with Ellen. She looked unchanged from the last time he had seen her, if a trifle more formidable, perhaps, in her purple gown and her enormous calash, which towered above her head, bright with diamonds.

"Good evening, Dr. Bancroft. You're looking better than the last time I saw you."

"Thank you, Madame. Paris agrees with me, especially this cool winter weather which is so pleasant for walking."

"Pleasant for you, perhaps, Doctor, but I would never go out in it myself. It does put color in the cheeks, but I find it simpler to use my vermilion. When one reaches my age, exercise is something one reads about. Tell me about your Dr. Franklin. Is he as fascinating as all Paris claims he is?"

"Madame, he is. He's certainly one of the most brilliant men of our time."

"I suppose he must be. He has captured the heart of Paris—there is no doubt of that. On the street one hears constantly the name Franklin. In the salons there is a rivalry for the honor of his presence which you would not believe possible."

During dinner, Edward told the old lady many stories about Franklin which only increased her desire to see the famous American.

"I thought I was beyond curiosity of this sort," she sighed, "but I see I am not. I have met him before, but that was at a large dinner where I spoke only a few words to him. I believe I shall invite him to dinner at my house. Perhaps, Dr. Bancroft, you might be able to convince him that my motive springs more from a desire to talk with him than from a vulgar wish to display him as a trophy."

Edward smiled. "I know I shall be able to do that, Madame. I shall whet his interest by saying that you have made many startling medical discoveries about indigestion."

"That will be kind of you, if not truthful," Madame laughed, turning toward her young hostess.

"Ellen, have you seen any plays recently that amused you?"

"Yes, Madame. We were at the theater only last week to see *The Barber of Seville*. It was most amusing, even during the fire."

"The fire?"

"Yes, there was a small fire. Figaro was dashing about so on the stage that his coattail knocked over a candle and started a small blaze in the carpet. It was quickly extinguished, and the play continued as if nothing had happened. I liked what I could hear of it over the noise from the pit."

"Fires, fires, fires," Madame said. "All over Paris one hears stories of fires. I have heard that Dr. Franklin is going to propose the establishment of a fire department in Paris. Is this true, Doctor?"

"I had not heard of that proposal. I would not be at all surprised, though, for I know he has visited the inspector of posts and made recommendations to him, based on his own experiences with the Colonial postal service."

"What an extraordinary person he is! He seems to be interested in everything. I wonder how it is that one man can encompass so many interests."

"I only say, Madame, that Dr. Franklin is constructed on what is called the heroic stature. Such men are increasingly rare, and thus even more unbelievable to their own contemporaries."

"Don't you believe that every generation makes the same complaint?"

"Perhaps so, Madame. Yet it seems that the world is becoming so complicated that we need more men of heroic stature than we ever did before."

"Alas, we are too serious tonight. Tell me, Doctor, have you ever met this Dr. Quaritch, of whom there is so much discussion in Paris?"

"He's the clairvoyant, isn't he? No, I never have."

"I've met him," Ellen said. "At the countess de Grere's. He was there for the afternoon, and he entertained all the guests by reading their minds. He's quite extraordinary: he told our hostess that she was thinking about replanting her apple trees around her estate in Provence; he warned Mme. de Ragnau that the man she was thinking about had an extremely jealous wife; but when the countess de Polignac asked him to read her mind he refused. She insisted, and he finally agreed. He said that the wagon she was thinking about was similar to the one that would carry her to her death. Everyone was horrified, of course, especially the lady whose death he had just prophesied.

"Just then a monkey that belonged to one of the ladies screeched and turned over a table with a vase on it. We all tried to capture the little beast and in the excitement quite forgot the unhappy prophecy."

"Shall we go into the drawing room?" Ellen asked. "I think it would be more comfortable and there is a warm fire, too."

"When I sit beside a fire," Madame said, settling herself comfortably in a large chair, "I am like a fat, lazy cat—too content to budge. I warn you: you may not be able to rouse me."

"We'll risk that, Madame," Ellen replied. "It would be a great pleasure if you would stay with us, but then think of the rumors Therese might start if you did not return."

"I know what she'd say," Madame exclaimed, settling herself further down in the chair. "First she'd say I was shameless, at my age, staying out all night. Then she'd moan and wail enough to disturb the whole house. Such an opportunity would be too good to waste without an audience."

"From the little I have seen of her," Ellen said, "she appears deeply devoted to you. How long has she been with you?"

"More than fifteen years. She's the most loyal and faithful person I've ever known; and in spite of the way she annoys me at times, I could not live happily without her. I never upbraid her too much for fear she'll leave me."

Mme. de Treymes said nothing for a few minutes. She stared into the fire, stretching comfortably as the warmth sank into her clothes and giving an occasional angry jab at her calash which had slipped a little to one side. As they watched her, they noticed the corners of her mouth curl up in a tiny smile. She gave a deep, rich chuckle and turned to look at them.

"A thousand pardons to you both. Fires make me dream, and I could not help smiling, for I was dreaming of the two of you."

She sat up a little in her chair and clasped her hands.

"What must it be like, to be in love and in Paris now, with your whole life before you? Older people sometimes dream like that, though you would never think so, from the advice they give so freely. I think I am a little jealous of you, really. I am old enough to be undisturbed by love, but not so old as to forget my memories of it."

Edward and Ellen remained silent, watching the fire and waiting for her to proceed.

"I remember, as I suppose most old people do, the time when I was just beginning my life with another.

"I was quite old—nearly thirty-five, an age when most women my age were fashionable young matrons with splendid salons. I had never met a man who interested me more than myself, until I met M. de Treymes. Why he should ever have noticed me, I cannot fathom to this day. He was so handsome, so tall and brown and healthy, so highly regarded by the world and so wildly sought after by mothers of marriageable daughters. I was even homelier than I am today—a timid, uncertain person with a strange predilection for books and conversation which did not center about the trivia of life.

"I believe he was first attracted to me when I told him, quite seriously, that I had committed myself to a life of thought. Secular thought, I remember adding quickly, lest he think I might soon be lost to a convent.

"He came to see me frequently after that, and then he left for Geneva. He stayed there five years without once returning to France. I had fallen in love with him, although I didn't realize it until after he had departed; those five years were the loneliest years in my life. When he returned, he came straight to me and asked me if I would marry him. He added that he did not wish to interfere with my thoughts. I told him I would marry him, and we arranged that I should have three months of every year to myself, when I could be alone to think what I liked. He was older than I and far wiser, so he insisted upon this compromise. We were married at once, but never, in all our life together, did I summon up enough courage to take my three months alone. I didn't want to, except on rare occasions. I knew he would have difficulty living without me, and I couldn't bear the thought of living without him. We were together for thirty years, constantly, and then, one morning, when he had seemed perfectly fine, he closed his eyes and died.

"God works in strange ways, indeed. He allowed me to live on, perfectly useless, battening on other people and growing fat with comfort, while he struck down my husband, as fine a man as there was in France. That particular injustice has always puzzled me; just after my husband's death, I thought about it a great deal, but I don't anymore."

Mme. de Treymes struggled to her feet and stood beside Ellen for a moment, her hand lightly stroking the girl's soft hair.

"I must leave. It is late and I have talked, as the old will, chiefly of myself. Forgive me. I hope you will both come for supper at my house some night. Try and stop in tomorrow afternoon, Ellen. There will be some people there who are rather interesting. You, too, Doctor, if you feel you could endure an afternoon of women's chatter. There will be other men there, so you will not be entirely alone."

They saw the old lady to her coach and returned to the house quickly, for the damp cold cut to the bone because of the fog that had descended over Paris.

"I love that old woman," Ellen declared, after they had gone upstairs. "She always seems to enjoy whatever she does, whether it's a coach ride or having dinner here with us. She makes me feel that she gives me a part of herself each time I see her."

"She has lived a very full life, and a happy one, from all she says. Considering her station in life, that's a remarkable achievement."

"What a queer thing to say!"

"Not at all. It's usually true that the more advantages one has, the less one enjoys life. People suffer deprivation as easily when they're rich as when they're poor, but it's a different sort of deprivation: a hunger of the brain instead of the stomach."

"I'd rather be rich than poor," Ellen observed with feeling. "You can feel very deprived when you've nothing to eat."

"Yes, but you do go on living. You fight against circumstances until you have enough to eat. When you suffer from hunger of the brain, you rarely realize what the trouble is. You're sick, but there's no medicine to help you."

Ellen shivered at his description. "You make it so clear, you must have seen a great deal of it."

"I have, but fortunately in others, not in myself," Edward replied. "It's a common disease, more common here than it is in England. We've been fortunate in the friends and acquaintances we've made, but just think of the lackwits at the French court. They are as useless a group as you could find. They have nothing to do, nothing to exercise their brains, so they make a fetish of pleasure. Someday all that pleasure will come back to haunt them."

THE NEXT MORNING was cold, clear, and delightfully crisp. Edward pulled his greatcoat about him and went down the Boulevard des Capucines, pleased that he had decided to walk.

The government buildings loomed against the blue sky as he moved toward the Pont Royal. The guards on the bridge, usually so dour and grumpy, smiled at him as he passed by. All Paris seemed to delight in the freshness of this December morning.

The anteroom of the little inn was crowded as Edward made his way through the waiting visitors toward the rooms in the rear which the American commissioners used for their offices. Carmichael informed him that Deane and Lee had already arrived.

When he entered, the two men were discussing Franklin's forthcoming visit to Versailles. After they had exchanged greetings, Lee turned back to Deane.

"Don't you think it's important?" Lee was saying. "After all, I'm one of the commissioners to France, just as you are, and I should be presented to Vergennes in my official capacity, as soon as I arrive at Versailles."

"Mr. Lee and I were discussing his introduction to Vergennes, Doctor," Deane explained to Edward. "He feels he should be presented to Vergennes immediately after Dr. Franklin is. What do you think?"

"I'm sure it is not for me to decide that, Mr. Deane. But since you ask my opinion, I would say that this interview has been arranged primarily for Dr. Franklin. Perhaps Mr. Lee could talk with M. Gerard while Dr. Franklin is with Vergennes. After they have finished, I know M. Gerard will present Mr. Lee if there is an opportunity."

While Edward was making his reply, he watched Lee and was not surprised to notice the anger mount in his face. Purposely, Edward kept the tone of his voice quite impersonal and took care to give no occasion for criticism in the words he used. It was quite clear that Lee was furious with his answer.

Just as Deane was about to speak, Lee broke in.

"I don't feel that Dr. Bancroft should be concerned in such a matter as this. I am here in an important position for our government. It is for you and Franklin to decide upon the best method of presenting me to the foreign minister. I am, of course, grateful for Dr. Bancroft's opinion, but I feel that this should be the concern of the commissioners."

Deane twisted angrily in his chair.

"Mr. Lee, it is quite clear to me that you have one thing still to learn about duty with a foreign government," he snapped angrily. "You are a complete stranger to its customs, just as I was. Dr. Bancroft has been invaluable to our cause. By his knowledge, I have learned how to deal with Vergennes and Beaumarchais, how to conduct myself in accordance with court tradition, and how to avoid making mistakes which might offend the French. I respect his judgment, and I depend upon it. I am certain that Dr. Franklin feels the same way, for it was he, you will remember, who was so eager for me to obtain Dr. Bancroft's assistance."

"I did not mean to give offense by my remarks," Lee replied, his face coloring violently. "I apologize, Doctor, if I appeared to do so. This matter is so important to me, however, that I cannot help feeling the decision should be made by the commissioners."

"Please, gentlemen," Edward injected, before Deane could explode further after this fresh clumsiness of Lee's, "please don't allow what I said to cause any difficulty. Mr. Lee is quite correct—it is a matter for the commissioners to decide. If I can be of any possible help, Mr. Deane knows that I shall be happy to do whatever I can."

"Indeed I do, Edward," Deane replied, as if he knew how much this use of Bancroft's Christian name would irritate Lee. "You've done splendid work for us, and we are all extremely grateful to you."

Edward was delighted this outburst had occurred. Lee had so antagonized Deane that Edward was certain the entire group would band together against this tactless Virginian.

"Good morning, gentlemen," Franklin said, hurrying into the room. "I am sorry to be so long delayed. What discussion has my tardy arrival interrupted?"

"We were discussing the coming visit to Vergennes," Deane explained. "What about Mr. Lee? Do you feel your visit to Vergennes would be the proper occasion for his formal presentation?"

"Hum," Franklin pondered, staring over the rims of his glasses at Lee, "possibly. It will depend on M. de Vergennes, however. He boasts of being the busiest man in France, so a formal introduction might be impossible during that visit. Suppose I try to arrange for it then, and if it should not be a suitable time, we shall arrange for a later meeting. How does that sound, Mr. Lee?"

Lee shifted in his chair. It was obvious that the thought of delaying his introduction to Vergennes displeased him greatly; Edward could tell by the way Lee coughed and continued to shift about that he was searching for some alternative by which he could achieve some success over Deane and himself and yet not offend Franklin.

"I think that is the only suitable solution," Franklin said, closing off any possible alternatives which Lee might suggest. "You may rest assured, Mr. Lee, that I shall present you to M. Vergennes as soon as I am able."

"When I saw him last," Deane recalled, "Vergennes asked that you be prepared to tell him about the strength and the finances of the army."

While Franklin and the others discussed his forthcoming conversation with Vergennes, the matter of Lee's presentation was forgotten. As always, the Virginian sat in the background, silent unless he was called upon directly for his opinion.

While Edward walked home that evening, his thoughts centered around Lee. What an impossible person he was to deal with. He was a man who didn't seem happy unless he had someone to fight against; from what Edward had seen of him thus far, he imagined that Lee could be a tenacious and cunning enemy.

CHAPTER VIII

WHEN THE DAY ARRIVED for Franklin's interview with Vergennes, Edward told him that he felt it wiser if he did not accompany him to Versailles.

There was always, as there had been when Deane went, the chance of meeting Stormont. It would be foolish, Edward said, to take such an unnecessary risk.

Franklin nodded when he heard Edward's suggestion and regretfully agreed. He climbed into the coach, followed by Deane and Lee, and as it moved off, he waved cheerfully to Edward.

The three men were warmly welcomed by Gerard, Vergennes's assistant, and they waited and chatted in his office until Vergennes was ready to receive Franklin.

Gerard was an attractive, agreeable young Frenchman, as pleasing in personality as he was brilliant in mind. Paris regarded him as a powerful influence behind Vergennes and gave him considerable credit for the reestablishment of France's prestige and power.

He was descended from an excellent and wealthy family. While still a youth, he and his tutor had traveled all over Europe; there was not a country on the Continent with whose customs and language and history he was not well acquainted. His family's position had secured him entree to every court, and his own charm soon endeared him to the distinguished people he met. He had been traveling in Russia when he was summoned home by Vergennes, who had made him his assistant in the foreign office.

Gerard had demonstrated at once that he was a man who did his work quietly, with great efficiency, while others frittered away their time at the Petit Trianon. Although he was not much more than thirty, his position at the foreign office had further developed a natural dignity which was evident in his respectful treatment of Franklin.

"I am so happy to meet you, Dr. Franklin," Gerard said after they were seated. "M. Voltaire has told me much about you, and that delightful M. Dubourg has told me still more. As you must know, M. Dubourg is one of your most ardent partisans. Once, I saw him rise to his feet, after someone had made a disparaging remark about the modern mind, and heard him extoll you as an example for all the guests to follow. He discussed your career and your achievements so completely that I feel there is little—"

He did not have an opportunity to finish what he was saying. The door of Vergennes's office opened, and the foreign minister stood in the doorway looking out.

"I will see Dr. Franklin now, M. Gerard."

Gerard led Franklin into the office, and the door closed behind them.

"The foreign minister doesn't waste time," Lee muttered.

"No, he does not," Deane agreed. "It is not for nothing that he boasts of being the busiest man in France. His enemies have a saying:The Devil never sleeps, so how can Vergennes?"

Gerard reappeared and sat down again with them.

"M. de Vergennes has just told me that I should discuss finances with you gentlemen while he talks with Dr. Franklin. Mr. Deane, I find that our original loan to you is nearly exhausted. Although M. de Vergennes was most unhappy to hear about the misfortunes of your troops at Fort Washington, he hopes that if you are given a little more assistance, matters may sufficiently improve to justify his faith."

On hearing from Gerard the secret news of the capture of Fort Washington, Deane was a study in amazement. He tightened his hands around the arms of his chair, and his chin trembled as he tried to control his emotion. He soon recovered sufficiently to reply.

"We ourselves have only just learned this unhappy news, M. Gerard. I agree with M. de Vergennes that with more funds at our disposal, the situation cannot but improve. It will, to be sure, improve without them, but with additional supplies, our successes will be more substantial. Perhaps Mr. Lee would like to add something to what I have said?"

"Such a loan would give fresh confidence to the people and to their leaders," Lee added eagerly. "I know in the case of Virginia that it would win to our cause a large number of people who today are still clinging to the British throne. If they were to be shown that France is willing to continue her support, even though these first battles go badly, they would be won over, I am sure."

"That is most interesting, Mr. Lee. I should like the opportunity of conversing with you at some later time about Virginia. It is a charming area that has always interested me."

Lee beamed with pleasure, and Deane smiled at the adroit way by which Gerard had won over Lee.

"Mr. Deane," Gerard continued. "M. de Vergennes has authorized me to tell you that the king is willing to lend America an additional two million livres. This will be put to your credit within the week."

While Deane and Lee were receiving this welcome news, Franklin was conversing with Vergennes and observing the man who must be won completely to the American cause. This was the one person in France, Franklin knew, who had the power to arrange a treaty between France and America. As he watched Vergennes, he realized his task would be difficult. Vergennes was clever; he would never commit himself or his country except when he stood to gain much by such commitment. Although friendly to America, he was completely dedicated to the interests and the prestige of France. While they talked, Franklin sensed that the news would have to improve—America would have to win a major victory—before the treaty could even be discussed.

"And so, Dr. Franklin, in the name of the king I have been instructed to welcome you to France and to convey His Majesty's regret that you cannot be welcomed officially as the representative of a sovereign nation. The king asked me to express to you his personal regret.

"His Majesty's life has lately become very difficult because of these innovations in thought that seem to be sweeping over Europe. As you know, he wishes to establish a reign of moderation here in France, to offset the unfortunate example of his grandfather. His success has been impaired by the ferment stirred up by these new philosophers, so many of whom seem, regretfully enough, to be French. These changes in government and society which they advocate cause His Most Christian Majesty great distress, since he is anxious to preserve in his court the ancient customs."

"I quite understand, M. de Vergennes. It will be better if I live quietly and work silently in Paris. So long as I may have the pleasure of meeting with you occasionally, I shall feel that my life here has some purpose."

"I am looking forward, Doctor, to the pleasure of discussing scientific matters with you, as well as the affairs of America, with which we are both so concerned. Frankly, these latest defeats, especially the fall of Fort Washington, have worried me greatly. It seems that the Colonists are not the equals of the British in military matters. I realize that is not a polite thing to say to one who visits me in amity, but the reason I mention it at all is to show you the importance of victory. Continued defeats may cost us both the confidence of His Majesty."

"The fall of Fort Washington is tragic," Franklin admitted, too wise to betray his curiosity as to the source of Vergennes's information. "But, sir, America is just beginning. She cannot hope at the outset to achieve victories over experienced British troops. There are bound to be some defeats."

"Some, yes," Vergennes agreed, "but thus far there has been nothing else. No good news to carry to His Majesty. No word of shining victories or even of successful skirmishes. Believe me, Doctor, I want the Colonies to achieve their independence—frankly, it will mean a weaker England, and it will enhance the importance of our West Indian colonies. But my enthusiasm, which I hope to communicate to His Majesty, must be implemented with happy facts; it cannot endure if it remains a recital of defeats and disasters."

"My position is also made more difficult by Stormont," Vergennes continued after a brief pause. "No opportunity escapes him to put me in an unfortunate light. Much as I dislike the man, I admit that he is clever. His ripostes at court, his jests and subtle satires about the Sans Culottes in America, are bearing fruit."

Franklin nodded sympathetically. "I understand what it must be like, Monsieur. Here in Paris, I cannot promise victories. Were I in the fighting, knowing all that you have told me, I am certain I would achieve at least one major triumph. It would occur just after I had told my troops that a British official had scorned them as warriors without pants. The men of our Southern colonies, the Virginians especially, would be so infuriated that no troops could stand against them. But I am not in America. The best I can do is pray, which I do constantly, and fly to you whenever there is favorable news."

"We shall both pray then, Doctor," Vergennes sighed, rising to his feet. "I am delighted that you are in France. I hope that you will come to Versailles soon again, bursting with good news for me."

"I am convinced I will," Franklin stated. "Good-bye, M. de Vergennes. Thank you for your frankness."

On the way back to Paris, Deane informed Franklin of the loan which Gerard had mentioned, and for a moment Franklin seemed happy and pleased. He soon fell silent, however, his distress mirrored on his face as he meditated on his interview with Vergennes and realized the impossibility of expecting good news for quite some time. Winter had already covered America with snow; the army must dig in and endure. It would have to wait for spring as best it could, with too little equipment, too little food, and no hope. When he thought of Washington commanding those ragged, unhappy troops that somehow had to be kept ready to fight, he could not conceal the torment he felt.

"I believed hearing about the loan would cheer you, Doctor," Deane sighed mournfully, "but it only appears to have made you sadder than you were. We can pay it back easily. Gerard said that the French would accept goods in return for it, to be sent after the war is over."

"For once," Franklin said, smiling a little, "it's not the return of the money that worries me. I was thinking of another, sadder subject, something for which there seems to be no remedy. But about the loan—when will the money be available?"

"Within a week."

"Fine. Perhaps we shall be able to secure enough new equipment to load ships at once. We must send uniforms and woolens as soon as possible . . . ."

"How was your interview with Vergennes?" Lee asked.

"Satisfactory," Franklin replied. "A most agreeable man, I feel. He is extremely sympathetic to us, although we have so far given him little reason for his confidence. A more valuable ally we could not have in France, except for the king himself."

AS WINTER SETTLED over Paris, life centered around the warm rooms of the city. Theatres were always crowded, and dinner parties and gatherings at the famous salons defied the chilling wetness outside.

Edward and Ellen were much sought after by the hostesses of Paris. They found their greatest pleasure at the homes of Mme. de Treymes and the countess de Grere; unless Edward felt it politic to accept another invitation, they passed most of their time at one house or the other.

Although the appointed time for the weekly gathering at Mme. de Treymes's salon was Thursday afternoon, Ellen had formed the habit of visiting the old lady during the morning, when she was comparatively undisturbed by callers bubbling with gossip and scandal. She loved to listen to stories of her friend's life and would sit for hours while Madame wove a colorful web of events and people she had known.

Edward had been asked to contribute to several of the important Parisian journals; his article on investments in the Colonies had occasioned much comment, and several times at Chacot's he had been asked by his banker acquaintances to explain certain aspects of it to them.

Franklin had also read the article, for the journal had printed a piece of his in the same issue.

He was much interested by it, and he told Edward he would like to discuss it privately with him. Edward, recalling Ellen's hopes, asked the Doctor to come to their house for supper.

"I shall be delighted, Dr. Bancroft," Franklin replied.

Franklin arrived promptly at nine, his fur cap brushed, his neat, freshly pressed clothes showing the assiduous attention of Champagne, the servant Dubourg had sent to him.

"I am happy to make your acquaintance, Miss Vaughn," Franklin said as he bowed to Ellen. "I have been extremely jealous of Mr. Deane, who has told me of the pleasant evenings he has enjoyed here."

"We hope that you will come often, Dr. Franklin; you know that you will always be welcome."

"How do you like your man Champagne?" Edward asked as they walked into the drawing room.

"I distrust large statements that cannot be proved, Dr. Bancroft, but I shall risk making one myself: there is no finer servant in Paris than Champagne. The man is uncanny—I am certain he always knows what is going to happen to me on the morrow. He never lays out the wrong clothes for me; several times I have forgotten an engagement until suddenly, seeing the clothes that were waiting for me on my bed, I remembered it. Now he has acquired a new virtue: if I return home discouraged, I find brandy by my chair. If I am pleased with myself, I find water; if I am pleased with the world—wine. What could be more perfect?"

"He sounds unbelievable," Ellen laughed. "How could M. Dubourg bear to part with him?"

"Dubourg would crawl from here to Calais if he thought it would aid me," Franklin said with sudden warmth. "He is one of my oldest friends. He is convinced that I am a hostage to overwork and is certain that I will die here in France unless he personally takes care of me."

"I am certain you will live a great many more years, Doctor. I am told in the salons that all your rivals are under fifty."

"I am too old for rivals, Miss Vaughn, although the idea is flattering. I must be truthful and admit that I enjoy hearing these highly complimentary stories about myself. Often I feel that the reason for them is because I have dabbled with electricity. Everyone in Paris, especially the ladies, has a passion to touch me to see if I have electrified myself. Even that greatest George-lover of them all, Mme. du Deffand, claims that lightning has made me younger. It is all quite ridiculous, but I enjoy it, especially when the prettier ladies insist that they must find out for themselves."

They walked into the dining room and sat down to a meal for which Ellen and Bertram had searched all over Paris. Edward had advised her well in advance what dishes Franklin preferred, and each course, as it was brought to the table, made the old man's eyes shine brighter with pleasure. There was a fine, cold paté to start, then a steaming soup made with greens and peppery spices. Next came sole, then partridge *champenoise*. After his first bite, Franklin adjusted his glasses, stared at his plate, and muttered, "Incredible." A *tarte aux pommes* appeared, followed by cheeses and preserved fruits— oranges, figs, and apricots. When they returned to the drawing room, coffee was served, after which Ellen poured a fragrant, sugary liqueur.

Over his coffee, Franklin peered at Ellen, his eyes round and questioning.

"Miss Vaughn, may I ask a question and then a favor?"

"Certainly, Dr. Franklin."

"First, where did you ever find all these lovely things? I have combed all Paris for such food—Champagne has searched wildly—yet I have been unable to find enough for even a single course of this superb meal."

"If I did not feel that it might keep you from coming here again, Doctor, I would show you. But yours is not a fair question to ask a hostess."

"I realize that full well, but it would not keep me from enjoying another dinner here, believe me. That is my request: may I be permitted to come again, sometime when I cannot bear the food at the Hotel d'Entrague any longer?"

"I hope you will come before that happens, Doctor."

"I shall. I know that this is a house where I do not have to labor to create a favorable sentiment for my country. In other houses, I must be grave yet cheerful, wise but not dull, witty but not scornful. That is a difficult, tiresome occupation, and I need a rest from it occasionally. Tonight you have made me more comfortable than I have been since I arrived.

"As if that were not enough, you have given me the finest dinner I have had here. I would like to feel that I can return and talk with you and Dr. Bancroft. Here, I feel that if I wish to say something indiscreet, I may say it and not suffer remorse."

Later in the evening, after they had discussed Edward's article, Franklin unexpectedly suggested that Edward go to London.

"I have some money," he said, "which I wish you would invest for me. Silas told me how successful you were with the funds he gave you. I have enough money for myself and my few wants, but I find that I am spending so much in my position as commissioner that I am rapidly depleting my resources. I do not expect the Congress to reimburse me for many of these expenses, the nature of which they would be unable to understand, so I must set about securing additional income. If you can manage to do something with my funds, I shall be most grateful."

"I will be happy to do whatever I can," Edward replied. "My associate in London, Mr. Wharton, is a member of the Exchange. He usually knows when there is a profit to be made. He may have some suggestions."

"Please understand," Franklin explained, "that this journey I wish you to undertake is not only on my account. I am curious to find out what is happening in Parliament now. I believe there is soon to be a change in the ministry, which may affect our position considerably."

"I shall find out as much as I can. When do you wish me to leave?"

"As soon as possible, if this dear lady will forgive me. I realize it is quite unpardonable of me, Miss Vaughn, to ask Dr. Bancroft to go to England, especially when you have just received me with such charming hospitality. But we serve a cause, Dr. Bancroft and I. When that cause requires our help, we must obey, whatever the inconvenience."

When Franklin had left, Ellen turned to Edward with a petulant expression.

"Why must you leave now?" she asked. "The Neckers are giving a supper at the end of the week, and I was so looking forward to going with you."

"I'm sorry, darling, but since he wants me to go, I must. Don't worry about the supper—I'll arrange for someone to take you."

A mournful expression appeared on Edward's face, and the tone of his voice became as sepulchral as Bertram's announcing a distinguished visitor.

"Who would you prefer as your escort, Miss Vaughn?"

She frowned at him for his foolishness, but could not repress a smile.

"I don't know," she sighed, "you suggest someone. It was your idea."

"What about Carmichael?"

"Oh, no! I couldn't stand him for an entire evening."

"Deane?"

"No. He's a bit dull."

"Very well, then, what about Dr. Franklin?"

"Oh, Edward! Be serious," she cried.

"I am, my dear, perfectly serious. Is he your choice?"

"Of course he would be, but he won't go. He's too busy, too famous. He would want to go alone and gather compliments for himself."

"You could hardly be further from the truth, my dear," Edward laughed. "There is nothing in the world that Dr. Franklin would rather be fettered with than a pretty woman. His own glory shines ten times brighter when men are jealous of him for reasons other than his own brilliance. Shall I ask him?"

"Of course, if you think he would be willing. It might be embarrassing if he isn't, or if he feels you're taking advantage of him."

"I shall arrange it so that he won't feel that way," Edward promised.

Before leaving, Edward stopped by the Hotel d'Entrague. There he wondered aloud whether Beaumarchais would be willing to escort Ellen to supper at the Neckers. Franklin protested vehemently against sacrificing such a lovely victim to an evening of Beaumarchais's self-adulation and offered to escort Ellen himself. Edward demurred, saying he would not think of imposing upon Franklin's generosity.

"Generosity? Nonsense, Doctor," Franklin chortled. "It's a very calculating move on my part, I assure you. I want to startle Paris by escorting a lady. When the lady is as lovely as Miss Vaughn, we shall"—Franklin paused for a second, his eyes twinkling—"electrify them."

CHAPTER IX

E DWARD WAS JUST SITTING down to breakfast at his club in London several days later when he was handed a note by one of the servants. He opened it and spread it out on the cloth. The paper was of the cheapest sort and wrinkled at the edges as if it had been folded many times. The writing was small and so poor that he had to squint at it and shift it about in the light before he was able to read:

> Dear Sir:
> I have a Matter of Vital Importance to Discuss with you. I have Spoken to Mr. Deane who told me to Speak with You when You were in London. I have Waited for more than a Week without Seeing You so I shall leave this note for You at Your Club. You will find Me usually at the Three Crowns at Ten in the Morning.
>
> John Aiken

Edward called a servant to his table as soon as he finished deciphering the message.

"Who received this note?" he asked.

"I don't know, sir. I imagine it was the head porter, sir."

"Tell him I wish to speak with him."

"Very good, sir."

When Edward had finished his breakfast, the head porter was waiting for him outside.

"This note was delivered here nearly a month ago," Edward began, holding up the note for the man's inspection. "Did you receive it?"

"Yes, sir. I believe I remember it."

"Do you remember the circumstances? Do you remember who gave it to you, what he looked like?"

"No, sir," the man's answer was blunt and crisp. "I don't remember any of those things. So long ago, you know, sir, and there's many a note left here for the members."

"Quite right. Well, thank you."

As Edward walked to Sam Wharton's office, his mind kept reverting to Aiken's note. What a curious business it was, a note like that from a perfect stranger. What did he want, he wondered, and how had Deane got mixed up with him?

Peabody was just walking out of Wharton's office when Edward entered. He stared after the meek little man for a moment and then turned toward Wharton with a bewildered look.

"The last time I saw him here, you were threatening to dismember him."

"I know, I know," Sam grunted, "but I had to hire him back. He knows more about the office than I do myself. Besides, I couldn't risk having one of our competitors get hold of him."

"What has he done this time? It sounded extremely quiet, for you, when I walked in."

"Nothing much." Wharton gave an embarrassed smile. "Just mixed up the files a bit. I like to rave at him—he goes into the outer office like an avenging lion, and for a few days things run smoothly. He's a strange little fellow. I'm really quite fond of him, in spite of what I say."

"It's an odd way to demonstrate affection," Edward said with a shrug, "but that's your affair. What's been happening lately?"

"Nothing much," Wharton replied. "Too quiet for me. The news you sent about Fort Washington helped us a a little, but outside of that, there's been no activity at all."

"It's the same in Paris. There's been no news from America in weeks. Everyone is getting restless, the French as much as the Americans, waiting for spring. However, I brought this . . . ."

He put an envelope on the desk. Wharton opened it and riffled the bills with his fingers.

"Who's this from? Deane?"

"Part of it. The rest comes from a new customer—Dr. Franklin."

"Good, good," Wharton exclaimed. "He's one I want for a customer. I've always been certain that he would control a great amount of money someday. Not that this is it, but at least he'll know we're in business. What do you want me to do with it? We can't give him a profit such as we gave Deane."

"I don't think we need to. Let's say enough to make it worth his trouble of giving me the money."

"Very well. How long will you be here?"

"So far as I know, until the end of March. Something may happen before then to take me back to Paris, but I don't think so."

"Brockenhurst told me that Canada shares would be released soon. There might be some profit in those." Wharton looked up at him curiously. "How long will this waiting go on, Edward? How long before we hear that big news you've talked to me about?"

"I don't know, Sam. It's bound to come, reasonably soon, I would say. Sometime this summer or fall. When it does, we'll be able to engineer the coup we've planned. There'll be a fortune in it, for both of us. But you'll have to have patience, Sam. Wait until the Colonial army gets out of its winter quarters. I've seen the equipment France has been sending. The first ships carried a great deal of second-rate material, but in the last ships there was nothing but the best. When that gets to the soldiers, it will make a difference. By summer or fall, the Colonists should beat the British troops, badly. When that news comes, it will be the moment we've been waiting for."

Leaving Sam's office Edward noticed that he had less than half an hour to reach his destination. He walked rapidly, twisting through the winding streets, dodging chairs, and pressing himself against a wall whenever a lumbering cart loomed at him and threatened to drag him under its wheels.

The Three Crowns was crowded, and as he walked in, he suddenly realized that he had no idea what Aiken looked like. He inquired at the bar.

"Last table back on the other side," the barkeep said, peering toward the end of the room. "He's there, sure enough. No drunker than usual."

"Are you Aiken?" Edward asked when he reached the side of the man the barkeep pointed out.

The man jerked his head around, peering up at Edward so intently that his upper lip pulled back in a snarl.

"Who are you?"

"Bancroft."

"Oh," the man said, staggering to his feet and reaching out unsteadily. Edward ignored the grimy hand and seated himself at the small table. "I never thought you'd get here, Doctor. I've been waiting a long time."

"I received your note this morning at my club. Surely you haven't been here since you wrote that?"

"No, Doctor. I come in here every day, always at ten, like I said in the note. Mr. Deane told me you came to London often; I thought I'd see you before this. Now that you're here, I want you to listen to what I have to say, Doctor. First, I need fifty pounds. The sooner I get it, the quicker I can carry out my plan."

"Fifty pounds? You want fifty pounds from me?" Edward exploded, exasperated more by the amount requested than by the request itself. "What for? Why should you expect me to give you fifty pounds?"

"Because I'm going to do something for the Colonists, Doctor," Aiken replied, smirking, "something they want done but can't do themselves."

"If you want fifty pounds from me, you'll have to talk plainer than that."

"All right, all right, don't get angry. This is a good idea of mine. It will do the Colonists a lot of good, and it won't cost them but fifty pounds. What's the biggest Admiralty harbor?"

"Portsmouth, of course."

"Have you ever seen the docks at Portsmouth, Doctor?"

"No. What about them?"

"They're beautiful, Doctor, really beautiful." Aiken smirked again and swallowed his brandy. "But they're not very neat. The sailors don't clean up so well, especially around the rope yard. There's big piles of rubbish there, close to the ships, too. Those piles would burn, Doctor. It would be a hot fire, so hot I can't imagine what might happen to the ships that were tied up there."

"Go on," Edward said, nodding.

"That's all, Doctor. I'm just a poor ship's painter who needs work. I have a lot of friends who need work, too. Fifty pounds we get, for a one-night job like that."

Edward remained silent for a moment, considering Aiken's proposal. It might work, he admitted. This drunken fool's plan might be wild enough to succeed, where a more careful scheme might fail.

"How do you know you'll get a job there? And what about these friends? Can you trust them? Why won't they just take the money and hand you over?"

"I've got a job there now, Doctor. My brother's there, working in my name. I wouldn't worry about my friends—they're not the kind that likes officials. Are you willing?"

Fifty pounds was a small amount for such a gamble. Even if Aiken's plan did not succeed, it would give the Admiralty a shock. It would provide pleasure for Franklin and worry for the government.

He reached into his wallet, counted out fifty pounds, and handed them to Aiken.

"If you are successful, there will be an additional fifty pounds for you," he said. "But remember this: I am not concerned with this scheme in any way. You asked me for a fifty-pound loan, and I gave it to you, believing you were a friend of Deane's. If anyone should ask me, that is the story I'll tell them. If you try to implicate me in this, I'll have you hunted down, and one morning you'll float past Parliament and be picked out of the Thames by the surgeons' men. Is that clear?"

Aiken grinned. "I'll see you before the end of the month and collect those other fifty pounds, Doctor."

EDWARD WAS EXTREMELY busy the next few weeks.

There were conferences and plans to be made with Wharton, and there were long talks with Thomas Walpole. Walpole told him that an attempt had been made within the ministry to force the resignation of Lord North. The attempt had failed because of the king's undeviating support of his prime minister, and North's position had been immeasurably strengthened. This would result inevitably in harsher measures against the Colonies, for North was determined not to sacrifice any part of the British realm during his time in office.

One day, Edward received a note from Eden, asking him to call at his office as soon as possible. As Edward waited in the anteroom, he paced back and forth, curious as to why he had been summoned. Was the king complaining about his speculations again? Or did Eden merely wish to see him, to compliment him, perhaps, on his work in Paris?

He was bowed into the office by one of Eden's secretaries. As Edward entered, Eden looked up and indicated one of the chairs near his desk.

"Good morning, Dr. Bancroft. Sit down, please. I'll be finished with this in a moment."

Eden continued to write on a long sheet of parchment and at length put down his quill and stared expectantly at Edward.

"What is the news from Paris?"

Edward shifted in his chair. "There was nothing at all for weeks before I left. The rebellion seems to be stalled by cold. The Colonists aren't moving and neither, I judge, are we."

"Hmm. Perhaps the spring will bring a different story. Tell me, Doctor, are you acquainted with a man known as John the Painter?"

Edward puzzled over the name. "No, I'm not. At least not so far as I know. The name is unfamiliar."

"Perhaps, then," Eden continued, "you might remember him better if I told you he also used the name John Aiken."

"John Aiken. Hmm," Edward mused, keeping his eyes on his boots. "The name is familiar, but then, it's a very common name. Perhaps he is one of the people who came into the office in Paris. There are so many of them that it's difficult to remember their names. Deane frequently sends people to me whom he doesn't want to bother with himself and yet doesn't want to offend by ignoring them."

"John Aiken," Eden continued in a dry, factual tone, "has just been arrested at Portsmouth, charged with attempting to fire the piers there. In his confession, which we obtained without too much difficulty, he implicated two other people—Silas Deane and you."

"Me?" Edward exclaimed, looking up at Eden. "Why, that's absurd. I don't even know the man." He stared so intently at Eden that in a few seconds, he was relieved to see Eden raise his eyebrows, sigh, and look back at the paper before him.

"He claims that he told you all about his plans," Eden went on remorselessly, "and that you gave him fifty pounds for his expenses."

"If he's the same man I'm thinking of, I did give him fifty pounds."

Eden looked up quickly, his eyebrows arched like rooftrees.

"But there was no question of firing the Portsmouth Yards," Edward continued. "He was shabby, this man, and a little drunk. He had a letter from

Deane, authorizing me to pay him fifty pounds if I believed the story he had told Deane."

"And what was his story?"

"He had been drinking for some time, obviously, and what he said was not entirely clear—it was difficult to separate his facts from his liquor. He claimed that he had worked for Thomas Morris here in London and that he had painted his house. When Morris was called to France, he left and forgot to pay this man. Deane's note mentioned that since Morris was away, there was no way of proving whether the man's story was true or false. If I believed him, the note went on, I was to pay him the fifty pounds. This attempt at arson which you mention was of course unknown to me—had I known what he was planning, I should have informed the Admiralty at once."

"Of course," Eden replied. "This confession is unfortunate, however; it puts you in a very bad light. It might even interfere appreciably with the splendid work you have been doing for us. On the other hand, if we handle the affair subtly, we can make capital of it and install you even more securely in the esteem of Franklin and Deane."

"What do you mean?"

"This is bound to appear in the journals, probably tomorrow. I suggest that you defend yourself, angrily, as an outraged and loyal English subject. Write letters to the journals—deny everything. Trade on your English residence, your membership in the Royal Society and the Royal College of Surgeons. Publish for all to read your unassailable loyalty to England, despite the unhappy fact that you chanced to be born in the Colonies."

"What about Franklin and Deane?" Edward asked. "They'll hear about these letters of mine. They have friends in England who will send them copies."

"So much the better. I have thought of a means to offset that. After your letters have been published, I shall arrange for Lord Mansfield or Lord Suffolk, or perhaps both, to defend you in Parliament. Then, after that is over, you will go to prison."

"Prison? Whatever for?"

"Don't be nervous, Doctor," Eden replied soothingly. "It's a very nice prison, compared with most of them, and you won't be there too long."

"But . . . I don't understand. Why should I go to prison?"

"Doctor, you interest me," Eden rasped in sudden irritation. "Why is it that clever men like you can never seem to appreciate the obvious? You are going to prison because the British don't trust you. Even after you've been defended by peers of the realm, you'll land in jail. Now—answer me this: when you're released, after a day or so, from lack of evidence, and allowed to return to France, what will be Deane's and Franklin's attitude toward you?"

"I'm sure I don't know. I'm not acquainted with the form of greeting that occurs on one's release from prison."

"I fear you're a little too skeptical," Eden said, pressing his fingertips together. "If I say so myself, this is really a brilliant maneuver. I'll tell you how they'll regard you: like a Christian martyr, Doctor, a Christian martyr recently escaped from the jaws of His Britannic Majesty. You'll be held in even higher esteem than before you left France."

"That's possibly true, but what about returning to England, after I've been banished to France?"

"That is easily arranged. I shall have your sentence vacated, for lack of evidence, and you will be free to return whenever you wish."

"It sounds almost too perfect, almost too simple. How can I be sure that nothing will go wrong? That I won't just stay there in jail and rot?"

"Surely you trust me, Doctor?" Eden smiled. "It is my duty to plan and make matters easier for those who work for me. There must be complete trust between us, Doctor, at all times; otherwise, we shall certainly fail in our task. I have believed everything you have told me. Surely you believe what I tell you, don't you?"

"Certainly," Edward replied, after a pause, uncomfortably aware that there was nothing else to say. "I'll do what you recommend—it is a clever maneuver."

When Edward left Eden's office, he had become more reconciled to the thought of spending a few days in prison, but as the day passed and he remained at his club in comparative solitude, he experienced that feeling he had known once before in France.

The physical symptoms appeared first: a dry throat, a constant pounding in his ears, a pressing weight in his chest that seemed to stifle him. But worse by far was the mental suffering. The dangers of his present life became so magnified and distorted that he had to fight against an urge to run away, to disappear. He became convinced that Eden knew the truth of the Aiken affair, that he had been like a spider, watching him from behind his desk, spinning strands of entrapment.

What saved him from despair and the foolish, desperate plans he made and discarded in an instant was the recollection of his conversation with Wharton. That strengthened him; it was like discovering water in a desert. Patience— that was all that was required. Soon the goal would be reached. In the meantime, he too must have patience; he must be willing to wait. He saw then how foolish it would be to sacrifice all he had accomplished because of an unfounded distrust of Eden. His courage returned, and when a journalist called to see him, he vilified Aiken and protected his own reputation with a fury that cowed his visitor.

The next morning he read the journals carefully.

Finally he found what he was searching for; a long article headlined, "The Late Horrendous and Unsuccessful Incendiarism at the Portsmouth Yards." It was not until he reached the last paragraph that he saw his own name.

"After a careful questioning," he read, "the culprit revealed that his horrid plot was known to a certain Silas Deane, so-called Commissioner to France from the Colonies, and to a Dr. Bancroft of this City, author and friend to many eminent people. A correspondent who talked with Dr. Bancroft says he absolutely denies any connection with this arsonist."

Edward's letter of reply was printed in the journal the next day and appeared for two days thereafter. This had been done at his request, so that as many people might read his answer as possible.

He had been able to convince the editor of the journal, whom he had invited to dinner at his club, that this was the only equitable method of repaying him for the distress caused by the original article. After the editor had departed, Edward picked up the copy of the journal he had saved and reread his letter, printed prominently at the top of the inside page:

In the *London Evening Post* for March 7, 1777, my name was mentioned in connection with the confession of one John Aiken, author of the plot to destroy the Portsmouth Dockyard.

The vindication of one's good name and reputation is the primary concern of every gentleman who becomes innocently involved in scandal. I therefore take this opportunity to make the following statement to my many distinguished friends who may have been concerned by this regrettable and untruthful statement of the culprit Aiken:

I have never been concerned in any plot against the government. I am a loyal Englishman, and although I chanced to be born in the Colonies, I have by preference made my home here for many years. The Royal Society and the Royal College of Surgeons have honoured me with membership and regard me, as I regard myself, as a loyal subject of His Majesty.

I have spoken to Aiken only once, at which time he begged money of me because he was starving and in great distress. I gave him money because his pitiful tale illumined for me my own good fortune. I knew nothing of the dastardly scheme to burn the Portsmouth Dockyards, nor did Aiken reveal to me his foul intentions.

I am entirely innocent and much maligned in this matter and do hereby attest my willingness to prove my innocence in the courts.

To my friends, I can only say that if there has been a fault on my part, it was the fault of generosity.

—Dr. Edward Bancroft,
Coventry House

A few days later, Edward read in the journals that he had been defended in Parliament by lords Mansfield and Suffolk. His complicity in the "Aiken Affair" was characterized by these gentlemen as utterly nonexistent; each of them stressed that there had been nothing improper in his conduct. Edward was relieved to read this. His reputation could not have had better defenders than these two men. The following day he received a message from Eden, asking him to appear at his office that afternoon, "with sufficient reading material and clothes for a two-day rest," as the message was phrased. He was shown into Eden's office as soon as he arrived.

"Good afternoon, Doctor. I have arranged for you to be placed in the prisoner's room at Lambeth, above the porter's lodge. The porter, Mr. Earnshaw, has been instructed to make your stay there as comfortable as possible. You will not be locked in. You may spend the days in his house, and you are free to walk about the grounds at Lambeth."

"That sounds quite pleasant."

"I think you will find it so. Today is Wednesday. On Friday I expect to send word to you that you are free to leave for France. Do you have any questions?"

"I should like to ask you one thing: how will Franklin and Deane know that I've been in prison, if there isn't any proper trial?"

"Oh, I did forget that. You had a trial this morning, a most private trial at Westminster Hall. You were found guilty of suspected treason and remanded to prison for the security of His Majesty's government. I had a man from my office stand up for you in court."

"Please don't look so distressed, Doctor," Eden continued as Edward stiffened in his chair. "Everything has worked out splendidly; when Friday comes, you'll be on your way to France. I would like to have a special report from you as soon as possible after you reach Paris. I wish to know whether Arthur Lee receives as much information as the other commissioners. Do they discuss every important matter with him? I am not yet clear about his status. I shall depend upon you to investigate and clarify this situation for me."

"I shall do what I can," Edward replied, considerably heartened by Eden's changed attitude. "I will send you a report as quickly as possible after I return."

"Good. You will find a Mr. Hedges waiting for you in the anteroom. He will conduct you to Lambeth and acquaint you with Earnshaw, the jailer. Good-bye, Doctor. Have a pleasant sojourn."

When the coach drew up before the ivied porter's lodge that guarded the gates of Lambeth Palace, Earnshaw appeared on the steps. Hedges handed him a paper and, without breaking the silence he had maintained from the moment he and Edward had begun their journey, stepped back into the coach.

"Good afternoon, Dr. Bancroft," Earnshaw said with a slight bow. "I am delighted to meet you, sir, though I regret you should have to spend any time in our little jail."

"I won't be here for long, Earnshaw, just until Friday."

"Yes, sir. That's what I've been given to understand. Most of our guests remain for a much longer time than that. Some of them come to like it—they tell me it gives them time to think and write their recollections."

"And the others?"

"The minute they arrive, they say: 'How long?' I have no way of knowing that in most cases. Some of them get angry at me—call me queer names like Charon. But I don't mind. The government takes care of its business, and I take care of mine. These men, begging your pardon, Doctor, are here through their own doing, not mine. I try to make their visit as comfortable as possible, but some of them are never satisfied. I hope you won't be like that, sir."

"No, I don't think I shall," Edward grunted as they climbed up the stairs of the old gate tower.

Earnshaw wheezed and muttered to himself as he climbed the stairs. Edward noticed that he was much older than he had first seemed. His face was tired and wrinkled and his long, gray hair crudely cut. His clothes hung on him like sails in the doldrums.

When they reached the top of the stairs, Earnshaw walked to a large oak door and pushed it open.

"This will be your room, Doctor. I've fixed it as comfortable for you as I could. That musty smell you notice—it won't leave. It's been here too long."

"Just below," he continued, pointing back down the stairs, "is where I live—the door on the right at the foot of the stairs. You're welcome to come there at any time except at night, when my instructions say you should remain here. You'll take your meals with us, sir. We eat our big meal at night, sir. Dinner at seven, breakfast at eight, tea at three."

Earnshaw nodded and left.

Edward's room was dark. After he had lighted candles, he stopped short at the sight of a row of iron rings fastened in the wall before him. At least I don't have to wear those, he consoled himself. The room was small, not more than twelve feet in any direction. The walls and floors were made of sturdy oak planks, and everywhere were scars from knives or whatever other cutting instruments long-forgotten prisoners had used to record the passing days.

There were three pieces of furniture in the room—a bed, a table, and a chair, all of which must have been provided by Earnshaw, Edward guessed, for they looked too new to have undergone much prison use. As Edward sat down in the chair, his eye was caught by an inscription at the far end of the room. Picking up a candle, he went over to it and scrutinized it carefully. It was in old script, and all that was clearly legible was the date: 1642. He traced over the worn letters with a fingertip. Finally recognizing the name, he spoke it aloud: Lovelace.

This must have been another place of that unhappy cavalier's confinement, he thought. He remembered hearing that Lovelace had been imprisoned in the Lollard's Tower, as this was called; perhaps in this room he had dreamed about and then written about Althea, the girl he immortalized. His interest aroused, Edward walked about with his candle, examining the more distinct inscriptions. He saw many names famous in history: Mollott, Cranston, Huffard, Choate, Osborne, and others whose owners had been too wearied by their fetters or too broken by the rack to write distinctly, for there were many scrawled, illegible names, as well as an abundance of burns on the floor.

Edward went downstairs at seven o'clock. Entering Earnshaw's dwelling by the door which the jailer had pointed out, he found himself in the living room, the obvious realm of Mrs. Earnshaw. The walls were nearly obscured by fashion plates cut from journals and pasted clumsily onto the plaster. It was not a neat collection, but it was comprehensive—all the styles from the beginning of the century to the present day were represented. No one was in a more favored position than another, unless it was the lady of 1730, who sat peeping over the desk. This poor woman had undergone the rough treatment of amateur coloring—her white wig had turned blue, and her costume, which had probably been charming in its day, was now a divided battleground of violet and orange.

While Edward contemplated this monstrosity, Earnshaw hurried forward to greet him. Swaying up behind him, like an overloaded galleon in a strong breeze, came his wife.

Mrs. Earnshaw was enormously fat. She was so tightly bound and strapped and pinned together that her arms and neck puffed over the edges of her gown like pieces of ripe fruit ready to fall from a basket. Her face was puffed and heavy, and her mouth so pushed together by her bulging cheeks that it was always pursed, as if expecting an unlikely kiss.

Edward's hostess was a relentless dispenser of small talk. After an hour in her company, Edward felt that there was no place he would rather be than in his bare, quiet room upstairs. They waited and waited for a dinner which threatened never to appear; and all the while, this monstrous woman babbled on about books and politics and events of the day of which she was completely ignorant. As he watched her grotesque little mouth continue to wiggle, a feeling of deadly weariness stole over him. She hardly seemed to draw breath before she was halfway through her next sentence.

Her more absurd statements were punctuated by a rumbling noise, as if she were challenging her listeners to dispute her words.

Mr. Earnshaw sat quietly through his wife's monologue. He looked, Edward thought, as if marriage had taught him not only the necessity for silence but the futility of argument. He chewed absently on an end of his ragged mustache. Occasionally his eyes closed in weariness, as if they would shut out what his ears could not. Edward sensed that he had Earnshaw's sympathy; a nod of the head or a quick gesture of the hand passed between them periodically, a sort of mutual distress signal.

When Edward felt he could endure no more, he shook his head slightly, as if to clear his brain.

Mrs. Earnshaw, taking his gesture for a denial, redoubled her volume.

"You don't believe there is a God?" she asked, incredulous but eager.

"I beg your pardon, Mrs. Earnshaw. I was just stretching my neck. I did not intend to imply that I do not believe in God. I do."

"Well, that's better," she replied. "For a minute, Dr. Bancroft, I thought you were a freethinker, like Dr. Johnson or Martin Luther. Dreadful people. I don't see how the world goes on, with such people to catch the fancy of the young. I'm a good woman, Dr. Bancroft, but I wouldn't trust myself to listen to one of those ambassadors of the Devil. Always try to be polite, I do, but sometimes when I hear what they say, I feel like going down the streets of London crying out: 'Shun them, good people, shun them, these messengers from Beelzebub.' I was raised a true Christian, Dr. Bancroft. I don't hold with the Pope any more than with that Luther—the two of them are leagued together against us true Christians. Don't you agree?"

"I have never considered religion on quite those terms, Mrs. Earnshaw, but yours is an interesting point of view. You should write a pamphlet."

"Oh, I have, Doctor, several. But no one will publish them. They're not the trash that people want to read today. I wish you would read them and see if they don't make you feel like smiting these dreadful freethinkers."

"Later, I certainly shall," Edward said feebly.

There seemed to be no escape. Every word he said was another log on the fire of her logorrhea. "Perhaps," he added, "you can send them to me."

"Oh, but I couldn't do that," Mrs. Earnshaw replied with some asperity. "What if they were lost, what then?"

"What indeed?" Edward repeated, suddenly coughing.

"What I mean is, I could never replace them. No, I couldn't consider sending them to you, Doctor, though it is kind of you to say how much you would like to read them. That's what I've always wanted Mr. Earnshaw to say, but he's never interested in what I'm doing or thinking; just sits there in his chair like he is tonight, waiting for Rose to get supper ready. Then he bolts his food down and rushes to bed without a civil word to me. I must say, Doctor, I can't think what's happening to his insides, eatin' the way he does, without feeling a bit sick myself. All that food thrown into the belly without any warning, so fast it doesn't have time to figure out where it's going before it's too late. Don't you agree, Doctor? You're a medicine man, you should know more about that than I do.

"Wake up, Jim, and listen to what the doctor wants to tell you. Wake up! There, you see, he thinks he knows it all. He'd rather sleep than listen. He'll repent, Doctor, I know he will. My father died from bolting his food. Many a night I've talked and talked to Jim here and warned him about how horribly Father suffered. Wait till Rose calls supper—he'll be out of his chair and shoveling his food down so fast it'll make you dizzy to watch him."

Mercifully, Rose appeared in the living room. She was a mangy looking, gap-toothed slattern who proclaimed in a kind of swineherd yowl that supper was ready.

True to his wife's prediction, Earnshaw was out of his chair and seated in the dining room almost before the echoes of Rose's announcement had faded.

Mrs. Earnshaw was not far behind him, and when Edward had seated himself at the table, his host and hostess were already half a course ahead. He stared glumly at the greasy mutton and the water-soaked potatoes.

There was nothing else on the table.

"Do you suppose I might have some bread?"

"Bread? Bread?" Mrs. Earnshaw asked. "Oh, bread. Yes, Doctor. Rose! Bring bread for the doctor."

In a moment Rose appeared, a large loaf of bread under her arm. She banged it down in front of him and withdrew again to the kitchen. He broke off a piece and placed the remainder in the center of the table. The Earnshaws paid no attention; they were now a full course ahead.

The meal continued in silence until Mrs. Earnshaw, trying desperately to finish before her husband, took too big a bite and began to choke. Mr. Earnshaw peered up at her out of the corner of his eye. He was almost ready to go back to gobbling when he noticed that she really required assistance. Slowly he got to his feet, and walking over behind her chair, he clapped her on the back. It was a hard, resounding slap; Mrs. Earnshaw heaved forward onto the edge of the table like a ship cast up on a reef. Her face was purple, and as she tried to catch her breath, Mr. Earnshaw delivered another blow.

"Gets like this sometimes," he shouted over the tumult of gasping and choking. "Have to treat her a mite rough, but she's hardy."

Edward nodded understandingly, but as he watched the lady's eyes focus suddenly and angrily on her husband's face, he judged that Mr. Earnshaw would not be quickly forgiven. Mrs. Earnshaw was blubbering with rage and surprise. As she drew in her breath in great, shuddering gasps, she seemed to be summoning her strength to attack her husband. A moment later, the difficulty had passed; she turned in her chair and faced her husband. Although he could see nothing but the back of her head and the straggling wisps of hair that stood almost erect, Edward guessed that her face was not a pretty sight. And indeed, it must not have been, for Earnshaw made a grimace of despair and, bending over his plate, began shoveling food into his mouth.

"Did you see him, Doctor, that murderer? Someday I'll have one of these attacks and be too weak to defend myself; he'll stand behind me and beat me to death. Such a man! What kind of a husband is it, Doctor, that beats his poor, helpless, choking wife to death?"

"Now, Cleonine, the doctor is our guest. Don't go on like that."

"She's like this sometimes, Doctor," Earnshaw confided to Edward in a low voice. "Sometimes she don't think what she's saying, and it sounds a mite queer to our guests. She don't mean no harm, though. She's just a woman of strong feelings."

"I'm sure she is," Edward replied, choking a little himself.

"I'd like to know what you're whispering about," Mrs. Earnshaw thundered across the table. "You might think there was something wrong with me, the way you nod and mumble at each other. Speak up, dear, speak up."

"The doctor and I were just discussing taxes."

"Taxes? Taxes? Frightful things, taxes," she sputtered. "I should know. It seems to me I'm paying a new one every day. Pay a tax to post something, pay a tax to buy something, pay a tax to eat something and to drink something. What do they do with all these taxes I pay, Doctor?"

"Various things, Mrs. Earnshaw," Edward answered. "They use the money for government expenses, for armies and navies, for wars, for assistance to the poor, for the court and such."

"Humph," Mrs. Earnshaw snorted violently. "Wars—the court—the navy and such frills. Why not use the money for something worthwhile? Why must I support all these people with my money? If I had my way, Doctor, I'd use those taxes for just one thing. Do you know what? Well, don't guess—I'll tell you: for plays and masquerades for the people, for the people who can't afford to go to plays and masquerades. Think of the pleasure they'd get, Doctor. A happier London—that's what I'd make, a happier London with free plays and free masquerades. Have you ever been to a theater, Doctor? You have? How nice. Did you like it? You did? Well, imagine. I'm terribly fond of the theater. I go every chance I have, and Jim goes with me. Theaters thrill me, Doctor, just thrill me. All those people on that little stage, the long speeches—I don't see how they remember all those words. I like to look up at the boxes, too, at all the ladies and their tall gentlemen and their jewels that sparkle in the candlelight. Once we went to the theater, and Mr. Pitt was there. Oh, but he was a fine looking man, Mr. Pitt. I looked and looked at him. I couldn't seem to watch the play. Finally I looked at my husband, and then I looked right back at Mr. Pitt again. A fine looking man he was. They say he took dope.

Would you believe it? Every day, sometimes twice when he was having a special discomfiture in Parliament. Isn't that terrible? Leading England and taking dope—sounds almost disrespectful, don't it? But that's what I say: how can England be happy when the men who lead are dope takers. Don't you agree, Doctor? It's a shameful state when a great country like ours can't find anyone but dopers to take charge.

"I'd like the job—just for a day. I think about it every week. I'd spend the first hour discharging the dopers. The next hour, I'd hire back the good men, like my father's friend, old Percy Quarles, the hostler. He's the man they need to take charge of those horses the king's guards ride. Just the man! Have you ever seen those horses, Doctor? You haven't? Well, you should, being a doctor. It's a shame the way they treat those horses. I'd be mortified to be seen riding such a poor beast. You wouldn't think I ever rode a horse, would you, Doctor? Oh, you would? Why, how nice of you to say that! Well, I did. I used to ride all the time when my poor father was alive. He was a hostler too, like Percy Quarles, only he had a bit of sense which is something you could never accuse old Percy of; Father put a bit of money aside before he died. He used to let me ride the horses before he stabled them for the night. He'd pick me up and put me on the horse's back and say— 'Wake up, Mr. Earnshaw! Wake up! Heavens, how can he go to sleep on the table when we have guests?' "

"Mrs. Earnshaw," Edward interrupted desperately, "this has been a charming supper, but I'm very tired. If you will excuse me, I think I shall go upstairs."

"Why, of course, Doctor. Jim! Jim! Wake up! The doctor's leaving. See what your bad manners have done—sleeping on the table!"

Edward bade a hasty farewell to his hostess as they walked back into the living room and hurried upstairs before she could commence another harangue. When he closed the door, he gave a sigh of relief and sank exhausted onto his bed.

As he lay resting, he recalled scraps of Mrs. Earnshaw's dinner monologue—Percy Quarles, the Pope and Luther, the dopers, Mrs. Earnshaw on a horse. He had met many people during his life whom he considered bores. They were a dull, gray lot, full of pretention, but little more than passing irritations. It was impossible, however, to ignore Mrs. Earnshaw. In just one evening, he had acquired a curious respect for her. She was a bore, too, but such a monumental one that she was unique. He imagined her transported from England and set down on a primitive island; within a few days she would be exalted as a goddess. Natives would travel miles to view this spectacular mass of flesh that never stopped making sounds. She would become an object of pilgrimage, a bloated obelisk, and probably end up cowing the natives in the same way she had Mr. Earnshaw.

Sighing, he reached into his luggage and pulled out the copy of Mr. Cibber's plays that he had brought along. The first play he turned to was *The Ladies' Philosophy*. He hurled it back into the bag with a groan and took out a copy of Mr. Sterne's whimsy. Settling himself as comfortably as he could on the hard bed, he began to follow the life of Tristram Shandy. For a long time he read, until the spluttering of his last candle forced him to close the book. He blew out the candle end with a sigh of regret. As he stretched out in bed, he heard the watch cry out: "Pa-a-ast two o'clock and a rainy morning."

Breakfast the next morning was a more endurable meal for Edward—Mrs. Earnshaw spent most of her time in the kitchen upbraiding Rose. The girl had returned to the house only an hour or two before breakfast, drunk and accompanied by rowdy friends. Edward could not avoid hearing the details as Mrs. Earnshaw's voice grew louder and louder:

"What a thing for you to do, Rose, here in this neighborhood, next to Lambeth House itself, where the church finds its repose. How do you think His Grace the archbishop would feel if he heard of this? Don't stand there ogling me, you slut. Answer! What? How dare you say that! His Grace is a Christian gentleman. A fine figure of a man he was, too, when he was a mite younger."

Earnshaw, his eyebrows lowered like a portcullis, frowned and shook his head sadly.

"Terrible, ain't it, Doctor? Never stops—all day and most of the night. Talk, talk, talk. Jabber, jabber, jabber. It's enough to drive me to Bedlam. Sometimes when I walks by there and hears those creatures laughin' so foolish and screamin' at each other, it seems almost like home."

Mrs. Earnshaw must have heard her husband's melancholy murmurs, for she appeared in the kitchen doorway and bellowed cheerfully at Edward.

"Good morning, Doctor. How did you sleep? Fine? That's good. That's the way it should be. Sometimes I have a sleepless night, and I say to myself—"

She was interrupted by a small commotion behind her. Rose, still trembling from the effects of her night out, had dropped a platter. Mrs. Earnshaw's eyes grew large; she swung about like a leviathan and surged back into the kitchen. Edward looked sympathetically at Earnshaw.

"Has she always been like this?"

"Always," he answered mournfully. "Of course it didn't used to be so bad. She went about a lot before she got so heavy, and I used to have a bit of peace in the daytime. But for near ten years, she's been home all the time. I used to think about goin' to sea, but I don't anymore. I'm too old for young thoughts like that."

Edward hurried through his breakfast and left the table before Mrs. Earnshaw had an opportunity to return. As he was leaving, he informed Earnshaw that he would be walking about the grounds of Lambeth House. He started down a path which led toward the river.

The sun was shining dimly through the haze, but the wind was strong and cold. As he approached the river, he noticed the water blacken with squall. He stood watching the boats for a few minutes and saw that whenever a boatman passed by Lambeth, he would raise his cap and make a slight bow. It was an unexpected and curiously touching obeisance.

He hunched down in his great coat at a particularly severe blast of wind and turned his back to the river to escape the chill. As his eyes roamed over the outlines of Lambeth House, he noticed a small group of men coming toward him. They were walking slowly, their breath like little jets of steam above their heads. Each was bundled up in a coat, and several wore heavy fur caps and mitts.

When they drew closer, Edward recognized the man in the center of the group. He was Archbishop Cornwallis, whom he had seen several times on his way to Parliament. The group of men reached him, and Cornwallis spoke.

"Good morning, Dr. Bancroft. I was advised that you would be staying a short time with our good Earnshaw. I hope your accommodations are comfortable."

"It is kind of Your Grace to trouble about me," Edward replied, making what he hoped was a sufficiently low bow for the eminence of Cornwallis's position.

"An invigorating morning, is it not?" the archbishop continued. His companions had moved along toward the river, leaving him alone with Edward. "I am fond of walking out here, when the wind is as fresh as it is today, and one cannot smell the fish. It seems to clear the stuffy air from my brain."

"I have the same feeling," Edward replied. "I also find that walking makes my present situation more tolerable."

"You are in excellent company here, Dr. Bancroft," the archbishop said, smiling. "Many famous men have visited Lambeth under circumstances similar to your own. I do not, of course, know the exact reasons behind your visit, for my informant was not overly explicit when he told me that you were coming. Did you know that there once was an archbishop of your name at Lambeth? His portrait is inside—a most agreeable appearing gentleman."

"His association with Lambeth was more noteworthy than my own, I fear," Edward said, smiling. "I had heard of him. As I remember, he was rather intolerant."

"You are extremely generous when you say that," Cornwallis said. "Richard Bancroft was a good man, but a most severe one. He is certainly not remembered for his tolerance, but he was most learned in Greek and Hebrew, so perhaps we can forgive him much. However, let us talk of other matters. You lack for nothing, in your quarters?"

"Nothing at all, Your Grace, save liberty, which I expect tomorrow morning. A messenger should arrive from the gentleman who arranged my visit here."

"You are fortunate, Doctor, not only to know the date of your freedom, but to be so considerately treated." Cornwallis shook his head and sighed. "There is much about our prisons today that is frightful; they are even more terrible than the word itself implies. Have you ever been in a real prison, Doctor, like Fleet or Newgate or Bedlam?"

"Only once, Your Grace. I was summoned to Newgate to treat a guard who had fallen into a fit. I never went farther than the guards' rooms, however."

"Then you were spared a sight, sir. I do not believe I have seen anywhere— and I have traveled far—a place more horrible than Fleet Prison. It is unbelievable, the conditions that those poor wretches, so many of them unjustly condemned, must endure. Little water, food that is always crawling with maggots, waste and filth on the floors and in the pallets. It makes a stench frightful enough to crack the skull. I have tried to do something, but every time I speak, someone speaks against me, denouncing me as a friend of criminals or claiming that I am trying to make the burdens of the wicked lighter."

"Aren't there always people who say such things?"

"Too many of them. There is a man here with us today, John Howard, who has labored for years to better the conditions in the prisons. He has battled hard against the cries and complaints of those who believe that sin can be conquered by torture and death alone. Last night he was reading us a part of the book he has just written. It is intensely interesting, a detailed record of all his observations here and in Europe of the prisons he has visited. One can scarce credit some of the stories he tells, yet I believe him, for his eyes shine so. Do you know what I mean?"

"Yes, I do, Your Grace. Howard must be a crusader. You speak of his eyes shining—I have noticed that quality in a few other men, all of whom I would call crusaders. Mr. Burke is such a one."

"I had not thought of him, but you are right. He is. There are other qualities about such people, too, as you have undoubtedly noticed. Small marks which distinguish them from their less impassioned and, perhaps, duller-witted fellows. I have found, for one thing, that they are invariably distrusted. They are considered unreliable . . . ."

The archbishop paused and raised his hand in the air to make the sign of the cross.

"A delightful custom, is it not? Each time a boatman passes Lambeth, I feel the church has grown a little closer to its people."

The archbishop stared after the boat a moment, then turned back to Edward. "We were speaking of crusaders. Have you ever wondered, Dr. Bancroft, what would become of us if suddenly there were no more crusaders? What a dreadful condition we would be in! But I ramble—I must rejoin my friends. This has been most pleasant, Dr. Bancroft. I am delighted to meet you, and I hope we shall meet again under happier auspices."

Edward bowed, and the archbishop walked toward his friends.

Luncheon and supper at the Earnshaw's table passed in remarkable quiet, with only minor harangues booming out of the kitchen. Mrs. Earnshaw was obliged to assist Rose, as the combined effects of the servant's all-night celebration and her mistress's wrath had proved too onerous for the girl. She had turned into a whimpering blob of misery. Mrs. Earnshaw did not refer to the trial she was undergoing in the kitchen, but Edward gathered from the majesty of her contempt that all would have been hopeless without the mistress's guiding hand.

When he came downstairs for breakfast the next morning, Edward saw Hedges standing in the living room.

"Mr. Eden sent me to tell you that you may leave whenever you wish, sir." Hedges paused and took a deep breath. "The authorities at Dover have been notified that you are released."

"That's good news, Hedges," Edward cried. "I don't know anyone I would rather hear that news from than a man of few words like yourself. Thank Mr. Eden for me, please. You might tell him that I shall leave for Dover at once."

Edward sat down to his breakfast rejoicing. Free again! He calculated how long it would take him to reach Paris—no later than Monday, certainly, and probably before that. He went upstairs and packed hurriedly.

That afternoon he was on his way toward Dover.

CHAPTER X

IT WAS NOT UNTIL they were almost finished with their dinner that Edward told Ellen about his two days at Lambeth.

"In prison?" she cried. "Oh, Edward, what happened?"

"Nothing at all, really. There was trouble at the Portsmouth Dockyards— someone tried to start a fire. The police caught him, and he named me in his confession. I had seen the man only once before—he told me that he wanted money to do something for Deane. The authorities kept me at Lambeth while they checked further. Actually, it was a rather amusing two days. When they were satisfied as to my innocence, they set me free."

"But wasn't it awful, the prison? They're such dreadful places."

"This was a rather special prison. I was told before I went there that I would be following an illustrious company. Although the food was deplorable, I was rather comfortable. Also, I met the archbishop."

He laughed and filled their glasses.

"Let us drink to Lambeth, darling. To my jailer, Mr. Earnshaw, and his formidable wife, and to Archbishop Cornwallis—the companions of my misfortune."

He had swallowed half his wine before he noticed that Ellen was not drinking hers. She was staring at him, shocked by his toast.

"I'm sorry, Edward, but that doesn't amuse me," she said seriously. "Ever since we've been in France, I've wondered how long it would be before something like this, or something even worse, happened to you. I've never pried into your affairs. I don't know what you do, and I don't want to know, but all these trips and these strange people you meet. And now—prison. Most of all, this sense of danger I feel. I worry about you, Edward; I love you and I don't like—in fact, I hate—the idea of you taking terrible risks."

"Come now, Ellen. There are dangers in what I'm doing, I don't deny that, but you can't make them any less by worrying about them. It's like chess, Ellen. If you're clever enough, you can always discover a way to move out of danger. Death, if that's what you're thinking about, isn't staring me in the face yet."

"How do you know? How can you be sure? Suppose you betrayed someone—why couldn't you be found some morning, stabbed to death in an alley?"

"You're straining your imagination, Ellen."

"But it does happen, Edward, you must admit that. How I wish you could have lived where I did, Edward, over that tavern, for just a week. You would see what people do, how they act when all their money is stolen or when they're cheated or when someone runs away with their wife. You wouldn't see civilized people there, murmuring about justice. You'd hear them bellow with rage, rush downstairs and out into the street with knives in their hands. It's not because they're poor or mean—it's because they're human. They act as all people do when they suffer too much. That's what I don't think you understand, darling. Even from the little I know of him, I'd say a man like Paul Wentworth would kill without a qualm if he thought he'd been betrayed."

Edward sat in surprised silence during this outburst. The sudden vehemence and passion in her voice was a shock to him; he knew she was trying desperately to convince him of something she had been thinking for a long time.

"I don't think you need fear that Wentworth will try to kill me." He smiled, trying to soothe her.

"Paul Wentworth is more cunning than that," she replied, her eyes bright with tears. "He would hire a man to do it for him, which is worse. When you told me that you'd been sent to prison, it was like feeling the first link of that chain I've dreamed about, a long, heavy chain that has begun to wind around you. Darling, I'm afraid it will keep winding until it kills you."

With a little sob, she jumped up from the table and knelt beside his chair. Her tears fell softly on his hand. After her shoulders stopped trembling, he raised her face and kissed her very gently.

"I won't mention it again, Edward, but please, for my sake, be careful."

They walked into the drawing room together, his arm around her waist. They were just about to sit down when there was a knock on the door. A murmur of conversation followed as the door opened. Then Bertram appeared, announcing the arrival of Silas Deane.

"Hello, Edward," Deane exclaimed, striding across the room and seizing Edward's hand. "I'm delighted to see that you're safe, after all the stories I've been hearing."

"Stories, Mr. Deane?"

Deane interrupted his reply to bow to Ellen. "Good evening, Miss Vaughn. Please pardon my bad manners—it's because I'm so happy to see this gentleman."

"Yes, stories," Deane continued, turning toward Edward. "A man in the office this afternoon told me all about you—about Aiken and your letter in the *Post*. He said there was a rumor you'd been sent to prison."

"That's a fair summary," Edward laughed. "It's true, too. I did see Aiken, who, incidentally, told me that he had seen you and informed you of his plans to fire Portsmouth."

"Aiken? Burn Portsmouth? The fellow's mad—never knew an Aiken in my life, as far as I can remember. I can't be positive, though; there's at least one madman in the office every day. What did he look like?"

Edward described Aiken as well as he could. Deane nodded his head.

"Yes, he's vaguely familiar, but I don't remember anything about him. What exactly was he trying to do?"

While Edward described Aiken's plan, Deane's face changed from surprise to amazement to disappointment when he learned that nothing had resulted.

"Ho, ho!" he chortled. "What a scheme! I don't blame you for giving him the money, Edward. What a laugh we would have had if it had worked! It's too bad he was caught. What's this about your being sent to prison?"

"It's quite true. I was sent to Lambeth on suspicion of complicity in the arson attempt. They weren't able to prove anything, so they released me. As soon as I was freed, I took the packet for France."

"But what about returning to England? Will they permit that? I should think you'd be on probation of some sort, that they'd be keeping an eye on you."

"They were going to do that, I believe," Edward replied, "but I went to some of my friends in the government and complained, saying that was no way to treat a loyal subject. They agreed with me after Lord Mansfield defended my conduct in Parliament. My papers were returned with apologies, and I was given full permission to continue traveling back and forth between London and Paris."

Deane slapped his leg with enthusiasm.

"Damn, that's clever, Edward. I'm glad you're working for us. Well, I'll go along now. I just wanted to stop by and see if you were really back. Lee said he thought he had seen you get off the Calais coach."

The two men walked to the door. After Deane had left, Edward stood in the hall for several minutes, puzzling over Deane's last remark. Lee had seen him get out of the Calais coach? He had stopped the coach at this street, getting out here instead of at the regular coaching station. How had Lee seen him? He tried to remember if there had been anyone in the street when he had walked to his house; he could remember no one.

He looked out into the street. It was a dark night; fingers of mist from the river crept along the street and between the houses. Opening the front door, he stepped out and pulled it gently toward him, leaving it slightly ajar. He listened for a moment, then very quietly walked down the steps. The street was absolutely quiet until he came through the little front garden and stood on the sidewalk. Then, down toward the corner, he saw a figure hurrying away.

So that was it, he thought. Lee had hired someone to watch him. How else would he have known about the Calais coach? He walked back into the house, resolved to make the watcher's life miserable.

"You look tired, darling," Ellen said when he returned. "Don't you think it would be a good idea to go to bed early?"

"I am tired. That coach trip left me rather limp."

Edward stretched out comfortably on the soft bed and watched Ellen braid her hair. Almost at the same moment that he was thinking how glad he was to be home and how long he had been away, he fell into a sound sleep. He was lying on his back, breathing heavily, when Ellen blew out the candle. She slid under the covers quietly and lay beside him for a moment without speaking.

"Are you glad to be home, darling?"

As she waited for his answer, she heard his deep, regular breathing and felt him turn over on his side, away from her.

"Damn," she whispered. She closed her eyes and tried to sleep.

SEVERAL DAYS LATER, Edward received a letter from Sam Wharton:

Dear Edward,

I noticed your letter in the *Post* with some concern, but when I read Lord Mansfield's speech, I worried no longer. Mr. Walpole was in to see me and said you had probably returned to France; I shall address this to you there.

The money you left with me was put to good account. I put it into something at just the right time and was able to get it out again, in spite of Peabody, before anything interfered with our profit. I have forwarded the money to the Paris branch of the Bank de Lyons. The amount of profit I allowed our friends was 300 pounds, a worthy return, I feel, considering the short time the money was available.

Let me hear from you when there is worthwhile news; I am trying on the patience you mentioned, but it does not fit me well.

Yr. Friend,
Saml. Wharton

Deane was working over a large pile of papers at the Hotel d'Entrague when Edward returned from the bank.

"Paperwork!" he snorted. "Look at these reports I have to fill out for the Congress, Edward. Is that all they expect me to do?"

"Perhaps I have some news that will cheer you, Mr. Deane. I have the money you gave me—and also a profit of one hundred pounds."

"You know, Edward," Deane smiled, "it's beginning to give me great pleasure, handing money to you. Every time it returns, it's always larger than when it started out."

"It may not always be like that, Mr. Deane. Someday there'll be a loss."

"I'm a merchant, Edward; I know such things happen. I'm grateful that you handle this money for me, but I feel you should take a larger share of the profits."

"I take a fair share. Your money means business for our firm. The more business we do, the greater profit we make. If we took too much profit, we would soon lose our customers."

"I have a friend in America, Edward, who talks like that. His name is Robert Morris. He's one of the richest men in the Colonies and one of the smartest. You work in much the same fashion that he does. When you have a chance to go back to America, you should stop in to see him."

"I would like to."

"Have you thought about returning?"

"Oh, yes, many times. As soon as the war is over, I would like to go back."

"When I'm home again, come to Hartford and see me. I can put you to work for me, if you would like that, or set you up as a doctor. With your experience and your membership in those London societies, you would soon have a fine practice."

"I shall think about it, Mr. Deane. You make it sound most attractive. But I did want to ask you about my present salary. When I came here, we agreed, if I remember rightly, that I was to be paid 200 pounds per annum. Since I haven't yet been paid, I wondered if it had slipped your mind?"

"I haven't forgotten it, Edward," Deane said, frowning. "It has been very much on my mind. Frankly, we are having considerable difficulty about funds. I haven't been paid myself for almost a year, and I'm sure that Franklin and Lee have not received anything either. We receive enough for our official expenses, but no more. There's one other difficulty so far as your salary is concerned."

"Yes?"

"Lee," Deane said bluntly. "He claims we have no authority to pay you, since the Congress has made no provision for it. I know he's wrong about this, and so does Franklin, but we haven't received word from Philadelphia yet. I can't say when your salary will be paid, Edward, but I guarantee that it will, if I have to pay it from my own pocket."

"That's very kind, Mr. Deane. The money means less to me than the satisfaction in being paid for the work I do. That is what upsets me—receiving nothing for my efforts."

They said no more about money that day. Edward left early and went home. As he walked toward his house, he felt extremely disgruntled. It was not that two hundred pounds made any particular difference. What he disliked most was the thought of Lee—appearing again, like a stone in his path—interfering and making himself obnoxious. To be sure, Lee's protests would only further solidify the dislike that was felt for him by everyone; nonetheless, he was becoming more than just a nuisance.

"What is it, darling?" Ellen asked when he walked in. "You look depressed."

"Oh, there was a discussion about my salary. No one seems to know who is to pay it. Meanwhile, I'm to go on working as though everything was settled."

"What a shame! But is it really so important, this money? Is it such a large amount?"

"That's not the point," Edward said sharply. "The fact is that I have done my work and done it well, if I may say so. I should be paid for it, not put off with poor excuses."

"You're right. It is unfair. But don't fret about it any longer, darling. You'll spoil your supper."

Ellen's remark amused him, and his laughter helped dispel his depression.

"You sound as though we'd been married ten years," he said. "Very well, I promise to forget it all."

After they had finished supper, Edward read aloud from *Tristram Shandy.* Ellen listened, eyes half closed, until finally Edward closed the book with a sigh.

"My eyes are tired," he said. "I think I'll stop now."

"Of course, darling. Do you like it as much as I do?"

"Yes, I do. There was a great deal of discussion about it when I was in London. Many people claim it's poorly written and full of conceits."

"I don't believe that," Ellen protested. "Why do people always have to carp so?"

"It's the easiest thing to do. Whenever a book is published that people don't instantly understand, it's always the book's fault, not theirs."

"I wish I had read more, Edward. When I hear you talking sometimes, with Mme. de Treymes or Dr. Franklin, I feel dreadfully ignorant."

Ellen sighed, then turned to him. "I have a surprise for you tonight."

"What is it?"

"I'll show you. Let's go upstairs."

They went up the stairway, but as they reached the top of the stairs, she turned and led him to the bathroom.

As Edward entered, he stopped short and began to laugh. Surrounded by pails of steaming hot water was a glorious copper bathtub, arched at one end. It had been polished to a superb brightness.

"Where did you ever find that?" Edward chuckled.

"Never mind. Tonight we're going to try it—together. We'll see if it's as comfortable as the shop owner said. Now let's undress, before the water becomes cold."

She went into the bedroom. Edward followed and arrived in time to see her clothes cascading around her ankles. He undressed hurriedly and followed her back to the bathroom. Naked as a naiad, she was already pouring water into the tub.

"Help me with these," she laughed. "You have to work a little for your pleasure, you know."

As he poured water into the tub, he felt himself growing aroused. She glanced at him and smiled.

"You see, there are times when you don't need my little hand. Look at you. And you don't even know the game yet."

She made him enter the tub first.

"Be careful," she cautioned, "or you'll tip the tub over. Then all that water will stream downstairs, and Bertram will surely guess what's been going on."

Edward leaned back against the tub. She climbed in carefully, settled herself on him and guided him into her. He remained still and let her move slowly up and down on him, her feet pushing up until he slipped out of her; then, with the pressure of her body, she made him slide along her, pressing against her where she was most sensitive. She gasped, then pushed him inside and moved until he filled her completely.

She tightened around him and slowly began to milk him.

Her moans of pleasure increased, and he heard that guttural sound in her throat which told him she was ready. Swiftly he pushed into her. Reaching down, he spread her cheeks, then pressed them together.

The more he did this, the louder she moaned until, in a frenzy, she tightened around him and with short, frantic movements brought them both to a climax.

They were still for several minutes, their arms around each other. Then, very carefully, they moved out of the tub.

"Did you like your surprise?" she smiled.

"I loved it. And you?"

"More than I had thought possible. We didn't tip over the tub, we had a splendid bath—and lots more. Now we'll go to sleep together, and I love that."

ONLY CARMICHAEL WAS in evidence the next morning when Edward entered the Hotel d'Entrague. The secretary informed him that Deane would not be in until afternoon, and Franklin was at Passy and not expected until the next day. As Edward walked into the rear room and closed the door behind him, he noticed that Deane's desk was covered with papers which had not been there the previous day. Curious, he went over to look at them.

The papers were manifests which had just arrived from Wickes and Nicholson, detailing all the prizes which they had seized. Edward was surprised to note the length of the lists and was soon busily engaged in copying down the information which had been so carefully detailed. There was even a closely written list of the contents of the pouches which Wickes had seized when he captured the mail packet.

When he had finished, Edward laid the original of the list he had made on Deane's desk and carefully placed the second copy in his pocket, together with a roster he had made of the ships sailing to America and the cargo each carried. He stopped at Lee's desk, listened for a moment, then opened the drawers one by one and inspected them carefully. He pulled out a piece of paper from one of them and took it back to his desk. After making a copy of it, he put it back in the drawer in its original position.

As he went out into Carmichael's office, he said to the young secretary, "When Mr. Deane arrives, tell him that I have finished all the work there was to do. I may be back late this afternoon, but there's nothing more to do unless dispatches arrive from Philadelphia."

Carmichael nodded and continued with his work as Edward went out the door.

He walked to the Tuileries Gardens, intending to put his papers into the bottle in the plane tree. But the walk was so pleasant and his spirits so high, he decided he would take the papers to Wentworth himself. As he walked down the narrow street that led to Paul's house, he was surprised to see a familiar figure walking toward him.

Edward recognized him as the man who had come one day to see Franklin—Lupton, a discharged first mate.

He had asked for a berth on a privateer, but Edward recollected that he had not been too sober at the time, and Franklin had dismissed him angrily. He did not look drunk now, Edward thought as the man raised his hat and bowed with a faint smile. Lupton and Wentworth, he mused.

You never know, do you? He suddenly shivered and remembered the phrase that went with the shiver: Someone just walked on your grave.

Paul greeted him cheerily. After they had sat down in the study, Edward pulled the papers out of his pocket and handed them to Wentworth. "There were too many for that small bottle," he laughed, "and also, I thought you might have some questions to ask about them."

"A very sensible thought," Paul said, nodding. "I'll go through them now, if you can wait, and see if there is any question."

As Paul skimmed through the papers, his face darkened. "This is bad news, Edward, but you've done marvelously well to gather it all together like this. Wickes and Nicholson have been terrorizing the shipping in the channel. I had heard about the mail packet—it caused quite a panic in London—but I didn't know about all these others."

He let the papers fall to his lap.

"We must figure out a way to stop these privateers, Edward. If we can't protect shipping in the channel, we will lose an immense amount of prestige. Successes like these are bound to make the French more agreeable to an alliance. We must stop them as soon as possible."

"It's a rather large order, isn't it," Edward asked, "wanting to stop privateering when they have the whole French coast to use for asylum?"

"It is, but it is important enough to warrant our best efforts. If we can destroy the privateers in a swift, methodical fashion, we will ruin Colonial prestige in France."

"That is true," Edward agreed. "What do you plan to do?"

"I have been thinking about baiting a trap for them. Suppose we started a rumor that a large amount of specie was being transferred to France. We might even mention the boat it was to be carried on. We could send the boat out alone, with a strong escort of sloops and cutters behind. As soon as the privateer committed itself, we could encircle it. Outnumbered and outgunned as the privateer would be, it would be only a matter of time before we destroyed it. Then we could write a long account of the fight, describing the cowardice and bad seamanship of the privateer and have it printed in all the journals here and in London. After one or two actions like that, our worries would disappear. What I want you to do, Edward, is to find out which harbors the privateers—especially Wickes and Nicholson—use for refuge. Also, how their crews are recruited: where, how often, and by whom. If we can put some of our own men aboard, our task will be simpler."

"I have heard that Wickes is partial to Nantes—that's where he put in first when he brought Franklin to France. Very little is heard from Nicholson."

"Keep working on it. I have just remembered something else—have you discovered the names of the people in England whom Franklin and Deane are using as sources of information?"

"No, unless this means something to you. It's a copy of something I found in Lee's desk this morning." Edward handed Paul the piece of paper on which appeared a series of numbers:

474161—
808191 313281 647112 486042 839222 599041 573061 858211
0 599041 364191 395262 330191 405211 636132 346241 505182
—715012

Paul puzzled over the note for a long time and finally placed it on the table.

"I don't make any sense of it," he said. "One must have the key to read it, or the original letter to which this is obviously the answer. There was nothing more?"

"Nothing. It's in Lee's handwriting, if that helps you."

"Perhaps I'll think of something if I work on it long enough. When these ciphers are carefully fashioned, one doesn't solve them on the first attempt."

"I suppose you heard about my being in prison?"

"Yes," Paul laughed. "I had a note from Eden telling me about it. You had a very short stay, Edward."

"If I had been forced to endure a fortnight of Mrs. Earnshaw, I should have lost my mind."

"Earnshaw? Oh, the jailer. Yes, I remember. I'm glad you're out of it so easily. You must be extremely careful, Edward, to avoid more notoriety. It can completely ruin your value to the service. The important thing is to stay out of the public eye, to remain unknown except to the group with which you work."

After Edward left Paul's house, he walked to a nearby cafe which he knew. He was too hungry to go far and attributed his hunger to the long stroll he had taken through the Tuileries Gardens.

A waiter whom he did not recognize took his order.

"Wine," Edward said, "and an omelette. Don't cook it too long."

"*Oui, Monsieur.*" The waiter went to the bar and, picking out a bottle of wine, brought it back to the table for Edward's approval. When he nodded, the waiter uncorked it and poured a glass for him.

Edward sipped at his wine and looked about the cafe while his omelette was being prepared. Several tables away, next to the wall, a young man, blond and light bearded, was bent over a book, whispering the lines aloud with much feeling and pausing periodically to take another sip of wine. In the front of the cafe, at a table near the window, two men were heatedly discussing some matter of politics. Periodically, Edward overheard a name repeated which sounded like that of a prominent statesman. He tried to hear more of the conversation, but the voices of the two men were pitched too low for eavesdropping.

The waiter interrupted Edward's attempted eavesdropping. He carried a large platter which he set down carefully on the table. It was the omelette, superbly cooked, with the butter still running down the soft, creamy sides. Edward bent toward it and sniffed; the delicious aroma made him close his eyes and sigh with pleasure.

"Pardon, Monsieur, but it makes me happy to see a man who so enjoys his omelette."

"It makes me happy to see such an omelette. A bottle of his favorite wine for the chef."

"Monsieur is generous. The chef will be most happy."

He had not taken more than two bites of the omelette when he became conscious that someone was standing beside him. Looking up, he saw Captain Hynson, perfectly sober and cleanly dressed, with fresh ruffles at his neck.

"Good afternoon, Doctor. Surprised to see me?"

"Surprised and delighted, Hynson. Sit down, won't you? Have some wine. I must say, I do admire those ruffles."

Hynson pulled up a chair. Twirling it around, he straddled it, his hands clasped on the top.

"You're kind to say a good word about the ruffles, Doctor. They feel queer to me; I'm wearing 'em as a promise—she said I wouldn't dare. It's been a long time, Doctor, since we crossed from Dover."

"Yes, it has. What are you doing in Paris? I thought you didn't come any farther south than Calais."

"Usually I don't, but this time I had to. My pretty little boat was wrecked a few weeks back. Badly anchored, she was; a stiff wind blew her up on the beach—tore the bottom right out of her. No good tryin' to fix 'er, even; she was dead gone. Thought I'd come here and see if I could find some work;

it takes money to buy a new boat. You haven't heard of anyone who wants things transported, careful-like, across the channel, have you, Doctor?"

"No, I haven't. There must be someone, though. People are trying to send things to England all the time, things they wouldn't want the customs to see."

"That's what I figured. I've taken enough of it back and forth to know it's a thriving trade. I thought I might be able to get an advance payment from someone—enough to buy a new boat."

"I'm sorry I can't help you myself, Hynson. I'm not sending anything to England except letters. I might be able to give you a few commissions later, but there's nothing now."

"I'm grieved to hear that. When I came across you here, sitting in front of that beautiful omelette, I said to myself, Joe Hynson, providence is mixed up in this. Here's your old passenger, Dr. Bancroft, sittin' right in front of you, just when you need him most."

"It does look like providence, I must admit," Edward said, smiling. "There is one man you might try, Hynson. His name is du Maistre, Alain du Maistre. He lives on the Rue Descombes. I have been told that he is interested in jewels. It's possible he might have something for you."

"Thank you, Doctor. I'll try him. I'd do anything to get another boat." Hynson's voice was almost a whisper when he mentioned the word *boat.*

"I want to get another fast little one like the last, one that'll step away from these channel-wallowin' cows. Some day I want a ship of my own. I don't suppose you'd understand, Doctor, not bein' a sea-lovin' man like me, but I dream about havin' a ship of my own."

Hynson rose to his feet and slid his chair back into place. "I'll look up this man du Maistre, Doctor. Thank you for your kindness and for the wine, too."

Edward stuffed some bills into Hynson's palm.

"You're most welcome, Hynson. I'm glad to see you again, though I'm sorry to hear about your boat. Here's a bit toward the new one. See du Maistre—maybe he'll have something for you to do."

Hynson strode out, and as Edward stared after him, he could not help feeling a bit sad. The man should never be forced to come ashore, he thought; Hynson was out of his element and looked it, like a hawk in a cage.

Carmichael was still alone when Edward returned late that afternoon. Closing the door behind him, Edward waited a few minutes to be sure that Carmichael was not going to disturb him. Satisfied, he pulled a key from his pocket and opened Franklin's strongbox.

He hoped that in checking through the papers again, he would find something to explain the cipher message he had left with Wentworth. He searched through the box carefully, but there was nothing.

Leaning back in the chair, his eyes suddenly fell on Franklin's old dispatch case hanging on the wall.

Edward knew that Franklin stuffed papers into it that he didn't want to throw away, but was sometimes too busy to bother with when they were first received.

There were bills, minutes of meetings in America, old journals, and notes of scientific lectures which Franklin had attended since his arrival in Paris.

Franklin was true to his principles, Edward thought—he saved every scrap of usable paper. There was nothing of interest until, turning over an envelope, Edward found a strange notation on the back in Lee's handwriting. It was in cipher and, like the other, a jumble of numbers:

715012—
410171 553132 093112 6531120548121 386211 260152 701082
808191 4841510326142 636132 414152 923321 110131 45111
326142 539211 414152 387261 450061 252102
—475161

Edward hastily copied down the numbers on a piece of paper and put the envelope back in the dispatch case. If Wentworth couldn't figure out the code, perhaps he could, Edward thought, so he made a copy for himself.

Nodding good-bye to Carmichael, he walked out and turned toward the Tuileries Gardens again. When he arrived at the large basin near the plane tree, the children were just starting home. Edward sat down and watched them fade away like sprites, skipping down the paths and shouting in high, tired voices to their friends. When they had all disappeared, he looked about to make sure he was unobserved.

Taking the bottle out of the tree, he put in the copy of the other cipher letter.

At the office the next morning, Edward had hardly seated himself at his desk before Carmichael was at his side.

"Pardon me, Doctor. Mr. Deane has just sent a message. He's at the Hotel Sans Souci, and he asks that you join him there. His coach is waiting outside."

When Edward arrived, he found Deane pacing restlessly before the proprietor's desk. Seeing Edward enter, his face brightened.

"I might have known I couldn't do this by myself," he said, hurrying over to Edward. "Franklin's moving—to Passy. I don't want to stay at the Hotel d'Entrague any longer—the food's terrible. I thought I'd look around and find a place for myself this morning, but I haven't had any luck. What do you think of this one?"

"I'm not acquainted with it, Mr. Deane. I've heard the food isn't too good, however."

"I won't bother with it any longer, if that's the case. Where would you recommend?"

"Have you looked at the Hotel d'Hambourg?"

They departed and entered the Hotel d'Hambourg just as the proprietor came out of the kitchen. He bowed politely and walked over to them, a platter in his hands.

"If you gentlemen don't mind waiting one moment . . . "

The proprietor's polite request was interrupted by Deane. He was leaning forward, sniffing. Suddenly he put out his hand and raised the cover of the platter.

"*Tiens, Monsieur*," the proprietor hissed, "you will make it cold."

He walked away rapidly and set the platter down before a waiting guest.

"*Poule au vin*," Deane murmured. "Delicious, too, from the aroma. Shall we have lunch here, Edward, before we look further?"

After they had given their order, Deane introduced himself to the proprietor and inquired after lodgings. The proprietor beamed with delight at the prospect of sheltering Colonial officials. He took Deane upstairs after the *poule au vin* was finished and showed him the quarters. Deane displayed only the slightest interest; his lunch had already determined the issue. This would be his future home in Paris. He descended the stairs jubilantly and called to Edward: "I'll stay here, Doctor. Would you ask Carmichael to start sending my things over?"

Carmichael was not pleased with the message Deane had sent.

"Moving? He wants me to move all these things? Damn! Aren't there any servants in Paris, Doctor? Why must he always send for me when I have something to do? I had an appointment this afternoon with a man I thought Nicholson could use—now we'll lose him, probably, because I have to help Mr. Deane move."

"Perhaps I could take this man a message for you, Carmichael," Edward suggested. "Where were you to meet him? It might not be too far out of my way."

"Could you, Doctor? That would be splendid of you. His name is Agnew.

I was to meet him this afternoon in the Blue Boar. He's a rather tough-looking person—has a beard, about as tall as you, black hair, and a scar on his right cheek. He's an Englishman, a sailor they threw out because they suspected he was connected with a mutiny. He's not very happy about it, and he wants to work for us. Deane said to give him a job with Nicholson. Agnew must be told he should go to Havre and report to Nicholson there. He can find a man from the crew at Mme. Bouton's boarding house."

"I'll tell him."

"It's extremely kind of you, Doctor. You're certain it's no trouble?"

"Not at all, Carmichael."

Later that afternoon, as Edward walked inside the tavern designated for the meeting place, the noise hammered at him until his ears ached. Standing at the bar, he ordered a glass of wine and looked about for the man he had come to meet.

The Blue Boar was a rendezvous for those whom society had struck down or cast aside. Each of these men, according to his specialty, was waging his individual war against the rich and the well-fed. There were thieves and murderers, schemers and promoters of graft and chicanery, blackmailers, cut-purse poets and painters, restless soldiers and sailors, and the hard, ubiquitous little group of haggard intellectuals, some who looked like priests defrocked and others whose smoldering eyes cursed the world's indifference to their talents.

Many of them were ragged; all but a few were noisy and garrulous. For years the guardians of the peace in Paris had looked uneasily at the Blue Boar, but since it collected all the perpetrators of the most recent crimes, they allowed it to exist because it made their work easier.

Smoke eddied around the room and made it seem to Edward that he was seeing their faces through the filter of a dream; they were dim, fragmentary, like faces half-remembered on awakening.

One man he did see clearly. He was sitting at a table, halfway across the room. Old, perhaps sixty or more, with a full white beard and an absolutely bald, shining pate on which there was not even the faintest memory of hair. His eyes were intensely dark and his face, though handsome, was terribly disfigured by the scar branded on his forehead. What sort of blackmail had it been, he wondered? The man looked imposing enough to blackmail only the richest or the most powerful.

Where was Agnew? Looking around the room, Edward noticed a man busily writing at a small table. Sheets of paper covered the surface in front of him, and quills were scattered about like warriors on a battlefield.

He was about thirty, wearing the small blue cap affected by sailors, a heavy blue sweater, and stained, worn pants. Since he was the only man in the room who approximated Carmichael's description, Edward picked up his glass and walked over to him. The man stared angrily out of the corner of his eye when he noticed Edward beside his table. As if determined to ignore the intrusion, he bent down to his writing again, biting his quill fiercely.

"Is your name Agnew?"

The man started, dropped his quill, and cursed vehemently when he saw the ink spatter on a clean sheet of paper.

"Who are you?" His face was a hard mask of suspicion.

"Mr. Carmichael asked me to find you and give you a message."

"Oh." The man's face lost the look of strain that had drawn it tight; he rose clumsily to his feet.

"Sit down, won't you?" he half apologized. "I'm sorry I was so short with you. It's hard to tell these days what people want."

"I should have introduced myself first," Edward replied, sitting down on the uncomfortable little stool across the table from Agnew.

"Never know people's business today," Agnew complained. "Used to be that you could tell a sailor or a presser, but today everyone's beginning to look the same. Where's Carmichael?"

"He couldn't come. He had to finish some work, so he asked me to come instead. He said to tell you that the Americans want you to sail for them; you're to report to Captain Nicholson as soon as possible."

Agnew nodded but did not speak. He picked up the paper from the table and crumpled it up in his fist; he took a deep breath, and Edward noticed that he seemed to grow younger as he watched him.

"Thanks for telling me, Mr—"

"Doctor, Dr. Bancroft."

"Thanks very much, Doctor," Agnew continued. "This means a lot to me, this chance to go back to sea. When I spend so much time on land, I think after a time that I'm rotting away, that I'll forget everything I ever knew about ships and sailing."

"Living on land must be hard for you."

"It's hell, if you're as fond of ships as I am. Started when I was a boy, going out in channel fishing smacks. Since then I've traveled over most of the world."

"If you've traveled so far, perhaps you got to Surinam?"

"I did. Spent some time in port there—at Paramaribo. Lousy town, that; but whiskey's cheap, so you don't mind it as much as you would if you were sober.

"Surinam's a funny place—hotter than sin, greenest jungle I ever saw, and full of people who ought to know better than to live in such a hole. When we were in port, there must have been a score of Englishmen who came to the captain, trying to get passage back home.

"Funny, you never expect to see white people in a place like that, except around the customs and the government buildings; but down there you saw them everywhere you looked. I never could understand how they got there in the first place."

"It's a bit like your sailing, Agnew. People go to Surinam because there's something inside them that's too strong to resist—a craving for adventure, if you want to call it that."

"You speak like a knowing man, Doctor, especially about Surinam. Were you ever there?"

"Once. I spent four years there, about twenty miles from Paramaribo, up in the hills you mentioned."

"Christ! What made you do that?"

"Just what I've been talking about. Adventure, an urge, or whatever you want to call it. The Indians there are strange—primitive, dirty, and ignorant. But there was something beyond that. They were always happy, unless they were drunk."

"I'm damned. I never thought I'd meet someone from Surinam who had a kind word for the Indians. All I heard was how wild and savage they were. The knives they carried made me believe those stories."

"I suppose those knives would make you fearful. They didn't use them for anything except cutting brush."

"Did they ever come to you, Doctor? To be sewed up?"

"No, not once," Edward recalled, smiling. "They didn't have much faith in our medicines. In certain things they knew far more than we did—what herbs to use for bruises, what grasses for cuts, which powdered rocks for skin infections. Those were ancient remedies, all of them, passed down for generations through the chiefs and the old people. They worked, too—those herbs and grasses."

"Did you ever find out what they were? Ever bring any of them back with you?"

"I couldn't bring them back. They were native to Surinam."

"It's too bad you couldn't," Agnew said, grinning. "With all the brawling in the streets and taverns here and in London, those herbs would be very handy now, wouldn't they?"

"I guess they would, but I haven't worked as a doctor since I left Surinam. Besides, I don't know whether I'd be willing to spend all my time patching up these people."

"I can't blame you for feeling that way. But maybe we don't have the right to judge them."

"That's an interesting remark. You know, Agnew, you talk too well to be a common sailor."

Agnew looked up at him, and Edward noticed again the mask he had first seen on the man's face. It had appeared instantly, after his last remark; he was reminded of the manner in which some animals protected themselves when danger threatened. The reaction was the same, the transformation just as rapid. Agnew relaxed suddenly, and his eyes circled the room cynically before he replied.

"Perhaps I wasn't a common sailor to start with, Doctor, but that's what I am now."

His remark put an abrupt halt to the conversation.

Edward sighed a little as he rose. He had enjoyed talking with this man; he had brought back vivid memories.

"I'm pleased to have seen you, Agnew. I hope you have many pleasant voyages with Nicholson. You'll find a man from his crew at Mme. Bouton's in Havre."

"Thank you, Doctor, and thank you for bringing me good news."

There was a message from Ellen when Edward arrived home, saying that she had gone on to Mme. de Treymes's house for supper and asking him to come as soon as he could. He arrived to find a large supper party in progress. There were so many guests that it was with some difficulty that he finally found Ellen and sat down beside her.

"I'm sorry I couldn't let you know before, darling. Madame sent a message this afternoon, saying she wanted very much to have us here tonight. I didn't know when you would return, so I came over alone."

"How is Madame? I haven't had an opportunity to speak with her yet."

"She's just the same, a bit more direct, if that's possible," Ellen laughed.

Edward began eating and Ellen was drawn away at once to listen to the stories of M. de Bouvilcais, the supper partner on her left.

M. de Bouvilcais was noted for his family and notorious for the deadliness of his conversation.

Edward had just decided that Ellen seemed to be enduring M. de Bouvilcais with great tact when he heard the lady on his right address him.

"I beg your pardon. I didn't . . . " He stopped in surprise. The lady whom he had so completely ignored while speaking with Ellen was Lady Downes.

He had not noticed anything in sitting down except a graceful head which had been turned away from him and a lovely pair of shoulders. He had thought no more about it at the time, these two delights being rather common coin in Paris. As he looked at her now, he did not understand how he could have confused this head and these shoulders with any others.

"It has been a long time, Dr. Bancroft, since we have sat beside each other at supper. Much has happened in the Colonies since we last discussed them."

"Indeed it has, Lady Downes. The rebellion once scoffed at has come in earnest, has it not?"

"Yes, it has. I can't help feeling what a sorry figure England cuts before the world by using all those Hessians. Many people in London are bitterly opposed, but there is nothing that can be done, apparently, to prevent it. I have heard much about you recently, Doctor."

"Yes? I trust it was nothing too dreadful."

"Would you be surprised if I said it was?" She paused and glanced at him, but Edward remained silent, preferring to allow her to continue the conversation.

"It wasn't at all. It was an extremely dull discussion for the most part, but your name was mentioned, and in a highly complimentary manner. Tell me, Doctor, do you feel that the Colonies will succeed in this rebellion?"

"I do not know, Lady Downes. It is extremely difficult to predict anything, so long as both sides are immobilized by winter. I do feel that the Colonies will continue to rebel until England shows herself more willing to consider their demands."

"I have always hated rebellion in any form, but this one seems different to me. I don't know why—perhaps the stories of bravery and hardship I have heard have influenced my opinion. I did hear that they were willing to negotiate for peace, if England would grant them a sufficient degree of independence."

"That might be true. I have become acquainted with some of the Americans here in Paris, and from what they have told me, peace would be welcome to them."

"I have heard, Doctor, that you are now a banker, too."

"Not a banker, exactly. I have done some financial work here, but actually I am only a cautious investor."

"M. Necker told me that you had a better grasp of the intricacies of finance than any Englishman he had ever known."

"That was more than kind of him, Lady Downes," Edward smiled, "and a bit more than the truth. For my part, I admire M. Necker's ability—he is truly a brilliant man, one whom I am proud and happy to call a friend."

"I could not help noticing, Doctor, that the young lady I saw with you at Vauxhall is here with you tonight."

"She has become extremely fond of Paris, Lady Downes. I don't know that I shall be able to persuade her to return to London."

The guests began walking toward the drawing room, from which the sounds of a string orchestra were issuing.

Lady Downes turned to her other supper companion, and Edward rose and walked out with Ellen. His last remark was still in his mind, and it puzzled him. He had not meant to say it; it had been one of those remarks that suddenly appears at the tip of the tongue and falls before it can be caught, its real meaning apprehended only as it fades into silence. He looked down at Ellen and thought how remarkably well she had done in Paris.

Her manners and her bearing were beyond reproach, and if an echo picked up on the London streets crept into her speech occasionally, it was regarded as unusual and quite charming by the ever-polite French.

As they reached the drawing room, Mme. de Treymes left the group of guests with whom she had been talking and hurried toward them.

"Dr. Bancroft, I am angry with you. Why haven't you come to see me before this? It's weeks since you were here last with Ellen."

"I have no excuse, Madame, so I shall not try to invent one."

"A good thing," she replied heatedly, holding on to Ellen's arm. "It's unfair and inexcusable, and you know it. I've wanted you to come more often— every time people come to my salon, at least one of them is certain to mention your name. Don't forget, if you will excuse this vulgar phrase, that I have a share in you, having pulled you bodily out of the grave."

"I have not forgotten. Every time I have a moment, I say to myself, 'Edward, you have Mme. de Treymes to thank for all this. Pray for her tonight.'"

"That's a pretty story, Doctor, but not as flattering as you might think. It is what has been happening for years. Someone is always praying for me. My greatest ambition is to have someone pray to me, and not make it seem that I am a creature of constant sin."

"I know that is untrue, Madame," Ellen protested. "There is not another woman in Paris who is more admired and respected than yourself."

"Then I truly need someone to pray for me," Madame sighed. "How dull that makes me sound! They are playing vingt-et-un upstairs, Doctor. Would you care to watch that for awhile? I want to introduce Ellen to some people I think she might like to know."

"Don't let Madame involve you in any of her schemes, Ellen," Edward laughed. "She has a reputation for using pretty girls as pawns in the games of diplomacy that are played in this house."

Madame stamped her foot and was about to protest when he turned and walked upstairs. There was laughter in her voice as she called after him, "I shall demand an apology when you return, Doctor."

The room that had been set aside for vingt-et-un and other games of chance was filled. Men milled about the tables, but there was little excitement—most of the men present were accustomed to playing for large stakes, but tonight they regarded the games with a bored air.

Edward watched the play at the roulette wheel for a few minutes and then decided on the red. Taking a louis out of his pocket, he threw it down on the board, on red. The wheel spun. Talking quieted, then died; all the spectators were watching, voicing through their eyes the silent words and prayers that would halt the wheel at their chosen number. It stopped, and the croupier called, "Number 41, red." Edward reached out and picked up his winnings.

For the next few turns, he made no bets. Reaching out suddenly, he placed both louis on Number 23. The wheel spun, the conversation died, and the little ball circled noisily about.

"Number 35, red."

With a faint smile, Edward turned and left the table.

He walked downstairs and found Ellen and Mme. de Treymes with a little group near the center of the room. As he walked toward them, Edward was surprised to find many of the Americans in Paris there: Lee, Deane, Carmichael, and several others.

"Ah, Doctor," Madame exclaimed as she saw him approach, "I'm so glad you're here. Mr. Lee was just telling us about Virginia. It sounds so lovely that I want to go there at once. M. le Marquis, may I present Dr. Bancroft. Doctor, M. le Marquis de la Fayette."

Edward bowed to the smiling young Frenchman. He was pleased to meet this young man of whom Franklin had often spoken. At first glance, he seemed as charming as he had been described. Edward knew that Franklin had already given him letters of introduction to various people in the Colonies; he wondered how soon he would be sailing for America.

"I am informed that you were born in America, Doctor," la Fayette said, "in Massachusetts, I believe. Mr. Lee has told us about Virginia—indeed, he has made it seem the most charming place in all the Colonies. Is this true, or do you prefer Massachusetts?"

"I was born in Massachusetts, sir, and have been to Virginia several times. I think, however, that it is unfair to draw a comparison between the two colonies."

"Unfair? What do you mean?" Lee asked, thrusting his chin forward suddenly.

"Why, unfair to Virginia, Mr. Lee."

"You see, M. le Marquis," Edward continued, turning to the young Frenchman while Lee stared at him suspiciously, "Massachusetts and Virginia are the oldest and most powerful of all the colonies. Virginia represents the southern section and Massachusetts the northern. To draw a comparison between the two would be the same as trying to decide which head was more important to a two-headed calf. Both heads are essential; if either one is removed, the Colonies perish. I must admit that there are fewer people in Massachusetts who are trying to sever their connection with the Colonies than in Virginia, which has a large number of persons who are still loyal to England."

Lee's face colored when Edward mentioned the Virginia loyalists, and his lips curled into their accustomed sneer.

"What you have said about Virginia, Doctor, was fairly true until your last statement. We have loyalists, I admit that—not so many in number, perhaps, as Massachusetts, where the British give them asylum—but we have some.

"Unfortunately, M. le Marquis," he said, turning to the attentive Frenchman, "in Virginia, we would not subscribe to Doctor Bancroft's belief in the two-headed calf. Virginia, being the oldest colony, discovered long ago that the best government was that instituted and carried on by the best people. I believe if you look at the most prominent Americans today, you will soon notice the superiority of Virginia: General Washington, Mr. Jefferson, Mr. Henry, and, if I may presume, my own brothers, Harry and Richard Henry Lee.

"In Massachusetts, however, the situation is not the same. There the people are allowed to run their own government, with unfortunate results; people of no brains and less manners—whose only claim to superiority is the uncertain power they wield over their fellows—are entrusted with the affairs of the colony. It is little wonder that Boston is such a nest of rabble-rousers and brigands."

"Gentlemen, gentlemen," Madame protested, "I'm certain that each of these colonies is more pleasant even than its partisans describe it. You will soon be going to America, M. le Marquis; you can write and tell us which you prefer."

"That is true. For me, that is a better way to decide, for I shall not run the risk of incurring the disfavor of either of these gentlemen."

"Since we are discussing the merits of the colonies," Deane interrupted, "it would be disloyal of me not to mention the many attractions of Connecticut."

The relieved laughter which followed Deane's words dispelled the discomfort Lee's remarks had created.

"It is not at all a jesting matter," Deane continued, a slight smile on his lips, "to me, it is quite serious. I truly believe Connecticut has more advantages than any of the colonies. It isn't as famous, perhaps, as Massachusetts or Virginia, but the people are just as pleasant, if not more so, and if you live there, you're judged by what you do, not by what someone in your family might have done fifty years before."

"Bravo, Mr. Deane," Madame said, "that seems to me the real spirit of the Colonies. If I contrast the people I see here or in England with those who live in the Colonies—whether they live in Massachusetts, Connecticut, or Virginia—I cannot help but feel you really *are* the New World. How fortunate you Americans are, wherever you live."

Startled by this acute comment from one so totally French, the Americans fell silent.

"Ellen," Madame continued, attempting to bridge the sudden silence, "what do you think of M. le Marquis's plan to go to America?"

"It's a splendid idea, I think. With his spirit and his famous name, M. le Marquis will be of great service to the cause of the Colonies."

"Well said, Miss Vaughn, well said," Deane beamed. "I have thought the same thing, though I have not expressed it so clearly."

"I am delighted that you approve my plan," la Fayette said, bowing to Ellen. "I hope I shall be of service to the American cause."

"Dr. Franklin is positive you will be of great service," Madame put in. "I wish he could be here tonight. I had a note from him, expressing his regrets. Much as I treasure the note, I would treasure his presence more."

"Dr. Franklin is extremely occupied with his Masonic brethren," Lee explained with a patronizing air. "He has little time for innocent pleasures."

Madame peered at the Virginian for a moment, then turned to regard her guests across the room. The only member of the group, Edward noticed, who remained unfailingly polite and interested in all that was said was la Fayette.

One must give credit to the French, Edward mused, who could erect such a solid structure of social poise and grace over their feelings that they never appeared embarrassed or angry. Mme. de Treymes was old enough to have acquired an undeniable right to individuality, but already the young marquis had acquired such a patina of aplomb that nothing seemed to disturb him.

Edward admired him for his unfailing interest and politeness. La Fayette would do well in the Colonies. He was young enough to be strong and active, wise enough to be silent and observing, and cultivated enough to reconcile and accept the inconsistencies of the people he would meet there.

The marquis disturbed Edward's reflections by leading Ellen away. As Edward watched them walk down the drawing room, his face must have assumed a sad expression, for he was soon conscious that Madame, highly amused, was watching him.

"Don't worry, Doctor. His wife is charming, his child adorable, and he is soon leaving France."

Edward knew a flush had spread over his face. He cleared his throat before he glanced at Mme. de Treymes

"It is most kind of you to spare me anxiety on that score. I was not really thinking about that, Madame; I was puzzling over an older problem."

"Wondering if she was tiring of you, perhaps?" Madame said softly.

Edward started and glanced down to find her looking at him, her eyes full of understanding.

"Are you surprised to hear me say that? Do you suppose I could live as long as I have and not learn something about people? You make me very angry sometimes, Doctor. You seem to respect me, yet you set no more store by my judgment than if what I said was something spoken by a child."

"On the contrary, I have always respected your judgment, Madame."

Mollified, Madame patted his arm before continuing. "I have seen fifty Ellens in my life. Not so attractive, possibly, a few years younger or older, but essentially the same. I have been with her a great deal, Doctor, as you know, and I have wanted to talk to you about her. Through no fault of yours or hers, but no less irrevocably, I am sure you are going to lose her."

"What makes you think that, Madame?"

"It is difficult to say. She is happy with you and delighted by her life here. I know this is so, both from what she tells me and from my own observation of her. But that happiness is fading, Doctor; that delight is fast becoming habit. Oh, heavens, why is it always so hard to tell others what you see so clearly? You could not see yourself or Ellen as I see you; I am so fond of you both that I have watched you as if you were my own. And now, when I want to say something, I cannot find the proper words."

Edward waited for her to continue. He knew that his relationship with Ellen had lately undergone a change, yet he was no more able to put that change into words than one could adequately describe love or lack of love. He had a great respect for the judgments of this woman; she had lived fully and seen much.

"She is bored, Doctor," Madame continued suddenly, as if she had found fresh courage to speak and the words she had been seeking. "That is the only way I know to say it. The excitement of this new life that you have given her is not enough to take the place of her old one. The people she meets are beginning to seem dull and colorless to her. I have noticed this often when we have been riding through the streets. Sometimes she is like a child when we pass near one of the poor districts where there is so much life; the sight of a fight or an argument will excite her for the rest of the ride.

"This life you and I love, Dr. Bancroft, this matching of our wits against the world, means nothing to her. It is something she does not understand. She is too hot-blooded, too passionate an individual; she has respect for the mind, you have taught her that, but it has no great attraction for her. I am more and more convinced that someone will appear who will offer her the excitement she needs. She'll leave you then, and I shall be sad, for both of you."

Edward felt depressed as he listened to Madame's words. She was right, he knew almost by instinct; what she was saying was what he had been thinking, what he had felt as he watched Ellen walk away with la Fayette.

He had sensed that she might someday walk out of his life in just such a manner, but he had put off thinking about it.

"But there—I have ruined your evening. Forgive an old woman's chatter, Doctor. Perhaps we might find some solution, you and I, if you want badly enough to keep her. Come and see me some afternoon—we'll talk about it."

"I shall come, Madame. You have said much that was in my mind."

Mme. de Treymes pressed his arm tightly and then walked away to join her other guests.

He shrugged off his problem and looked about the room for Ellen and the marquis. They were sitting together at the far end of the room, the marquis looking as gay as he had when he first arrived. Ellen, beside him, was leaning slightly forward, listening to him and laughing at whatever he was saying to her. She was more beautiful tonight than he had ever seen her, Edward thought as he walked toward her. There was a radiance about her, a glorious vitality revealed by her eyes and her tense, supple figure. She seemed like some beautiful creature captured for but a single night by this world so unlike her own.

"We were just speaking of you, Doctor," the marquis said, rising to his feet and bowing to Edward. "Miss Vaughn informs me that you are the famous Dr. Bancroft who is a banker, an author, and an explorer as well as a doctor."

"Miss Vaughn has been exaggerating my few accomplishments, M. le Marquis, but hers is a weakness I will gladly forgive."

"I may have mentioned your virtues, Edward, but I included some of your faults as well."

"They are faults which I would like for my own," la Fayette said, smiling.

"I am afraid she has not been at all a trustworthy witness. Has she mentioned that I have a frightful temper, that I throw things when I am angry? Or that I play vingt-et-un poorly but consistently? Or that I cannot dance as well as some?"

"No, Doctor, she said nothing about those matters. But I consider them, if they should be true, not very serious flaws. I do not dance well either."

This last sally of la Fayette's made them both smile. He had an undeniable attraction, Edward admitted. Although he had been prepared to dislike la Fayette, thinking he was but another of the hundreds of idle and supercilious young bloods of Paris who were going to the Colonies for lack of anything better to do, he realized that la Fayette could not be so easily cataloged and forgotten.

"I'm afraid we must go, my dear," Edward said, turning to Ellen.

She rose, and la Fayette kissed her hand gallantly and bowed.

"Good night, Dr. Bancroft. I have enjoyed meeting you. I understand now why Dr. Franklin speaks of you in such glowing terms."

"You are very kind, M. le Marquis. I hope I shall see you again before you leave for the Colonies."

Mme. de Treymes walked them to the door to say good night. "You are both most fortunate," she said. "You are young, your star is rising, and you are fond of each other. I wish that any one of these things might be true of me now."

They drove away in silence that was at last broken by Ellen, who was vainly trying to burrow into the warm robes in the carriage. Edward put his arm around her and drew her closer to him.

"A lovely party, wasn't it, Edward?"

"Perfect. Just the right number of people. Madame seems the only woman in Paris wise enough not to invite too many guests. I liked your Marquise de la Fayette."

"My marquis? Oh, Edward, don't be silly. He spent the entire evening telling me how much in love he was with his wife and what a torment it was for him to leave her and go to America."

"I thought him charming. I confess I had the wrong opinion of him before I met him. What I had heard about the other aristocrats made me suspicious of his trip to America."

"He really seems to be looking forward to the chance to help the Colonies. He talked of many things I knew nothing about, but there was no mistaking his sincerity, or his desire to be of service."

Just before they reached home, Ellen looked up at him. Pulling his face down to hers, she kissed him warmly.

"Let's not forget what Madame said to us when we left tonight," she whispered. "We have so much, darling, you and I. It would be shameful to spoil it."

THE SKY WAS BLACK with storm as Edward walked to the Hotel d'Entrague the next morning; occasional drops of what promised to be a heavy spring rain fell on his coat. Winter was over, and spring was eager to arrive.

In the Tuileries Gardens the earth was moist and black; trees were getting their first buds; and faint shoots of grass, defiantly green, braved their way through the soil.

As he walked inside the door, the storm broke behind him. Through the window he saw the rain cascading in sheets, and a fine mist suddenly blotted out the other side of the street. The rain fell with increasing violence, and even the gutters, which were swirling with water, were blotted out of sight. He could see nothing outside except the rain—Paris had disappeared. This little building had become an island, only precariously safe.

The mist cleared for a moment, and he saw a passerby hurrying along the street. He was bent low, shielding his face as best he could against the lashing water, his collar turned up and tight around his neck. His feet sloshed through the water and left no impression on the pavement behind, as if a ghost were passing by. A wagon appeared, the rain spattering on the bowed, sorrowful back of the horse. Stumbling over a loose stone, the horse almost fell before it could recover its balance. The driver, ineffectually covered by a small canopy which had been stretched above his seat, whipped the poor beast forward, cursing and flicking the water from his hands. The rain lashed at him, leaving his clothes sodden and hanging on him like rags on a skeleton.

"Quite a downpour, isn't it, Dr. Bancroft?"

Franklin was standing at the next window, shaking his head as he watched the wagon disappear down the street.

"Yes, it is. A good omen, though, Doctor—the first spring storm."

"It might well be," Franklin agreed. "Let's go into the office. There are several matters I want to discuss with you before I leave for Versailles, and before the people arrive who are to move the rest of our belongings to the Hotel d'Hambourg."

After they had seated themselves, Franklin turned to Edward, a quizzical smile on his face.

"Deane told me, Edward, about the discussion you and Lee had at the reception last night."

"You would have enjoyed it, I think, Doctor. You could have added something about the merits of Pennsylvania, unless, as an old Massachusetts man, you might have sided with me."

"Had I entered the discussion," Franklin said, "it would have been as a representative from Pennsylvania. However, that is not what concerns me. Deane said it was a rather bitter few minutes."

"It became that. What started as a rather humorous discussion turned into a full-fashioned argument. There was no harm done, however. The bitterness disappeared as quickly as it arose. But I speak only for myself; I cannot vouch for Mr. Lee's sentiments."

"Mr. Lee's sentiments provide the reason why I mention something so inconsequential," Franklin said, frowning. "Deane informed me that he had sided with you, not merely because you are from his section of America, but because, to quote him, Lee is 'a narrow, bigoted, sidesaddle specimen from the place where only the best people are named Lee.' "

Edward could not help laughing, and Franklin was forced to chuckle after he had finished.

"There are few people who seem fond of or tolerant of Mr. Lee," Franklin continued, "and I fear our group is no different. That does not allow us to forget, however, that he is a man with position and responsibility similar to mine and Deane's. We must not let ourselves be sundered by personal bitterness. We have too much to do."

"Mr. Lee and I are not friendly," Edward admitted, "but I have always tried to be as cordial as he would allow me to be. If it will make things easier for you, Dr. Franklin, I shall try my best to avoid any discussion such as that which we had last night."

"I had hoped you would feel this way, Edward. You know I am extremely fond of you and extremely grateful, too, for all the assistance you have given us. Lee is a problem we all must solve. If he continues to feel that we have banded against him, he is in a position to do incalculable harm."

"I understand."

"Another matter I wish to discuss is the recruiting that Carmichael is now engaged in for Nicholson. He has been able to assemble a complete crew, except for the first mate."

"I think that has been arranged, Doctor. I sent a man off to Nicholson yesterday, a George Agnew."

"Agnew? Never heard of him."

"Carmichael was busy with Mr. Deane and asked me to meet Agnew in his stead. He seemed a good man, so I gave him instructions to go to Havre and contact Nicholson there."

"Good. I didn't know about that. Since you have already helped with this task of recruiting, Edward, I shall ask another favor of you. What I want to do, if you are willing, is to give you a few instructions which should be passed on to the men whom we select for privateer crews. Carmichael and I have been the only ones here familiar with this information. Because I am so frequently at Versailles or Passy, it would be of great assistance to me if you were able to direct these men who come here for their instructions."

"I should be glad to help, Dr. Franklin."

"Very well. Perhaps you had better write this down. It's rather complicated."

While Edward gathered writing materials, Franklin called in Carmichael and secured from him a large folder which Edward had not seen before. Seeing that Edward was ready, Franklin began dictating:

"All crews for our privateers working out of Calais will be directed to Captain Wickes. He may be found at the Cafe de Normandie or at the Cafe des Anglais. If he is not at either place, his ship the *Reprisal* may be found by contacting the ship's boat, which calls at the foot of the Rue de la Mer at seven each morning and at nine each night."

Franklin paused to allow Edward to finish. The quill scratched over the paper, the only sound in the room. At length Edward nodded to signify that he had finished.

"Those crews which report to Havre will find Captain Nicholson at the Cafe de Rouen or the Cafe de Marins.

"His ship, the *Intrepid*, lies about one mile off Trouville-sur-Mer and may be reached by ship's boat, which calls at the Trouville dock at nine in the evening."

Again Franklin paused.

"The next instructions are for those who are to report to Captain Cunningham. They will probably be changed shortly, because his present anchorage is both unsafe and unwise. Crew members will find him at St. Nazaire, in the Pension d'Alain or the Cafe Martinet.

His ship, the *Surprise*, is anchored several miles up the river. The ship's boat comes to the dock in front of the cafe at ten o'clock at night."

When Edward had finished writing, Franklin put down the quill which he had been chewing.

"Cunningham's position is a dangerous one," he said, frowning, "and I hope we shall be able to change it before many weeks have passed; he can be too easily trapped where he is. If I do not happen to be here myself, Carmichael will let you know when we receive word from him regarding any change . Now, a few things for the captains who may stop in.

"Reports of prizes captured should be sent here at once by all captains. Captains will make their own arrangements for selling prizes."

"Please make a special note of this, Doctor," Franklin said, interrupting his previous thought. "Prizes of special importance, such as mail packets, men-of-war, and specie carriers, are to be taken directly to Nantes. Under no circumstances will a captain delay removing his ship from the area where a prize of this sort has been captured. Now, to continue with our former subject:

"The percentages originally agreed upon with each ship's captain will remain the same, subject only to minor changes made by the agent with whom the prize is left. If any word is received from the Continental Congress changing this agreement, all captains will be promptly notified."

"Finished?" Franklin asked after a moment of waiting.

"Very well, this is the last item: Any member of a ship's crew who is discovered working for the English as spy, informer, or in any other capacity, will be disposed of as the ship's captain concerned may deem advisable. Record of such action will not appear in the ship's log."

Franklin stood up and hurriedly put on his coat.

"I'm late, now, I'm afraid. It's too bad Versailles isn't closer to Paris."

After Franklin had left, Edward made a careful copy of the instructions he had written out. When it was finished, he walked around to the front of his desk and, reaching down, inserted his paper knife in a crack in the wood. As he twisted it slightly, there was a scraping sound. The front panel of the desk swung open, revealing a compartment already well filled with bulging packets. He placed the original instructions on the top of the pile and closed the compartment door quietly. A half hour later, he was standing at the door of Paul Wentworth's house.

"Mr. Wentworth is out, Doctor. I expect he'll be back shortly, however, if you care to wait for him, sir."

Edward nodded and walked into the little study where he settled himself with a book and began reading. He read for some time before the door opened and Paul Wentworth stepped into the room.

"Every time I see you here, Edward," Paul smiled, "it makes me happy. You never bring me news that's unimportant."

"How much money do you have with you, Paul?"

Wentworth stared at him for a moment in bewilderment. Then, opening his wallet, he counted the notes in it.

"Two hundred livres, I make it. Why?"

Edward did not reply until he had opened his own wallet and placed a pile of notes on the table beside him.

"There are two hundred livres there," he said, pointing to the money. "I will wager you that amount that you cannot guess the news I have brought you."

Wentworth's brows wrinkled. Suddenly, he stepped forward and placed the money he was holding beside Edward's.

"Done. How many guesses?"

"Three?"

"Fair enough. Franklin's dead."

"No, not that. Two more."

"America is willing to make peace on any basis."

"One more."

"Hmm. Two hundred livres is a fair amount of money. There's no sense in wasting my last chance. At least tell me what it's about."

"It concerns your major interest at the moment—the privateers, and one of them especially."

"Cunningham's been captured."

"No, not that," Edward replied, picking up the money and putting it into his wallet. "But something just as good. I can show you how to capture him. Here, read this."

Paul took the copy of Franklin's instructions which Edward held out to him and sat down to read it. Folding it up after he had finished, he glanced at Edward and shook his head.

"You couldn't have done better than this, Edward. It's exactly what I wanted to know. We'll have men on every privateer they own within a month. But what about Cunningham? I don't quite see what you mean."

"His ship is up the river. Your ships can lie off the coast, on the alert, so that when he does come out, all you have to do is close in on him. There's nothing he can do except fight until he's been sunk or he founders on the rocks. Franklin said he didn't expect him to change his anchorage for at least two weeks. Surely you can assemble ships by that time."

"If we can get Cunningham, it will even the score," Wentworth mused. "His Majesty may forgive us the loss of the packet. If, as you say, we do this quickly enough, Cunningham won't have a chance. I'd rather take him and his men alive, however. They'd be more valuable to us as prisoners rotting away in England than they would be as martyrs drowned off the coast. However, that's for the Admiralty to decide. I'll send this to them by courier."

CHAPTER XI

L ATER THAT WEEK, Edward was traveling north of Paris, jolting uncomfortably along the road in the Calais stage. Franklin had asked him to go to London.

The old man was worried by the lack of news from America. He was especially eager to learn what the British planned to do during the approaching spring and summer months. General Burgoyne was his chief concern. Franklin realized, because of his trips to Canada and his familiarity with the geography of the Colonies, the terrible possibilities of a British attack from the far north, an attack which might split the Colonies and force each to make peace individually.

Shortly after he arrived in London, Edward stopped by the foreign office to see Eden.

"I'm delighted to see you, Doctor. Are the Americans still hoping to sign a treaty with France?"

"There is much talk of it in Paris, Mr. Eden, in spite of the few scraps of bad news that have been received this winter. Dr. Franklin is worried, however. He does not seem as optimistic as he did when he first arrived in France."

"Franklin is a most astute man. How do you think the Americans would react toward an offer of peace at this time?"

"The news is not bad enough yet for that. They are committed to negotiate only if England is willing to grant the Colonies their independence. They must suffer at least one disaster before those orders from the Continental Congress can be changed."

"With the news we receive from Howe, such a disaster cannot be far distant."

"Perhaps not, but I wonder ... " Edward left his thought unsaid.

"Wonder, Doctor? Wonder what?"

"I wonder, Mr. Eden, how accurate these dispatches from Howe really are. I have read some of them. General Howe has killed and captured more men than ever lived in the Colonies."

"Perhaps so. It is difficult sometimes not to count the casualties who might have been. However, Doctor, I feel that when one side wins so consistently, as we have been doing, it becomes only a matter of time before the other side is too weak to continue."

"If it were not for the privateers, the Colonies would be much weaker today than they are."

"That is quite true, Doctor. Thanks to you, the privateers will be one fewer within a week. We have already cast our net for Cunningham; it should not be long before he blunders into it."

"I am glad to hear it. The two I am presently concerned with are Wickes and Nicholson—I cannot afford to allow thousand-pound bounties to slip through my fingers."

"You did not do that, Doctor," Eden smiled, "when you gave us the information on Cunningham. Ever since we captured the mail packet, I have posted that amount against his name. When we capture him, I shall forward your thousand pounds to Mr. Wentworth."

"I shall be very happy to receive it. Paris is an expensive place in which to live."

"I have heard that. There is also, I understand, the possibility of a famine among the poor because of prices rising so swiftly. We are delighted by that prospect. If there is trouble at home, Vergennes will have less opportunity for provoking trouble abroad."

"I shall see you again, Mr. Eden, before I return to France. Perhaps the net will have closed around Cunningham by that time."

"I hope so, Doctor. That will be a bounty which I shall pay with great pleasure."

Wharton had not yet arrived when Edward entered Jonathan's for their luncheon appointment. As he looked about the coffeehouse, he could not help contrasting it with Chacot's in Paris. Both served the same customers—stockjobbers, bankers, speculators, and financiers—but that was the only similarity between them. Jonathan's was an old establishment, perhaps sixty years older than Chacot's, and there was a vast difference between the proprietors of the two. Chacot and his wife were definite, unmistakable individuals, but Mr. Sebastian Pidge, the proprietor of Jonathan's, was remarkable chiefly for his self-effacement.

Edward could not calculate the number of times he had been in Jonathan's, yet he remembered noticing Mr. Pidge not more than five or six times.

Edward began to wonder whether Sam had forgotten about lunch when suddenly he saw the bulky figure of his partner in the doorway. Wharton saw him at almost the same time and, waving a greeting, hurried over to Edward's table.

"Afternoon, Edward." Sam stretched back in his chair. "Damn, I wish I was in bed now. I'm tired."

"A bad day, Sam?"

"No, not too bad. Just busy, all morning long. People wandering in to see me with some of the most harebrained schemes you ever heard of. The last one finished me. After he left, I told Peabody I wouldn't see anyone else. I ducked out and came straight here."

"What did the last one want?"

"Money, I suppose. He wanted to start a company to make some new kind of coach. Claimed they'd go faster than any coach on the roads today. Get crowds of customers, be boasted. Everyone wants to be first today, he told me, as if I hadn't realized that—first on the boat, first off the boat, first to business, first to the theater. He said people were spending their money for speed. Everyone would want to buy his coaches because they were the fastest. Humph! Not much they would! He showed me some sketches—damndest looking things I ever saw."

"They couldn't be any more uncomfortable than the coaches we have today, could they?"

"They looked dangerous to me, Edward. They had springs everywhere you looked. Go over a bump or hit a pothole, and you'd fly fifty feet in the air."

"What was his name?"

"Macadam. Son of a friend of mine in Edinburgh. I told him the damned thing would never work. Afraid I insulted him with that. He's stubborn, just like his father. But what about you, how long will you be here this trip?"

"I don't know exactly, Sam. A week or two, I should think."

"Good. Are you going to stay in London?"

"No. I'm going out to Carshalton tomorrow. I think I'll spend my time there."

"You're fortunate. I wish I could find a place as pleasant as that to spend my time. How are the Americans?"

"As you might expect. The news they hear from the Colonies doesn't cheer them much."

"You don't look as though it cheers you much, either. What you need is a change." Wharton smiled suddenly and began to laugh. "I'm a fine one to be telling you that, Edward. You had to cheer me up the last time. Tell you what, how would you like to see a cockfight tonight?"

"Fine. Where?"

"At the Pillars of Hercules. Nine o'clock, downstairs from the bar. It will do you good. Take your mind off the rebels. Can you meet me there at eight-thirty?"

"Yes."

"I'll be in a stall if I can find one empty. Eight-thirty will give us time enough to place our wagers."

Edward passed a quiet afternoon at his club and after supper went into the library. He skimmed through the copies of the journals, but the day's events were dull, and the news of hangings and debtors depressed him. He was delighted when it came time to leave for the Pillars of Hercules. Going outside, he hailed a linkman.

"Here you are," he said as they started, holding a coin out to the man. "I've a pistol in my pocket and no pity for street thieves."

The linkman moved the torch closer and stretched out his free hand, into which Edward dropped a shilling.

He glanced at Edward for a second, and as his eyes took in Edward's shoulders and the convenient pockets on his coat, the man nodded understanding.

They moved toward the tavern without a further word being spoken. As they passed one of the more wretched alleys, the entrance cluttered with rags and filth, Edward noticed that the linkman had started to lower his torch. Swiftly, he put his hand inside the pocket of his coat. The linkman, noticing this, gave a long whistle which ended in a sharp discord. At the same time he raised his torch higher.

This proved the only incident of the walk, and Edward was greatly relieved that he had given the man a warning. He remembered his battle with the gang of street thieves the previous year. The Irish chairmen loved nothing better than to split the skulls of thieves, but linkmen were of a different breed. Many of them were or had been thieves themselves and guided their unsuspecting patrons into alleyways where they could be more conveniently assaulted and robbed.

The Pillars of Hercules was crowded. As Edward glanced about the tavern looking for Sam, he saw people pushing their way toward the bar, slopping pots of ale on their neighbors and bellowing to make themselves heard over the clamor in the packed room. All the tables were taken and the stalls as well, but as he made his way around the side of the room, he recognized Sam's face in a far stall.

"That's better," he exclaimed, after he had drained half the pot of ale Sam had waiting for him. "Am I late, Sam?"

"Right on time, by my watch."

"All these people here for the cockfight?"

"I should think not. The proprietor lets only a few downstairs. The price of admission keeps most of them out. Much as they love cockfighting, they'd rather spend their shillings on ale."

"If you've come for the fight, gentlemen," the proprietor said, stopping beside their table, "it's time to go to the pit. Twenty minutes you have for placing your wagers. If you'd care to follow me, I'll take you there now."

The proprietor conveyed them to the far side of the pit, directly across from the man who was taking wagers. He stared at them attentively for a moment as they stood next to the railing around the sand pit. Then, judging it would be a few minutes before they had inspected the birds and settled on their choice, he turned back to the men who pressed around him, waving notes and thrusting tightly clenched fistfuls of coins at him.

The space around the small cockpit was filling rapidly as Edward and Sam, along with the others, made their wagers and then moved to a spot where they could see the fight better. Edward was beginning to find it difficult to distinguish faces across the pit from him. Although the other side was not more than fifteen or twenty feet away, a heavy veil of smoke already obscured it; the smoke hung like a soft, undulant curtain above the birds, which had already been put in position, one at each end of the pit.

A handler held each bird, turning it first this way and then that to reveal the power of the shoulders and the wings and to prove the presence of its sharp, shining spurs. Occasionally, the handlers would tap at the fierce beaks of their birds, which made them snap angrily and caused a new ripple of excitement among the spectators.

It was becoming more and more difficult to move in the crush about the pit. Just as Edward was considering the possibility of moving farther to one side, he felt a hand slide down his jacket toward the pocket of his breeches. Quickly, he pushed his neighbor slightly to one side and thrust his hand behind him.

He was not able to turn about, but he felt his hand touch another and his fingers closed tight. He exerted all the pressure he could from such a cramped position and had the satisfaction of hearing a stifled groan as he twisted the man's wrist far to the left. Suddenly the hand tightened and freed itself from his grasp with a jerk.

"What's the matter, Edward? You look as if someone had stepped on your foot."

"It's nothing, Sam," Edward sighed, turning back toward the pit again. "Someone tried to pick my pocket, that's all."

"You have to be careful here. There's always one of them about. Look! They've started!"

The two fighting cocks had been released by their handlers and were advancing toward each other. One was moving more swiftly than the other, his legs stiff and his head low.

The second cock waited restlessly for his opponent to approach; his spurs scraped on the floor of the pit and threw up little bursts of sand as he shifted from side to side. This second cock, which both Edward and Sam had chosen, looked like a devil's toy. He was a shining blue black, iridescent in the candlelight. His spurs were decorated with a fiery, blood-red line, and his beak seemed longer and sharper than the other bird's.

When they were no more than a foot apart, both birds hurled themselves into the air and dashed against each other. No harm was done—both recovered at once and resumed their exploratory stalking. The spectators grew quiet as the birds approached each other again.

Almost so quickly that the human eye could not follow it, the brown bird dashed forward, raised itself a bit off the ground, and, whipping its fierce beak around, tore out the eye of the black bird. The injured bird ran about the pit wildly, frantic with shock.

Glittering crimson splashes marked the sand, but the black bird recovered too swiftly for the brown bird to press his advantage.

The black bird paused at the far end of the pit. Spinning about suddenly, he came pounding across the ring in a sudden attack. Lifting himself into the air, he dashed at his opponent, both spurs churning a mortal path through the air. The vicious attack just missed the brown bird, but so great was the momentum of it that the birds crashed against each other and rolled over on their backs.

They recovered instantly and began hissing at each other, their beaks only a few inches apart while they circled about. Their claws scraped desperately for the small purchase the sand in the pit afforded.

In the next moment, the fight ended so swiftly that the spectators were taken by complete surprise. They could only gape toward the center of the ring, hardly believing what they saw.

The black bird had risen straight in the air and dashed at his opponent before the brown bird could defend himself. His razorlike spurs ripped open the ruff of green feathers, and a cascade of blood fell on the sand like a sudden shower on the desert. The brown bird lay limp while the victor fluttered triumphantly through the path of blood, until his handler seized him and thrust him into a sack.

When they realized what had happened, those who had bet on the black bird began cheering. They had endured an uneasy beginning, when their favorite had lost his eye, so their shouts contained a large portion of relief.

Edward and Sam collected their money from the dour-faced wagerer and, by thrusting and pushing, finally made their way outside the Pillars of Hercules.

"Well, Edward, we won. How did you like it?"

"Most exciting, Sam.I wouldn't care to watch every match, but I like one as exciting as that we saw."

"Winning money is always a nice feeling, too," Wharton laughed. "For a moment there at the start, I was about ready to look around for a good bird for the second match. Ah, here's a coach that's going toward my house. Can I take you anywhere?"

"No, thank you, Sam. I'm going the other way."

"Have a good rest at Carshalton, and don't forget to stop by and see me before you return to France."

EDWARD SPENT THE NEXT fortnight at Carshalton. He had been there almost a week when General Crowder, one of Thomas Walpole's friends, came to dinner. After Mrs. Walpole left them, they sat in the library discussing the war against the Colonies for several hours. During the conversation, Edward learned quite by chance what he had come to England to discover.

General Crowder was a retired British Army officer who had served with distinction on the Continent. He was a man of more than sixty, white-haired and surprisingly small in stature. This smallness had given him an advantage in combat, but it had worked to his detriment in peacetime. As a result of it, he had never attained the position he felt was due him because of his military knowledge and attainments.

Crowder was not at first glance a very impressive man, Edward conceded, as he sat and watched the general explain a battle by the diligent use of fire tongs and canes. Yet there was a force and a vehemence about him, a belligerence, too, as if he resented being thought too old to continue to fight for his country. The war office had been for him a most unsatisfactory substitute for the battlefield.

"Thomas," Crowder said, looking up from his tongs and his canes, "this is confusing Dr. Bancroft, I can see. I can't possibly explain what is happening over there with only these things to use. Don't you have some maps somewhere?"

Walpole fetched an atlas and laid it out on a bare table. Crowder gave a sigh of relief and, riffling through the pages, opened the book and spread it flat.

"There, that's what I needed all the time. You see, gentlemen, by looking at this map, my point becomes immediately clear to you. Here is New York...."

Edward was watching so intently that it was several minutes before he noticed Walpole leaning on the edge of the table opposite him, his jowls quivering in his effort to suppress a yawn.

"Burgoyne, a fair general, but not always clear in his orders, I must say, will come down through northern New York, trying to separate these colonies—Massachusetts and Connecticut and the others—from the ones that lie farther to the south."

"And General Howe will march north from New York to meet him? Is that the plan?" Walpole asked, scratching his head.

"Not at all, Thomas. Burgoyne will come all the way to New York. The Colonists have no one to stop him. You see, their army, such as it is, will be contained in New Jersey. That's what General Howe is to do—wage a fight there which will keep Washington too busy to move. While that is going on, the general's brother, Admiral Howe, will sail from New York against Philadelphia. He'll land marines there and capture the defenseless city as well as that insufferable Congress. A simple yet beautiful plan, is it not, Doctor?"

"Yes, it seems feasible. What will prevent the Colonists from falling back to Philadelphia and defending it?"

"Nothing. They can if they like. But it would be useless, for then Howe's army will be there, too, as well as the marines I mentioned before."

"There's no one to interfere with Burgoyne up north?"

"They have a few rifles perhaps, here and there, but only frontier people, not soldiers. We did hear that Schuyler was in the north, but he's in bad odor at the moment because of a row among their generals."

"They're beginning this maneuver now?" Walpole asked.

"It has already started. Burgoyne is supposed to be at Fort Ticonderoga—there, on that lake—at the beginning of June. He is already on his way down from Canada. He may take a little time to get there, perhaps he will not reach it until after the first of June.

"After all, his troops have had nothing to do but sleep all winter, and they're probably fat and lazy. Getting through those forests will make men out of them, I dare say, better men than the Colonists can find to put against them."

Before he went to bed that night, Edward carefully wrote down every word he could remember of Crowder's conversation. He had a vivid picture still in his mind of the general's blunt finger as it traced the course of the future on the map, blotting out the line of Colonial forts that lay between Canada and New York, the only protection for Franklin's beloved Philadelphia.

A week later, Edward was aboard the packet, headed for France. He was glad to leave England, for the last week of his visit had been depressing. His desire to rest at Carshalton had vanished abruptly after Crowder's discussion, and when he returned to London he found Eden bitter because Cunningham had escaped the trap laid for him. The one morning Edward spent with Wharton going over his assets had shown him to be 50,000 pounds richer than he had known; but it had taken him four hours to extract this truth from his partner, who was occupationally opposed to direct speech. He felt greatly fatigued when he left Sam's office, and he stepped into the Dover coach with a sigh of relief.

The weather had not improved his disposition; indeed, he realized it was probably the cause for the general discontent he had encountered. Winter was departing regretfully, threatening to stay on like an unwanted guest; the days were bleak and cold, with gray skies and blustering, chill winds.

The morning after his return to Paris, Edward entered the Hotel d'Hambourg to find Carmichael sitting resignedly at his desk while a flood of protest and invective swirled past him. He raised his head from his hands when Edward entered, smiled ruefully, and shrugged his shoulders. Through the open door of the office, Edward could see Deane pacing back and forth.

He remained beside the entrance door. As he listened, a smile crept slowly across his face. There was no mistaking the cause of Deane's discontent—in every sentence there was Arthur Lee's name or a biting description of him.

Carmichael breathed a sigh of relief as Edward walked past him into the office and closed the door. "Bancroft! Thank God you're back at last. I never needed your help as much as I do now."

"I'm sorry you're so upset, Mr. Deane."

"It's Lee. The damned fellow is causing all kinds of trouble for us. No wonder his brothers sent him over here. I don't blame them a bit."

"What has he done?"

"Vergennes wants one of us to go to Holland; he thinks we should be able to raise a loan and also arrange to use Dutch ports for our privateers. Franklin can't go because he wants to stay near Versailles, so he asked me to go. Lee had his heart set on going, so he's been making trouble ever since. Claims I'm needed here because Franklin is usually at Passy. He's been badgering Franklin to let him go in my place. I don't care who goes, but Lee thinks I like to travel about like royalty. Also, he's convinced that I have business with firms in Rotterdam, which is utterly false. I haven't said I wouldn't go because he irritates me so much I don't want to give him that satisfaction."

"How does Dr. Franklin feel about it?"

"He doesn't want Lee to go. He's convinced that Lee will blunder somehow. You remember when he went to Spain—how he blabbed about his mission there and gave away our plans to the English? Franklin is still upset about that. This mission will require tact and diplomacy for which Lee has never been noted. If he should make a mess of the business, it would have serious repercussions at the French court."

"How soon must someone leave?"

"Within the next few weeks. Gerard told Franklin that Vergennes was annoyed no one had left yet."

"I'm sorry to hear all this, but I cannot say I am surprised. I have had less important, but no less annoying, altercations with Mr. Lee myself. He is a man determined to have things his own way."

"He is an ambitious, stubborn, prideful fool," Deane exploded. "Why should we be forced to endure the spite and jealousy of this creature when there are other men in the Colonies much more agreeable and better fitted for this position?"

"We've had bad luck with younger brothers of eminent men, you'll recall. Morris, the agent in Nantes, falls in somewhat the same category as Lee."

"That's true," Deane agreed, his face darkening. "Thomas Morris is no more like his brother Robert than Beelzebub is like St. Francis. You might think we had enough to worry about, with Lee to plague us, without having Morris too. What made you think of him? Did you hear something in England?"

"Yes, a conversation at my club. Someone described Morris as a magnificent choice for the Colonists to make. He said that the agent was drunk to stupefaction every day, lewd and filthy in his habits."

"Magnificent choice, indeed!" Deane snorted. "He's done us more harm than half of Howe's army."

"Several of my acquaintances here have had the misfortune of dealing with him. Usually he was too bleary to appear at his office when they wished to see him. If the matter was urgent and they went to his home, they were forced to see him in bed, foggyeyed, with trollops around him like buzzards around a corpse."

"Ugh," Deane grunted. "I can't understand degradation like that, Edward. When I think of his brother, one of the finest and most respected men in the Colonies, I don't understand how they can be related. Let's not dwell on it any longer. There's nothing we can do. Have you heard about the marquis de la Fayette?"

"No, I haven't. The last I knew he was almost ready to leave for the Colonies."

"A most unfortunate affair. He started, with letters from us to Congress and to General Washington, but he was afraid some difficulty might arise because his father-in-law, the duke d'Ayen, opposed his venture.

"He planned to sail to Spain, where he would make the last-minute preparations for his voyage. But before he could leave, the king signed an order for his recall, so now he must return to see His Majesty."

"If his father-in-law is still opposed to his going, I doubt if he will secure the king's permission."

"Perhaps not," Deane replied, "but I fancy he will be able to win the king to his side. His wife, even though she's expecting another child, wants him to be free to go, so I believe she will be able to persuade her father. One of the reasons for the duke's disapproval is that he does not believe young la Fayette will receive a position commensurate with his position here in France, even though I've commissioned him a major general. The duke has said General Washington will never agree—and he may be right."

"It is becoming harder, Dr. Franklin told me, to find suitable posts for all the young nobles who are going to the Colonies."

"It's impossible!" Deane exclaimed. "Every one of them wants to command at least a brigade, except la Fayette, who told me he'd hand his commission back to Washington and then ask how he could help. But enough of that—was your trip to England successful?"

"Very," Edward replied. "I discovered precisely what Dr. Franklin wants to know. I hoped he would be here this morning, so that I could explain the news to both of you."

He gave Deane a brief summary of Crowder's remarks. When he had finished, Deane paced about the room, his hands clasped behind his back.

"Fortunately for my peace of mind," Deane said at last, stopping in front of the map that was placed on the wall, "I can find certain flaws in that plan. Otherwise I should sink into complete despair. It's an excellent plan, but there are mistakes in it, mistakes which arise because of the British attitude toward us. Since we are not a nation, in their eyes, it is impossible for them to believe that we could have an army that was a real military force. I believe that is what will spoil this plan of theirs, for we do have such an army. It will be something to reckon with this spring and summer."

"When this plan was explained to me," Edward said, "it seemed at the time almost too pat, too simple to be possible."

"They have forgotten that there are troops available for that northern section," Deane explained, pointing to the top of New York. "Men can be sent there from Connecticut and Massachusetts and the other New England colonies. However, I'm no general, so I shall not try to be one. My concern is with what happens over here. Did you hear anything about our privateers?"

"Something I'm afraid you won't like. The English government is considering a proclamation which would declare all privateers to be pirates, subject to hanging upon capture."

"That's infamous!" Deane stormed, gasping with rage. "It's completely contrary to law! If they do that to us, it will only lead to the bitterest sort of strife, the worst butchery and murder imaginable."

"There was little doubt that His Majesty would sign the proclamation."

"We must do something, otherwise no man will be willing to serve aboard one of our ships. Until now, the English have been content to place our captured sailors in filthy prisons, to starve and mistreat them until they died from neglect and cruelty. That was bad enough—it served to deter hundreds who might otherwise have served on our ships. But this is summary execution! The king would be a butcher if he signed such an order."

"I have heard that he has reached that state already, so far as the privateers are concerned. Cunningham's capture of that mail packet seems to have been the final provocation. His Majesty has focused his entire wrath upon that one incident."

"Perhaps Franklin can write another pamphlet, like the one he wrote about the Hessians," Deane mused. "I have heard that he was successful in upsetting Frederick of Prussia as well as the English. Frederick, of course, loathes the idea of his name being connected with mercenary soldiers, and Franklin's pamphlet was so brilliantly written that the Prussian monarch has ever since blamed his English cousins for the unwanted notoriety. I must make a note of that. If I could persuade Mme. Helvetius of the pamphlet's importance, she would be able to persuade Franklin to write it."

"It's been a long time since you first arrived in France," Edward laughed. "Anyone could tell that from your last remark. The idea of persuading Franklin through Mme. Helvetius is truly a French inspiration."

"Possibly," Deane chuckled, pleased by Edward's compliment. Growing serious, he added, "I'm afraid Franklin's age is finally beginning to show. His work here has been so much more difficult than he supposed, and the discouragement and despair have been so continuous and unrelenting that he no longer has the strength he once had. He would never forgive me for expressing such a thought, I know. We're all like Franklin in one respect—we need some good news from America to hearten us."

After Deane had left for Passy, Edward walked over to his desk and searched quickly through the pile of recent dispatches. Finding what he was searching for, he made several notes on a piece of paper and then replaced the dispatch exactly as he had found it.

He smiled cheerfully at Carmichael as he went out, then walked quickly toward Paul Wentworth's house. Paul was not at home, but Sylvestre informed him that he was expected to return by late afternoon. The day had suddenly become warm and fragrant with the promise of spring. Edward told Sylvestre that he would return about five and walked back down the Rue d'Angouleme.

How pleasant a walk through the Tuileries would be on such a day as this, he thought. Spring was finally coming to Paris, and its magic therapy could already be detected in the faces of those he passed on the street. They were happier and more cheerful than he could remember seeing, so long had the winter seemed. The streets were cleaner, too, and he was grateful that there were no puddles and no piles of mud which passing coaches might splash over his clothes.

Edward was convinced that the coachmen of Paris found their greatest pleasure in splashing pedestrians. It was probably amusing for the coachmen to bump the people or knock them down, too, but splashing required a good eye and just the right amount of turning in a puddle in order to get the pedestrian as wet as possible. This one winter in Paris had almost destroyed his love for walking. If he had not had Walpole as a horrible example of what lack of exercise did to a man, he might have given up his morning walk entirely. Yet, he realized with a smile, he would miss the excitement of matching his wits against an approaching coachman.

As he reached the entrance to the gardens, Edward saw that much of Paris felt as he did about this day. Crowds of children were galloping madly about on the paths, playing games that had no end and no beginning, absurd games that were perfect outlets for the children's bottled up energy. Old men and women sat watching them from the benches. Many had taken off their hats and were letting the sun's faint rays stream down on their bare heads while they dozed.

Edward found an empty bench. Sitting down, he opened his coat and threw back his head to catch the sunlight on his face. He drank it in for more than an hour, changing his position only often enough to relieve the cramped muscles in his neck.

When five o'clock came, he rose regretfully and started toward Paul's house. The sunlight, although it was not strong, had beaten down on his face for so long that he had difficulty in seeing clearly at first. There was a golden curtain between his eyes and the world. He had never seen Paris so beautiful as it was this afternoon.

"Mr. Wentworth is here, Doctor," Sylvestre told him. "He's waiting for you in the library."

Paul looked up from his book when Edward walked in.

"Hello, Edward. Glad to see you."

"Good afternoon, Paul. I thought I'd drop in and find out how everything was going. Have they caught Cunningham yet?"

"Not yet. He escaped from our first trap, you know. He's been as shy as a girl for several weeks, not daring to venture far into the channel. If he escapes a second time, I think Eden will hang a few of the captains concerned."

"When I saw him, he was angry enough to do just that," Edward said. "I was upset myself. I can't imagine how he escaped if the trap was well set."

"It was. There were more than enough ships to take care of Cunningham, but he didn't make his run until one extremely foggy night. It was impossible to follow him once he got out of the harbor. In fact, we lost one of our ships that ventured too close to shore in search of him."

"Take a look at this, Paul," Edward said, pulling a piece of paper out of his pocket, the one with the notes he had made in the office.

Wentworth scrutinized it carefully before he spoke.

"It won't be your fault if we don't catch him this time, Edward. This is what we need—everything we need—harbor, anchorage, and expected time of departure."

"I thought you would find it helpful. This time he must be caught, Paul. I won't be able to obtain information as precise as this every time he slips past the British navy."

Paul looked up at him sharply, then turned his head toward the paper again without saying what had been in his mind.

"We'll take him, Edward. There won't be another chance for Captain Cunningham. Then we'll go after Nicholson and Wickes. Once they are disposed of, our hardest work will be done.

"While you're here, I would like to discuss with you something Stormont and I were speaking of several nights ago. Stormont says he must have more information about prizes, and he needs it as quickly as it can be sent to him. If we can learn the locations of prizes before they are sold, Stormont may be able to block the sale by his protests. You receive this information, don't you?"

"Regularly, but just as a notice from one of the captains that a prize had been seized, brought to port, and sold for so much money. There would be no point in Stormont's protest if he had only that. I don't know what you can do, unless you station watchers in every port."

"England has a treaty with France that denies asylum to ships of any nation at war with us or with them. We'll have to proceed on this basis. The word *nation* will, of course, create a legal quagmire. Nevertheless, I would like you to spend the next few weeks making careful lists of all prizes. It's what you have done in the past, but I have a special reason for wanting every prize and its cargo listed during the near future. It's an idea of Stormont's, and I think it will work. The French will have to deny their ports to the privateers or risk war with us. I know they don't want war, at least not for a few years."

"Before I leave, Paul," Edward said as they walked toward the door, "I want to mention something else. A mission is being sent to Holland for a loan and for permission to use Dutch harbors as refuges for privateers. It hasn't been decided yet who's to go—Deane or Lee—but whoever goes will be leaving shortly."

"Tell me as soon as the date is set, and I'll send word to Holland. I might also send one of my men after whoever goes. It might be wise to check his luggage periodically."

The information Wentworth wanted came into the office during the next few days in bulging manifests from the privateer captains. Every day Edward made a complete list of all such information received and placed it in the top drawer of Deane's desk. Every night he took away a duplicate of this list and left it in the bottom of the plane tree in the Tuileries. He knew he had sent enough information for Stormont to have weeks of audiences with Vergennes and was wondering what use was being made of it when Franklin called him aside one day.

"Dr. Bancroft, do you remember one day some weeks ago when we made a list of the prizes taken during the month of April?"

"Yes, Doctor, I do. If I am correct, it was nearly two pages long when we finished it."

"Look at this. See if you recognize it."

Franklin handed him a copy of the Hague's court circular and pointed to the left-hand column on the page. The circular was dated May 10, 1777:

The following prizes were recently seized by Colonial merchantmen operating in European waters against English commerce...

There followed a listing in fine print of all prizes seized, with complete details as to the place of seizure, port used, and cargo sold.

As he studied the familiar list, Edward felt a muscle in his cheek begin to twitch.

"Does it look familiar to you, Doctor?" Franklin demanded.

"Yes it does. I believe it is the same list we prepared. I don't remember the other exactly, but well enough to be nearly certain this is a duplicate."

"That was my impression also," Franklin said in a harsh, clipped tone. "You realize what this means, don't you?"

Franklin went on without waiting for Edward's reply.

"It means we have a spy in this office. Or if not that, someone who visits us frequently is a spy. One of the two must be true; otherwise, how could this information be so complete?"

Edward decided not to answer, unless an answer seemed desired by Franklin. It seemed wiser to let the old man carry the conversation by himself, rather than hunt for a reply which might prove suspicious.

"We should have expected it, I suppose. It was only a matter of time before the British learned to do to us what we had been doing to them through you. What do you think, Edward? Do you have any idea who it might be?"

"No, I do not. You will recall that I exposed Mercer and Williamson, but that was some time ago. They could not have been concerned in this," Edward replied, pointing to the circular in his hand.

"We work so closely together here," Franklin mused, "that it is difficult even to consider one of us as a spy. I could never suspect Deane, or you, or even young Carmichael...."

His voice trailed off, but Edward saw his advantage and pressed it at once.

"All of us here work too hard for our cause to be guilty of betraying it,"

Edward declared. "There are so many people who visit this office, Doctor—any of them might be able to steal papers that were lying about."

"You are right, unfortunately. I have often felt that we were careless in this respect. Let safeguarding our papers be our first step then, Doctor. After we have seen to that, we can set about discovering this spy, if there is one, which I hope is not the case."

"For safeguarding the papers, I have a suggestion that might work."

"What is that?"

"Most of us are careless about locking up our papers when we are not using them. I would suggest that they always be locked up except when they are being used."

"An excellent suggestion. I always lock mine, as does Mr. Lee; but I have noticed that Silas is inclined to be rather careless in this. I shall speak to him about it. Keys should be limited also, don't you agree?"

"It would make everything much simpler and much safer."

"There are two keys for my dispatch pouch—I have one and you have the other. Mr. Lee keeps the key for his own case, which is the only one I know of. As far as I can recollect, Deane and Carmichael have keys for Deane's pouch."

"I also have one. There is so much that I help him with, that even before your arrival, I had a key."

"I see. Well, it's no matter, so long as we know where all the keys are. You spoke of not allowing strangers to come into the office."

"My feeling is that we should never leave anyone alone in here. If the person they have come to see is not in, they should wait outside. Usually Carmichael has them do this, but occasionally I have found them here alone—people like Beaumarchais or his secretary."

"Surely you can't suspect M. Beaumarchais."

"Not at all, but I cannot vouch for his secretary."

"I see."

"If we do allow anyone here except ourselves, they might be able to make off with some of our papers or, if there is time enough, even copy them, as they must have done with this list in the court circular."

"That is a prudent suggestion. I shall inform Carmichael of it," Franklin declared. "He will allow no one in here, except ourselves."

"Finally, I would recommend a lockbox. At night, when we are ready to leave, all dispatch pouches and papers should be placed in it until morning.

In that way, we could eliminate the possibility of someone entering during the night and breaking the rather insecure locks of the pouches."

"A capital idea! I'll send Carmichael after one at once. Carmichael!"

The secretary hurried into the office at Franklin's call. Edward watched amused as the young man's hands went through their habitual chores of straightening the perfectly fitting coat and smoothing the unruffled wig.

"Yes, Dr. Franklin?"

"Carmichael, I want you to go out and purchase a lockbox at once. Buy one about two feet wide and two or three feet long, if you can. Be certain that there are strong bolts on it."

"Very well, sir. Would it be permissible for me to take your coach?"

"By all means, do so."

After Carmichael left, Edward noticed the desire for action seem to desert Franklin. Looking at the old man slumped in his chair with one hand supporting his head, Edward realized that age was really beginning to subdue Franklin. His eyes were closed, and on his face there was an expression of weariness which one did not notice when talking with him.

Edward asked if there was anything more that Franklin wanted of him at the moment. After Franklin shook his head so slightly that he seemed to be answering in his sleep, Edward said he was going out for lunch.

Franklin sighed and opened his eyes, smiling. "I didn't mean to keep you here while I napped, Doctor. My age sometimes overwhelms my brain and demands this restful oblivion you have just witnessed. Go ahead; I shall wait here until Carmichael returns."

Edward hurried to Wentworth's house, heedless of the other pedestrians. Several times he almost collided with passing carts and carriages, so occupied was he by his thoughts. His face was white, and every few seconds a muscle twitched in his cheek; his hands had been clenched since the moment he stepped out of the office.

People who noticed him coming toward them moved swiftly out of his way and, when he had passed, stared after his tall figure.

The look on Edward's face as he was shown into the house spoke of trouble to Sylvestre also. Wordlessly, the servant showed him into the library and disappeared at once. Paul entered shortly afterward.

"What's the trouble, Edward? Sylvestre told me you had arrived and looked as if you were prepared to murder someone."

"I am, Paul. I've just had a bad time with Franklin, thanks to a blunder of yours. Except for my own quick wits, it might have been calamitous. Do you remember the list of prizes I gave you last month, the one that was almost two pages long?"

"Yes, I do. A most useful document it was, too. Stormont caused all kinds of trouble when he presented it and asked for an explanation."

"I should say he did cause trouble," Edward thundered, rising to his feet and glaring down at Wentworth. "Do you know what that damned fool did with the list?"

Paul's face revealed his surprise. Detecting the fury in Edward's voice, he wisely kept his seat and answered quietly. "No, I don't, if he did anything except what I have told you. I merely gave it to him, thinking it would be useful."

"It wasn't enough for him to show it to Vergennes. He had to send it to Holland, too, where it appeared in the court circular, verbatim. Just as Franklin and I had written it, word for word, phrase for phrase—not even the order of prizes had been changed."

Edward paused for a second to allow the full import of his words to sink into Paul's mind.

"And now," he concluded bitterly, "the not so stupid Dr. Franklin believes that there is a spy in his office."

"Ahh," Paul groaned in disgust. "If I had known that was what Stormont intended..."

The force of Edward's rage exploded, trampling over Paul's excuse. "If you had known! Why did you allow this jackass to put me in such a position?" he thundered. "I agreed to work for Eden; I even agreed to live outside England, which is something I detest. I work for a pittance, a ridiculous figure that doesn't pay in a year's time for a single month's expenses there. And now this! I could train children from the streets to work more efficiently."

"Edward, Edward, quiet down," Paul soothed. "I don't blame you a bit for feeling as you do. If I had known what Stormont was going to do, I never would have given him your information."

"That's easy enough to say," Edward snapped, "but what about the future? How do I know that this won't happen again? That I won't suddenly find myself faced by another, even worse, predicament?"

"I'll be personally responsible for the information I receive from you, Edward. It will be used only as I direct. Does that satisfy you?"

"Yes, it does. At least I will feel that my information will not strike me down like a boomerang. Also, you might tell Eden that I want more money. I'm through working for a pittance, especially when I have to take such chances because of the stupidities of Stormont."

"I've been thinking about an increase for you, Edward. I'll tell Eden everything that's happened today. I'm certain he'll be reasonable."

Edward returned home and had been there only a short time when Ellen entered.

"Good afternoon, darling," she said, bending over him and kissing him lightly on the cheek. "I'm glad you're here so early."

"This is one of those days when I want to do just as I please. What would you like to do, my dear?"

"I'd love to drive toward St. Germain—it's such a beautiful day. I feel a need for fresh air and a change from Paris."

"Do you mind if I go along with you?" His eyes were suddenly warm and full of gentle humor.

"I want you to," she laughed. "It will be the first time we've been free like this since we came to Paris."

"Then let's go to St. Germain. We can have supper there and return later tonight."

IT WAS AN IDEAL afternoon for a drive. Once they passed beyond the crowds and the carts that filled the streets of Paris, it seemed as though they had come to another land. The air was fresh, the fields were dappled with spring flowers, and the trees were young again with new leaves.

When the coach stopped in front of the inn where they were to dine, Ellen hurried around the side of the building so she could enjoy every moment of the sunset. Edward had chairs brought around, and they sat there for almost an hour, reminiscing nostalgically of other sunsets they had witnessed in England.

What perverse creatures we are, Edward thought, when the last long rays of the sun had thrown a curtain of red and gold before their eyes. Here we sit and delight our souls with the most beautiful sight in all France, and yet we speak of no place but England.

The proprietor interrupted to inform them that supper had been prepared.

After Ellen had taken a last look at the darkening countryside, she slipped her arm about Edward's waist, and they walked back toward the inn together.

"That was so beautiful, darling. I'm happy we came today."

"It makes the city seem a vile place, doesn't it?" Edward replied. "Sometimes I wonder how people endure living so separated from the beauty you and I have just seen."

"When I'm at one of the Parisian salons," Ellen mused, "being bored to death, I find myself sometimes looking around and wondering: what do all these people think about when they're alone? Have you ever seen such uneasy people as there are in Paris? Not the little people—I don't mean them—but most of the ones we know, and especially those connected with the court."

"It seems to me the atmosphere in London is more relaxed; there isn't the tension one feels here. Strangely enough, I think the people in Massachusetts, at least those who were not too closely tied to the church, were the happiest I have ever seen. They lived as they wanted to, not as habit or custom decreed."

"It takes determination and courage," Ellen said softly, "not to follow what everyone else does."

"Indeed it does, and more of both than most people can muster. Think of all the ones who would try to dissuade us if we decided to spend the rest of our lives in Surinam."

"I know one person who wouldn't," Ellen declared.

"Who?"

"Mme. de Treymes. She'd insist that we take her with us. That's what she would love to do, I know, if she could do without her footbaths. They are her one indulgence, and from the way she speaks of them, I don't believe she'd ever be able to give them up."

"Footbaths?" Edward chuckled at the thought. "I never suspected her of such a weakness. I shall have to ask her about them when I see her again."

"Oh, Edward, you mustn't!" Ellen cried. "It's an absolute secret—no one knows except Therese and me. Madame only told me, I think, because she was tired one day and didn't want to talk about anything that would make her think. Therese gives them to her. She calls them Madame's secret vice."

"I won't mention them then," Edward promised. "You're right about her going to Surinam, however. She once made me tell her everything I could remember about the people there. The natives fascinated her."

On the way back to Paris, they suddenly spoke of the future, as people will when present delights seem too ephemeral to endure.

"Will there be many nights for us as happy as this one?" Ellen whispered. "Sometimes, darling, I am afraid to think of the future."

"You shouldn't be. There will be many other nights like this."

"I wonder. What will happen when your work here is finished? What about your wife? Suppose we move back to London—would you live with me or with her? Would—"

She broke off her questioning with a deep sigh and moved closer to him, grasping his hand tightly and holding it against her lips.

"Why do we women talk love to death?" she asked in a whisper. "Do we enjoy risking our happiness? Do we have to hazard our future, not once, but over and over again, with all our what ifs?"

"Perhaps you're trying to shape the future," Edward suggested.

"Possibly," she agreed. "We do love to feel we have some control over it. Yet the power to decide is the last thing we want. Isn't that strange?"

"How do you mean?"

"We're always the first to say, 'You decide.' If a man tells us we must decide, we resent it, because we feel he should be the one. That way he'll get the blame if anything goes wrong."

Edward laughed and tightened his arm around her.

"I'm serious," she said, pulling back a little. "The simple truth is we love to be taken care of. Do you understand what I'm trying to say, darling, or am I simply confused?"

"A woman's mind is never easy for a man to understand. I think I understand what you're saying, yet I'm not certain. Men think so differently. I often wonder about you and our life in Paris—are you really happy? Or are you sorry that I took you away from London?"

"When I know you need me, and when I realize that you love the woman who is Ellen," she said softly, "then I'm happy, very happy. If I could feel like that every day, I don't think I'd ever be unhappy. Just to be able to look over at you when you are still asleep and tell myself: he loves you and he needs you. That's what I like most. And I think that's what every woman wants, really. To feel that she is necessary to a man—because she is a woman, and because she's the woman she is."

CHAPTER XII

C ARMICHAEL BURST EXCITEDLY into the office waving a letter, just as Edward was about to reply to a question Franklin had asked. "Here's a letter from Mr. Hodge, Dr. Franklin. It just arrived. Perhaps it will tell us something about Captain Cunningham."

"Let's hope so," Franklin replied as he took the letter and tore it open.

Edward watched Franklin's face while he read it. He had been waiting as anxiously as Franklin to receive word from Hodge, who was the American agent in Dunkirk. No report had been received from Cunningham since his ship escaped a pursuing British squadron several weeks before, thus avoiding Wentworth's second trap. Hodge had written one letter shortly after the escape, saying that he expected Cunningham to put in to Dunkirk for repairs, but no further word had been received.

The look on Franklin's face when he finished reading the letter was a grim enough indication to Carmichael, who had been standing inside the door waiting to hear the news. He turned swiftly and shut the door behind him.

"Mr. Hodge advises us that Cunningham and his crew have been imprisoned by the French at Dunkirk, charged with piracy on the request of the British minister."

Franklin slapped his breeches several times. Still silent, he took off his glasses and polished them carefully.

"Damnable, damnable," he fumed at last. "Pirates! Humbug! It's ridiculous, Doctor, calling those men pirates. I'm going to see Vergennes and try to have them released. At least we can be grateful that they are in a French prison and not an English one."

"Do you think Vergennes will agree to release them?"

"I shall have to convince him. We need those men, especially Cunningham. He's one of the finest captains we have, and we can't afford to let him rot in some dungeon. Once I have him released, however, I'm going to send him back to America. He can do the English almost as much harm there and not risk prison for his efforts."

"How will the other captains feel," Edward asked quickly, "if Cunningham is sent back? Won't it seem to them that the only real protection is that afforded by their own coastline?"

"Possibly, but we must risk that. Cunningham has captured so many prizes that he appears to be a special target for the Admiralty. We can't risk losing him altogether by keeping him here. We have other men who can take his place. Perhaps they don't have his experience, but they're not so well known to Stormont, either."

"It seems too bad to send Cunningham back to America. His ability and his daring have become famous among the privateers, I am told. If he were sent away, it might weaken the morale of the others."

"You may be right, Doctor," Franklin sighed. "I would like him to stay here as much as you would, but the English are concentrating their efforts on capturing him, so it would hardly be fair to his crew to make them run such an additional risk. I think I had better take care of that now. Carmichael?"

"Yes, Dr. Franklin," the secretary answered, hurrying into the office.

"Write a letter to Mr. Hodge. Tell him to advise Captain Cunningham and his crew that they are ordered to return to the Colonies as soon as they have been released from prison. Under no circumstances are they to begin raiding channel shipping. Say that I shall arrange for their release as soon as possible. Put the letter in cipher—I don't want Stormont to know about this.

"Now," Franklin mused, after the secretary had gone into the outer office, "who shall take Cunningham's place? Johnson? No, too much Maine in him—wants to stand and fight when he should have the sense to run. Burrall? No, he won't do. Wickes! That's the man for us, Doctor, Lambert Wickes.

Even if he is a relation of mine, he's a fine captain. One of the best we have, though I have never understood how our family managed to produce such a good sailor. He's at Nantes. Has a good ship and a fine crew."

"The harbor there is blocked, I believe," Edward said.

"Yes, but not very effectively. Pinet told me that Wickes could get out at night without any trouble."

Franklin suddenly straightened from a slump and turned to face Edward. "I must send new instructions to Wickes, now that Cunningham is to return to America. Would you mind writing a letter for me, since Carmichael is busy with that letter for Hodge?"

"Not at all, Dr. Franklin." Edward crossed to his desk. After sharpening a quill, he took out paper and looked back at Franklin.

"Tell him first that Cunningham, with or without his ship, is returning to America. He is to take Cunningham's place, harassing channel shipping."

"Finished?" Franklin asked in a moment. When Edward nodded, he continued, "He will start operations at once, upon receipt of the letter. Last, and most important, he is not to bring prizes back to the same port from which he sailed—that's what put Cunningham in jail, and we don't want it to happen again."

Edward brought the letter over and laid it on Franklin's desk. The old man read it carefully and nodded his approval.

"I've been thinking, Doctor," he said, looking up at Edward, "that it would be wiser not to trust this to a courier. Could you deliver it to Wickes yourself without too much difficulty?"

Edward tapped his fingers on the edge of the desk.

His eyes fell on the lockbox.

"Yes, I think so," he replied.

"I realize that it is extremely short notice, but could you take the afternoon coach for Nantes? Wickes must receive this as quickly as possible. Every day we delay means we have no vessel operating in the area assigned to Cunningham."

"I can leave this afternoon."

"Fine. I'm extremely grateful to you, Edward." Franklin stood and, walking over to the newly installed lockbox, raised the lid and pulled out an envelope.

"This should be sufficient for your expenses," he said, handing Edward a sheaf of notes. "If it is not, I shall reimburse you on your return. When you arrive in Nantes, go to M. Pinet's office. He will advise you as to the quickest way to contact Wickes, but I believe you are already familiar with that."

"Yes, I am, Doctor, quite familiar," Edward said, smiling. "I shall visit M. Pinet, however, and pay him your respects."

"I don't think I would mention Cunningham's present plight to Wickes," Franklin suggested as they walked toward the door. "Lambert wouldn't mind, but it might make his crew nervous if they should discover the charge against Cunningham's men. I am hoping to have the charge dismissed before rumors of it reach our other crews."

When Edward arrived home, he found that Ellen had gone shopping with Mme. de Treymes. While Bertram packed his clothes for the journey, Edward wrote a note explaining that he had been called away suddenly on business and that he expected to return sometime within the week.

He was already inside his coach before he remembered that he had not sent word to Wentworth.

He was just stretching his legs out in front of him after giving Philippe the address of Paul's house when he sat up and called to Philippe again.

"Don't bother to stop there, Philippe. Go right on to the Nantes coach. It's too late."

"*Oui, Monsieur,*" Philippe called down.

When they arrived, the Nantes coach had already left. They followed its route and were almost within sight of Versailles before they saw it on the road ahead. Philippe whipped the horses forward, and when the diligence stopped in Versailles for another passenger, Edward climbed aboard.

The trip lasted three days, during which time Edward dozed fitfully and uncomfortably in the crowded coach or watched the countryside, which seemed to become more beautiful as they moved farther west.

A day away from Nantes, after the coach had been bumping and swaying along in its usual fashion, it suddenly crunched to a halt. The rear of the coach had swung off the road and part way down a ditch.

After the passengers climbed out and discovered that their injuries amounted to nothing more than surprise, they noticed that a rear wheel had come off.

It lay about fifty yards down the road, at the foot of the tree into which it had crashed. The coachman, flushed with the tot he had taken to assure himself that nothing too serious had happened to his vehicle, began to roll back the vagrant wheel and soon was trying to rock the coach by himself and fit the wheel back onto the axle.

The passengers, under the direction of Edward and another man, soon added their strength to the coachman's efforts. The coach rose up slowly, and finally the wheel was slipped back in place and a new linchpin inserted.

They started off again, and Edward fell asleep despite the awkward motion caused by the loose wheel. He was awakened suddenly by hoarse shouting. As he struggled back to consciousness, his first thoughts were of highwaymen. His hand was moving toward his wallet when his eyes opened. He relaxed as he looked out of the coach. He could see they were in the courtyard of a small inn and the shouting he heard was the voice of the coachman bellowing orders at the stableboys. The boys were only shadows in the darkness, scampering like mice between the coach and the stable.

Edward climbed out of the coach and stretched gratefully. His muscles were cramped from the long ride. It was pleasant to be able to move about and stretch his arms up toward the night sky. The air was filled with the warm, rich scent of freshly plowed earth and the faint fragrance of spring flowers. The moon stole through an orchard beside the inn, silvering the trunks and branches of the trees.

The landlord ushered all the passengers into the dining room and led Edward toward a small table.

After he had finished dinner, Edward was led along the upstairs hall by a small boy he judged to be the landlord's son, for he had the same squat stature and the same dark complexion. The boy flung open the door of a room near the end of the hall, and, as he led Edward inside, the light from his candle disclosed a small but extremely neat and clean bedroom. Edward breathed a sigh of relief; the room was not like most such rooms in France, which were usually filthy and ridden with pests. Edward undressed quickly and, sliding into bed, stretched out and pulled the coverlet to his chin.

In what seemed an instant, he was awakened by a loud knocking at his door. The erratic treble of the landlord's son informed him it was time for breakfast. Edward crawled out of bed and stumbled over to the crock basin, into which he poured the water that had been left there.

The coolness of it revived him. Spluttering, he wiped his face, shaved, and in several minutes was walking downstairs to breakfast.

The diligence started toward Nantes just as the church bells began to sound the hour. The call to the farmer, Edward thought as he listened to the bells; we should be at Nantes before ten, if there are no more accidents.

There was little conversation in the diligence. The passengers were still sleepy from their early rising; as the coach proceeded, Edward noticed heads lolling about and heard someone in the front of the coach snoring loudly. They are missing a lovely sight, he thought to himself, as he looked out across the fields. The sun was just rising, and the fields were glittering with dew. Coveys of birds circled around the coach and then sped toward the west.

People were beginning the day's work—here, an early plowman trudged behind his enormous Percheron; there, a milkmaid moved across the fields toward the little town they had just left, the milk buckets swinging from the pole on her shoulder in cadence with her walk. The farmhouses at the far edge of Ancenis were busy with early morning activity.

Children ran about doing their chores. Cows were herded out to pasture. Horses were bridled. Over each farmhouse rose a tiny column of light smoke that quickly disappeared in the enormous blue of the sky.

Once, they were halted by a herd of cows being driven across the road. Edward listened to the conversation between the coachman and the herder and smiled suddenly as he realized how gladly the coachman had stopped and how gaily he was speaking. The two men discussed the weather and the crops and the condition of the fields as the cows ambled over the road. When the last of the herd was passed, the farmer called a cheery farewell.

They proceeded without further interruption and reached Nantes nearly half an hour early. The coachman helped the passengers from the coach, and Edward smiled at the proud look on his face as the passengers congratulated him on the excellence of his driving.

The confusion that attended the arrival—passengers being welcomed, baggage being sorted and carried away, vendors moving among the passengers, and stableboys and coachmen and horses adding to the melee— gave Edward time to arrange for a room at the inn where the coach had stopped and, without bothering even to inspect it, he hurried down the main street toward the offices of Pinet and Company.

Edward presented the letter of introduction from Franklin to a clerk, who glanced carelessly at the signature, then gulped and bounded off to find the owner of the firm. While he was waiting, Edward glanced around at the activity surrounding him on every side.

Pinet and Company was an old firm and a very busy one. He judged that there were about fifty clerks in the office, all dressed alike in dark breeches and jackets. They all wore the same expression, too, a harried, nervous look. Bent over their ledgers, they perched on tall stools while supervisors walked about. The supervisors paused now and again to inspect the work and nod or point angrily at an incorrect figure. From time to time one of the clerks would slide off his stool and dash into an inner office with a sheaf of papers or a ledger in his hand.

Pinet's firm had done much work for the American commissioners, although it was not officially recognized like Hodge's company at Dunkirk or Eyries's at Havre. Through the efforts of Beaumarchais, much of the business for the Americans in Nantes was handled by the firm of DeVine and Damblier. Edward remembered hearing Franklin say that this was a great disappointment to Pinet, who was eager to make his firm the largest in Nantes. Nevertheless, he worked assiduously for the Americans, conducting prize sales and obtaining cargoes for vessels bound for the Colonies.

A tiny little man, immaculate in dark green breeches and jacket, bobbed across the office to where Edward was sitting. He wore a cluster of delicate lace at his throat, and Edward noticed the curious buckles on his shoes were fashioned like heads of deer.

"Good day, Dr. Bancroft, I am M. Pinet."

"Good day, M. Pinet," Edward replied. The shrill piping of the little man's voice had nearly shocked him into silence; it reminded him of the birds he had heard on the coach trip. "Dr. Franklin asked me to pay his respects to you. It is most important for me to find Captain Wickes as soon as possible. He said you would be able to tell me Wickes's location."

"I see," Pinet said, nodding. He grasped his jacket lapel and ran his hand nervously up and down. "Dr. Franklin mentioned that in his note. I cannot tell you for certain where he is, Doctor, but he can usually be found at the Hotel des Etrangers, near the waterfront. Many of your captains who visit Nantes stop there. Just now—" Pinet's voice dropped so low that it was almost inaudible. He moved closer to Edward lest he be overheard. "Just now, Doctor, he is fitting out his ship before going to sea again. If you do not find him at the hotel, ask the proprietor about him. Be discreet, however. Spies are everywhere, just as in Paris. You understand?"

"Yes, I do," Edward said softly. "I am grateful to you for your assistance, Monsieur."

Pinet looked up at him and smiled. "It is no trouble at all, Doctor. I am delighted to do all I can for the Americans. I only wish I could do more."

Pinet's face tightened as he made this last remark. The loss of so much American business seemed to wound him; his hand stole toward his lapel again, and his eyes grew sad.

"How I wish I could do more!" Pinet exclaimed softly. "But prominent people league against me. You must not think, Dr. Bancroft, that I am in the habit of burdening innocent visitors with my personal cares. Such is not the case, I assure you. It is only that certain foolish regulations are unfair to an honest man like myself. That pains me. But no matter—you remember the directions?"

"Yes, M. Pinet. Thank you again for your kindness."

"Not at all. I am delighted to have met you, Doctor."

They bowed, and as Edward turned to go, he noticed out of the corner of his eye that Pinet was looking after him, his hand still stroking the soft lapel of his jacket.

The streets of Nantes surprised Edward because they were so different from the familiar streets of London and Paris. Here, where the interests and the business of the city revolved principally about ships and shipping, the streets were filled with sailors. Some carried bulky sea bags filled with articles from distant lands. Some had their arms full of purchases made for journeys about to begin. Edward imagined that others, wandering and weaving through the streets between cafe bars, were trying to forget the sea that had stolen their comrades or shattered their sleep.

Edward asked an old man the direction toward the Hotel des Etrangers and was told to proceed halfway down the Quai de l'Aiquillon, as far as the Rue de la Reine. The inn, the old man said, was close by the junction of the two. He walked along the Quai de l'Aiquillon, which skirted the Loire, and at last saw the inn he was searching for. A large board swayed in the breeze, bearing a faded legend under coats of grime and salt and spray.

Edward entered and summoned the proprietor by ringing a small bell on the desk. The proprietor, wiping the traces of an early lunch from his chin, hurried toward him.

"M. Pinet told me to find you," Edward said. "I am looking for Captain Wickes."

The proprietor stared at him for a moment, a dull look of surprise on his face, and then asked him to repeat the question.

"Captain Wickes. I am looking for him. Where can I find him?"

"I do not know, Monsieur. So many people look for the captains who visit Nantes. I do not know where they are. They stop here on occasion—but they do not tell me where they are going. Perhaps if Monsieur would care to leave a message for this captain, I can give it to him if he should come here again."

Edward reached inside his coat and pulled out his wallet. He removed a piece of paper from it, which he handed to the proprietor. The man stared down at it for a moment, turning it this way and that.

"Dr. Franklin sent me to find Captain Wickes," Edward said, hoping to move the proprietor to some sort of activity.

Motioning Edward to follow him, the proprietor walked into the kitchen. He called to his wife, who was stirring a pot on the stove. She came over to them and, drying her hands swiftly on her apron, took the paper from her husband.

"Read it to me, *cherie*," the proprietor said.

The lady puzzled over Franklin's elegantly simple calligraphy and then read aloud, "Dr. Bancroft is an authorized representative of the American commissioners in France—signed Silas Deane and Benjamin Franklin."

"Monsieur," the proprietor said, "I hope you will forgive me for being so cautious. We must be most careful with our tongues in Nantes—the English spies are everywhere. Only last week they managed, through lies and devils' tricks, to kidnap five of Captain Wickes's crew who were on their way to their ship.

"Poor fellows," he sighed, cocking his head to one side, "what will happen to them now? Thrown in prison, taken to England perhaps—and all because they were too trusting. You see, Monsieur, I take no risk with the safety of my good friend Captain Wickes."

"You are quite right to be so careful," Edward assured him. "Captain Wickes is too good a man to lose through careless speech. Is he in Nantes now?"

"Not at present, Monsieur. He left several days ago to board his ship. He did not expect to return for some time—that is what he told me. However, his ship is still anchored down the Loire. It lies some distance away, but the ship's boat will be here tonight at nine. You could visit the *Reprisal* by that means."

"Where does the boat tie up?"

"Just opposite the Ile Lemaire. About one-half kilometer west of here. The mate, M. Bishop, is usually in charge; he gathers up the sailors who have spent the day in Nantes. Sometimes, you know, Monsieur, they are not entirely correct. M. Bishop has no trouble with them; he carries a heavy stick he calls his persuader. A strange man, M. Bishop, but honest and always most correct with us."

"I shall meet the boat tonight, then," Edward said as he walked toward the entrance of the inn with the proprietor. "The information I have for Captain Wickes cannot be delayed. Good-bye, Monsieur."

Edward walked about the city during the afternoon and had a late supper at the inn where the coach had stopped. As the hour for the arrival of the ship's boat neared, he walked down to the quay and continued toward the spot the innkeeper had mentioned.

The Ile Lemaire loomed up out of the river like some prehistoric beast, its outline etched by the waning moon.

Walking a little farther, he saw a figure standing at the edge of the wharf. The clouds that scudded across the moon obscured the figure momentarily, but not before Edward had noticed the long stick in his hand.

"Mr. Bishop?" he called out.

"Who's there?"

"A friend," Edward replied. Moving closer, keeping an eye on the stick, he whispered, "I have a message for Lambert." The sound of Wickes's name reassured the suspicious man. He straightened up and his stick made a light tapping noise as its point dropped back to the wooden wharf.

"Come closer," he said.

Edward moved across the quay until he stood beside the stranger. The man was large—the innkeeper had only hinted how large—for he towered over Edward. As the moon peered out again over the tops of the clouds, the sudden light revealed more details of the *Reprisal*'s mate—a powerfully built man with hulking shoulders and a clipped head barely covered with stiff hairs, like the bristles of a boar. He stared grimly at Edward.

"What do you want?"

"You're Bishop?"

"What if I am?" the man grunted. The stick in his hand was raised a trifle; it swung gently back and forth like a warning.

"I have a message for your captain," Edward said. He was relieved to see the stick lowered again to the wharf.

"Who sent you? How do I know your business is with my captain?"

"Dr. Franklin sent me. I've seen Pinet here in Nantes. Then I talked to the innkeeper at the Hotel des Etrangers. He didn't trust me at first, either; when he read this note from Franklin though, or when his wife did"—Edward took the note from his coat and held it out toward Bishop—"he told me where to find you. Is that good enough?"

"I guess so. What's the message?"

"I have been ordered to give it to Captain Wickes personally, Mr. Bishop. I thought I might go back to the *Reprisal* in the ship's boat."

"Oh, you did? How do I—well, I guess it can't do no harm, not with one of you against all of us. We'll leave in another five minutes, as soon as I round up these drunken fools some call a crew."

The mate grew more and more angry as they waited ten minutes longer than he had estimated. He paced up and down the wharf while his stick beat a furious tattoo on the wooden planks.

Soon down the quay there echoed the sound of voices singing. As Edward stared toward the city, he could distinguish five or six figures weaving and turning and wandering from one side to the other. Behind them, like a shepherd behind his flock, walked another figure. Several times as he watched the group approach, Edward saw one of the men stray far to one side. When the shepherd called out a few words, the wanderer would return to the group. The last time it happened, he heard the shepherd say that the next offender would be mentioned to Mr. Bishop.

Edward heard the men grunt in disgust, but he noticed that the weaving group stayed together after that.

They finally arrived at the spot where Bishop and Edward were standing. As each man approached the angry mate, Bishop held his stick half aloft. At the sight of that terrible instrument, each of the men, however stupified and incapable of thought he might have seemed a moment before, grew instantly quiet, saluted the mate, and clambered hurriedly down the ladder to take his place in the boat.

As they rowed swiftly down the river, Edward felt the chill of the light mist that hung above the water and pulled his coat closer around his neck. The longboat drew up beside the dark bulk of a ship that lay almost in midstream. Edward was directed up the rope ladder by Bishop, who came close behind him.

"This way," Bishop said when they had reached the deck. He led Edward aft and up another ladder. They paused before the door of a cabin, and Bishop rapped. His knocking echoed over the quiet ship.

"Come in."

They entered and Edward found himself standing in a small, extremely tidy cabin. Captain Wickes sat behind a gleaming lamp, a quill in his hand and an unfinished letter before him on the desk. He stared at Bishop questioningly and did not seem to notice Edward.

"This man hailed me on the wharf, sir. He said he had a message for you from the people in Paris. I thought you might want it while there was still time."

"Damn it, Bishop," Wickes thundered, throwing the quill on the desk, "there isn't time. Are all the men back?"

"Every one, sir," Bishop answered quietly. "I thought it might be important, sir, that's why—"

"All right, Bishop, all right. One more passenger won't make much difference. He may be of some use. That'll be all."

"Yes, sir."

Bishop went out without another look at Edward and closed the door silently behind him.

"Now," Wickes exclaimed, "who are you, sir? And what message do you have for me? I suppose they want the English navy delivered to Havre."

"I'm a bit confused by your remarks to Mr. Bishop, Captain. Do you think I'm a passenger?"

"You haven't done too much sailing, have you?" Wickes asked with a sudden chuckle. "Can't you feel her moving?"

"Moving?" Edward dashed to the porthole. The trees along the riverbank were gliding past.

"I can't sail with you, Captain. I must return to Paris. I only wanted to make sure that you received the letter from Dr. Franklin."

"Don't be upset, sir. I don't plan to be at sea too long. Where's the letter?"

Edward reached into his pocket automatically and placed the letter on the desk before Wickes. The captain tore it open and began to read, but stopped almost immediately.

"You are Dr. Bancroft?" he asked.

"Yes."

"Glad to know you, Doctor." Wickes shook Edward's limp hand vigorously. "I'll be finished with this in a moment. Please sit down."

Wickes returned to the letter as Edward slumped into a chair, his mind still spinning with the sudden change in his plans.

As he sat there, waiting for Wickes to finish reading and thinking of the voyage he was about to make, he suddenly perceived how fortunate this mischance might prove to be. Whatever happened, it would not last more than a week or two, and it could not fail to strengthen his position in Paris. When he returned, after a voyage on a privateer, and especially on the privateer commanded by Franklin's nephew, Lee's enmity and suspicions would be of little use to him.

"Hmm," Wickes murmured, tossing the letter on the desk and leaning back in his chair, his head cradled in his hands, "there does seem to be an error in your accompanying us, Doctor. I must offer my apologies for speaking so brusquely. I did not realize how valuable you were to Dr. Franklin. We can arrange to put you ashore in the longboat just before we reach St. Nazaire."

"I have had a change of heart, Captain," Edward said, smiling. "I would like to go with you, if it's not to be too long a voyage. Perhaps I could be useful to you as a surgeon."

"Glad to have you with us, Doctor," Wickes cried, his face lighting up. "I should be most grateful for your company, sir. Our surgeon sometimes has more work than he can handle. Possibly you're a chess player, too?"

"Yes," Edward laughed, "I play."

"Splendid, splendid. We'll have chess, too, in addition to our normal excitement."

"You understand what Dr. Franklin wants you to do?" Edward asked.

"I certainly do. I've been wanting to do it now for some time—I was always a little jealous of Cunningham, up there in the channel. The coasting craft and the Spanish traffic don't provide much sport. No fight in them. I've always wanted to test this ship against an English man o'war. Not that I underestimate the obstinacy of the English—they can be stupid enough to charge head on into fire that would curl an Indian's scalp lock. It would please me mightily to cripple a few of them."

"What port will you make for when the voyage is over?" Edward asked.

"Whichever is most convenient—that's all I can say," Wickes replied with a sudden scowl. "I don't look forward to working with another agent, I can tell you that, Doctor. It took me a long time to feel that Devince wasn't cheating me every chance he had. What a stupid rule that is—not to return to the same port. Here we prey on the English trade, burning and sinking and capturing their vessels. We fit out in French ports with French money, return to French ports, fit out again with more French money, and so on. Now we can't come back to the same port anymore because the English might protest to the French that they were harboring unfriendly ships! If the French don't want war with England, why let us do this in the first place?"

"There are certain rules in diplomacy, Captain. The French must appear to conform to them, so that the English will have to conform also."

"Damned foolishness," Wickes snorted. "I prefer to fight honestly and openly. All these technicalities are so much scupper scum."

"At least you're not often concerned by them, Captain. You should be thankful you're not ashore, where you'd have these troubles every day."

"Oh, I couldn't stand that," Wickes groaned, rising to his feet. "Go crazy, I would. How about a tot, Doctor?"

"Thank you. I am a bit chilled from that mist on the river."

"Here you are," Wickes said cheerfully, setting down a full cup in front of Edward. "That's Jamaica. As strong as shipfitter's glue, but better tasting. That'll knock the chill right out of you, I warrant."

Wickes tossed off his glass with a single gulp, refilled it, and set it down on his desk. He stood there, bottle in hand, waiting for Edward to finish. Edward tilted back his head, drained the glass, then held it out to Wickes. He could hear the liquor pouring into the glass, but he couldn't see it—he could hardly see Wickes. His eyes filled with tears, and his throat felt as if he had swallowed a cupful of molten lead.

"Ha, that's good rum," he gasped when he recovered his breath. "A bit strong, though, if you're not accustomed to it."

"Yes, a bit," Wickes agreed, "but I wager you'll soon get used to it, Doctor. I bought it last year—still have another keg of it below. We'll have to try that one—it may prove more to your taste."

Wickes picked up his glass and sipped slowly.

"Ever have any family in Massachusetts, Doctor? I used to know some Bancrofts there. One was an old man, one of the finest skippers ever fashioned—Nathaniel Bancroft. Used to sail in the Indies trade—sugar and slaves and rum. Any kin to you?"

"He was my grandfather," Edward replied.

A sudden warmth rose in Edward at the memory of the old man. He had not thought of his grandfather for many years, except occasionally, when something reminded him of Westfield or a stranger's speech or appearance unaccountably brought to mind his childhood. He still remembered his grandfather vividly—his beard so long and impressive, his clothes always smelling of the sea air, and his wizened old servant Nero, whom he had freed and brought to the house at Westfield. Nero had always tried to take the blame for Edward's mistakes, because he hated to see the boy caned by his grandfather.

"I thought so," Wickes grunted. "You favor the Bancrofts—the same look about your eyes. The way you stood here, when you first came in, reminded me of the captain. How'd it happen you came to be a doctor?"

"I wasn't at first," Edward laughed. "I was pure Bancroft—like all the others. I ran away to sea, too. Went to Surinam. That was where I first took an interest in medicine. There isn't as much of my grandfather in me as there should be—at least I don't have his craving for the sea. I stayed some time in Surinam and finally went to London. About a year ago I went to Paris to help Silas Deane."

"You've had quite a life," Wickes said, "though it's too bad you quit the sea. You might have made as good a captain as your grandfather. You seem to like excitement, and he was an old hand at that. Used to tell me stories, sometimes, about his trips to the Indies and about all the troubles he'd had carrying slaves. Fancy stories they were, some of them. A bit enlarged from the truth, perhaps, but exciting—Lord, were they!"

Wickes smiled at his recollections and drew on his pipe.

"Every now and then he'd show up unexpectedly at our house in Boston, for he was an old friend of my father's. I was young then, and I'd sit in a corner as long as they'd let me, drinking in those wild tales as a young boy will. My mother would come in to shoo me off to bed."

"How strange it seems," Edward mused, "that we should meet for the first time—on a French river."

"Strange is a mild word, Doctor. Think of all that's taken place since I last saw your grandfather—where I've been, where you've been, and what has happened since those quiet days."

"Quiet? I don't think of them as quiet."

"I guess they weren't, really, but they seem quiet to me today. There was excitement, but only at times. It wasn't like it is today, when you never know what will happen next. Tonight, for example. How could I guess that you'd be coming aboard, bringing a message that would change all my plans? Instead of sailing toward Spain, I'm turned about toward England. Instead of coming back to Nantes, I'll have to make for Calais or Havre or some other port. Instead of one surgeon aboard, I have two. Instead of playing myself at chess, I can challenge you." Wickes laughed as he finished. Reaching out, he picked up the bottle of rum and pointed it toward Edward's glass.

"No, thank you, Captain," Edward said, shaking his head. "I still have most of my second tot."

"That's the first thing I've seen you do"—Wickes smiled as he refilled his own glass—"that makes me think you're not all Bancroft. If your grandfather saw you do that, he'd refuse to acknowledge you."

"I've been in France so long, I've lost my taste for rum. Before the voyage is over, I hope to have it back again."

"It won't be any fault of mine if you don't."

There was a knock on the door, and, after Wickes called out, Bishop entered. His eyes flicked nervously from Wickes to Bancroft and back to Wickes again.

"Yes, Mr. Bishop, what is it?"

"About St. Nazaire, Captain. We expect to pass the town at three or four in the morning. Shall we pick up a pilot, sir?"

"No, we won't need to. The helmsman knows the channel well enough. The fewer people who know we're moving, the better. I don't want word to reach the English. Their ships are just offshore. If anyone seems curious, Mr. Bishop, tell them we have a Nantes man aboard. If they're not satisfied, call me at once. Oh—have the other cabin prepared for Dr. Bancroft."

"Very good, sir." As the mate passed him, Edward was conscious that Bishop was staring down at him as if puzzled by the captain's sudden friendliness toward a stranger. The cabin door closed noiselessly behind him.

"I think it would be a good idea, Doctor, if you were to win Bishop over to your side. I was watching him just now as he went out—he doesn't know quite what to make of you. He's a fine mate, Mr. Bishop is. Knows more about cannon than the best officer in the king's artillery. On our last voyage we had a completely new crew on one of the cannon. Bishop tended them like they were children, and damned if they didn't blow holes through every enemy quarterdeck we saw. He's a good man."

"From what I saw of him ashore, I gathered that was the case. He seems a bit dour at first glance, but I imagine that's chiefly for the benefit of new members of the crew."

Wickes nodded. "Usually it is, but he can be hard, Doctor. Several men have stayed ashore because of him. Not that we haven't been better off without them. Lazy fellows they were, all of them, and laziness is something Bishop won't tolerate."

"He must be invaluable."

"I don't know what I'd do without him. He's been with me ever since I came over from America. Several of the prizes we've captured have been due entirely to him: one of them he spotted after the lookout missed it, and the other he got by some of the smartest shooting I've ever seen." Wickes poured himself more rum.

"What do you expect it will be like in the channel, Captain?" Edward asked.

"I expect trouble, Doctor, and that's all I know. What I'd like most would be to take a packet like the one Cunningham captured, or a ship carrying specie. Those are the best ones for us. Cargo ships are often hard to sell— these agents demand huge commissions for taking them off our hands. I'd also like to meet a man o'war about our size. If we ever do that, Doctor, keep your eye on Bishop."

Wickes stood up and stretched. "The cabin I spoke of is next to this one. Let's see if it's ready."

They went outside and paused momentarily to observe the progress of the ship. The moon lit up the riverbank and as Edward stared out into the semidarkness, his eyes could make out groves of trees beside the river. Now and then, a night cry floated on the air, from the animals in the woods or from those stabled and secure. There was no evidence of man, although as he listened, he heard the sound of hooves on a hard packed road.

Wickes turned from his own silent scrutiny and entered the cabin. Edward, following behind him, saw the cabin boy busily making the bunk. The cabin was nearly identical to that of Wickes; although not quite as large and without a desk, it seemed equally comfortable. As Edward's eyes fell on the bunk, he felt a weariness steal over him. It was, he assured himself, as much the result of his excitement as the result of the rum.

"Enough, enough," Wickes called out. "What hasn't been done tonight can be finished tomorrow."

The cabin boy stopped his work at once. "Aye, sir," he said, and left the cabin hurriedly, before the captain could change his mind.

"I think you'll find this comfortable," Wickes said to Edward. "If there's anything you lack, let me know."

Edward explained that his luggage had been left ashore. Wickes disappeared and returned in a few moments with a large bundle in his arms.

"We're about the same size," he declared. "The officers will be glad to provide you with anything else you may need, if you don't find it here. I'll see you in the morning, Doctor. I should be glad for your company at breakfast."

"Delighted."

"Very well, then. Knock at my cabin at five. Good night."

Edward was barely able to conceal his dismay. Five o'clock—what an ungodly hour for breakfast! Well, it was his own fault. He had agreed to go on this voyage.

He undressed and climbed into bed, determined not to lose a minute of the few hours' sleep that still remained.

CHAPTER XIII

S
IR, THE CAPTAIN'S COMPLIMENTS to you," piped a young voice. "Breakfast in ten minutes."

For a moment, the sound of the voice had made Edward think he was back in the inn at Chalonnes. He turned over with a groan. It was pitch dark in the cabin, and he realized that if he did not get up at once, he would go right back to sleep. Wearily, he thrust his legs out of the bed and banged his shin against a chair. Cursing, he fumbled for the candle. In a few moments he was at the captain's cabin.

"Good morning, Doctor. Come in. Breakfast is on the way."

Edward walked into Wickes' cabin and sat down.

"Where are we now, Captain?"

"At sea. We passed St. Nazaire several hours ago."

"Was there any difficulty about the pilot?"

"No, they hailed us but seemed satisfied when we said we had a Nantes man aboard. Bishop was just here. He said there was no sign of English ships about, which is a blessing to us. We need space to maneuver, to say nothing of time to train our new men. If they'd caught us coming past St. Nazaire, we wouldn't have had a chance."

"I'm delighted they didn't. I'm afraid I would have been too sleepy to be of much service."

"I doubt that, Doctor," Wickes chuckled. "You'll be amazed at how quickly a man reacts to danger. Every voyage, these green men we take on surprise me. Never been in a battle before, any of them. They know nothing about cannon and boarding parties, yet when the time comes, they all act like old hands. It's partly drill, to be sure. You'll see a great deal of that while you're with us."

"How often do they have drill?"

"Every day. Mornings, they have gun drill. Afternoons, ship's drill, when they learn how to handle themselves when they're not at their guns. Then we also have boarding drill where we rope off a part of the deck and use that as the enemy ship. They learn how to jump from one vessel to another, how to carry their weapons so they don't trip and fall between ships. You'll understand it better when you see them practicing."

A cabin boy entered as Wickes finished speaking and set a large tray down on the captain's desk. He brought a smaller tray over to Edward's chair, then stood against the wall, alert for any instructions from Wickes.

There were slices of ham, apples, a thick gruel, and coffee on Edward's tray. Following Wickes's example, he gave his entire attention to the food. After he had finished, he leaned back in his chair and sighed contentedly.

As soon as the cabin boy saw that both the men had finished, he replaced the dishes on the trays. He was about to leave when Wickes called to him, "Bring another pot of coffee."

"Very good, sir," the boy replied and hurried out the door.

"Well, Doctor, did you have enough?"

"Indeed I did. It was excellent."

"We have a good man in the galley, for a change," Wickes said with a wry smile, "a Frenchman I was able to coax into coming with us. He used to be the proprietor of an inn where my men stayed. They persuaded him to play vingt-et-un with them one night and won everything he had, including the inn. We let his wife keep the inn, but he came along with us to work out the rest of the money."

"I imagine good food is essential on a ship," Edward mused.

"It is, it is. The men work hard, and they need food. If it isn't fit to eat, they can't do their work. To me, the galley ranks next to the quarterdeck; a bad cook can do almost as much harm as a bad captain."

After they had finished the second pot of coffee, they went out on deck. It had grown light. Edward noticed that France was but a small blur on the horizon. Members of the crew were already busy repairing sails, washing down the decks, and climbing up into the rigging. Others were coiling ropes which seemed to be everywhere he looked.

Forward, he noticed Bishop, his head bright in the sunlight, hurrying about the deck. He watched the mate point angrily at something on the deck while several of the crew stood about him in an uneasy semicircle.

"Mr. Bishop," Wickes cried.

The mate raised his head. Seeing the captain on the quarterdeck, he barked a final word that sent his audience scurrying.

"Yes, Captain?" Bishop said, when he had come aft.

"At what time will you hold gun drill?"

"In another half hour, Captain—unless the captain wants it sooner?"

"No, that will be satisfactory. I wanted to let you know that Dr. Bancroft will be with us, too."

"I'll tell the men, sir. It will make them look alive."

Bishop grinned and turned to Edward. "I hope you'll find it interesting, Doctor. The men do better when they have an audience."

"Come back here about five minutes before drill, Mr. Bishop," Wickes ordered. "We'll go with you."

"Aye, sir," Bishop replied, then left for the main deck to resume his inspection of the work.

"When I told him last night that you were going to remain aboard," Wickes said after Bishop left, "he was surprised, but also a little pleased, I think. He couldn't believe that anyone connected with the commissioners in Paris would risk going on a privateer with a mission like ours."

"I'm grateful to you, Captain. He seems more friendly this morning."

While Wickes busied himself with his sextant, Edward stared out over the ocean. At first, he saw a sail every few minutes; but as he watched, his eyes adjusted themselves to the vast expanse of water and he realized that each sail was only the rise and fall of the sea at the horizon. Lookouts had been posted fore and aft, and he watched them as they scanned the ocean. Their glasses described slow, careful half circles, which were repeated at short intervals. The sea had assumed a bluish cast, having lost the green which denoted the shoaling water near the coast of France.

Bishop reappeared beneath the quarterdeck to remind the captain that the time for gun drill had arrived. Wickes and Bancroft climbed down the ladder and walked forward on the main deck to a place beside one of the sixteen-pounders, where they waited for Bishop to give the signal for drill to his crews.

The mate raised a small whistle to his lips. As the shrill note sounded over the deck, the sailors dropped whatever they were doing and ran to their places beside the cannon. In an instant the deck had been cleared, and Bishop began bellowing out the orders:

"Prepare for broadside—seven hundred yards. One ball — load — aim — Fire!"

The men around the cannon near Edward sprang into new activity at each shouted command. They pushed the cannon around, leveled the tube, and loaded the powder and the shot. Behind the cannon, the fuse setter stood by, in his hand a cane-length rod with a wick smoldering in the breeze.

"Understand it, Doctor?" Wickes asked. "It's a bit strange at first, with all these men running about, but you'll soon be accustomed to it."

"It all seems very clear, except for the work of the man who aims the cannon. I don't see how he can figure out when to shoot."

"He knows the range," Wickes explained. "You may have heard Bishop call that out. He knows that the tube, when it is set at a certain angle to the sea,will fire a certain distance. All he does is set the tube where he judges it should be and fire when we're riding a wave."

Bishop ran from gun to gun, checking the angles of the tubes and giving whatever praise or blame was merited.

While Edward was watching him, he stopped beside one of the crew who was standing next to a cannon with a rammer in his hand. Evidently, the man had been standing too close, for Bishop moved him back about three feet. Edward could see the mate point to the mouth of the cannon, then at the man's head. The man wiped his face nervously as he listened to the mate. He took another step backward, but Bishop seized his arm and moved him back where he had first placed him.

The mate blew his whistle again, and the men returned to the tasks they had been performing before gun drill. Just as they picked up the tools they had been using, the whistle blew once more.

They went through the same drill again, using the same signals. It seemed to Edward that they were already becoming more proficient.

Bishop kept on barking out commands, changing the range, changing the direction; before the drill was finished the cannon had been pointed up and down the entire length of the deck. The men were sweating and rubbing their sore arms.

One tube setter, a young man with bushy hair and broad, capable hands, kept nervously rubbing his hands on his pants after each change in direction.

"Mr. Bishop," Wickes cried, during a lull in the mate's activities.

Bishop ran over to the captain, and after the two had talked together for a moment, the mate ran back to the starboard side. He blew three times on his whistle and began shouting new orders.

"Watch them now, Doctor," Wickes said quietly.

"This is their most difficult task, but also the one they like the best."

The deck suddenly came alive with activity. Formerly, the cannon had been evenly distributed along each side of the deck. But as Edward watched, he saw the crews unlimber their cannon and then, with pulleys and ropes and muscle, strain them back onto rollers and move them carefully to new positions. When all the cannon had been secured in their new locations, there were two groups of three and one group of two on each side of the deck.

"Bishop prefers to fight them like this," Wickes explained. "He says it is easier for him to control the firing."

While Wickes was speaking, Edward observed Bishop hopping about, orders tumbling out of the mate's mouth so fast that the crews had difficulty keeping up with his commands. Bishop's eyes missed nothing; he scurried up and down the deck cautioning this rammer, damning that fuse setter for taking too long, readjusting guns, and pointing out errors. Bishop blew again on his whistle, and as suddenly as the frantic activity had begun, it stopped. The crews unlimbered their cannon and rolled them back to their old positions. After the guns were secured, Edward noticed as he walked back toward the quarterdeck with Wickes and Bishop that one man in each crew stayed beside each cannon, testing and tightening the braces and ropes which held it firmly in position.

"I suppose if one of those cannon came loose, it would be a disaster," Edward commented when he and Wickes were alone again on the quarterdeck.

"Each of them weighs over five hundred pounds, Doctor. A weight like that, loose on the deck, can do more damage than a dozen broadsides." Wickes paused to check on the lookouts, then continued. "One of the first ships I served on had that experience. One night there was a storm, and one of the cannon worked loose. Before we could secure it, it had smashed up every bit of gear on deck and cracked the foremast as well."

Ship's drill took place early in the afternoon and boarding drill directly after that. But by then the men seemed listless and tired from their efforts, and Wickes soon dismissed them. Late in the afternoon, a lookout cried excitedly, "Sail ho!" The *Reprisal* was brought about, but even after every possible scrap of canvas had been lofted, the sail which the lookout had seen disappeared over the horizon, and they came about again on their former course.

"Too bad we missed that one this afternoon," Wickes muttered that evening as he and Edward sat down to dinner in his cabin. "Thought for a moment she was a Jamaicaman, until we started to chase her. Moved too fast for a ship of that size. Perhaps we'll have better luck tomorrow."

"Bishop certainly does a fine job with those gun crews," Edward said. "I never realized how quickly cannon could be shifted, nor how easily one man could control them all."

"That wasn't a very good drill, Doctor," Wickes said, smiling. "You'll see them work faster than that before this voyage is over."

"Many of the men are green," he continued. "Did you notice the rammer that Bishop had to pull back out of danger? He's never been on a ship before, Bishop tells me. One good fight and he'll feel and act like a veteran, but now he's green and careless. The first time that cannon goes off next to him, he'll be petrified. But he'll work out. Most of them do. It takes time, that's all, time and patience. Bishop, God be praised, has both. More patience than I could ever have."

Edward laughed and began eating his dinner. While they ate, Wickes talked about his life at sea, the vessels he had served on and the captains he had known.

Some of the stories were so full of Wickes's rough humor that Edward had difficulty swallowing without choking.

"There are more characters at sea, I warrant," Wickes said finally, "than anywhere else in the world. Every captain that's ever sailed a ship has stories told about him. There are probably some about me, too, but I haven't heard them yet. There's a flock of legends about Cunningham, as I suppose you know."

"I heard some of them when I was in Paris," Edward said, nodding.

"Every time we had a visitor from Dunkerque or Havre, there'd be a new one."

"That's how it usually happens. The stories start off fairly close to the truth, but after they've traveled a ways, they get too big to be believed. Then a new one's made up out of the pieces of the old."

"Captain, while I was watching the gun drill this morning, I wondered about your other officers. What do they do during a fight?"

"They have almost as much to do as Bishop, though you don't see so much of them. He's first mate and shouldn't really be in charge of the gun crews at all. That's the gunnery officer's duty. But Bishop is so good and he likes it so much, I haven't the heart to take him off it.

"One of the other officers stays here on the quarterdeck with me—usually the second mate, Mr. Watkins—so that there'll be someone to direct the ship if anything happens to me. Then there's the gunnery officer, Mr. Halstead, who's taking Bishop's regular duties, supervising the setting of sails and carrying out the orders I give him. If we decide to board the other ship, he has charge of distributing small arms—and he leads the men over. Below, there's the quartermaster, Mr. Greenough, who handles our stores and takes charge of sending ammunition on deck during a battle. Each of these officers has another man by his side all the time during a battle, so that if there's an accident to one, the other can take over his duties."

"Don't they get in each other's way?" Edward asked, imagining a scene of utter chaos.

"No. They learn to step fast—the smoother they can work together, the easier it is for them. Tonight I've asked the surgeon to come by. You'll have a chance to talk with him and find out about his duties."

There was a sound of running along the deck as Wickes finished speaking. Suddenly a loud drumming sounded on the captain's door. Wickes was across the cabin in two bounds.

"Sir," a voice gasped from the darkness outside, "the lookout's seen a sail. It's on our course, coming this way. Looks like a frigate, he says."

Wickes muttered an oath. He turned, called to Edward to put out the light, and then disappeared into the darkness outside. When Edward came out, he found the captain beside the rail, scanning the sea ahead of them first with his eyes, then with his long glass.

"He's right," Wickes exclaimed. "It is a frigate, and a big one. Looks almost big enough for a man o'war in this light. We can't take any chances on being outgunned."

"Quarter turn to port," he cried suddenly to the helmsman.

"Aye, sir," came the soft reply.

The ship veered and trembled as she fought her way through heavier waves onto her new course. Edward saw more and more faces appearing at the rail, squinting through the night to make out the ship that was coming toward them. She was still better than two miles distant, but in the moonlight which reflected on her sides and sails, she seemed enormous as she bore down on them. While they watched, they saw the other ship swing about on a starboard tack, a course which would intercept their own.

"Damnation," Wickes cried. "They want trouble, I guess. We'll run for it and fire as we pass, if it's a fight they want. I know we can outrun them."

"Hard to port!" he shouted to the helmsman. "Threequarter turn!"

"Aye, sir," the helmsman grunted as he wrestled with the stubborn wheel.

The *Reprisal* shook like a wet dog before she settled. Edward saw that their new course would carry them clear of the other ship, which had not even started to come about as yet.

"Mr. Bishop!" Wickes cried into the darkness on the deck below. "Prepare to fire a salvo from the starboard quarter. They'll be about in a minute, and you'll find them square in your sights."

"Aye, sir," came the mate's reply, a second before the noise of his whistle disturbed the silence below.

Edward's eyes had become fully accustomed to the half-light, and as he looked down at the deck, he saw the crews were already in position. Men were standing beside the cannon with ammunition at their feet. The fuse setters were ready, their sticks clutched tight in their hands. The lighted tips gleamed in the darkness like little red eyes.

"Rammer on number three," Bishop called out, "don't stand there like a statue, move back! Look alive, man!"

"Aye, sir."

As the crews waited silently beside their cannon, their tension communicated itself to the quarterdeck. Edward felt sweat breaking out on his palms and his forehead; he rubbed his face with his sleeve and then turned to watch the other ship. She was just coming about. Edward could hear the noise of her sails flapping and the loose gear banging about on her deck. There was not more than a thousand yards between the two ships.

Suddenly, with a flash of red and a rumble of sound, a shot sent up a harmless column of water far short of the starboard side of the *Reprisal.*

"Ha!" Wickes jeered. "Think they can reach us from there, do they? Not much!"

Wickes turned to Edward. "They should close to within five hundred yards. That'll be as close as they'll get. We're upwind now; we have the advantage. We'll begin to move away from them fast in another ten minutes."

Wickes's prophecy about the five hundred yards was accurate. The other ship steadied on her new course and drew closer to them. More sail was being set on the *Reprisal,* however, and she began to pull away slightly.

Another flash and rumble came from the pursuing vessel.

This time, the shot was more accurate; it fell directly astern, and the water it flung into the air splashed against the hull. Wickes cursed and turned to the officer beside him.

"More sail, Mr. Watkins. As fast as you can set it."

Watkins leaped recklessly down the dark ladder. Soon Edward heard his voice, exhorting, cajoling, demanding that the men be swift about their tasks.

The other ship was drawing closer and had almost narrowed the distance to the five hundred yards when Wickes cried out, "Take over, Mr. Bishop! Fire as you see fit. She won't come any closer than that!"

"Prepare for salvo—six hundred yards. One shot—load—aim—fire!"

The *Reprisal* vibrated under the cannonade. Edward's eyes closed from the sudden shock. He opened them just in time to see several of the shots falling astern of their pursuer. The last two struck her flush at the rail. The mizzenmast swayed very slightly against the sky. Over the water he could hear the shouts and curses of the enemy crew as they tried to clear the wreckage.

"Fair, Mr. Bishop, only fair! Two astern. Try another."

"Aye, sir," Bishop called back. He cursed at someone, but before he could finish his next order, the enemy ship opened fire again.

This cannonade caught the *Reprisal* slightly aft, on the starboard side. Edward was flung against a cabin door and fell on his face to the deck. Splintered pieces of wood hurtled through the air. As he rose to his feet, still dizzy, he saw that Wickes and the helmsman had both escaped injury. One of the gun crews had been hit almost square. Of the four men in the crew, only one was alive when Edward reached the deck. Two of them lay beside the gun like grotesque and broken puppets. A third had been hurled across the deck and lay there without moving. The fourth was crawling painfully toward the center of the deck.

Edward knelt beside him and gently turned him over on his back. Ripping open the wet, red leg of his breeches, he found that a piece of splintered wood had dug a deep gash in his thigh. He made a tourniquet of his kerchief and had just finished tightening it when Dr. Temple arrived. The surgeon gave a quick look at what Edward was doing, then nodded his approval and his thanks at the same time.

"Take this man below," he called to the two men following him. "Loosen that bandage when you get him below, then tighten it again if the leg is still bleeding. Get some coffee for him from the galley."

They bent down and hoisted the man up between them. The injured man started to cry out, but the cry died in his throat as he passed out from the pain. His head bobbed limp between the bearers.

As he climbed up the ladder, he heard Bishop cry, "Fire!" Edward crouched against the top of the ladder, his shoulders tensed to protect him from the shock of the blast. After the cannon had fired, he straightened up and looked toward the other ship. Its mizzenmast swayed more perceptibly this time. Then, so slowly that it looked almost regretful, the mast leaned forward and fell toward the mainmast. Wickes, from his position near the helmsman where he had gone to observe the barrage, hopped about with glee.

"Damn, Mr. Bishop," he cried out as he watched the mizzenmast topple and crash. "A tot for the crew that fired that round!"

They began to pull ahead of the other ship now, and Wickes stood watching until it had almost disappeared from view.

"Well, you've seen your first fight, Doctor," Wickes said, turning toward Edward, who had joined him at the rail. "How did you like it?"

"For a moment," Edward exclaimed, "I thought they were coming closer to us than that five hundred yards you mentioned."

"To be truthful, Doctor, so did I. After that shot of theirs hit us, I didn't know how much headway we'd lose. I'm glad this happened at night. It might have ended much differently in the daytime. You probably didn't count the guns they carried, the way I did."

"No," Edward admitted, "I didn't."

"That was a thirty-six gun ship, Doctor. Bigger than a frigate, she was. A class I haven't seen before."

As if he had been reminded of something, Wickes hurried forward. "Mr. Bishop," he called.

"Aye, sir?"

"Which crew was it?"

"I can't be sure, Captain. Could have been any one of them."

"Very well, then," Wickes chuckled. "Give them all a tot. When they drink it, make sure they know they've been blooded. They're veterans now, to the greenest man among them."

Wickes walked back to Edward. They stood quietly for a few minutes, staring out over the sea.

"A lovely night, Doctor, and all the prettier now for having helped us take the bloom off an Englishman."

The moon cast a wide, sparkling path across the sea toward the *Reprisal*, a path that climbed right up the side of the ship, transforming the darkness of the deck into a shadow stage. All the sailors and the rigging and the sails were etched with a faint radiance which shimmered one moment and grew dark the next.

On Wickes's invitation, Edward followed him into his cabin and noted the reappearance of the bottle of dark Jamaica rum. Tonight, he felt, he would be in better condition to enjoy it, especially now that he was more accustomed to its strength.

The captain raised his glass. "To the gunners, Doctor, who did a fine night's work."

Edward raised his glass, too, then took a deep pull at his drink. The warmth of it stole through his tired body, and as he relaxed in his chair he realized for the first time the tension he had felt. He was completely worn out, but it was an agreeable sensation.

Dr. Temple entered the cabin with a paper in his hand. Wickes had another glass filled before the surgeon could protest.

"I know you don't like rum, Mr. Temple, but that's an unnatural aversion for a man to have. Besides, tonight you look as if you need at least one tot, maybe two."

"Perhaps I do, Captain," Temple admitted. "I am tired. Our losses, sir, are three men killed and two injured."

"Three killed?" Wickes said with surprise. "I saw only two there beside the gun."

"The ammunition man on that cannon was knocked clean across the deck, sir. He broke his back on the rail."

"Poor chap," Wickes said, shaking his head. "What a freakish way to die. Did he suffer?"

"No, sir. Killed him right off, as near as I could tell. He was dead when I reached him, and that wasn't more than a minute after it happened."

"Well, it's better than lying there in agony. What about the injured?"

"One man had his hand torn slightly, and the other got part of a plank in his leg. Chewed out the meat, but didn't touch the bone, fortunately."

"That's the man you helped, Doctor," Temple said, turning to Edward. "Dr. Bancroft fixed him up right away, Captain; he should recover without any difficulty."

"So you've been at work already," Wickes said with a smile. "Good for you. I didn't think you'd spend your time watching. A good thing for us, too."

"I did very little," Edward protested. "Dr. Temple's bearers were there almost as soon as I reached him."

"Between the two of you," Wickes chuckled, "I don't think we'll have much difficulty with our medical arrangements. Thank you for your report, Dr. Temple. You'd better get some rest."

As the door closed behind the ship's surgeon, Edward rose, yawning.

"I think I shall leave you too, Captain."

"Good night, Dr. Bancroft. Get as much rest as you can. This little affair tonight was nothing compared to what will probably happen later. I'm very grateful for your assistance tonight. It means a great deal to the crew, too."

THE NEXT MORNING Edward awoke with a start and wondered if he had overslept and missed his breakfast with Captain Wickes. A sudden knocking on the door reassured him, followed as it was by a familiar, piping voice which told him there were but ten minutes until breakfast. Stepping out on deck, he was astonished to find the sun well up in the sky. He pulled out his watch and discovered it was nearly eight o'clock. As he hurried into Wickes' cabin, he found the captain sitting behind his desk, writing busily in the log.

"Good morning, Doctor. Sit down, please. I'll be finished with this in a moment."

Edward sat down and noticed that the breakfast tray beside Wickes' desk was still untouched.

"Damn, but I hate this eternal writing," Wickes fumed, as he banged down his quill and thrust the log into his desk. "Every time I put to sea there's more of it to do than the last time. How do you turn out, Doctor?"

"Late but fit, Captain. I hope I haven't kept your breakfast waiting."

"Not at all. I always have my breakfast late after a night of fighting. I need the sleep, and so do the men. The whole ship's rested now and ready to go it again."

Wickes took a spoonful of gruel and as he swallowed, he began to smile.

"That's what the English can't do," he said after he had finished most of his gruel. "The ship that chased us last night—they were all up, I warrant, at five this morning and they'll go around all day stumbling over their feet and seeing with only one eye, if they see at all. Imagine what would happen to them today if they were in another fracas. That's why I sleep and let my officers and crew sleep later than normal. We're ready for anyone now."

There was a knock on the door. The cabin boy ran over and opened it, admitting Mr. Bishop.

"Good morning, Mr. Bishop. Everything all right?"

"Yes, Captain, everything's shipshape again. The men asked me to thank you for the rum. They said it helped them sleep better."

"Wouldn't be surprised if it did," Wickes said with a smile. "It helped me, I know. How do they feel about the men who were killed?"

Bishop's face lengthened a little.

"Two of them were new men, sir, so they don't miss them so much. Dodson was killed, though—he was the gunner—they don't feel so good about him."

"Hmm. That's too bad—this was his fourth trip with us, wasn't it?"

"Fifth, sir. He was one of the old-timers. He made that first trip to Barbados."

"Oh, yes, I remember now. Wasn't he the one who could never count the powder barrels correctly?"

Bishop grinned suddenly, then his face grew solemn again.

"That's too bad, Mr. Bishop. I don't like losing old hands."

"No, sir," Bishop shook his head sadly. "Dodson had a fair crew until last night. Trained 'em himself, with a bit of help from me. One minute they was a crew, and then—bang!—three dead men and two that could hardly crawl."

"We have to expect things like that, Bishop," Wickes said brusquely. "We're lucky we didn't have more trouble than we did. Did you notice the lines of her?"

"I did, sir. Never seen another like her before. When I was ashore at Nantes a few days before we sailed, a man told me about some new ships the English were building. Heavy-armed craft to use against us. Suppose she could be one of them, sir?"

"She might be. I wish you'd make me a sketch of her, everything you can remember, especially the gun positions. I've made one myself already. When you've finished yours, we'll send them both on to Paris with Dr. Bancroft here, after we land. They can send copies out to all our other ships."

"Very good, sir. I'll get to it at once."

After Bishop had left, Wickes stared at his breakfast a moment, as if he disliked the thought of it.

He picked up a fork, however, and began eating again.

"Too bad about Dodson," he said, half-aloud, "a good man and an experienced hand. We need men like that, need them badly."

"That's one of our principal jobs in Paris," Edward said, "getting men for you and the other captains. Not too many of the sailors we talk to are anxious to sail on a privateer."

"If they're Americans, they're cowards, then," Wickes snapped, "and if they're anything else, they're stupid. A voyage like this should net each man at least forty pounds over his pay, if we have our usual luck.

"Bringing a prize into port means that much nearly every time. As you probably know, this ship, like all the other privateers, is privately owned. After the owner's share is taken out, whatever is left of the profits—and there's usually a good, fat amount—is divided between the officers and the crew."

"I should think sailors would be eager for the chance to go. Perhaps the rumors the British spread in the ports are what prevent them from signing up. You can't be in a port long without hearing of the might of the British navy."

"Might! Bah!" Wickes snorted. "They have more ships than we do, but they can't handle them worth a damn. At least most of them can't. They have a few good captains, I admit. But they should have, after all the years they've had a navy. Gun for gun, an American ship will outshoot and outfight any British ship."

"After what I saw last night," Edward said with a smile, "I agree with you. You and Captain Cunningham are setting the standard for the American navy."

"That's too flattering, Doctor. We're just doing what we like most to do: giving His Majesty fits. If you've finished your breakfast, let's go on deck."

"What is our position?" Edward asked as they walked out of the cabin.

"I'll be able to tell you better after I take a reading," Wickes replied, nodding toward the sextant in his hand. "We should be somewhere off Point du Raz, just south of the westernmost tip of France. Tonight we'll be in the channel."

While Wickes was working with his sextant, Edward stood at the rail gazing out over the water. A breeze had sprung up from the northwest, and the *Reprisal* was proceeding swiftly. Wherever he looked, there was nothing but ocean, miles and miles of it, empty and silent except for the gulls which circled over the masts and plummeted down whenever scraps from the galley were thrown overboard. A few minutes later, Wickes had his reading:

"Sixty miles off the coast, Doctor," he announced, "twenty miles south of Point du Raz. Sometime today we'll circle while we wait for darkness, then head into the channel about ten this evening."

"Is this the route that ships follow to the south?" Edward asked.

"We never can tell that. This used to be their route, but since we've been after them, they've been taking different routes, most of them farther out to sea. Packets come this way, though; there's usually a brig and a cutter with them. If they're attacked, the escort ships keep the attacker busy while the packet escapes. We've seen them once or twice with a frigate for escort, or one of the bigger ones, forty guns or more. We let that combination go by without bothering it, unless two of us happen to be sailing together."

"Might there be another American ship around here now?"

"I don't rightly know. I wish I did. Captain Johnson works in this area, but he was in some sort of trouble with the French authorities at Brest, so I don't know if he's been able to sail. Burrall was expected to leave Lorient this week, but he rarely comes this far north. I didn't make arrangements to meet anyone on this trip, though. I find it's wiser to make it by yourself usually—if we sail in pairs too often the men are inclined to depend on another ship being with them."

"Sail ho off the starboard quarter!"

As the cry echoed over the ship, Wickes ran aft, picked up his long glass, and hurried toward the starboard side. Edward ran after him and reached him just as he brought his glass down.

"Mr. Bishop!" the captain yelled.

"Aye, sir," Bishop cried as he came running aft.

"A merchantman," Wickes told the mate. "She's heavy in the water, too, so she may have guns as well as cargo. Prepare your crews, and be ready to board after we've taken her."

"Aye, sir," Bishop replied. Turning, he blew his whistle. All the men on deck sprang into familiar action, uncovering the cannons, preparing for firing, and checking to be certain all was instantly ready for use. Men began spilling out from below decks, powder bags in their arms. The piles beside each gun grew larger and larger as they approached the merchantman.

"A big one, Doctor," Wickes said, pointing toward the ship they were approaching. "She's still a good distance away, so I can't make out who she is. Should be English, but she might be French or Spanish. If she is, the men won't be very happy."

"It would be a disappointment to me, too," Edward laughed.

"It's good for them. Serves better than gun drill, for now they've a target to lay on, even if it does prove friendly."

"Mr. Bishop!" Wickes cried again. "Prepare to put a shot across her."

Edward heard Bishop shouting new orders to one of his crews. When Wickes called out several minutes later, a single cannon blasted and dropped a shot into the sea, safely forward of the unknown ship.

The merchantman turned slightly in her course, and a standard rose to the top of her mainmast. Wickes scrutinized the flag through his glass and then cursed, loud and hard.

"Mr. Bishop! Recall your crews. It's a Frenchman."

A groan of disappointment rose from the deck below, and Edward felt like joining in. Bishop, after sounding his whistle, ordered a man to raise the Grand Union flag. While this was being done, the merchantman tacked again. Soon the two vessels were following the same course, the *Reprisal* moving with much greater speed. When they were even with each other, a charge was set off in one of the port cannon. A moment later an answering report echoed over the water. Several of the men at the rail of the privateer glumly waved their caps.

They followed the same course for the remainder of the morning and part of the afternoon. About three o'clock, Wickes began to maneuver the ship in the great circle he had mentioned to Edward.

"This will bring us back to the channel entrance about eight," he told Edward. "Two hours after that, we'll be well into it. If the moon isn't too bright we should get past the entrance easily, even if they've tried to block it."

"Block it?" Edward asked. "Isn't the channel a bit large for that this far to the west?"

"They don't block it quite the way you're thinking, Doctor. The English have a great many vessels about near the entrance, smaller craft, most of them. When they see one of our ships coming in, they signal to one of the groups of men-of-war which are stationed near them."

"Even so, I don't see how they could watch effectively over so much water."

"They can't really. We have found that it is safer near the French coast than anywhere else, although you might think the English would have stationed vessels near there. They do have one group close to the center of the channel—Nicholson ran into them one night when he was coming in. He had a hard fight to pull clear of them; ever since, we've all avoided doing that."

They ate supper early that night, for, as Wickes explained to Edward, the coming night would be one of constant alert. When they came out on deck again after finishing their supper, the sun had vanished behind a bank of low, dark clouds. A fine mist settled over everyone and covered the ship with a glistening patina.

The deck had become slippery, and, as Edward paced about to keep his muscles from growing too taut with the nervousness, he found it difficult to keep from sliding on the wet planks. Wickes stayed close to the helmsman, leaving him only to come forward, first on the port and then on the starboard side, as if trying to force his gaze through the increasing mist and darkness to discover any lurking English vessels.

Once, the sound of waves pounding against rocks reached them. At least that was what Edward thought it was. He stood motionless, holding his breath and listening so intently that his neck began to ache. Wickes must have thought the same thing, Edward thought, for he saw the captain hurry into his cabin where he had taken his charts. When he reappeared, he seemed relieved.

"That was Ushant Island," the captain said quietly. "We're on course."

The silence aboard the *Reprisal* was absolute and ominous. The only sound was the washing of the sea against the hull. There were men on deck, Edward knew; sometimes he noticed a dark shadow move from one side of the ship to the other or heard a muffled curse as one of them struck a piece of gear. Yet these occasions were so infrequent that as he stood there, in the eerie, chilling mist, he imagined they were moving as a ghost ship might move. He felt a mad urge to talk or to shout, longing to dispel this oppression which was eating into him.

As the wind freshened, the ship responded, surging faster through the tumbling waves and rolling more noticeably. He heard something slide across the deck below; it tumbled over and over and crashed against the rail. The noise was a welcome diversion, but when it ceased, the silence became even more oppressive.

Wickes was also affected by the strange quiet. The captain strode about the quarterdeck, his hands clasped behind his back. His steps sounded muffled, as if he were wearing cloths around his boots to deaden the noise.

He paused at the rail occasionally, gripping it with both hands and staring out into the darkness, his face a white blur. Edward shivered suddenly and, to warm himself, began walking around the quarterdeck. Just as he reached the starboard side, he heard Wickes gasp.

He hurried back and stood beside the captain, peering out into the darkness. He started violently when he perceived what Wickes had seen.

About three hundred yards from them, nearly obscured by fog, a ship rode at anchor. It was a bark, he judged, about their size. He could detect no movement aboard her, and the *Reprisal* swiftly passed her by without challenge. Only hints of the ship could be discerned—the masts were dark smudges, and along the decks there was a line of black circles which Wickes, in a whisper, informed him were cannon. There had not been a sound as they passed her, except the noise of the sea against their hull; but as the other ship faded from sight, a long sigh rose from the deck below them. Wickes shook his head when he heard it.

"A close one, Doctor," he said, still in a whisper.

He wiped his sleeve across his face. "Thought their lookout would see us for sure, even with that fog around them. Much as I would be glad of a fight at this moment, I don't want to risk rousing more of their ships.

"They've changed their tactics, I guess, leaving that one as close to shore as she is. If we started battling, there'd be five more here before we had a chance to finish her."

"Then that may not be the only one we meet tonight?"

"No, indeed. We may not get past so easily the next time."

"If the men are feeling the way I am, they would probably welcome a fight now," Edward admitted. "Anything to relieve this tension."

"They're feeling it, never fear. So am I. But they're not as eager now as they are in daytime. It's difficult to see in a night battle—cannon going off can blind you for several minutes. You can't afford to be clumsy around all that powder." Bishop suddenly came up the ladder and stood beside them.

"Are the men getting coffee from the galley?" Wickes asked.

"Yes, sir. They're mighty glad of it, too, it being so wet."

"They'd better stay where they are until the night's over, all of them. We don't know what's ahead of us, and we don't want trouble if we're not ready for it."

"They don't mind, sir. They have blankets. They're only changing the bad air below for some fresh sea air."

"You'd better see if you can get some rest, Mr. Bishop. I'll be up until morning, and you can take charge tomorrow when I feel I can catch up on my sleep."

"Aye, sir, as you wish. Good night, Captain. Good night, Doctor."

Bishop saluted and climbed down the ladder. Edward felt a little glow of pleasure at Bishop's acceptance of him.

"You may not know, Doctor, that Bishop saw you helping the man who was hurt,"Wickes said, breaking in on Edward's thoughts. "He told me yesterday he'd never seen any surgeon, except Mr. Temple, who was so swift and who seemed to know so well what he was doing. Bishop's a slow-speaking man, as you have seen. You should feel complimented."

"I do, Captain," Edward replied swiftly. "I never knew he had noticed me."

"Not much happens on deck that Bishop doesn't see," Wickes said dryly. "His men discover that fast, sometimes to their sorrow." He leaned out over the rail and peered through the darkness again.

Edward stood beside him, gazing into the fog, wondering while he watched how much more Wickes's trained eyes could see than his. On a night such as this, when visibility was nonexistent and when every move seemed to depend upon instinct, Edward realized how totally dependent everyone now was upon Wickes's abilities. It was an unfamiliar situation to him, one that he found disquieting.

The two men waited through the long hours for dawn. The fog, which never lifted, was like a clammy rag on their faces. Their clothing was saturated with mist and spray, chilling them when they paced about the deck to keep themselves from growing numb. Their only solace was the steaming coffee which a cabin boy brought several times during that long watch. They drank it avidly, heedless of the scalding in their mouths.

Finally, the blackness turned to gray. A wind sprang up and dispersed the fog. In the east, the sun was just beginning to pull itself up out of the sea; across the waves, bright bands of red-gold light were running westward. The channel stretched before them, quiet and untenanted, a vast expanse of open water.

CHAPTER XIV

F OR SOME DAYS they sailed along the French coast, the lookouts keeping sharp eyes on the sea. Many ships were sighted, but if they were not accompanied by men-of-war, they were too close to the haven of either coast to make pursuit rewarding. At night, the *Reprisal* circled and doubled back on her course, so that the distance they progressed each day toward the narrows of the channel was very slight.

As the days passed, the crew became restless and quarrelsome. Arguments erupted, and above the soft pounding of the waves against the hull, angry voices lashed at each other in sudden fury. Even Wickes had lost his usual serenity—he was silent at his meals now, and when Edward spoke, the captain rarely answered with more than a few words. His attention was concentrated on the lookouts, whom he shuffled and changed about so often he seemed to be seeking a man in the crew with a magnetic power which would draw prizes toward his ship.

Mr. Bishop had also succumbed to the general pessimism. He went about his duties with his head lowered, his eyes focused on the planks beneath his feet. He held gun drill each day, but there was a lack of spirit in it; the men performed their duties only because they were under the mate's cold scrutiny.

There was little else, besides gun drill, to keep the crew alert—they were like children with a whole year of holidays.

They had been in the channel almost a week when, one night at dinner, Wickes said to Edward,

"We're going farther up the channel, Doctor. We don't seem to be finding any prizes here. I plan to put into port in the next three days. Do you care whether it's Havre or Calais?"

"If it makes no difference to you, Captain, I think I would prefer Havre. I'm pleased to hear we're putting in; I have been feeling that I should return to Paris soon."

"There's no telling what we may find farther east. We may even find that English trap I mentioned. However, I feel it's worth the risk, merely to find some action. The men are beginning to snap at each other. They need a good fight to cheer them up."

"Poor Bishop," Edward said with a smile, "has suffered more than the rest, I fear. He even cursed his gunner yesterday. Unless his crews are firing shot instead of practicing on cold cannon, I imagine he always has that doleful air. What is your plan?"

"I'm going as close to the narrows as I dare, hoping to find a packet boat, though I doubt if I'll be that lucky. With a packet or even a Jamaicaman, I'll be happy to head for port."

That night the *Reprisal* sailed steadily toward the east. The crew had been expecting the ship to circle; when she stayed firm on her course, moving swiftly up the channel toward the principal ship lanes between France and England, the atmosphere on deck changed noticeably.

Edward came out on deck that night sensing a new attitude in the men from the quiet, determined way they went about their duties. They kept silent, in accordance with Wickes's orders; the only sounds that rose from the *Reprisal* were the whispered orders to the helmsman.

Wickes and Edward retired early. The captain explained that they might have their greatest amount of activity in the early morning hours, unless they chanced to run upon another ship tonight. The crew turned in early as well; and when Edward came out on deck again, just before dawn, he noticed that all the gun crews were already at their stations, conversing quietly and looking out at the channel. Wickes was near the wheel directing the helmsman. Mr. Bishop moved about the deck from gun to gun, checking on ammunition and the alertness of his crews.

"Sail ho! Off the port quarter!"

Wickes peered through his glass toward the east and the oncoming dawn.

"A Jamaicaman," he cried jubilantly. "A fine piece of luck for us, Doctor."

"Be ready to fire, Mr. Bishop, but wait for my signal," Wickes shouted down to the deck.

"Sail ho! Half a mile over the first!" the lookout cried again.

Wickes spun in his tracks and swept the port quarter with his glass. A moment later, after searching the sea carefully, he lowered his glass and cursed.

"What I feared might happen," Edward heard him mutter. "A corvette, about our size, but heavier gunned from the look of her. Mr. Bishop!"

"Aye, Captain?"

"A corvette our size, Mr. Bishop. We'll cripple that merchantman first, so she can't run for port and then we'll deal with the other."

Bishop ran back toward the forward crews.

"All gunners aim for the mainmast. Two rounds—soon as she's abreast of us. Load and wait for the captain's signal to fire!"

Wickes had already begun to maneuver the *Reprisal* so that Bishop could deliver the first cannonade against the merchantman and still have time to reload and lay a barrage on the swiftly approaching corvette. She had put on more sail since the lookout had first seen her and was now trying desperately to close the distance between herself and the merchantman. The captain of the Jamaicaman was also maneuvering, veering hard to port in order to lessen the distance between his ship and the shore and to give his escort an opportunity to slip in front of him to protect him from the privateer.

Wickes ordered more sail lofted and Edward felt the ship surge forward. Before the merchantman was able to complete its maneuver, the *Reprisal* had swooped in between it and the shore. As she drew abreast of the slow cargo vessel, Wickes cried out, "Fire!"

The cannon roared in one tremendous explosion; a cloud of smoke enveloped the forward area of the deck. When it cleared, the merchantman was slightly aft of them, her foremast swaying precariously, but still aloft. Bishop hopped up and down with rage. His curse had hardly died away when he gave another order to fire. This time, after the cannon had belched again, it was the merchantman's mainmast that swayed, yet both of the masts that had been struck were still aloft. Bishop's renewed cursing sounded over the suddenly quiet deck; he pounded his forehead in despair.

"Forget the merchantman, Mr. Bishop," Wickes shouted down at the frenzied mate. "Ready your crews for the corvette. We'll be on her in no time."

"We don't have to worry about that merchantman," Wickes explained to Edward. "With her masts like that, she can't carry any canvas. She'll just drift until she's been patched up, which won't be for at least an hour."

The captain of the English corvette was an experienced adversary. The skill with which he maneuvered past the crippled merchantman toward the *Reprisal* evoked a grunt of admiration from Wickes. They had been watching him approach from the port quarter; and just as Wickes was about to turn farther to port to rake the approaching craft with a broadside, the Englishman veered sharply. His ship steadied, and it was his barrage that sounded first, pounding the *Reprisal*'s forward deck space with well placed shot.

Although two of the cannon had been temporarily silenced, Bishop was able to fire the others. One shot was low, striking the enemy just above the waterline; from the deck of the *Reprisal,* they noticed the wood in the corvette's side splinter. When Wickes saw this, he jumped up and down in sudden excitement.

"Look alive down there," he cried. "She'll be back in another minute. Aim for the waterline, Mr. Bishop. Forget the masts."

The *Reprisal* turned and headed directly for the corvette, which had not changed its course as quickly as Wickes had expected. At an order from Wickes, the helmsman swung the wheel hard; and as the ship steadied on a starboard tack, they caught the corvette with a broadside which did visible damage. Four shots struck her at the waterline, while one wild shot struck the fore-topmast and toppled it toward the deck. Before they could turn and lessen the target they presented, the Englishman had fired again, but this barrage was not as accurate as the first. One shot smashed the railing, but the others whistled harmlessly through the rigging and fell to starboard, throwing up high columns of spray.

After another exchange, the corvette headed north into the channel, the *Reprisal* in close pursuit. Severe damage seemed to have been inflicted on the English ship. She labored forward like a wounded animal, though there was little visible damage.

"How close did you observe our fire, Doctor?" Wickes asked, puzzled.

"I saw a few hits, Captain. Some at the waterline, some above, and one on the foremast."

"That's what I thought. Mr. Bishop!"

"Aye, sir?"

"Where did our last barrage hit the enemy?"

"All but two shots landed just at the waterline, Captain," Bishop replied. "I followed your orders, sir, and told the crews to aim low instead of at the masts."

"That must be what's slowing her, then. They can't pump fast enough."

"It may be, Captain. She's thin hulled. If those shots got through her, she'll be taking on a lot of water."

"I think she did. She must have been built for speed, not safety."

The *Reprisal* was gaining rapidly on the corvette when Wickes suddenly spun about and looked back at the merchantman. Sail had been raised on the still unsteady masts, and the vessel was beginning to move.

"Alter course," Wickes cried to the helmsman. "Make for the merchantman."

The *Reprisal* turned in a tight circle, and Wickes's face relaxed as he saw the distance between the ships diminish rapidly.

"Prepare to board that vessel, Mr. Bishop. If they try to fight before we reach them, clean her deck with grape. But no more shot unless we have to use it. The better shape she's in, the more money we'll have in our pockets."

"Aye, sir." Bishop gave orders to his crews. The men stood by their guns, waiting; faint plumes of smoke rose from the fuse setters' rods and drifted lazily across the deck.

They had closed to within a few hundred yards of the merchantman when a musket blasted. One of the men beside a forward cannon yelped like a dog in pain.

He dropped to his knees, clutching his arm.

"God damn 'em," Wickes stormed. "All right, Mr. Bishop. If that's all the sense they have, give 'em a round of grape."

The cannon which Bishop designated to fire blasted and belched smoke and flame. The shell landed just below the quarterdeck of the merchantman; those on the *Reprisal* first saw holes appear in the sails, then heard the cries of those who had been hit by the flying scraps of glass and iron. A white flag suddenly rose below the ensign that flew at the stern of the ship.

At the sight of it, the men aboard the privateer broke into loud cheers.

"That's finished," Wickes said, turning toward Edward. "Her captain will be here in a few minutes; we'll send a party aboard to take her into port with us."

"Mr. Bishop," Wickes called down. "Select your party for boarding and be prepared to leave at once, armed. We can't take any chances out here or waste any time. That ship we let free will probably send help."

"The men are ready now, sir."

"After her captain comes aboard, shove off as soon as I give you the word."

"Aye, sir."

Across the water, a small boat was lowered over the side of the merchantman. Men climbed down a swaying Jacob's ladder, dropped into the boat, then pulled away toward the *Reprisal*. In another five minutes, the captain of the merchantman was aboard.

He was a tiny fighting-cock of a man, this captain, not more than five feet tall and dressed in colorful, tight-fitting green breeches. He wore a white shirt with a silk scarf at his throat; his heavily embroidered three-cornered hat was tilted slightly on his head. Edward thought this gave him the look of a small boy masquerading as a sailor, an impression woefully contrary to fact.

His face was scrunched up in wrath; he shook his small fist under Wickes's astonished eyes and pointed eloquently at his drifting, debris-strewn vessel. All the while tears of rage ran down his cheeks and dripped off the tip of his jutting chin.

Wickes stood beside him, a little baffled, while Bishop waited impatiently in the boat below for the captain's signal to depart. Wickes's face grew more and more perplexed while the little man harangued and gesticulated and expressed with enormous energy his disapproval of the attack upon his ship.

"Furthermore, you pirate," he screamed wildly at Wickes, "you've injured one of my men. I have no one aboard to take care of him; and if he dies, I'll hunt you down and string you up for murder."

"Don't worry about that, Captain," Wickes replied soothingly. "We have a surgeon who can take care of your man."

"Temple is busy with our injured, Captain," Edward said. "Shall I go with Mr. Bishop's boat?"

Wickes nodded gratefully and turned to the rail.

Edward's offer of assistance had momentarily calmed the furious bantam.

"Mr. Bishop, take Dr. Bancroft with you. There's a man aboard the merchantman who needs care."

"Aye, sir. We'll wait on the doctor."

Edward went inside his cabin and picked up the little bag of medicines and instruments that had been made available to him after the first fight. He hurried to the rail and carefully lowered the bag by rope into Bishop's waiting hands. After clambering over the side, he let himself down the swinging ladder until, feeling in space with a frantic toe, he heard Bishop say, "Drop, Doctor. Just drop."

He let go and landed with a thump. The men at the oars pushed away from the side of the ship and began to row toward the merchantman.

Edward was led aft to the side of a young seaman who lay stretched out on a piece of bloody canvas. He had been struck in the chest by a piece of iron, and Edward saw at once that he had lost a dangerous amount of blood. His face was chalky white and his pulse so feeble that Edward could hardly detect it. The pain he suffered must have been considerable, for he moaned intermittently, although his eyes did not open when Edward tore away his shirt and exposed the wound. The iron had left a deep hole just below his shoulder.

Not a fatal wound, Edward thought as he peered into his kit, unless he's lost too much blood. Pulling out some forceps, he hastily cleaned them with a length of bandage. Probing as gently as he could, he felt the forceps strike against the metal. Very slowly, intent for any fresh spurting of blood, he tugged and pulled at the metal. Several times the forceps slipped and he was forced to start over again, but at last he succeeded in drawing out the piece of metal. The fragment rang on the deck, and Edward quickly inserted a large swab of bandage in the wound, keeping it in place by a strap which he wound tightly around the man's chest.

"He should be as good as new in another ten days," Edward said, rising beside the old sailor who had stood next to him during the entire operation. The other sailors who had come to watch had departed; Edward smiled as he saw several of them bent over the rail, vomiting into the sea.

"Give him a good, stiff tot of rum," he told the old man, "and keep him on his bunk as much as possible. He shouldn't walk about for at least ten days."

"Aye, sir," the old man agreed. "I'll tell the mate. Thank you, sir. What you did means a lot to me—that lad's my own son."

Edward noticed the tears on his rough cheeks. He reached out and patted him on the shoulder.

"He'll be all right. He's a strong boy."

The old man brushed his sleeve across his face and nodded his gratitude, too upset to say more.

"Mr. Bishop," Edward said when he met the mate on the quarterdeck, "my work's done aboard this ship. I'm ready to return whenever the boat is."

"Very good, Doctor. About five minutes."

The mate turned and continued to bark orders to the members of the *Reprisal's* crew who had come aboard the merchantman with him. Edward watched them as they took over all the necessary duties to ready the ship for sailing and directed groups of English sailors to repair sails or to brace the weakened masts. Aloft, sailors swarmed in the rigging, replacing the snapped shrouds.

The English officers stood grouped on the quarterdeck, the expressions on their faces fluctuating between disdain and fear. Occasionally, Bishop would dispatch one of them to supervise a group on the deck below. The officers selected for such duties were slow to comply with Bishop's orders, but the mate was prepared for such difficulties. Resting one hand lightly on the pistol in his belt.

"You heard my order—look alive!" he would roar. "Or you'll swim to shore."

Under such threats of primitive justice, understanding was immediate. The officers hurried to their designated tasks.

"Boat's returning now, Doctor. Would you tell the captain we're ready to sail?"

"Certainly, Mr. Bishop. That man I patched up should be kept off his feet."

"Very well, Doctor. I'll give orders for it."

The boat into which Edward climbed was rocking even more than it had been against the side of the *Reprisal.*

The sky was clouding, and a breeze had sprung up from the northwest. They rowed across the choppy water between the ships. Edward, as soon as he was aboard, made his way to Wickes with Bishop's information.

Wickes nodded, stared toward the north for a moment, then shouted orders to his officers to get the ship underway.

"We'll lead her in," he called back to the helmsman.

"Pass her and come in close on her starboard side. I want to speak with Mr. Bishop."

"Aye, sir."

When the maneuver had been made and the two ships were close to each other, Wickes called across the little water that separated them with a speaking trumpet.

"Mr. Bishop, we'll make for Havre at once. All the sail you can carry. I'll go into the harbor, you drop anchor outside the breakwater. I'll let you know later where to go."

"Aye, sir," the mate's reply came faintly on the wind.

The ships began to move, the merchantman slowly, for she was still not fully repaired and had difficulty gaining headway. Wickes watched her progress intently; when he saw the *Reprisal* pull away faster and faster from the other vessel, he beat his fist on the rail and looked again toward the north. Turning, he gave orders to Mr. Watkins to lower some of the canvas.

Watkins raced forward. Wickes scowled, turning to Edward.

"I don't like this, Doctor. It may give the English a chance to catch us before we can reach port. That one we let escape will make trouble for us, I warrant."

"We aren't too far from Havre, are we?"

"Far enough to cause us all sorts of grief if they can catch us," Wickes muttered in reply. "We should make port in a few hours, even at this rate of crawl. But a few hours, with some of their fast ships, will be time enough to catch us."

They watched the water to the north for some time, Wickes scanning the sea constantly with his glass.

"As far as we can tell now," Wickes said finally, "it will take them an hour or more to reach us, even creeping along the way we are."

The ships moved steadily to the east along the coast. Coffee was brought to the quarterdeck several times during the morning. They gulped it eagerly, keeping one eye on the open sea to the north and the other on the sloshing liquid in their cups. Wickes grew more relaxed as they came closer to Havre. Several times Edward noticed him with his back to the north and his glass to his eye as he inspected the merchantman, perhaps estimating the price she might bring.

"I guess we'll make it without any trouble," Wickes said about noon. "In another hour we'll be turning in for Havre, and as yet there's no sign of the English. I wonder if that corvette could have sunk."

THE REPRISAL MOORED at three that afternoon. Both Edward and Wickes had sighed with considerable relief when they passed safely inside the breakwater. When they finally tied up, Wickes stared down at the wharf with a smile on his lips. The merchantman rested just off the breakwater, awaiting orders from Wickes.

"I think I'll go ashore, Captain," Edward said. "I want to find out about getting to Paris as quickly as possible."

"Very well, Doctor. I'll be ready to go ashore myself in an hour. Would you mind meeting me at Eyries's office? I'd be grateful if you were there to help me while we talked. I've never done business with him before, and I've heard he could be more honest than he is."

Edward met Wickes outside the entrance to Eyries's offices promptly at four. The captain had changed his clothes and looked highly uncomfortable in a dark blue jacket and dark breeches. His square brimmed captain's hat lent a further air of unreality to his appearance. He looked profoundly grateful when Edward appeared.

A clerk led them into the small inner office that Eyries, the Havre agent for the commissioners in Paris, used for transacting confidential matters. Eyries greeted them with a slight bow and motioned them to be seated.

Eyries was a tall, dark man, almost too fashionably dressed. His languid fingers played incessantly with the ruffles at his throat as he listened to Wickes's description of the captured merchantman. When the captain explained the present location of the merchantman, Eyries leaned forward, his gray eyes suddenly alert.

"Lying just outside the breakwater now, eh?" he asked.

"Yes, Mr. Eyries. I told my mate, Mr. Bishop, to hold her there until he received orders from me."

"A wise move, Captain." Eyries spoke with a strange, barely detectable wheeze in his voice. "Affairs in Havre have been most unsettled lately. The English have made strong protests to the authorities about prizes being towed into our ports. Perhaps it would be better now to register the merchantman in the name of my firm. These papers which you have brought"—he waved toward the manifests which were scattered carelessly on his desk—"will give us sufficient information. We will be responsible for selling the vessel and returning the proceeds to you, less, of course, our usual commission of twenty percent."

Wickes started violently. "Twenty percent! Not on your life, Mr. Eyries. Not when you haven't lost a minute's sleep or risked a pound to take that vessel."

"Our commission may seem high at first glance," Eyries admitted with a shrug, "but, you see, we must give our entire attention to selling the vessel for you. We must not only pay wharf and storage charges, but, more important, we must circumvent the legal difficulties which the English are certain to put in our way. You are quite correct when you say we risk no money, but we agree to assume the entire responsibility for selling the vessel and its cargo. That requires effort, Captain, on the part of many people. When difficulties arise, as they always do, we spend our time and our money to smooth them out. Legal advice, as you know, is extremely dear, but we pay for that. I do not believe twenty percent too high a figure, Captain. It is our regular charge for selling any prize that is brought to us."

"What do you think, Doctor?" Wickes asked. "Twenty percent seems outrageous to me."

"It does seem high, Captain," Edward said, nodding, "but because of the strong English protests there have been increasing problems in all the ports. It's more difficult to dispose of prizes—not only more difficult, but more expensive as well."

Eyries nodded with approval at Edward's statement; his gray eyes watched Wickes's face intently as the captain listened to Edward.

"However," Edward continued, and Eyries sat up slightly in his chair, "I know that if M. Eyries, who is most friendly to our cause, realized the bravery necessary to obtain such a prize, he would perhaps lessen his fee to, say, eighteen percent."

Eyries frowned and his busy fingers left the ruffles to drum on the top of his desk. He was just about to speak when Edward continued:

"Such a generous act on your part, Monsieur, would be gratefully received in Paris and long remembered by the commissioners, I can assure you."

"Dr. Bancroft knows how much I esteem bravery such as yours, Captain. To prove my belief in the cause you serve so well, I am willing to lower my usual fee to the figure which he has suggested."

"I trust, Doctor," he added, "that word of my generosity will be communicated to the commissioners."

"I shall inform them myself," Edward assured him. "I know that they will be even more regardful of your integrity and your honesty, Monsieur."

"I shall begin negotiations immediately, Captain. From your description of the vessel and from what I have read in the manifests concerning the cargo, the sale should bring in a substantial amount. The ship should be moored at Pier 7, where we have our warehouse. She can be unloaded at once, for the warehouse is empty; but be certain that your crew guards the cargo after it has been transferred. There has been much thievery here recently."

"I shall arrange for that, Mr. Eyries," Wickes replied firmly. "There'll be none of this cargo stolen, save at the price of a broken neck."

When they had walked outside Eyries's office, Wickes asked Edward if he would care to have supper aboard the *Reprisal.*

"I'll walk back to the ship with you, Captain. A walk now will do me good, with that long coach ride ahead of me; but I'm afraid I can't stay for supper."

"I still think that buzzard cheated me," Wickes complained as they walked down toward the waterfront. "I'm grateful for the way you took my part, Doctor, but it galls me to think of paying that vulture so much."

"It can't be helped, Captain. It's part of the system today. You have to pay people like Eyries the price they ask if you can't sell the prize yourself."

"I suppose so," Wickes sighed. "I'm glad you were with me—you saved my men a few hundred pounds by forcing him down."

"I was happy to be able to do it. It is little enough to repay you for the kindness you have shown me."

After they came aboard, a boat was immediately dispatched to the merchantman with orders for Mr. Bishop to tie up at Pier 7. Edward went to his cabin to obtain his greatcoat and his few belongings. When he was ready to leave, Wickes walked to the ladder with him.

"I'm sorry to see you go, Doctor. You've brought us good luck from the minute you arrived."

"If they feel they don't need me in Paris, Captain, I'll plead for a chance to serve with you again."

"Mr. Bishop would be pleased if you did. I don't know a higher compliment I can pay than that."

"Knowing how carefully Mr. Bishop guards his compliments," Edward said with a smile, "I feel honored. I hope you'll say good-bye to him for me."

"I'll do that. I hope you'll be able to make another voyage with us, Doctor; I've been happy to have you aboard."

"Thank you, Captain. Good luck, and good luck to the *Reprisal.*"

Edward stopped on the wharf and gazed up at the ship and at Wickes who still stood at the rail, watching him. They waved and Edward turned away toward Havre, toward the coach which would take him back to Paris.

Before he had gone a great distance, he turned again, for a last look at the ship. His eyes clouded as he stood there, looking at her. A fine ship, a fine crew, a fine life, he thought to himself. When he turned again toward Havre, his eyes were clear and there was no longer hesitation or reluctance in his step.

On his face there was an expression which Wickes would not have recognized, unless he could remember back to the night when Edward had first come aboard the *Reprisal*.

Just after Edward finished his supper at the inn from which the Paris coach was to leave, the proprietor stopped at his table.

"There is a gentleman waiting to see you, Monsieur. In the small room to the right of the stairs."

Edward nodded, put some money on the table, and walked quickly out of the dining room. When he opened the door of the little room, he saw Eyries seated opposite, his legs stretched out comfortably. He closed the door behind him and stood there, watching the Frenchman without a word. Finally, reluctantly, Eyries rose to his feet.

"Good evening, Doctor. I have brought what I promised you this afternoon, before our meeting with Captain Wickes. After I checked the manifests, I decided the first payment should be a bit more than we had agreed upon. I found that there were several thousand yards of woolens, which always fetch a good price."

"How much is it?"

"Five hundred pounds. It would have been more, but you yourself changed the percentage we had agreed upon. He knew nothing—he would have accepted twenty percent in the end."

"Perhaps so, but it is not wise to antagonize such a man. He is Dr. Franklin's nephew."

"I see. You are right, of course. I didn't know that. Good night, Doctor. The other payments will follow as I dispose of the cargo."

"You know where to send them?"

"Yes. I have your address."

After Eyries had departed, Edward sat down and opened the package. He counted the money carefully and deposited it in his wallet.

The fire in the little room was warm; it threw a reddish light on the chairs and table. As Edward watched it flicker, he was reminded of that first explosion aboard the *Reprisal*. He thought of the gun crew that had been struck. Quickly, he walked out of the inn and climbed inside the Paris coach. Feeling a sudden chill, he drew his greatcoat about him.

CHAPTER XV

O N HIS WAY HOME after his arrival in Paris, Edward stopped at the
Hotel d'Hambourg. Just as he walked inside, he heard Carmichael's
voice coming through the open door of the inner office.

"But something must have happened to him, Dr. Franklin. He's been gone
a week longer than anyone expected, and not a word has reached anyone."

"Dr. Bancroft is quite capable of handling his own affairs without our
worrying about him, Carmichael," Franklin answered. "I feel we must
concentrate on our business here. Besides, has it ever occurred to you that
perhaps he may not want to be found? There are times when I feel like
disappearing, I know, and I would not be surprised if he feels the same way."

Before Carmichael had an opportunity to reply to Franklin's remarks,
Edward stepped inside the open door. Carmichael's mouth fell slack when
he saw Edward standing beside him. Deane rocked back in his chair,
astonished. Franklin rose to greet him.

"I was telling Carmichael and Deane that they shouldn't worry about you,
Doctor. Now you appear to prove me right."

He reached out and shook Edward's hand heartily. Franklin's movements
seemed to awaken Deane and Carmichael; they crowded around him,
stammering greetings and blurting questions. Only Lee remained seated, his

face twitching between disbelief and disappointment. Edward laughed and raised his hands to fend off the questions.

"Please, gentlemen, let's sit down. I'll be delighted to tell you what happened."

They resumed their seats and Edward gave them a brief resume of his voyage with Wickes. Franklin chortled and slapped his leg.

"Damn, Bancroft, what a lucky fellow you are! I've always wanted to go on a real chase with that nephew of mine—coming over here with me, he was as careful as a hen with chicks."

Because they insisted, Edward explained in more detail the most exciting events that had occurred during the voyage. Lee paced up and down while Edward was speaking, his hands clenched behind his back, his head shaking back and forth as if the whole story was too incredible.

When Edward told about the interview with M. Eyries, Franklin exploded with rage and thumped on the table.

"Silas, we must rid ourselves of that hyena. It's bad enough to charge us twice the value of what he does, but when he tries to steal from my own family, that's unforgivable."

"I agree," Deane said, nodding his head vigorously. "I hadn't dismissed him, because I had no one to put in his place. Beaumarchais might be able to recommend someone."

"I don't think I'd discharge him yet, gentlemen," Edward advised. "Any agent at Havre is in a difficult position. The English are keeping a very close watch on the port. Consequently, his expenses are higher than they might be at Nantes or St. Nazaire. Wouldn't it be a better idea to let Eyries continue, but to watch his charges more carefully? If he seems to be obtaining more from our captains than any other agent, we can let him know and warn him to lower his fees. As Mr. Deane has said, he is the only man we have."

"What happened to that bark you mentioned," Lee interrupted, "the escort for the merchantman that was captured?"

Lee's suspicious voice grated so harshly that everyone felt suddenly uncomfortable. Franklin, shifting about in his chair, gave the Virginian a perplexed look. Edward concealed the rush of exultation he felt when he heard Lee's question. He did not know what might be behind such a question, but knowing Lee, he expected the worst.

"After we forced her out of the fight," Edward replied, "she made for the English coast. Captain Wickes thought it wiser to capture the merchantman if he could, rather than allow her to escape while he engaged the bark. Other men-of-war were in that vicinity, and we might not have escaped if they had all descended upon us."

Lee raised his hands in despair.

"I can't understand these brave captains of ours," he complained. "Here was an opportunity to do great harm to English prestige, and it was wasted for a merchantman. Surely it would be better for our cause if our captains would forget prizes and sink a few men-of-war, don't you agree, Dr. Franklin?"

"No, Mr. Lee, I do not," Franklin snapped. "It is always easy to impute questionable motives to a man who fights and risks his neck if one is sitting in an office. Since you ask, sir, I'd say Wickes did exactly what he should have. He is the captain of a privateer, not an American man-of-war."

The conversation soon turned to other channels; and before long, Lee bowed to them all and took his leave. When he had departed, Franklin gave a long sigh and leaned back in his chair, his hands pressed against his head.

"Oh, how fortunate you were to be away for two weeks, Edward, especially these last two weeks. Have you heard about Lee's mission to Holland?"

"I heard before I left that he might go. Mr. Deane told me, I believe."

"Well, he went. He was gone almost as long as you were. He might still be there if his papers hadn't been stolen."

"His papers stolen?" Edward asked in amazement.

"Yes, while he was at court someone ransacked his rooms and made off with all his papers, all the plans that we had so carefully prepared here. He returned moaning about treachery and insisting on knowing where you were."

"Where I was? Whatever for?"

"I don't know. I really don't. We had a difficult time here, trying to reason with him. I was surprised he was as moderate toward you today as he was. I don't know what we can do about Mr. Lee, Doctor, truly I don't. He harbors an intense distrust of you, as I dare say you have noticed."

Later, as Edward reached his house, he saw a carriage pull away from the door.

"Welcome home, Doctor," Bertram said with unusual enthusiasm. "We were concerned about you, sir, if I may say so. Especially Miss Vaughn, sir. She's been most worried these last few days, not hearing from you."

Edward hurried into the drawing room. At the sight of him, Ellen gave a little cry. She ran from her chair across the room to him. For several minutes she said nothing, content to nestle in his arms.

Her hands caressed his sleeve as if only through the feel of the cloth could she convince herself that he was really home again. Her eyes, when he held her away from him to look at her, were wet. Seeing the tears on her cheeks, he closed his arms about her and drew her to him again.

"Oh, darling, I've been so worried about you. What happened? Where were you?"

"Poor Ellen. I'm sorry I worried you. I thought that note I left would explain matters, but I suppose I've been away too long for you not to worry."

She shifted in his arms and wiped the tears angrily from her cheeks.

"Where were you, Edward? Couldn't you let me know? Couldn't you even send a message?"

"No, I couldn't. I've been aboard a ship, darling. I took a message to a privateer, but I had no chance to get off before she sailed. I reached port only a few days ago."

They walked across the room and sat down. Ellen kept her arm about his waist as he told her of his days aboard the *Reprisal*, touching him as if she wanted to reassure herself that he was safe and back with her again.

"I can understand now why you didn't let me know," she said after he had finished recounting his voyage. "I was so terribly worried, though. No one knew where you were. I sent a note to Dr. Franklin. He stopped by to see me, but he couldn't tell me anything either. It was as if you had suddenly dropped off the earth; for two weeks I was positive I'd never see you again."

"You mustn't worry like this, Ellen. I told you when we first came to France that there would be times when I would be called away and it would be impossible to write or send a message. There may be other times like this, darling; I don't want to feel that you are here worrying to death about me."

"I'll try to remember, Edward," she said, smiling at him as her hand tightened on his sleeve.

"What has happened while I've been gone?" he asked suddenly. "How is Mme. de Treymes?"

"She was here this afternoon. She left only a little while before you arrived. She has been here several times. Mr. Carmichael was here once, and Paul Wentworth came for supper one night."

"Paul?" Edward asked, surprised. "That's nice. How was he?"

"Very well, as he always is."

"Was it just a friendly call?" Edward asked, "or did he have something to discuss with me?"

"I couldn't tell. After he discovered you weren't here, we chatted for a while. It was time for supper, so I casually asked him if he would care to stay. To my surprise, he did. We had an interesting conversation about people he knew in France and England, fashions and plays and so on. Not a serious talk at all. I never imagined that he was so well acquainted with actors and actresses. He told me some amusing stories about Mrs. Cibber."

"Nothing Paul says or does surprises me any longer," Edward laughed. "He's able to discuss almost any subject, even the most unlikely, with knowledge and complete assurance."

"I noticed that," Ellen said, smiling. "He did seem most informed, though. It isn't all a pose, is it?"

"Oh, no, it isn't a pose at all. Those who know him well realize that, but I should imagine that a person meeting him for the first time would find him disconcerting, to say the least."

"He talked a little about the country house he has in Kent. From his description of it, it must be quite elegant."

"It is. I've been there once."

"Why did he leave that colony, New Hampshire, wasn't it?"

"Yes, New Hampshire. That's where he was born. I don't know. Knowing Paul, I'd say that he didn't care much for the primitive life. He's a man who isn't happy except in a place like London or Paris, or possibly in an establishment as comfortable as his Kent house. He has little inclination for a simple way of life."

Bertram interrupted their discussion to ask Ellen about supper.

"Meat for the doctor, Bertram," she said with a smile. "That is the most important thing of all. The rest I shall leave to you."

"Very good, miss," Bertram replied gravely, although the good humor in his heavy face belied his solemnity.

"I believe Bertram is as happy to see you as I am. He has been like a mourner ever since I first began worrying about you."

"I would never expect him to show emotion," Edward chuckled, "unless it was a catastrophe in the kitchen or a monkey loose in the house. I'm very flattered to hear it, nonetheless."

"Mme. de Treymes keeps trying to steal him from us. He told me that much as he admires her, he is more content here with us than he could ever be with her. She always watches him when she is here, and he says that makes him nervous."

As they sat together after supper, Ellen made him repeat every part of his voyage to her. The capture of the merchantman and the battle at sea did not interest her nearly as much as Edward's stories about Mr. Bishop and the vessel they had passed so silently that night in the fog. She was delighted to hear that he had taken Wickes's part against Eyries and had been able to help the wounded sailor aboard the merchantman.

"It must have been exciting, darling. How I envy you! All I did here was to go to salons where I had gone before and see people I had just seen the previous day. Your story makes me jealous."

"You wouldn't really like the life aboard a privateer. It's rather crude."

She laughed, and Edward rose to blow out the candles in the drawing room. As they undressed upstairs, Ellen seemed even happier than she had been earlier in the evening. While she told him all the amusing gossip she had overheard in the various salons, he finished his preparations and climbed into bed. Stretching out, he watched with a smile as she arranged her hair for the night.

She took out the pins and the jewels. Letting it fall over her shoulders, she combed it vigorously, until it shone and sparkled in the candlelight. As he looked at her and noticed the grace of her movements and the beauty of her figure beneath the nightgown she wore, Edward reflected on his good fortune in keeping her with him for such a length of time. He had not expected, that day when they set out together from London, that their relationship would last as long or as well.

Ellen finished combing her hair and slipped off her nightgown to wash. Edward closed his eyes. How did women expect men to behave like reasonable, rational creatures when they did things like that?

Or did they?

Leaving her nightgown where it had fallen, she slipped into bed and put her arms around him. As he kissed her, he whispered, "It was never like this on the *Reprisal*."

"And a good thing it wasn't," she murmured, pressing against him. "Otherwise, I would be very angry."

As she felt him respond to her caresses, she laughed quietly. "I know, my busy little hand again—but you've been away such a long time, my darling."

THE NEXT MORNING, Franklin sent word that he would remain at Passy for a few days of rest. Deane frowned when he read the note, but resolved to continue the discussion he had just begun with Edward and Carmichael.

"I regret that Dr. Franklin can't be here to give us his advice. But we must act on this immediately, or there will be further difficulties."

Deane turned to Edward to explain. "You see, Doctor, there was a letter from Hodge this morning. He said that although Cunningham had received the instructions Franklin sent him, he was determined to take a devastating revenge on the English for forcing him and his men into a French prison. Hodge apparently heard this from one of the crew and wrote to advise me of the situation. Cunningham must return to the Colonies at once—he's to be released from prison at the end of the week. Vergennes doesn't want him making any more trouble; apparently Stormont has been bothersome again.

"I'm sending Carmichael to Dunkirk with orders to Cunningham to return to the Colonies the moment his cargo is loaded. I specifically state in the orders that he is not to fight, except in self-defense, on pain of losing his commission. He's so intent on revenge that I can think of no other way to make certain that he won't take a week to sail down the channel, burning and sinking as he goes."

Deane looked up at Carmichael. "Be most careful he understands what you tell him. He must *not* fight, and he must leave as quickly as possible. Be very definite, Carmichael, about my orders. We must placate Vergennes; that damned Stormont has him in an uproar. We can't afford to offend him."

Carmichael nodded his understanding. "Are there any other instructions you wish me to give Captain Cunningham?"

"No, I don't believe so. It will be hard enough for him to endure these. He should tell no one when he is leaving; and when he does sail, he should make for open sea as fast as possible. His ship, the *Revenge,* is said to be a fast vessel, fast enough to elude larger ships."

"Very good. I shall leave at once."

When Carmichael had stepped out of the office, Deane stared after him, scratching his head and muttering to himself.

Edward interrupted, "Don't you think Captain Cunningham will be able to escape?"

"No, Edward, I don't," Deane sighed. "I mean—no, I don't know what I mean. I hope he can; I think he can. But I can't help wondering if he's not too pigheaded. He and that crew of his hate the English so much that I doubt if they will be able to resist making just one raid on their way out of the channel. Cunningham is angry with us, too—he feels we didn't do enough here to keep him at sea and out of prison."

"I can't blame him for feeling angry about that. I've been in a prison myself."

"Yes, I'd forgotten that. His prison experience in France has been much pleasanter than it would have been in England. From the stories that I've heard, there's no bar on the door, and all he must do is promise to return to his cell at sunset every day. Well, enough of Cunningham. I must finish the work I have to do before I go to Passy to see Dr. Franklin."

"Is he suffering from gout again?"

"Yes—his gout has returned. I don't know how much he really suffers from it. He never complains to me about it; whenever he can't move, he's always surrounded by a crowd of pretty women."

"I have seen several of those attentive ladies," Edward recalled with a smile. "They are lovely enough to turn young Carmichael's head."

"Several of them have," Deane chortled, his eyes lighting up. "Poor Carmichael cannot understand how they can prefer Franklin to him."

He reached out and picked up a thick bundle of papers from his desk.

"These are the latest reports from our agents," he said. "While I write a report to the Congress, Edward, I wonder if you would be kind enough to make a listing for me. All I want is the name of each prize captured, her type, and her principal cargo, not everything on these manifests."

"I'll be glad to do it," Edward replied. He rose, and taking the papers from Deane sat down at his desk to make the list.

He was still writing when Deane glanced at his watch.

"Thunderation! I shall be late again! I meant to ask you, Edward: do you suppose you could find another good investment for some capital of mine? It seems a pity to let it remain idle."

"I don't know, Mr. Deane. I'd be glad to send it off for you. Perhaps my partner can put it to work."

"Fine. I should appreciate that. I've invested quite an amount in that new ship of Cunningham's—Robert Morris and I bought it together. I would like to hedge a bit with other investments."

Deane placed several bills of exchange on Edward's desk, thanked him again, and left the office.

Before Edward had finished copying the list of prizes, Arthur Lee walked into the room. Edward acknowledged Lee's curt nod and continued writing, although he was fully conscious of Lee's curious and constant stare. Suddenly the Virginian gave a loud sigh and walked toward the window near Edward's desk.

Passing behind Edward, his eyes scanned the papers zealously, but he said nothing and soon returned to his desk.

When Edward had finished the list, he leaned back in his chair and studied it carefully. There would be no chance to put the duplicate he had made into his pocket as long as Lee was in the office. He decided to wait at his desk for Lee to leave.

Out of the corner of his eye, he noticed that the Virginian had placed several papers on his desk to which he was giving only fragmentary attention. His hand wandered from time to time toward the bulky, calf-bound dictionary on his desk; but each time, he glanced toward Edward and bent over his papers again. Edward watched this curious behavior for almost an hour before Lee finally rose and, without a word to him, left the office.

Leaning back and looking out the window, Edward watched Lee until he disappeared from view. He swiftly put his copy of the prize list in his pocket. Opening the lockbox, he placed the first copy securely inside, then the original prize list on top. As a precaution, he looked out of the window again before walking swiftly toward Lee's desk. Opening the dictionary, he rifled through the pages, but discovered nothing inside. Again he opened the bulky volume, but this time slowly, carefully, so that the pages separated naturally, to the point of most frequent reference.

He glanced at the page—the words ranged from *sure* through *surrender*. For some time he puzzled over the page, trying to find on it a word of special meaning or importance to Lee.

After stopping for lunch at a nearby cafe, he hurried to Paul Wentworth's house. It was late afternoon when Sylvestre opened the door to admit him.

"This is the newest list of prizes," he said to Paul. "I had some trouble getting it out of the office. Lee was there, determined to discover what I was doing. He stayed for nearly two hours, most of which time he spent watching me. When he finally left, in some hurry, I was able to put this in my pocket."

"Mr. Lee is becoming rather a nuisance, isn't he? If I were you, Edward, I would consider how I might rid myself of that man as quickly as possible."

"I do, constantly, but every time I think I have a solution, I find something wrong with it."

"Perhaps that's because you plan to take care of him yourself. If I may say so, that is foolish and reckless, too. There are many people in Paris who make their living at such things. You should hire one of them."

"The only reason I haven't done so is because I can't risk exposure, through some accident. If I hired a man to kill him or merely to injure him, I have a feeling Lee might be fortunate enough to stumble his way out of the trap. An exposure of that sort would ruin me."

"Nonsense, Edward. Many in Paris have used these people and never been suspected of complicity."

"That's a risk I don't care to chance. Something must be done about Lee, it's true. He appears to be more suspicious every day. If he could find any proof, I think he'd strike at once. That must be why he has done nothing thus far—he doesn't dare say anything he can't prove."

"You must remember that I am concerned in this problem also, Edward. If Lee should manage to trap you, I should lose a most important source of information."

Edward shrugged and was about to reply when Sylvestre entered the room. The servant walked quickly to Paul's side. Leaning down, he whispered something in his ear. Wentworth looked up at Edward with sudden alarm.

"You were not too careful coming here today, Edward," he said. "Sylvestre tells me that there has been a man watching this house since you first arrived. He believes he was in the garden once, listening to us; but when Sylvestre looked out, the man was back in the street. Come upstairs with me."

When they had reached a window in one of the rooms upstairs, they cautiously looked below. Edward gasped when he saw the man who was pacing back and forth across the street.

"You know him?" Paul asked.

"I'm not certain, but I think that's the same fellow I saw outside my house one night. He looks about the right size, though I didn't get too clear a view of him then."

They went back downstairs. Wentworth's expression was brooding and preoccupied. Finally, he called in Sylvestre.

"Dr. Bancroft will stay for supper, Sylvestre. Keep an eye on that man outside. If he is still there when it is dark, fetch my coach. Be careful that only Thomas comes with you. He knows how to drive and what to do in an emergency like this. Is that clear?"

"Yes, Mr. Wentworth," Sylvestre answered, nodding. "You want him here first?"

"Yes."

A few hours later, when they had finished supper, Edward and Paul were playing chess together when the noise of a coach rolling along the street outside was followed by a sudden cry. Strangely muffled, the sound drove all thought of the game out of Edward's mind. When he started to rise to find out what it was, Paul stretched out his arm and gently pushed him back into his chair.

"Patience, Edward, patience. Your move, I believe."

Edward moved his bishop without thought. Paul chuckled as he saw the piece moved into jeopardy.

"I fear your mind is not on the game, Edward. This is most unfair."

Paul reached out, and with a deft motion swept Edward's bishop off the board. A slow smile spread over his face.

"What was that noise, Paul?" Edward demanded. "You weren't at all surprised by it."

"No, I wasn't. Now please be patient, Edward. Let us finish our game first. There will be time to discuss the noise later."

They had not made more than two moves when the door opened and Sylvestre looked in toward Paul. Seeing the servant nod, Paul rose to his feet and motioned Edward to follow him.

"Was there any difficulty?" Paul asked Sylvestre.

"No, sir. Thomas caught him next to the wall, sir. I only had to open the door of the coach to pull him in. One jab was all it took. We hardly stopped."

"Fine. Well done. I don't like this to happen right here, but we had no choice."

Both men followed Sylvestre to the kitchen, where in in one corner lay the body of the man who had been watching the house. Sylvestre placed a burlap sack beneath it so the blood would not stain the shining floor.

Paul knelt beside the body and went through each pocket, feeling in the jacket and shirt for anything that might be hidden there. Sylvestre took off the man's boots and inspected them carefully. When they had finished, Paul held a small pile of papers in his hand.

"Put him back in the coach," he told his servant. "Thomas knows what to do."

"Yes, sir."

A careful study of the papers revealed very little at first. They were pieces which had been torn from journals, concerned mostly with the opinions of one of the popular writers of the day. Midway in the pile, however, Paul drew in his breath suddenly. Over his shoulder, Edward read:

> The bearer of this paper, Mr. Rush, will be allowed to come to my rooms at the Hotel de' Riome at any hour. Arthur Lee

"That's what we needed," Paul said with satisfaction, looking up into Edward's eyes. "Now, Edward, you see why you can't delay much longer. If you do, Lee will trap you. This man was working for him; he may have others as well."

Edward nodded. Walking over to the window, he stared out into the empty street. The brutal efficiency of Paul's methods had startled him. Death was not the same, here in Paris, as it had been aboard the *Reprisal*. It was a cold, brutal fact, without glory or excitement, as cruel and as simple as crushing a man against a wall with a coach, then stabbing him as he lay at one's feet, helpless and in agony.

"Before you go, Edward, tell me about your trip. I haven't seen you since you returned. I understand that you arrived at Havre trailing a prize behind you."

The unexpected change of topic took Edward by surprise. His mind had been on Rush, and for a moment he stared perplexedly at Paul before he could recover himself sufficiently to answer.

"How did you hear about that? It was only a few days ago."

"I have friends all over France," Paul answered with a smile, "as I thought you realized. They also informed me that you boarded the *Reprisal* at Nantes. How did you enjoy the voyage?"

"The change of air was good for me. Wickes was very pleasant company."

"I'm delighted to hear it. What did you learn of interest to us? What will Wickes's next port be? How long does he plan to remain at Havre? What route did he follow from Nantes?"

"Those are all rather technical questions, Paul, which I can't answer. I know nothing about ships. I was only a visitor aboard the *Reprisal*. Wickes told me nothing about the route we were following. To me, it was merely ocean—and a great deal of it."

"Can you draw me a plan of the *Reprisal*? What about the cannon that are said to shift position during a fight? Surely you can answer that, Edward."

"Yes, I can, Paul. I watched the battles and the gun drills as well. But I'm not going to give you that information—yet."

"Not going to? What on earth do you mean?"

Paul wavered between astonishment and anger. The quill he was holding slipped from his fingers. He rose from the desk.

"Do you remember the last conversation I had with you, Paul?" Edward asked. "It was just after Stormont had made that monumental blunder of publishing the prize list in the court circular. We agreed then there was to be an increase in my salary, an increase which Eden and I had previously discussed, but which had never been made."

"Yes, I remember that, Edward. But I don't see how that—"

"That increase has not come," Edward interrupted brusquely. "There has been no evidence that it will come. I told you then that I was tired of working for a pittance. I say it again. If you want to find out this information about the *Reprisal*, you will have to pay for it. I want that money, and I want it before I say anything about the *Reprisal* or my voyage."

Paul's anger had changed to irritation.

He paced up and down the small room, his hands tightly clasped behind his back. When he stopped, finally, in front of Edward, his face was rigid and his voice curiously soft.

"I have not advised you, Edward, on anything you wanted to do here in Paris. I shall advise you, at least slightly, on this matter. We all work for money in this business, but I had supposed that all of us were wise enough to know that it takes time for a person like Eden to implement his promises. He's extremely busy, and if he has not had the opportunity to send your money, it is not because he has forgotten it or because he wishes to ignore it. Finally, I deplore such an attitude on your part."

"The point is that nothing has been done about my salary," Edward stated flatly. "I don't care how good Eden's intentions may be. He has not kept his promise, and I feel relieved of all responsibility for furnishing further information until that promise is kept. I want at least a demonstration of good faith, a sign that the promise will be kept."

"Very well. Suppose I pay you half of the thousand pounds Eden promised? I will write to him and have him send you the remaining half. Would that satisfy you?"

"Yes, it would. At least it would be a sign that the promise was still good. It's not that I don't trust you, Paul—you know that—or Eden, for that matter.

But I know quite well how much and how rapidly political power can shift, and I don't feel that a promise made by Eden—who is subject to the whims of the court—can be counted upon indefinitely. He might be replaced tomorrow by someone who had never heard of the promise and who would refuse to honor it."

"I must admit you have a sound argument. Eden, however, is in a different position from most of those in public office. He has held his office for so long that I doubt if they could find another man to do his work. If the arrangement I have suggested is satisfactory to you, Edward, I suggest that you return tomorrow for the five hundred pounds."

As Edward neared the Hotel d'Hambourg the next morning, he heard shouts and cries from people walking ahead of him. They moved close to the walls to allow a long line of wagons to pass down the street.

The wagons were crammed with people, massed together as tight as powder in a musket. As he stared at them, he realized that this was the day when convicts were transported from Paris to the ports, on their way to exile in the Colonies. There they would be worked like cattle, beaten, starved, and mistreated until they died or outlasted the system. Dressed in rags of all kinds and colors, those on the wagon train epitomized the most abject human misery. The prisoners were filthy, their faces black and their hair matted. Their hands and nails were ceaselessly busy picking and plucking at the lice which spotted them.

Edward shuddered as the wagons continued to rumble past, the clatter of the wheels joining with the rattling of the chains which secured each prisoner. As the wagons moved over the uneven street, the mass of prisoners swayed back and forth like one man. Save for a long beard here or white hair there or a singularly evil countenance, there was no individuality among them— they had been beaten witless, and most of them stared without expression at those they passed on the street. Some of them had retained their speech, or enough of it to beg for bread or alms.

"Alms, gentleman," one man cried to him, a lout of a fellow with scabs that twisted the skin of his face.

Edward turned aside in sudden disgust. The man in the wagon laughed in a high, crackling voice and called to him shrilly, "What is it, gentleman? Am I too dirty? Do I stink too high? A pity I offend you."

The convict's voice rose in a screech which seemed all the more frightful, so unexpected was it in that giant's body.

"Maybe you ought to be here with me, you with the pretty lace and the fine wig!"

A guard came running up. Seeing the man's hand outstretched, he gave it a fierce blow with the club he was carrying. The man shrieked and swayed back against his fellows, blubbering with pain.

"Keep your hand inside, you scum!" the guard shouted at him. "Next time I'll put a bayonet in it."

The injured man looked down at him, his face twisting with pain and hate. Very deliberately, he spat straight into the guard's face.

Wiping his face with his hand, the guard stared for a moment after the wagon as it moved slowly down the street.

Suddenly he smiled and pulled a bayonet from his belt.

He ran toward the lumbering wagon. The wounded convict tried vainly to press himself inside the mass of prisoners, straining at the chains which bound him in place.

Edward saw the sunlight glint on the moving blade as the guard caught up with the wagon. A high scream sounded along the street, and the man crumpled, one hand clutching at his injured arm while blood spurted to the cobblestones below. The guard laughed. After wiping the blade on his boot, he ran forward to inspect the other wagons.

Edward walked slowly on to the office, the scene burned in his mind. All morning long he continued to see the agony on the face of the wounded man and to hear above the noises of the city that terrible scream. He could not keep his mind on what he was doing. Whenever Deane spoke to him, he answered slowly, as though he had difficulty understanding what was being said to him.

He went to the Tuileries after lunch, hoping that in the fragrant gardens he might rid his mind of the nightmare of the convicts. He sat there nearly all afternoon, watching a group of children playing not too far from the bench on which he sat. One of the smallest children suddenly ran from the group and came up to him. Edward noticed that he was shivering slightly, in spite of the hot day; two lanes of tears had made their way through the dirt on his cheeks.

"Please sir, will you help me?" the little boy asked. "I found a bottle in a tree, and the other boys have taken it away."

Edward rose quickly to his feet. "Certainly," he said. The bottle had been found, as he knew someday it would be, but fortunately by these children who could do him no harm.

He walked over to the circle of children. The two largest boys were circling round each other like gamecocks. Apparently the larger of them, a boy about twelve years old, had gained possession of the bottle; there was a large bulge in the front of his tattered shirt. The other boy, a trifle shorter, but heavier and angrier from the look on his face, was circling round and round, rising from time to time on his toes and lunging at the other with a clawing hand.

Edward broke through the watching circle which had fallen silent at his approach. He walked up to the larger boy.

"There's no sense in fighting over a bottle," he said with a laugh. "Suppose you tell me what it's worth to you. I'll pay you, and then you'll have no need to fight."

The older boy glared at him, suspicious of his generosity, but glad of the chance to rest.

"Two francs for me, one for him," the boy answered, pointing at his puffing opponent, who only nodded, puzzled by this unexpected generosity.

"Let me have the bottle," Edward demanded.

"Oh, no. The francs first, Monsieur."

"Very well." Edward reached in his pocket and pulled out several coins.

The boy reached inside his shirt and placed the bottle in Edward's hand. Edward did not bother to conceal his relief. It was not his bottle, after all. This one was small and thin, a cordial bottle of dark green glass which kept its look of coolness even with the sun shining on it. As he sat down on the bench again, he peered into it and saw that it was empty. The little boy who had first spoken to him was standing before him, mute entreaty on his face. Edward handed him the bottle with a sudden smile.

"There it is, my boy. Don't let them take it away from you again."

"No, Monsieur. Thank you. They'll never see where I put it. I'll hide it under my shirt until I leave the gardens."

"That would be a good idea. There'll be less chance of your losing it. Where did you find it?"

"In that tree over there, the one with the birdhouse. It was inside the birdhouse. I was looking for a nest."

When the little boy had left, his hands carefully folded over the bulge in his shirt that marked the bottle, Edward leaned back and relaxed. He dozed as the sun beat down upon him, but woke just in time to catch himself from slipping off the bench. The gardens were quiet; the children had gone.

He shifted his position and was about to close his eyes again when he saw a man approaching. The stranger seemed another casual visitor to the gardens until Edward noticed that he kept turning his head slightly, as if he were scrutinizing the trees and the shrubs for someone who might be hiding there. Heading into the sun, he was walking down a path that would take him fifty yards or more in front of Edward. It was not until he had come almost directly in front of him that Edward recognized the man as Arthur Lee. He was in drab clothes, as usual; his wig was slightly askew on his head.

Edward was partially shielded from Lee's view by a row of trees that stretched along the path in front of his bench. Edward slid down on the bench to get a better view and to conceal himself from Lee's scrutiny.

Lee kept shaking his head angrily, as if he wanted to get the glare of the sun out of his eyes.

Edward could almost feel Lee's glance slide over him, stop, and then move away. After what he considered a reasonable interval, he looked out again and saw that Lee had apparently judged him harmless, for he was now hurrying across the grass toward the tree that held the birdhouse.

Edward saw a white blur as Lee pulled something from his pocket. The Virginian stretched up on his toes and felt inside the little house. He sank back on the soles of his feet and peered around suspiciously.

Again he stretched up, felt around desperately, and finally, stuffed the paper inside the little house.

As soon as Lee was out of sight, Edward walked over to the birdhouse. Reaching up, he extracted the paper. He read it quickly, then put it into his pocket. Within minutes he had made his way out of the gardens and was approaching Paul's house.

"Good afternoon, Sylvestre," Edward greeted the grave-faced servant. "Paris seems to agree with you. You look younger every time I see you."

The Negro's face changed from grave to pleased with a single slash of his white teeth.

"Thank you, Dr. Bancroft. I do love Paris, it's true."

When Sylvestre disappeared to fetch the wine his master had ordered, Paul turned to Edward with a smile. Edward was somewhat relieved at the smile, for he had not known whether he had overplayed his hand during the previous evening.

"I've been eager to tell you, Edward, that I've found a clue to the cipher among Rush's papers last night. It's no more than a clue, but at least it's something to work on. Here."

Paul handed Edward a scrap of paper. "Bancroft—" it read, "808."

"Does that mean anything to you, Edward?"

Edward studied the paper for a moment and suddenly looked up at Paul, his eyes shining.

"Yes," Edward cried jubilantly. "I think I can break the cipher now! Where is a dictionary?"

Paul rose, puzzled, and pulled down a heavy book from the shelf behind him. Edward opened it quickly and turned to page 808. He stopped in dismay, staring down at words which all began with *r*.

"Oh, of course not," he cried. "This is the wrong dictionary. I don't want Dr. Johnson's. I need Bailey's, in the octavo size."

"I'll send Sylvestre out for it."

"Good. Tell him to go to Durand's, on the Rue St. Jacques. They should have a copy; they have a great many books printed in English."

While they were waiting for Sylvestre to return, Paul handed Edward a sheaf of bank notes. "This is what I promised you last night. The other half will be here, I'm certain, as soon as Eden receives my letter."

"Thank you, Paul. I hope I did not offend you with my frankness last night?"

"To be truthful, Edward, you did a bit. I must say you seem to have acquired an unnatural regard for money. I don't mean that to sound so blunt, but I am perplexed. You never felt this way before. When you were working for me in Surinam, I sometimes had difficulty understanding how your expenses could be so low."

"It isn't miserliness, Paul. Nor is it 'an unnatural regard for money,' as you say. I'm merely determined that I shall be paid for the risks I take."

"But we pay you well, Edward. I don't understand why—"

"Don't try, Paul. I'm sorry if my demands for money have offended you, but that is how I feel."

"Very well. I shall say no more about it. I think I shall find those ciphered messages before Sylvestre returns. If you'll excuse me, I'll be back in a moment."

When Sylvestre returned, carrying the dictionary under his arm, both men breathed a sigh of relief. They sat down and carefully examined the first cipher note, which still seemed to both of them like a jumble of numbers. Suddenly Edward nodded with satisfaction when he noted the numbers 808 early in the text:

474171—808191 131281 647112 486042 839222 599041 573061
858211 0 599041 364191 395262 330191 405211 636132 346241
505182 715012.

While Paul read the note again and again, searching for a further clue, Edward leafed through the dictionary and periodically jotted down a word; his quill made a loud scratching that emphasized the silent concentration in the room.

At last he put down the quill and the dictionary and handed a piece of paper to Wentworth on which he'd written:

"Lee—Surgeon carried prize lists to Paul on Tuesday. Paul gave him 500 pounds from Mansfield. Rush"

Paul whistled as he read the message.

"How did you arrive at this, Edward? I still don't see what the cipher is."

"It's quite simple, but it's unbreakable as long as you don't know the source of this code. I knew it in a moment, though completely by accident, after you showed me that note you found in Rush's pocket. The number of it was familiar to me—it was the page number I had noticed in Lee's dictionary."

Edward explained Lee's curious actions in the office the previous morning.

"All the code consists of is putting down the page number of the word in the message."

"What about these other numbers?"

"The next two numbers are the number of lines down the page where the particular word lies. If there should be less than ten words, then a cipher is added, as in this fourth group."

Edward's finger pointed to the 486042.

"The final numbers, you will notice, are always alike, either 1 or 2. They signify which column the word appears in, 1 for the left, 2 for the right."

"It's unbelievably simple, isn't it," Paul said, somewhat in disgust. "When I think of the hours I've spent trying to break this code, I grow a little angry with myself."

"They chose an excellent system. No one, as I said, could possibly break this unless they found out about the dictionary. Where's the other message?"

Paul handed it to him. Edward smiled as he saw certain numbers repeated in it. In a few minutes he had worked it out and handed the result to Paul:

"Rush—I need better proof. Must have document to reveal surgeon's treachery. Fifty pounds if you bring it, fifty more when he is disgraced. Lee"

"Oh, I almost forgot," Edward said when Paul looked up from the second message. "I found Mr. Lee's hiding place in the Tuileries today. Apparently Rush knew about our bottle in the plane tree. He selected a hiding place of his own not fifty yards away. He probably wanted to copy down any messages he might find in the plane tree and leave them for Lee. Lee left this paper there this afternoon."

After Edward had decoded the newest message, he stared at it for a moment, then handed it to Paul. Paul read,

"Rush—Why didn't you keep your appointment last night? Come tonight without fail. Lee"

"I'm afraid Mr. Lee will have a long time to wait," Edward chuckled.

"Perhaps I was too hasty in thinking that Lee was ready to trap you," Paul mused. "From these messages, he doesn't seem to have any evidence against you. Now that he has lost Rush, I suspect that his task will be doubly difficult. Rush must have been a good man. He not only overheard conversations outside that window, but he was an excellent tracker as well. You only noticed him once, and he had probably followed you about for several months.

"I think you would be well advised, Edward, not to do anything at present about Lee. Let him commit himself first. You know the man well enough to be able to sense real danger in his attitude. If that time ever comes, remember this name and address: Madame Hartouque, Cafe Dijon, below the Hotel de Riome. Mention my name. For money, she will arrange any skulduggery."

"I'll remember her," Edward assured him. Then, musing, he added, "I wonder how Lee will act when Rush continues to not keep his appointment. He will automatically suspect me. Perhaps he may show his hand."

CHAPTER XVI

THROUGH THE SUMMER AND into the fall of 1777, Edward had little time to consider the problem of Arthur Lee.

When he was not on a mission to London, he was riding toward Passy to visit Franklin or snatching an afternoon to drive through the countryside with Ellen.

The few times he had been with Lee, he had noticed that the Virginian seemed strangely quiet since the disappearance of Mr. Rush. This had lulled Edward into relaxed compliance. He decided to let matters rest unless the Virginian should make action imperative.

One afternoon in November, after Carmichael had left the office, Silas Deane looked into the outer office to be certain that no one was there. He closed the door and sat down beside Edward's desk.

"Perhaps I should not tell you this, Edward, but I feel I must. You have been most kind and helpful to me ever since you arrived here; I cannot stand by and say nothing."

Edward turned in his chair to face Deane. His forehead was furrowed in puzzlement, and he studied Deane intently.

"Lee has spoken to Dr. Franklin about you," Deane continued. "I knew that the man would cause trouble; he's been altogether too quiet these last few months. He told Franklin that you were a spy for the British and that he had papers of some sort which would prove this claim. He insisted that Franklin summon you to Passy where Lee would bring the proof and, as he said, confront you with your treachery."

As Deane paused, Edward rose and paced silently about the room. He noticed that Deane had not moved from his chair or even glanced at him after making his startling declaration. Deane took out his kerchief and patted his cheeks with it, as if the room had suddenly turned oppressively warm. Edward walked back and stood before Deane, his arms folded across his chest, his mouth a thin line across his face.

"I appreciate your telling me this, Mr. Deane. I hope you will understand when I tell you that what you have said makes me want to walk out of this office and never return."

Deane nodded emphatically.

"That's what I told Franklin," he said with sudden fury. "I warned him this would happen. I said he should never listen to Lee, that Lee would cause us all manner of grief and trouble before we were finally rid of him. I don't blame you for feeling as you do, Edward. I would feel the same way if I were in your place. When a man has worked as hard and as faithfully for us as you have, a ridiculous accusation like this is monstrous."

Edward said nothing for several minutes; he strode up and down the room again, conscious of Deane's eyes following him. Suddenly, he paused and took his wallet from his coat. Taking out some bills, he placed them carefully on the desk beside Deane. Then he began taking papers from the various drawers of his desk. Deane looked from the money to the papers in bewilderment.

"What's this for?" he asked.

"When you paid me my salary last June, it included the month of December. Since I shall not be here any longer, it is only fair that I return that amount to you."

Deane's dismay deepened. He drew his hand back from the money with a jerk.

"I wish you'd stop a moment, Edward, and consider. If you leave now, you will be playing into Lee's hands. We don't believe him—Franklin and I. We know what he claims is nonsense. But if you go away suddenly like this, he can claim you were afraid to face him."

"Let him claim what he likes. I am not concerned by Mr. Lee's opinion."

"Do you want to give him the satisfaction of being able to boast about his cleverness? Do you want him to tell people that he was right and we were wrong?"

"No," Edward said bluntly, "I don't want that." He sat at his desk. "Very well, I shall stay and upset Mr. Lee's little scheme. I wonder what this proof is that he speaks about."

"I don't know. He told me yesterday that Franklin had agreed to call you to Passy next Monday. He intimated that he would confront you then with the papers I mentioned before."

"I see. What does Dr. Franklin propose to do when I refute these idiotic charges?"

"Lee was sent here by order of the Continental Congress, so there's no way we can rid ourselves of him without their approval. I believe Franklin's idea is the same as mine—we will find some unimportant mission for Lee which will take him far from Paris. Then, we shall arrange to have him recalled to America."

Edward spent the afternoon alone in his house, planning the action he should take against Arthur Lee.

The morning's conversation with Deane, although it had clearly revealed how Deane and Franklin felt toward him, had, nevertheless, shown him that it was important to act before the week was out, before the meeting at Passy. He must discover what papers Lee had obtained and, if necessary, destroy them. He still could not believe that Lee really possessed any evidence which could be used against him; he had always been scrupulously careful with the papers he had handled.

"Something is troubling you, Edward," Ellen said to him after they had finished supper that night. "Is it anything I can help you with, darling?"

"No, thank you, Ellen. I'm sorry to seem so depressed. It's Lee again. He's trying to lay a trap for me, and I can't imagine what it is. That's why I probably look a little haggard. I've been thinking about it all afternoon."

"Couldn't I help you?" Ellen asked with sudden excitement. "Surely there's something I could do."

"No, that's not a good idea," he replied brusquely. "I don't want you to have anything to do with Lee. He's a bad-mannered bore; but more than that, he doesn't like women."

"Be reasonable, Edward. If he means to do you harm, why shouldn't we find out anything we can—both of us? You should remember, darling, that women are rather clever at extracting information. Suppose I arrange to meet your Mr. Lee at one of the salons, or perhaps, accidentally encounter him at the theater. Isn't it possible that I might discover, through some inadvertent remark of his, exactly what you want to know?"

"You may be right," Edward admitted. "You might be able to find out something. Whatever it is that he's planning, I must know about it before the week is over. Do you think you will have time enough?"

"I'm certain of it," Ellen replied. "I shall see Mme. de Treymes in the morning. If she is willing to help me, I'll find out what you want to know before the end of the week."

After Edward left for the Hotel d'Hambourg the next morning, Ellen drove to Mme. de Treymes's house. The old lady was just rising when Ellen was shown to her room.

"Good morning, my dear," Madame grunted. "Sit down and have some coffee. I'm too old to apologize for the way I look at this hour; besides, it doesn't make any difference to me. You look quite beautiful, considering the hour of day. How is Dr. Bancroft?"

"He's fine, thank you."

"Has he told you anymore about his adventures at sea? Or murmured the names of wenches in his sleep?"

"Not so far," Ellen laughed.

"What brings you here so early?"

"I need your advice. You once told me that if ever I needed advice—"

"I remember," Madame interrupted with a chuckle. "I hope it's a boy. Have it, by all means. That's it, isn't it?"

"No, that's not it," Ellen replied with a sudden, bitter smile. "Something much less exciting than that: I have to obtain some information for Edward. I wanted your advice on how I should go about it."

Madame studied her for a moment, then reached across the table and pressed her hand.

"I'm sorry if I hurt you, my dear," she sighed. "I should not have said that."

She withdrew her hand. "Information, eh?" she asked. "Yes, perhaps I can help you with that. I've been obtaining information of one sort or another for as long as I can remember. Usually it was concerned with the fickleness of men, especially husbands. What information is it, and when must you obtain it?"

"There is a man in Paris who hates Edward and who is determined to ruin him. Edward has heard that this man intends to act against him next week. He wants me to find out what he plans to do."

"Next week? That does not give us much time. Unless you know the man well, I would say it is not nearly enough time. What have you thought of doing?"

"I don't really know. That's why I wanted to talk with you. I think he's too dull to be seduced, so I was wondering if there might not be another way."

Mme. de Treymes rocked in her chair with laughter.

"My dear Ellen," she smiled, wiping her eyes, "what an ingenuous creature you are. However dull this man may seem to you, you must remember that that is not the way he appears to himself. You might as well reconcile yourself to paying for this information in some fashion. None that is worth the hearing ever comes free."

"I wish he weren't so dreadful a man."

"How well do you know him?"

"I have met him several times, but I rarely exchanged more than a few words with him."

"Do I know him?"

"Yes, Madame. His name is Arthur Lee. He is a Virginian."

"Arthur Lee—oh, yes, I think I remember him. Therese!"

The door opened swiftly and Therese bustled in.

"Therese, do I know a M. Lee, from Virginia?"

"Yes, Madame." Therese stiffened noticeably. "He was here some time ago, at one of Madame's soirees."

"Describe him, Therese. I do not place him."

"Of medium height, Madame. Brown hair straggling out beneath an ill fitting wig. Breeches of a most beautiful green velvet, but abominably cut. An unbecoming thickness of accent. He became rather noisy, Madame; he disputed with certain of the other guests."

"That gives me a fair idea of the man, Therese. I take it you did not like Mr. Lee?"

"No, Madame. He had money—or so I gathered from that green velvet— but no manners, Madame. Once, when I was passing by, he held his glass toward me and called out, 'My good woman' as if I were a common serving wench. Rather than look at him, I bowed to M. le Comte de Varennes and walked on."

"Quite right, too," Madame said, nodding. "Very well, Therese, that is what I wanted to know."

After Therese left to resume her duties, Madame's face wrinkled with mirth.

"A harsh summary, wasn't it?," she said. "Not undeserved, I am sure. What a pity such a man as that should have the information when there are so many attractive men in Paris. Suppose I invited him here again? I'm giving a soiree on Friday. There will be just a small group here for supper and a little music. Would he accept?"

"If you made it appear a very special invitation, I know he would," Ellen replied. "He's rather a recluse, I understand, but he has a weakness for gatherings of prominent people. I believe that in his province the name of Lee is considered important."

"He is becoming a familiar type to me, the more you tell me. You will come alone, of course?"

"Yes. It will be difficult enough for me to approach him. It would be impossible if Edward were here."

"You're quite right. Whatever your plan may be, Edward must not be here. His absence would make the evening much easier for you."

"Lee knows of my relationship with Edward, I am quite sure. I plan to disarm him by admitting it before he can question me about it."

"That is as much as you need tell me. No man can resist a pretty woman who confides to him that she is bored with another man."

"I hope you're right. I feel I must obtain this information; I am certain that Edward is in greater danger than he has admitted to me."

"Dr. Bancroft has my complete admiration," Madame sighed. "I have never known a man quite like him. He has lived so many lives in his few years. Now you come to intrigue me further with this talk of imminent peril."

Ellen rose and, moving to Madame's chair, bent down and kissed her lightly on the cheek.

"I must return home. I am most grateful for your help."

"Rubbish, child. It's little enough that I've done; not nearly so much as I would like to do. Come at eight, will you? The others will come later, but perhaps we should plan a little before your Mr. Lee arrives."

"I shall be here. Thank you again."

"Say no more about it," Madame called after her. "There's enough adventure in it to fascinate me, as you knew there would be. Just don't worry about it—you'll spoil your face."

On the night of the soiree, Edward seemed preoccupied, even nervous during their early supper. Ellen had not realized how much he was counting upon her success tonight, until just before she left shortly before eight. He had kissed her and, with an effort that was painfully obvious, jokingly wished her good fortune.

When she arrived at Mme. de Treymes's, she hurried upstairs and knocked at Madame's door.

"Come in."

Madame was seated at her dressing table.

Behind her, Therese was busily arranging the calash on her mistress's head.

"Madame, please! Please!" Therese pleaded. "I cannot complete the coiffure if you insist on swinging your head about. Just another moment of quiet, Madame, and then all will be ready. Now, please."

"All right, Therese, but hurry. Heavens! You take so much time, I'll never be downstairs. Good evening, Ellen. You're late, my dear. Did you have difficulty leaving Dr. Bancroft?"

"No, none at all. I told him about our plans this morning, and he thoroughly approves."

"He should," Madame answered tartly. "It's all being done for his benefit. Therese! Aren't you finished yet?"

"Madame, Madame, please!" Therese cried desperately. "Remember what the doctor said: no excitement, Madame. No temper, no tantrums, Madame; otherwise you must remain in bed."

"Bah!" Madame exploded. "Don't you dare threaten me with what that silly man said. He has no more idea of the state of my health than my footman. He shouts at me, too, as if he were addressing someone who was passing beyond his ministrations."

Therese shuddered violently at Madame's remark and her eyes filled with tears. The top of the calash swayed perilously, coming to rest at an absurd angle.

When Madame saw this in her mirror, she pushed herself to her feet with an angry exclamation.

"Therese, you're a simpleminded, emotional fool. All one has to do is mention death, and you start slobbering like a peasant. Now, get out and try to come to your senses. When you've stopped your blubbering, you may return. Shoo! Shoo!"

Madame swept across the room, her calash rocking back and forth. She pushed Therese out the door, slammed it shut, and seated herself angrily at her dressing table.

"Such a trial!" she cried to Ellen. "Superstitious, ignorant peasant. I can't bear Therese when she's dripping all over herself like that. Will you help me, my dear?"

"Certainly," Ellen replied, straightening the calash as carefully as she could. "Hold still a moment, and I'll fasten it in place."

She pinned the swaying edifice securely, and stood back to observe the effect.

"Which would you prefer on top, the diamonds or the birds?"

"This is only a small party, so there'll be fewer thieves about. The diamonds, I think."

Madame reached out and picked up a chain of diamonds.

She handed them to Ellen, who began winding the jewels around the calash.

"How can there be so many thieves in Paris, Madame? I can't understand how they can slip into any house and take what they want without someone stopping them."

"House thieves aren't as bad as highwaymen, my dear," Madame snorted. "At least the thieves in one's house usually come unarmed, but those ruffians who hold up coaches and assault pedestrians are monstrous creatures. Several of my friends have lost all their jewels to the rascals. As to why there are so many house thieves, I should imagine it's simply because there's more to steal in Paris."

"How do they manage to get into the finest houses?"

"Many of our thieves come from the finest families, child," Madame laughed. "Men who have been ruined by gambling find stealing an easy method of paying their debts. They are really quite charming, some of them. A friend of mine was foolish enough to go out with one of them for a breath of air during a masquerade, and she was fortunate to lose no more than her jewels."

"Has anyone ever been robbed here?"

"No, my dear, not yet. At least I have not been informed of it. I have always thought there must have been one or two women robbed here; but their husbands were present, and, rather than reveal their indiscretion, they allowed the charming thief to go free."

"What would happen if they should see him again, at another house?"

"Nothing. They might remove their jewels before trusting themselves in the garden again, but that would be all."

"I don't understand them," Ellen sighed, shaking her head. "I can't imagine people being like that."

"Oh, Ellen, such nonsense!" Madame fumed. "What a silly thing for you to say! Here I hoped I had taught you something, but I seem to have failed completely. Don't you realize yet how few people are in the world who are of any use to it, except as part of the scenery?"

Madame looked into her mirror as she waited for Ellen to speak and then continued, "Look at me, my dear. I'm old and ugly and I have a sharper tongue than most. Why do you suppose intelligent people like to come to my house? Because I have more money or a bigger house or better food and wine? Not at all. They come because they know they'll be listened to with some degree of understanding and intelligence.

"The Duc de Choiseul, for instance—he comes frequently. Once he told me why. He's a crotchety, opinionated man with a certain savage cunning in his nature. He's interesting, though; he exercises his mind. I like him for that, much as I deplore his politics. He once said to me, 'Clothilde, I admire you greatly. You are the only woman in Paris who dares call me misguided and smile at me when I attempt to disprove it. Every time I come here, I look forward to an intellectual duel. When I leave, I feel a little wiser, though a great deal more tired than when I arrived.' That is why they come, Ellen. I hope they will continue to do so. Intelligent people sharpen my wits, as this encounter with Mr. Lee tonight will sharpen yours."

Madame paused to catch her breath. She had spoken longer and with more feeling than she intended. She cast anxious eyes at her towering calash and sighed with relief when she saw it still firmly centered on her head.

"At least it survived my harangue," she laughed. "I hope you have, too. As I am fond of saying, I am old and I want desperately to pass on to some young person what I have learned in my life, before it is too late."

"Don't say that, Madame. You have lots of time left."

"Ha! Indeed I don't," Madame sniffed. "I don't want lots of time. I've had enough. I shan't be at all sorry to die, though I would like to die in my own fashion."

"What do you mean?"

The corners of Madame's mouth curled upward a trifle, and her eyes sparkled suddenly.

"I should like to sponsor some revolt such as my impractical nephew is always talking about. Talk is all very well, but there must be action, too. Sometimes I dream of myself as the Jeanne d'Arc of a revolution. Usually my dream ends when I am killed by a revengeful member of the overthrown group—the court or the aristocracy or the bankers. Do you appreciate what that would mean, being killed at the moment of triumph? I would become a martyr, enshrined in a golden sepulcher, surrounded by weeping marble angels, and visited by thin pilgrims. A lovely idea, isn't it?"

"No, a terrible idea." Ellen made a little moue. "It's not like you at all. Besides, you're too fond of comfort to be a martyr."

"Nonsense. I'd make as good a martyr as anyone you've ever known. Because the comforts are here, does that mean I should not use them?"

"You were meant to use them, not go without them. In any case, you're too understanding to make a good martyr."

"You may be right. I talk too much," Madame said abruptly. "The guests will be arriving shortly and we want to be downstairs to greet them, especially Mr. Lee, although he said he would not arrive until after supper. Perhaps it is as well. You should not be forced to endure his table manners in addition to everything else."

Madame turned toward her mirror and took a last solicitous glance at her calash. All at once she made a horrible grimace and then rose with a laugh to take Ellen's arm.

"At my age, no sensible woman should care how she looks. What a waste of time it is—primping and painting and rigging a gutted ship. For what? I hate to recall how many years it has been since I deserted the lists."

Ellen was still laughing at her complaints as they descended the stairs. She pressed the old lady's hand affectionately.

"You must count the number of people tonight," she whispered, "who compliment you on your calash and then tell you how well you are looking."

"All they will really mean is what an extraordinary length of time to preserve such an ancient body," Madame finished.

Some of the guests had already arrived. When they reached the bottom of the staircase, the guests hurried over and gathered around Madame, bowing and greeting her with affection. Madame treated these first guests, Ellen noticed, as dear friends. She recognized only a few of them, and as Madame presented the others to her, she listened to their names and forgot most of them. One she did remember—Mlle. de Trouvillers, the daughter of a prominent merchant. She was a beautiful young girl whose gray silk dress Ellen coveted the moment she saw it.

As they stood talking, more and more people arrived until the entrance hall had become quite crowded. Madame moved toward the salon, and the newly arriving guests went there to greet her. Those who had come first stood about the entrance hall in small, congenial groups.

Soon all the guests who had any intention of appearing at a reasonable approximation of the designated hour had arrived. Madame walked out of the salon toward the dining room, surrounded by a circle of friends, then paused beside Ellen to gather her arm in her own and lead her on toward the dining room. A portly gentleman, with a long beard and beautiful wig, whispered something to Madame. She stopped abruptly and turned to him.

"You are the only man gallant enough to say that, Henri, so to you falls the honor of escorting Miss Vaughn. Monsieur le Comte, to you falls the more dubious honor of escorting your hostess."

Varennes stepped forward from the little group behind Madame, a wide smile on his face.

"I am honored, Madame. The last time you refused me because you said I was too fond of talking politics. Tonight I promise to discuss only music and painting."

"As the supreme authority, of course," Madame laughed as she took his arm. "Wasn't it clever of me to place M. Vernet at the far end of the table? You may enlighten me without fear of contradiction."

The gathering walked into the dining room behind Madame and Ellen and their escorts. The long, candle-lit room shimmered with reflections on the silver and the glasses—and music could be heard beneath the undulant hum of conversation. Servants formed an almost solid line around the room, each of them ready to serve behind his master's or mistress's chair.

All through the dinner, Henri Petre, who had been Ellen's escort, claimed her entire attention. He talked incessantly and somewhat pompously about taxes, for he was a man of affairs and keenly concerned by the constantly increasing expense of conducting his various enterprises.

"I fear you are speaking from behind your screen, Mr. Petre," Ellen said, smiling.

"From behind my screen? I do not understand."

"I have heard that you have a fondness for masquerading behind a screen of poverty, although you are very rich."

"That's not true at all," Petre protested. "Those who do not know the taxes I pay accuse me unjustly. I . . . "

Before the simmering Petre could finish his explanation, Mme. de Treymes had risen from the table; the other guests arose and followed her toward the salon.

The music they had heard until shortly before the end of supper began again. Hearing the unexpected strains of an old peasant dance, several of the guests smiled suddenly at each other, as people will when reminded of other, happier days. The tune seemed out of place in this gathering; in the midst of such splendor, it evoked a poignant vision of a simpler existence.

Soon after she entered the salon, Ellen noticed Arthur Lee come in and make his way toward Madame.

Ellen excused herself from her group and walked across the salon until she stood quite near Madame. She turned as if to study a cabinet of ancient and beautifully fashioned ivory statuettes, while straining to overhear the conversation between Lee and his hostess. In a moment she heard her name called; turning, she walked to Madame's side, smiling at an overtly eager Mr. Lee.

He was dressed tonight in what might have been the height of Virginia fashion, she decided, but a fashion forsaken by the shifting taste of Paris nearly a year ago. His breeches were neat and well brushed, but that was all that might be said in their favor.

They were extremely loose at the knees, so loose that they made him look as if he suffered from gout; his legs, beneath the puffs of cloth at the knees, were straight and thin as quills.

"My dear," Madame said, "I have been telling Mr. Lee how much you have wanted to meet him."

"I deem it a high compliment, Miss Vaughn," Lee added with an awkward bow. "It is not often, I must confess, that such a lovely lady desires to make an old Virginian's acquaintance."

Lee stared at her with that silly expression she had sometimes noticed in men who feel they have made a masterful reply. Although his nose was slightly tensed as if he were making an effort to smile, his lips defied the attempt—they cut across his face in a thin, hard line that did not alter.

"I am delighted to meet you, Mr. Lee," Ellen replied. "I have always regretted that we have never had an opportunity to converse. I have heard so much about you from Dr. Franklin and Mr. Deane."

A shadow of doubt darkened Lee's face; his glance became suspicious, his eyes cold and searching. A second later he relaxed, apparently deciding that Ellen was perfectly sincere and quite unaware of the hostility that existed between him and the other commissioners.

"I hope their reports were given in a friendly fashion, Miss Vaughn. Sometimes, I regret to say, their jests are not especially humorous except to themselves."

"Oh, they gave you nothing but the highest praise, Mr. Lee. Dr. Franklin said that your opinion was indispensible to him; once you had decided, he knew exactly what course to follow."

Madame left them together and walked toward the far end of the salon. There was a faint smile on her face, a smile which increased the more she thought of Ellen's last remark.

"I am surprised not to find Dr. Bancroft here tonight," Lee said after Madame had departed.

"Dr. Bancroft did not care to come tonight. He preferred to read some financial articles rather than enjoy himself. I came alone."

Ellen looked as petulant as she could, her eyes downcast and her mouth a small circle of disapproval.

Lee swallowed and began to stutter, so eager was he to make capital of this unexpected opportunity.

"Dr. Bancroft has been—that is to say, if you will forgive my boldness," Lee blurted, his eyes sweeping over Ellen. He started again. "It is singularly unwise to trust such a pretty woman to the lures of this sinful city. There's no telling what might happen to you alone, Miss Vaughn. You need a man's protection, certainly in this house, where I have already seen so many men of evil reputation."

"If you are offering yourself, Mr. Lee, that is most kind, but I don't feel that I need protection. I've always been remarkably successful in looking after myself."

"I'm certain of that, Miss Vaughn, yet I would be delighted if I could be of service to you."

"The first thing," Ellen laughed, "would be to fetch me some wine. My throat is quite dry."

"Certainly." Lee made an awkward bow, which further unsettled his wig. Nervously, he pushed it back and then crossed the room, a slight swagger in his walk. He returned in a moment and handed a glass to Ellen.

"While I was fetching the wine, Mme. de Treymes asked me to tell you that her nephew has arrived and is asking for you."

Lee sipped his wine moodily after making this announcement.

"Oh, that must be Pierre," Ellen murmured. Lee winced slightly.

"I don't wish to see him," she continued. "He's so young and much too talkative. He has just returned from Switzerland, so he fancies himself an authority on many subjects."

"He sounds quite unappealing."

"He is. He upsets me, too, the way he looks at me. Certainly I don't want to see him now, just when I'm having such a pleasant conversation."

"Couldn't we go someplace where he could not find us?" Lee suggested eagerly.

"Why, yes," Ellen replied. "There's no need to stand here waiting for him, is there? The library—we could go there. He wouldn't look for me there, I'm sure. Do you remember the entrance hall?"

Lee nodded.

"When you cross the entrance hall, you will see a little door on the right, at the far side of the staircase. Go through that, and walk down the corridor to the end, where there is another door. That opens into the library." Her voice had faded to a whisper. "I shall go first and wait there for you."

Lee nodded again, vigorously. He had lost the power of speech, and the color in his face had increased perceptibly.

Ellen saw Mme. de Treymes on the way to the entrance hall.

"It's almost too simple," she whispered a little breathlessly. "He's coming out in a moment. We're going to the library."

"Good," Madame chuckled. "Remember, my dear, these Virginians come from a warm climate."

"I shall, though he doesn't *look* strong. He's even less attractive than I thought. And he clicks his teeth!"

"My poor Ellen," Madame sighed. "Well, may you find some comfort in the thought that you make a beautiful sacrifice."

Ellen moved swiftly through the entrance hall, down the corridor she had described to Lee, and settled herself in the library. There was a fire, and that cheered her while she waited. Lee entered, casting a quick look down the corridor before he closed the door, as if he were afraid that someone was following him.

"A charming room," he said, rubbing his hands together as he stood near the fire.

"Isn't it? Someone laid a fire, too, which always makes a room so much more friendly."

"I should have brought some wine."

"That would have been nice. There are glasses there on that shelf. Do you suppose there could be some wine here, in one of those cupboards under the bookshelves?"

Lee inspected the cupboards carefully, tugging on several of the small walnut doors only to find them locked. He tugged violently at one which seemed slightly loose. The latch gave suddenly, throwing him back on his heels and almost toppling him into a small table. Recovering his balance, he cleared his throat and peered inside. With a pleased exclamation, he brought out a bottle which he studied carefully in the firelight.

"Brandy," he said, rising to his feet with a broad smile. He repeated the news, "Brandy."

Lee was obviously captivated by the seclusion and the air of conspiracy that enveloped them. Suddenly Ellen remembered Madame's warning in the hall. As Lee leaned toward her, a glass in one hand and mischief in the other, she said hurriedly, "How do you like your work in Paris, Mr. Lee? Do you find it as pleasant as you had hoped?"

Lee straightened up and sipped at his brandy.

His work was obviously the last thing he wanted to think about at this moment. He frowned.

"Pleasant? My work? No, I couldn't say that, Miss Vaughn, although why I could not must remain my secret."

"How unfair of you, Mr. Lee," she pouted. "I told you one of my secrets when you asked me why I came here alone."

"You did," Lee admitted, nodding. "Well, to be truthful, Dr. Bancroft is one reason why my work is not too pleasant."

"He can be most difficult at times, as I know all too well."

"Difficult?" Lee repeated, his voice rising. "That's the kindest thing that might be said of him. How long have you known him, Miss Vaughn?"

"A year or two."

"But I understood—that is, people say—"

"That I am Dr. Bancroft's mistress?" she finished for him sweetly. "That is true. You see, I was alone and he was the only man I knew who was willing to look after me. I suppose I'm a frivolous, expensive creature, really. I hope you won't judge me too harshly—life is so hard for orphans. One just doesn't know what to do sometimes, and when a man appears who is generous and kind like Dr. Bancroft ... "

She gazed pensively into the firelight, her teeth nipping the inside of her lip. Two large tears formed in her eyes and wandered slowly down her cheeks. Lee's hand reached out to cover hers.

"Poor girl. I appreciate how difficult it must have been for you. However, you know he isn't the only man in Paris who would be glad to take care of you."

"You're very gallant to say that, Mr. Lee. I hope it's true, because lately I have felt that the doctor is more interested in finance than he is in me. Tonight, when he said he would prefer to stay home and read those stupid journals—that was more than I could bear."

She dabbed at her eyes with a wisp of lace.

When she put her hand back in her lap, Lee seized that one, too.

"I think you would be wise to find someone else to look after you, my dear," he whispered, moving closer. "Dr. Bancroft is not what he seems to be, not at all the generous or kind person you believe he is. Nor is he as clever as he thinks...."

Lee paused for a brief instant, scowling at the fire. Ellen, watching him out of the corner of her eye, moved her hands slightly. His grasp on them tightened, and he turned back toward her.

"I should not tell you this, I suppose, but I feel a kindly interest toward you. I wouldn't like you to lack any care or comfort so long as I am in Paris. When Dr. Bancroft is disgraced, as he will be shortly, I hope you will come to me if you need assistance."

"I'm afraid I don't understand," Ellen whispered, bewildered. "Has he stolen money or borrowed too much? Does he owe a great amount for gambling?"

"I do not wish to confuse you by telling you something you would not comprehend," Lee said with a patronizing tone. "But I can say this much: I received papers today which will disgrace him. I don't want to feel that I have brought misfortune to you, so I hope you will allow me to act as a . . . a support until you have recovered from the shock of his disgrace."

Lee's eyes locked on hers, and as she gazed back, she noticed that he looked like nothing so much as an amorous beagle.

"Oh, Mr. Lee, you're so thoughtful," she sighed, yielding to the incessant pressure of his arm and resting her head against his shoulder. "Everyone in Paris says there's not a finer gentleman in the world than a Virginia gentleman."

"That's the truth," Lee began, his words groping their way out of his suddenly thickened accent. "We respect women in Virginia, and we show them the courtesy and the chivalry we feel they deserve as the Lord's loveliest creatures."

"I think I'd like to live in Virginia," Ellen mused. "It must be beautiful."

Lee stiffened, and she knew she had found his vulnerable spot.

"It is beautiful, Miss Vaughn." He straightened a bit as caution, that inner bugler, blew retreat. "I think you would soon tire of it, however. We don't have the amusements there which Paris can offer. There would never be a party as splendid as this one tonight."

"I adore simplicity, Mr. Lee," she said in pursuit. "From what you say, one might think my only interests were pleasure and parties and fine clothes. I would love to go to Virginia."

Lee's arm suddenly withdrew from her waist, and the Virginian bent over in a paroxysm of coughing.

As he covered his face with a kerchief, his mind sought frantically for a solution. Much as he would like to further the relationship, he could foresee an insoluble difficulty. Imagine news of her reaching Virginia—how his friends would pounce on that, to say nothing of the disapproval of his brother, Richard Henry. He would be the laughingstock of all Westmoreland; the mud of scandal would cling to the name of Lee for the first time since the days of Queen Caroline, who, like this girl next to him, had also been impetuous about a Lee.

He made one final, gasping cough, then shook his head sadly, as he thought of those soft shoulders. Such a pity, the way women could turn an innocent remark into a lifetime together. He straightened up and put his kerchief back in his pocket. Ellen was regarding him with concern.

"It's nothing," he said with a faint smile. "A complaint I've had since I was four days old. Sometimes I can't catch my breath. My brothers say it will be the death of me, especially if I don't stop drinking brandy."

A sudden coolness had come over her, a change he noticed with some relief. The prospect of nursing him through the remainder of her excessively healthy youth could not be very attractive to her. His worries about scandal reaching Virginia disappeared. He smiled, inspecting her beauty for perhaps the last time. Regret stabbed him. To turn the knife in his wound, Ellen kissed him lightly on the cheek and stood up before he had time to react.

"Perhaps we should join the others, Mr. Lee," she said. "I know Madame will be wondering what has happened to me."

"I hate to go back—this has been so delightful," Lee replied. "However, I know I have no right to keep you all to myself."

As they entered the salon, Lee excused himself and walked to the other side of the salon.

Ellen looked for Madame, and just as she noticed her at the end of the hall, Madame glanced in her direction. Ellen smiled and nodded. "Tomorrow," she mouthed, and Madame, her calash bobbing perilously, nodded her agreement.

Shortly thereafter, the soiree at Mme. de Treymes's ended. While the other guests waited in the entrance hall for their carriages, Ellen arrived home to find the house completely dark. Several minutes after she knocked on the door, Bertram appeared, his face contorted by a violent effort to keep from yawning.

"Good evening, Miss Vaughn."

"Has the doctor returned?"

"Yes, miss, a short while ago. He is upstairs." She hurried to the bedroom, and after lighting a candle, glanced across the room. Edward was there, fast asleep, one hand hanging over the edge of the bed. She undressed as quietly as she could, thinking that it would perhaps be better to tell him the result of her conversation with Lee in the morning.

CHAPTER XVII

ELLEN WOKE SHORTLY after dawn to find Edward gazing down at her, his face eager with questions.

"Good morning, darling. I didn't want to waken you, but this waiting is unbearable. How did you make out with Lee?"

"Fairly well, I think," she replied, raising herself far enough off the pillow to brush her lips against his cheek. Settling back down, she stretched and clasped her hands behind her head.

"I discovered nothing more than that he received papers yesterday which he feels will incriminate you. I'm not at all clear what he means, nor could I trick him into saying anything more than that. Even brandy didn't help. Mr. Lee is a close-mouthed, cautious person."

"I hope he didn't cause any trouble."

"No, none at all. I disconcerted him, I think, by saying that I should like to live in Virginia. It was too direct for him—he was bathed in a cold sweat at the very thought. He moved away from me then, and left me shortly afterwards."

"He didn't mention the source of those papers?"

"No. He only said that he had received them and intimated that I would do well to find another protector—someone like Arthur Lee, for example."

Edward stood up and began pacing around the room. His face was furrowed with concentration.

How baffled he looks, Ellen thought as she watched him.

"You're certain that he said nothing more," he asked, "that he made no mention of what the papers were about, who they came from, or where they were?"

"No, darling," she said with some petulance. "I've told you every word he said to me."

"Forgive me, Ellen," he said. "This affair worries me, and I am not being reasonable, I know. Somehow I have to find out about those papers. He must keep them in his rooms. From what you tell me, they would probably be too bulky to carry with him, and I know he wouldn't risk leaving them in the office."

Ellen realized then that Edward was talking more to himself than to her, so she got out of bed and began to dress. They walked downstairs together, Ellen holding his hand in hers.

"You will think of something, darling," she said later over breakfast. She noticed that he had not touched his food.

"You must eat, Edward. You'll be weak from worrying otherwise."

"I'm weak now," he laughed suddenly, "though I believe I finally have a plan that will work. If Lee went out in society instead of staying home every night, my task would be greatly simplified."

CARMICHAEL REACHED THE OFFICE shortly after Edward walked in. The two men greeted each other, and Carmichael said he expected Lee any minute, since he had just seen him at breakfast.

"I didn't know you lived where Mr. Lee does."

"Heavens no, Doctor! My rooms are across the street from his, and I saw him through the window. He lives at the Hotel de Riome. Mine is a smaller place, but one where I can have my friends visit me when I like. At Lee's place, where I lived for a short time, it is more like a club. Interruptions, you know; it's impossible to have a visitor without everyone else knowing of it."

"I understand," Edward smiled, amused by Carmichael's involved excuses. "Does Lee live alone?"

"Oh, yes," Carmichael chortled. "I can't imagine who would be able to endure those incessant references to Virginia. He talks of nothing else, unless it is the excellence of his family or the wealth of his neighbors. He does have a servant, fortunately deaf. He lives in the rear of the hotel, probably because it is more difficult for Lee to find him there."

"A French servant?"

"No, American. Lee brought him from Virginia."

"I should think Lee would prefer living in a house, since he is so accustomed to what he calls 'gracious living.' Are his rooms large enough for him?"

"I've only been in them once. They seemed quite small to me. They're at the corner of the hotel. His bedroom looks out over the lawn, and his sitting room faces the street. I shouldn't think they would be large enough for him, but, as you know, he's not careless with his money."

"He may not be accustomed to as much space as he would have us believe," Edward suggested, determined to keep Carmichael gossiping.

"No, Doctor, I know that's not the case. One of my friends stayed with the Lees once. He told me their lands seemed to stretch over half of Virginia. Everywhere he went, he met someone who was living on Lee property. Stratford, their house, was enormous, he said. He claimed that it must have been built with an eye to housing every Lee born in Virginia; there were three generations living in the wing where he had his room. The Lees may not be the wealthiest people in Virginia, but they're far from poor. From what I've heard, they economize whenever they're away from Stratford and then lavish their money on whatever suits their fancy when they're home."

"Mr. Lee seems to be following the family tradition here in Paris," Edward noted, then quickly continued. "I understand he rarely goes out at night, and from what I hear, he prefers not to."

"That's quite true. He told me once himself that he would rather go to bed at ten, by himself, than stay up until four with the prettiest woman in Paris."

"Does he mean every night?" Edward asked with a faint smile.

Carmichael laughed and shrugged his shoulders.

"I don't know. I would guess he's in more often than he's out."

Lee arrived just then, and the conversation ended abruptly. He grunted a good morning to them. As he walked past Edward to enter the office, he flashed a glance that was something like the look given by a duelist to his prostrate enemy. Edward could not conceal a smile after the door had closed behind Lee; Carmichael, noticing it, smiled back at him broadly, as though there existed a delightful secret between them.

Edward left the office immediately after Lee's arrival and devoted the remainder of the morning to perfecting his plan. He hired a coach and drove back and forth before the Hotel de Riome until he felt that he knew every stone in the building. He made a little sketch of Lee's rooms and the lawn which Carmichael had mentioned. There were trees quite close to the windows of Lee's rooms, he noted with satisfaction. That would simplify matters.

Someone was cleaning in the bedroom as he rode past the inn again; a fine spray of dust came cascading out of the open window and he saw a figure moving about in the shadow of the room. When he had completed his sketch, he dismissed his coach and walked to the Cafe Dijon.

The cafe was quite dim when he entered, as most of the shutters were still closed. The customers must not care to be seen too early, he thought as he walked across to the bar. A girl was serving, and, as he stood waiting for her to finish with another customer, he caught sight of a woman he judged to be the proprietress sitting behind a small counter not far from the bar. She was wearing a large shawl which nearly succeeded in covering her shoulders. As Edward glanced at her, his eyes fastened on those shoulders—they were unseemingly huge for a woman, and misshapen, too, he judged from the protruberance so poorly concealed by the shawl.

She was knitting with long, stained fingers that curved over her needles like claws.

She had lost her teeth, and her lips and mouth had sunk into her face, giving her a frozen expression of disgust.

"Marie!" she screamed suddenly, her voice scratching like a nail down Edward's spine. He shivered involuntarily and watched the barmaid hurry to the woman's side.

"That gentleman waits to be served," she snarled, cuffing the girl sharply with the back of her hand. "Stop playing trollop to that lout of yours and serve the gentleman."

"*Oui, Madame*," the girl whimpered, her face white except for the long marks of fingers. She returned to the bar so quickly that her feet seemed hardly to touch the floor.

"Yes, Monsieur?"

"Cognac." As the girl turned to select a bottle from the shelf behind her, Edward added, "A glass for Madame, also."

After the girl had placed the small glass of cognac on Madame's counter, Edward walked over to the suspicious proprietress.

"*Bon jour,* Mme. Hartouque."

"*Bon jour,*" she replied coldly, sipping at her cognac and staring at him. Her eyes had no life in them, no animation of any kind. They resembled glass pebbles carelessly inserted in a mask—one was brown and the other green.

While Edward watched the woman sip her drink, her eyes remained fastened on his face.

"I need assistance, Madame. A friend of mine recommended you as a most helpful and discreet person."

She did not speak nor did her eyes betray the slightest interest in what he was saying. Edward's fingers tightened around the stem of his glass.

"You will tell me the name of this person," she demanded, "this friend who recommended that you come to my cafe."

"M. Wentworth," Edward replied, "an Englishman."

She nodded and sipped at her cognac. Her eyes had not moved, but as he watched he saw life spring into them like a light onto an empty stage. When she placed her glass on the counter, the extreme slowness with which her hand moved made him inexplicably tense.

"You have a king's order in your pocket, perhaps?" she hissed at him viciously, leaning forward until she seemed to rise from behind the counter. Her mouth had sunk even deeper into her face, and her clawlike hands gripped the counter.

"King's order? I do not understand. I know nothing of a king's order, Madame. I come only to ask your assistance."

"You think you can trick me," she cried, her deformed shoulders trembling. "You are as stupid as the rest of your kind. Get out! If you come back, I shall arrange a reception such as your spying kind deserves."

Edward reached into his wallet and placed several bills on the counter.

"You are mistaken," he said hurriedly, before she could finish counting the bills. "I do not come to spy. I need help. If you will listen to me, you will understand."

"I understand all I need to know about you," she snapped, her fingers closing tightly around the notes, "except that I didn't know you could give bribes. I know you lie from what you have told me."

What had he told her? Edward was baffled by the woman's remark. Suddenly he understood what the difficulty might be.

"I see it now. A thousand pardons, Madame. M. Wentworth has lived so long in England that I sometimes forget he was born in the colony called New Hampshire."

The sound of those familiar syllables worked a miracle. Madame relaxed on her chair. The fire died from her eyes, but her fingers remained clenched around the money.

"Your name, Monsieur?"

"My name is Chalmers, George Chalmers," Edward answered.

She seemed satisfied and carefully lowered herself from the stool. When she stood in front of him, he had difficulty concealing his surprise. Except for her enormous shoulders, she was tiny.

"Come with me," she muttered.

Edward followed her through a door behind the bar. They entered a small room furnished with a table and six chairs. As she closed the door and motioned him to sit down, he felt that he had gained her confidence. This room must be the meeting place for those she accepted.

"For a moment, Monsieur," Madame began when she had eased herself into the chair opposite him, "you were in a most unenviable position. I thought you a king's man because you spoke incorrectly of M. Wentworth. I presume you forgot his advice to you to say New Hampshire before beginning your business with me. You see, I cannot be too careful here. My clients demand caution, and I myself have no desire, at my age, to join the galleys and travel to foreign shores."

Her mouth fell open in mirth, revealing a dark hole, a waste of black stumps of teeth and a spotted tongue. Edward looked quickly down at the table.

"You wish someone killed, Monsieur?" she asked, edging herself closer to the table.

"No, I definitely do not want this person killed. I want a fire set in his rooms—tonight."

"Only a fire? Oh, Monsieur. My friends do not like fires. The risk of being caught is just as great, and the reward, in satisfaction, much less. Wouldn't it be simpler to kill him?"

"It is absolutely necessary not to kill him, Madame. If he is killed, it will spoil a bit of work I have planned for your friends at a later date. They must understand that."

"I shall make them understand, Monsieur," she said, nodding. "You need have no fear of that. But they will be disappointed. They pride themselves on their excellence in killing; you will find no one so neat, so quick, so silent."

She continued sadly, "Ah, it is too bad. They lose their skills without practice. You said tonight, Monsieur? It will cost more to do it so quickly. Monsieur understands that?"

"I will pay any reasonable amount."

"Where is the fire to be set?"

Edward pulled out the sketch he had made and placed it on the table before the old woman. She studied the paper carefully, asking an occasional question about the trees and the number of inhabitants in the hotel.

Finally, she rose and opened the door. In a voice so low that it was impossible for Edward to overhear, she gave instructions to the barmaid.

A moment later she returned with a bottle of cognac and several glasses. She had scarcely finished pouring the cognac when the door opened and a man entered.

"Ah, Jean," she exclaimed. "Sit down with us. This gentleman has work for you."

Jean pulled out a chair and sat down beside Madame.

She pointed to the sketch, which he picked up and began studying carefully. As Madame outlined to him what Edward wanted, he nodded from time to time and marked places on the sketch with his fingernail.

He was about thirty, Edward guessed, very thin, but strong-looking and burning with fierce nervous energy. Edward had noticed when he first stepped into the room that he seemed to balance himself as he walked with a kind of springing motion. He walked as if ready at any moment to leap ten feet into the air. As Jean studied the sketch, he passed his hand across his face— it moved so quickly that it could scarcely be seen. His hair was long and black—it could not have been cut for months. As he bent over the map, it kept falling in front of his eyes; when he wanted to see more clearly, he would jerk his head back suddenly.

As Edward studied Jean's face, he was filled with a certainty that his plan would succeed. Although everything about this man seemed as unpredictable as his gestures, he exuded confidence. He seemed to only half listen to Madame's explanation, yet the questions he asked were pertinent and direct.

"How high from the ground is the first large branch on this tree?" he asked Edward suddenly in a flat monotone.

"About eight feet, I should say."

Jean grunted and turned back to the sketch again.

"You must have this done tonight, Monsieur?" Madame asked.

Edward nodded.

"In that case, Monsieur, Jean will do it for you; but it will, as I warned you, cost more. He tells me that it will be necessary to put one of his men in the hotel, which will make for additional expense. He says his price will be three hundred francs."

"Tell him I cannot pay more than two hundred," Edward replied calmly, determined not to pay without the bargaining which was expected.

Jean looked at Edward for a long moment after he heard two hundred francs. Muttering something out of the corner of his mouth, he rose to his feet.

"It is settled for two hundred?" Edward asked.

"No, Monsieur," Madame replied, spreading her hands in an eloquent gesture, "he says bargaining insults him. His price is now four hundred francs."

Edward sat up in his chair. The fellow was perfectly serious. It would be wiser to settle for four hundred and not risk a further, expensive display of temperament.

"Very well," he replied. "Four hundred francs then. Two hundred now and two hundred after his work is finished."

Madame whispered to Jean for a second, then nodded to Edward.

"That will be satisfactory. Usually he would ask for three hundred in advance; but you have been understanding, and he appreciates that."

Edward pulled out his wallet and extracted two hundred francs which he pushed across the table. Jean started to reach for the money, but Madame slapped his hand angrily. While he rubbed his hand, she took out several bills and handed him the remainder.

"He drinks much wine, Jean," she explained to Edward, "and his business is uncertain. I give him credit, sometimes."

She tucked the francs into her dress and stood up.

"At half after twelve, Monsieur," she said with a grimace, "there should be a lovely fire. Perhaps the gentleman may not wake in time."

"I don't want him to sleep that soundly," Edward cautioned.

They walked out into the cafe, and Jean disappeared at once. Edward soon followed, relieved to step outside into the clean, cold December air.

Carmichael was still alone when Edward entered the office. The young man told him that the others had been in during the morning and the early afternoon, but had all departed more than an hour before his arrival.

As Edward walked across the office, he saw that Lee and Deane had cleared their desk tops completely. There was not a loose paper in sight. When he opened the drawer of his desk, he was surprised to find it empty.

"Carmichael, did you borrow anything from my desk?" he called out.

"Why, no, Doctor, I didn't," the secretary exclaimed as he hurried in.

"Those manifests I was working on are gone. I left them here in the top drawer."

Edward rose and walked over to the lockbox. Opening it, he peered inside and then nodded.

"It's all right. They're here," he said with a sigh of relief. "Someone must have put them away for me, thinking I might not return."

"I was afraid for a moment that we had had an unknown visitor," Carmichael said with a nervous laugh. "It wouldn't surprise me at all to find that entire lockbox removed someday."

"Why do you say that?"

"I don't know. The British seem to find out everything we do here, however careful we try to be. It's discouraging, really."

"It's not quite that bad, Carmichael."

"I've always wondered where they get their information," Carmichael continued, warming to the subject. "Even Dr. Franklin was concerned about something this morning. After Mr. Lee talked with him, he seemed most upset."

"Perhaps Mr. Lee has discovered how the British obtain their information."

"That's possible," the young man replied. "There's no merit in fretting about it, I suppose. I'm happy you found your papers, Doctor. I couldn't imagine how they had been mislaid."

After Carmichael left, Edward stared moodily at his desk. The fire was not taking place any too soon. Those manifests had been moved for some inexplicable purpose, and Franklin's concern over Lee's words was another troubling indication. It might be wise to talk to Paul Wentworth—he might have another suggestion as to the course he should follow.

Edward hailed a coach and within a few minutes was walking down the street toward Paul's house.

He had entered the little garden and reached a clump of tall bushes when he heard the sound of voices coming through an open window of the front room. The timbre of one voice made him start.

"He has been most difficult lately, m'lord. I have felt for some time that he has reached the end of his usefulness to us. It has been especially true since he returned from his voyage with Wickes. That was why I took the action I mentioned to you."

Edward noticed that someone was walking about in the room, so before he could be detected he moved out of the bushes toward the side door. His heart was pounding with excitement, but his brain kept repeating *What action? What action? What action?* as he waited for the door to open.

He would brazen it out, this meeting with Paul. He realized his danger, but he also realized that Wentworth, unaware of what Edward had overheard, might be trapped into an inadvertent disclosure. He stifled the feeling of anger and resentment that had welled up in him.

There would be time enough later for anger; what mattered now was to discover the action Paul had taken.

Sylvestre opened the door and, smiling back at Edward, led him into the small library. Edward could feel his heart beat faster as he heard footsteps approaching the door. His blood pounded out a warning to him: *be careful, be careful,* it seemed to say. He took a deep breath and pressed his hands to his thighs.

The door opened, and Paul Wentworth stepped in.

"Edward," Paul exclaimed. "How nice to see you. "I hope it is good news that you bring. I was talking about you not long ago."

"Indeed? I hope in a complimentary way."

"Oh, yes. I was saying that you had done such splendid work for us that I thought you deserved a reward of some kind."

"That's most kind of you, Paul. Was it someone I know, this person?"

"No, I don't think you ever met him, though I've worked with him a number of years. How is Miss Vaughn?"

"Very well, thank you. Have you had any word from Eden recently about the five hundred pounds he was to send?"

"I had a letter from him several days ago. He said he already had spoken to Lord Mansfield and expected to send it within the week."

"Fine. It will be most useful to me just now. What I really wanted to see you about was the last prize list I gave you. I found after I checked the list in the office that I omitted several ships which were reported in the next letters we received from the ports. Do you have it here? I can remember the additions, I believe, and it would be better if we kept all those ships on the same list."

"True, but Stormont has the list now," Paul said. "Perhaps if you gave me the names, I could add them after he returns it."

"Well, it makes little difference. I'll put them on when you have the list available."

Edward had found the answer he was seeking in Paul's momentary hesitation. He drew a deep breath and looked at Paul with a faint smile.

"Good-bye, Paul. I am extremely grateful for your recommendation of a reward. I find it difficult not to ask you what it will be."

"You'll have to bridle your impatience, I'm afraid, Edward," Paul laughed, "but not for too long."

As Edward walked away from Paul's house, he had great difficulty moving past the bushes where he had stood earlier. It would be pointless, he realized; he had heard all he needed to know. Wentworth had betrayed him, had somehow passed along to Lee the proof he needed, so that Lee could crow in triumph and spare the British the necessity of dealing with him. He doubted that Paul would be smiling as easily tomorrow as he had been this afternoon, Edward reassured himself.

That night, Ellen had made plans to attend a musical, and would leave about eight.

"Why don't you go to bed early, darling?" she urged him. "You look so tired. I'd rather stay here with you, but I promised to be there, at least for a short while."

"Enjoy yourself, my dear," he said, rising and slipping his arm about her waist as they walked toward the door. "Please don't worry about me. I'm not really as tired as I look. I have an appointment later tonight, but that should not last too long. I shall go to bed, I promise you, as soon as I return home."

She searched his face for a moment, a sudden suspicion in her eyes.

"Lee?" she asked.

He nodded.

"Be careful, darling," she whispered. Reaching up, she pulled his head down to her lips and kissed him.

Edward tried to read after Ellen left, but it was useless.

All he saw on the page was the dark figure of Jean in the trees outside Lee's window. He could almost hear the scraping noise his breeches made as he climbed. He tried again to concentrate on his book, but with no more success. When he did not see Jean's figure on the page, he saw Paul Wentworth's smile, which was even more upsetting.

Cursing, he stood up and threw the book into his chair. He put on his hat and coat and strode out of the house, banging the door after him. The noise reverberated down the cold, quiet street; even after he had passed several houses, he imagined that he still heard the metallic, fretful banging of the knocker.

The night was so dark he could not see the hands of his watch. Stopping in the doorway of a cafe, he pulled it out again. Half after ten. Two hours more. The Hotel de Riome was no more than an hour's walk away. That left a whole hour to occupy somehow, an hour that would be agonizingly long. If he kept walking toward the Hotel de Riome, at least he would not have to think, which would be a blessing. He went on into the darkness.

Almost an hour later, he recognized a little bookstore with some Boucher prints in the window; the Hotel de Riome was no more than five minutes from here. He had an hour yet—where could he go?

He looked up and down the street and into a little alley just in front of him. The houses were shuttered tight; there was no light anywhere. He walked to the next block and peered through the blackness.

Far down on the right, he detected a slight reflection on the cobblestones. He hurried toward it, keeping one hand in his pocket as he passed some particularly menacing shadows. It was a small cafe, he judged, from the smell of wine that wafted toward him. One of the shutters had fallen loose, allowing a shaft of light to escape. The door was closed; when he tried the handle, he found it locked. He rapped and then waited, listening. Hearing nothing, he rapped again. A shutter creaked, and a head appeared at the window above him.

"What is it?"

"I would like some cognac."

"The cafe is closed, Monsieur."

"There is a light."

"A tall candle that guards us from thieves. If Monsieur will return tomorrow ... "

Edward reached into his pocket and pulled out some coins. He dropped then on the pavement, and they spoke with a clear, sharp ring. The shutter closed instantly, and as Edward stooped to pick up his coins he heard the noise of talking inside the cafe. The proprietor opened the door, and he walked in.

There were ten or twelve men in the room and several women. They stared at him in silence as he walked to the bar. He gave his order to the proprietor and stood there uncomfortably. He knew he had interrupted these people by knocking and bribing his way inside; he had not expected to find such a hostile silence, however. He shrugged and attributed his feelings to nervousness, to this damnable waiting he must endure for a little while longer.

When he reached out to pick up his glass of cognac, he noticed a small scrap of paper beneath it. He leaned forward to sip his drink, and looked down at the writing on the paper.

"It would be wise to leave at once."

Nothing could be more definite than that, he thought. He raised his eyes to find the proprietor looking at him from the other end of the bar. Almost imperceptibly, the man nodded and Edward reached into his pocket for a coin. Someone behind him coughed; the unexpected noise made him acutely conscious that no one had spoken a single word since his arrival.

He sipped at his cognac while he waited for his change, wondering what sort of cafe this was, who these people were, and what they had been discussing before he came.

They all must belong to the same group, he decided, for they had remained silent as if by previous agreement. A political group? Perhaps. There were all kinds of groups in Paris today, banded together to fight something—taxes or the court or the aristocrats or the watch. Whatever this group was doing or planning to do, he was an unwelcome intruder; the sooner he left, the more amicable would be the parting. It would be stupid to ignore the proprietor's warning; this was one night he could not risk misfortune of any sort.

The proprietor returned with his change, which he placed carefully next to Edward's glass, his forefinger tapping the message as if for emphasis. Edward finished his drink and turned to leave. He was too late.

A tall, swarthy man stood directly behind him. He frowned as Edward started to move past him, then shifted directly into his path.

"Pardon, Monsieur," Edward said calmly, "you are in my way."

Edward moved ahead slightly, only to find the swarthy man blocking his path again. The others had left their tables and were converging on the door, their eyes on the two men facing each other.

Edward felt his heart pounding; it sounded as if it had moved up into his throat. He knew he could expect no assistance, even from the proprietor who had warned him of his danger. He did look back for the man, but he was nowhere to be seen. Just as he was turning around again, he caught sight of an iron bar descending toward his head. He dodged, drew back his arm, and landed a hard blow on the chin of the swarthy man who had struck at him.

The man dropped like a tailor's dummy; there was a gasp of astonishment from the group gathered at the door.

Edward realized he must capitalize on his advantage immediately. Seeing other weapons in the hands of those in front of him, he felt escape not only impossible but unwise.

"Proprietor," he called, turning toward the bar, "cognac for your guests and water for him who cannot swallow."

There were several laughs at his remark, and he knew he had gained a little time. He selected the man he guessed to be second in command of the group.

"You there," he called, pointing to a small, stocky man whose fingers were wrapped about the neck of a bottle. "Come here."

The man moved toward him, scowling. His legs were in a curious crouch, as if he feared he might be walking into a trap.

"Put down that bottle and take a glass of cognac with me," Edward ordered. "There is no reason for you or your friends to fear me."

The man set the bottle down on the table but kept his scowl. His mind was working slowly on what Edward had said. Edward noticed that consciousness was returning to the man on the floor; his legs were beginning to move. The stocky man apparently decided to capitalize on his opportunity; he walked up to the bar and stood beside Edward.

"Tell your friends to drink their cognac," Edward said. "I will even treat the one there on the floor when he awakens."

The man grinned when Edward said this, then turned and addressed his companions. There was another burst of laughter, and the atmosphere in the little cafe cleared magically. Several of the men picked their fallen companion off the floor and heaved him onto a chair. The others crowded around the bar.

"You have no reason to fear me," Edward repeated to the little man beside him. "I am not your enemy. I am an American, a countryman of Dr. Franklin."

The stocky man choked on the cognac and stared at Edward in surprise.

"Ah, *mille* pardons, Monsieur," he whispered. "From your clothes and the way you spoke, we were certain you were one of the king's men. No one else would be abroad so late at night. No Frenchman not a king's man would have the courage to walk the dark streets of Paris alone."

"I understand your mistrust now," Edward laughed. "A king's man, eh? I don't blame you for feeling the way you did. Monsieur, more cognac."

While the proprietor filled their glasses, Edward wondered how he could discover more about this little group. He was still curious as to who they were and what they had been discussing when he had interrupted them.

"I regret that I interrupted your conversation tonight," he began. "I noticed you all stopped talking when I walked into the cafe."

"Yes, Monsieur, you did interrupt," the stocky man smiled, "and more than you perhaps realize."

"Dubois, there"—he pointed to his swarthy companion who was now bent over in his chair, holding his head in his hands—"was talking to us just before you came in. When he does not talk, no one talks. You understand, Monsieur?"

Edward nodded and took a sip of cognac, waiting for the other to continue.

"Dubois is our leader, Monsieur. He is biggest, though perhaps not smartest. When he speaks, all of us listen. He was telling about a companion of ours who was seized this week by the king's agents. They claimed he had eaten a partridge wounded in the king's chase. Because he did not give it up—he was hungry, you understand, Monsieur—he was brought back to Paris and sentenced to three years in prison. Dubois called us together tonight to see if we could find a way to assist our friend."

"Three years? For a single partridge? That's monstrous."

"Yes, Monsieur, but not unusual," the stocky man said with a shrug. "It has been happening for years. What are we to do, we little people who have nothing but our hands to fight with? When the old king died, we thought life would be happier for us. We hoped young Louis would be as good as people said he was . . . ."

He shrugged again and twirled his glass between his fingers.

"It is not so, unfortunately. He listens only to the queen and the foreigners at the court. He does not realize what is happening to his country. He cannot see beyond his windows. We feel he has lost touch with us, his people; otherwise our friend would not be forced to endure this injustice."

"Perhaps the king is still too young," Edward began. He stopped suddenly when he noticed Dubois standing near him. He was gazing at Edward in perplexity, unable to understand why everyone had gathered at the bar in such a friendly manner.

"Why do you speak with that man, Leon?" he demanded.

"He is not what we thought, Francois," Leon replied with a nervous smile. He reached out to Dubois and, holding his arm, guided him closer to the bar. "We were mistaken; he is from America, not a king's man. That is why he has a fist filled with thunder and fast as lightning, if you remember."

Leon chuckled as he remembered how Dubois had dropped to the floor.

"Bah! Idiot!" Dubois snarled. "How was I to know he was a Colonist full of savages' tricks?"

"Let us forget our misunderstanding, Monsieur Dubois," Edward interposed quickly. "We are friends now—we no longer mistrust each other—so there is no merit in fighting among ourselves."

Dubois grunted and stared moodily at the dirty floor.

"I have been telling him," Leon explained, "how we suffer today in France."

"You talk too much, Leon. Some day you will awake in the Bastille because of that flapping tongue."

Leon grunted and sipped at his cognac. Dubois resumed his scrutiny of Edward, as if trying to decide whether to risk talking with this stranger. Finally, he reached out and picked up the glass of cognac which had been poured for him.

"Your health, Monsieur," he said.

Edward drank his cognac with relief; now that Dubois had accepted him, he knew his difficulties here were over.

"Life is becoming more and more difficult for us, Monsieur. It is as Leon says, only worse. Every day there are new taxes, new restrictions, new laws that cheat us. As M. Rousseau has said, we are spiritual beggars here in France; a false face is more to be desired than truth or simplicity."

"You have studied Rousseau?" Edward asked, amazed that this man should be familiar with the writings of Rousseau.

"Of course," Dubois replied with dignity. "Who can be unaware of the great Jean Jacques Rousseau, who cries aloud what the people have been whispering for years? He is a great man. He describes the evil that saps the strength of France, and that is why the aristocrats hate him, why they mock him."

"It does not seem likely to me that many of your friends here would be so aware as you are of M. Rousseau," Edward suggested.

"You are correct, Monsieur. These friends of mine hear me talk about him, and they ask me, 'Francois, what does it mean, this book you are always telling us about?' I have told them many times, but they cannot comprehend its meaning. Ah, sometimes when I am very hungry, I do not comprehend it myself; I wonder then if bread is not more important than thought. I was not thinking of M. Rousseau when I raised that piece of iron. I was thinking only of prison. I apologize, Monsieur."

"You did what you thought best, M. Dubois," Edward replied with sudden warmth. "You thought first for the safety of your friends."

Dubois smiled in gratitude. Edward looked at his watch and started. He had but ten minutes to reach the Hotel de Riome.

"I must leave you and your friends now," he said. "I wish you success, M. Dubois. I hope we may meet again."

"Good-bye, Monsieur." Dubois grasped Edward's hand. "We are grateful to you for the cognac and for the chance to become acquainted with a Colonist. We do not see many of your countrymen, Monsieur, but we pray for them in their struggle against tyranny. I am happy we part as friends."

Edward walked out into the street and started for the Hotel de Riome. A strange group, he thought to himself. How many others were there like these in Paris, meeting and conspiring?

He kept close to the walls of the buildings as he walked. In the daytime, such a position was dangerous, for the residents of Paris tossed slop from their windows without a thought as to who might be passing below. At night, however, the shutters were closed tight and the walls afforded a defense against street thieves, being one direction by which they could not approach.

As he drew nearer and nearer Lee's hotel, several times he paused and pressed himself into a doorway or against a wall to let one of the watch go past. He had the advantage of seeing them first, outlined perfectly by their torches as they crossed the streets in front of him. When he did see one, he waited until the man had disappeared before proceeding.

Soon he reached the top of a small hill. Lee's hotel was not more than two hundred yards down the street. He moved forward carefully, keeping always in the shadows and ready to use one of the routes of escape he had planned along the way. He could hear the noise of cats as they prowled about in the gloom, pursuing their nocturnal interests of love and rats.

All at once his eye discerned the familiar gable on Lee's inn. The tree beside Lee's window was impossible to see, but so carefully had he memorized the locale that he had no difficulty in telling where it should be. His eyes were now fully accustomed to the blackness. He could see everything he needed to see; anyone entering the area would require several minutes to adjust to the dark shapes about him, minutes he could employ for escape.

It must be almost time, he thought. He opened his mouth to take a deep breath and closed it instantly; the beating of his heart startled him with its drumming intensity.

He remained crouched in the shadow of a building several doors up and across the street from the Hotel de Riome, his hat pulled down and his cloak gathered about him. He could distinguish Lee's windows and the small lawn beneath.

Lee was accustomed to fresh air; his windows were open.

A rustle struck his ears, as clearly and distinctly as if it had been a clock striking. He strained to hear it again, listening with every nerve in his body. All he heard was the beating of his heart. No! There it was again; a scraping noise, so soft it almost seemed a whisper. Jean must be climbing the tree. He drew a quick breath and strained to catch the sound again.

A door banged suddenly far down the street. Edward started violently and fell forward on his knees, a pace or two from the wall. Swiftly he rocked back, pressing himself into the wall again. The shock had been so great he felt scarcely able to breathe. He could feel each aching muscle, and his body was beginning to tremble because of its cramped position.

Footsteps suddenly alarmed him, but then he realized they were moving in the opposite direction. He sighed with relief. Looking toward the inn again, he saw a faint red glow reflected through one of the upstairs windows. That must be Jean's helper.

As he watched the glow become brighter and brighter, a cry sounded from inside the inn. There was a sudden shout, and Edward looked back toward Lee's windows again, wondering if there was still time for the plan to work.

He looked toward the tree just in time to see a small spark. There was a sudden hiss, then a glare that blinded him as the tree burst into view.

Jean was crouching in one of the branches, the firebrand in his hand. He drew back his arm, and the shadow of the tree lurched across the street. The brand flew through the air, banged against the window ledge, and, as

Edward watched—his breath a short, painful gasp, his heart rigid—the flaming torch fell inside the room.

For a moment he thought it had gone out. The red seemed to fade into blackness. Had its flight through the air put it out? His fist beat against his leg in frustration.

Lee's room blossomed suddenly with a furious red. The portieres caught fire, and the light they cast was startling. Smoke poured out of the room, and from inside came cries for help. The other fire had grown and seemed to be leaping forward to join its fellow.

Edward lingered as long as he dared, fascinated by the conflagration. He moved back toward the corner, his head still turned toward the inn which was bright with flame. Across the street from the burning building, shutters were being thrown open and people began tumbling out of the houses, moving out to the street and onto the lawn of the hotel. As he walked quickly down the side street which had not yet been awakened by the conflagration, he heard shouting behind him. He turned to look; no one was coming, yet the shouts continued. He hurried down the street again, and the noise died away.

The jubilation he felt at the success of his scheme swept away the tension he had experienced while waiting. He felt his breathing return to normal, and his long strides made short work of the distance between the hotel and his house.

As he bounded up the steps, there was a look of triumph on his face. Lee would no longer be so confident without those papers—if indeed Lee were still able to get about. Tomorrow he would pay Jean the remainder of his fee, and to it he would add another hundred francs, for his excellent work.

CHAPTER XVIII

D
EANE LOOKED UP and nodded when Edward entered the office
the next morning.

"Good morning, Edward. I have news for you."

"Yes? What news is that?" Edward asked as he sat down at his desk.

"I saw Dr. Franklin last night," Deane continued. "He asked me to tell you to come out to Passy this morning, as soon as I saw you."

"Oh. This must be the day for Mr. Lee's little inquisition."

"I regret to say that it is."

"Very well," Edward exclaimed. "There's no point in delaying. The sooner I reach Passy, the sooner I shall return here."

"Before you go, Edward, I want to say once again how sorry I am about this affair. I know you'll have no trouble with Lee, and I want you to know that you can count on my support."

"That's most kind of you, Mr. Deane. I don't expect I'll be there more than an hour. When I return, I'll tell you all about it."

"Excellent. I'll be waiting for you."

Edward's coach moved swiftly toward Passy until it crossed the Seine. The road farther out from the city had become extremely slippery, and Philippe proceeded with more care after they nearly slid into the ditch.

When they reached Passy, Edward directed his coachman from the Grande Rue de Passy onto the Rue du Marche. The streets were narrow and confusing, but finally Edward recognized the turn that led toward Franklin's dwelling. As his coach stopped, he jumped down to the street and gave instructions to Philippe to turn the coach about so that it headed for Paris and wait for his return. He climbed the small iron stairway and, entering a door, walked through a passageway to the Petit Hotel de Valentinois, Franklin's residence.

The doctor met him in the hall, his face wreathed in a smile.

"I was afraid I would not see you until after Lee arrived," Franklin said. "I wanted you to know, Dr. Bancroft, that I regard these charges of Lee's as utterly stupid; if it were not for his official position, I would refuse to listen to them."

"I am most grateful to you for saying that," Edward replied. "I do not know what is in Lee's mind, but I am well aware of the hatred he bears for me. I imagine our meeting this morning will not be a pleasant one. I am relieved to know your friendship for me has not changed."

They walked together to the drawing room. A man and a woman were seated before a small fire. At their approach the man rose, and Edward recognized Caron de Beaumarchais.

"Mlle. de Chaumont," Franklin began, "may I present Dr. Bancroft?"

Edward bowed to the young girl and understood at his first glance why the excessively polite Beaumarchais had been so slow to rise from her side when he and Franklin had entered the room. She was blonde and small and exquisitely formed. He looked at Franklin in envious astonishment: this was the girl who had been the doctor's close companion since his arrival at Passy.

"M. de Beaumarchais," Franklin continued, "I believe you have met Dr. Bancroft?"

"Yes, indeed. A pleasure, sir."

Beaumarchais was a triumph of silver cloth; he glistened in the firelight like a fabulous moth, and as he bowed toward Edward, the shimmer of light on his clothes was breathtaking. Today Beaumarchais had forsaken a waistcoat and was wearing around his waist a cloth of dull gold, wrapped tightly and secured in front by a beautifullly worked silver dagger. It was a symbol of the man's incredible self-assurance. Anyone else wearing a weapon like that dagger would be certain to do himself irreparable harm in sitting down.

Franklin seated himself in the large chair beside the fire, leaving the place on Mlle. de Chaumont's left to Edward. Beaumarchais had just started to tell them about the play he was writing when Yves, Dr. Franklin's household factotum, hurried into the room in obvious excitement.

"Dr. Franklin," he exclaimed, "there is a young man outside who says he must see you at once. I would think him mad except that his horses are so muddy and winded."

"What is his name?"

"Austine, he said. He spoke too quickly for me to be sure."

"Hmm. Austine? I know no one by that name."

"He is very dirty, Doctor. He has not shaved for several days. He does not look like one of the young men who usually come to call on you."

"Then what he has to say must be really important," Franklin chuckled. "Have him come in."

A young man entered the room a moment later and stood looking down at them. He was, as Yves had said, extremely dirty. He was also, as Yves had noted with disapproval, unshaven. Yet beneath the dirt and the slight growth of beard, he was an extremely handsome young man. He could not have been more than twenty-four, tall, broadshouldered, blond, and vibrant with energy and strength. He strode across the room, carelessly tossing his cloak over his shoulder as he neared Dr. Franklin. Edward heard Mlle. de Chaumont's intake of breath as she inspected the young man.

"I have hurried as fast as I could, sir. I have a dispatch for you from Boston."

Reaching into his pocket, he took out a paper and handed it to Franklin with a slight bow. Franklin remained looking at his visitor, ignoring the paper in his hand.

"Your name, sir? My man was not too clear."

"Jonathan Loring Austin at your service, sir."

"You left from Boston?"

"On the thirty-first of October, Doctor, aboard the *Perch*."

"When a man travels from America with news for me," Franklin sighed, sinking down into his chair, "I hardly dare listen to his words or read his dispatches. I am too old for shocks. Before I open this, Mr. Austin, tell me: do the British still hold Philadelphia?"

"Yes, Doctor, they do. But that is not important anymore."

"Not important?" Franklin cried, straightening up in his chair. "In God's name, young man, why not?"

"Because the Americans hold General Burgoyne, sir, with all his army and all his stores. That dispatch informs you that we won the battle at Saratoga, Doctor. The general and his entire army are prisoners of war."

The shocked silence was broken by Franklin. He leapt from his chair and embraced the messenger. Beaumarchais and Edward stood up and one by one embraced the delighted Mlle. de Chaumont.

"Ho! Ha! Formidable!" Beaumarchais shouted with delight as he capered about the room. "What wonderful news! I, Caron de Beaumarchais, swear that at this moment I am more American than French.

"Dr. Franklin, we shall have that treaty now! You will see Beaumarchais at Versailles as fast as his horses can gallop, running from room to room like a scandal, shouting the news, even to His Majesty."

"A fine idea," Franklin said with a grin. "Thank you."

"Thank me?" Beaumarchais asked incredulously. He laughed and ran up the stairs.

"Thank me?" he repeated, pausing at the top to fling out his arm in a magnificent gesture. "Not at all, Doctor. As well thank a father for acknowledging his own child. I shall go directly to le comte de Vergennes. To him I shall say: Sire, I, Pierre Caron de Beaumarchais, have the exquisite pleasure of being the midwife of joy. The British have fallen at Saratoga. Their entire army plods in chains across the snow to prison.

"Forgive me, Mademoiselle," he added, turning toward the girl. "I have waited so long and so impatiently for this day that I fear I am somewhat unbalanced."

"*Au revoir, Mademoiselle et messieurs,*" he cried, bowing to them. "Beaumarchais, the Mercury of Versailles, bids you good day."

As he disappeared through the doorway, the laughter of his three listeners echoed after him like applause.

"If I did not love you so much, Papa," Mlle. de Chaumont remarked, "I could become very fond of M. de Beaumarchais."

"I shall accept that as a gentle warning," Franklin chuckled, "and redouble my efforts to please you."

"Doctor," he said, peering at Edward, "I would like you to return to Paris at once and inform Mr. Deane of this news. Tell him to send messages and couriers to all our friends and all our agents—we cannot spread these tidings far enough or fast enough. The treaty for which we have worked so long and so hard will be ours now. We must move swiftly and arrange it while this enthusiasm burns over France like a fever."

"I shall be delighted to go, of course, Dr. Franklin, but have you forgotten ..."

"Lee's inquisition? Bah!" the old man snorted. "We have more important things to talk about now. In a month or two, perhaps, if he still insists. The most important thing is for you to go to Paris immediately."

"Very well, Doctor." Edward bowed to Mlle. de Chaumont and Franklin. He hurried through the passageway and reached his coach a moment later. Philippe was sitting patiently on the box. When he saw Edward coming down the steps, he smiled and threw off the robe with which he had covered himself.

"To the Auberge du Moulin, Philippe, at the end of Rue Montpelier— hurry."

They had just started down the street when another coach turned the corner in front of them. In approaching, it slipped toward the center of the street, blocking their way. Philippe cursed and pulled on the reins. The other coach moved slowly to one side, and as they passed it, Edward stared out curiously. They were abreast of it before he recognized Lee.

There were two others in the coach with him. One man he did not recognize, but the face of the other brought his heart into his throat. It was Jean. Why was he here? How had Lee found him? Lee saw him at that moment and sprang forward in his seat. He opened the door of his coach and cried out to Philippe to halt.

"Go on," Edward shouted desperately. Opening the little window in the front of the coach, he yelled and waved his hat wildly at the astonished horses. They bucked and in an instant were pulling madly against the reins.

"Don't stop for anyone, Philippe," Edward shouted up to the astonished coachman. "I must reach Paris as quickly as possible."

They jolted perilously around the corner, the coach wheels screaming in protest, and Edward fell back on his seat with a sigh of relief. He was safe now; he would reach Paris before Lee. It had been too narrow an escape. If Lee had kept his coach in the center of the street, he would have been trapped.

By the time he reached Paris, Edward had decided what he must do. He realized that with Jean as a witness, both the British and the Americans would be leagued against him now. He was alone, and there was nothing to help him except his own cunning. It was a challenge he enjoyed. He welcomed the excitement; it brought back to him the feeling he had experienced aboard the *Reprisal*.

The coach pulled up at the inn to which Edward had directed Philippe. He hurried inside and called for the proprietor.

"Is your son Claude here?" he asked M. du Mont.

"Yes, Monsieur."

"Good. Send him to me."

"Very well, Monsieur." Edward's urgency had communicated itself to du Mont, for he hurried off toward the kitchen and a moment later returned with Claude, who was still trying to swallow his lunch.

"I have something for you to do," he said to the youth. "It is extremely important, and for every hour you can cut from the time it usually takes you, I shall pay you five pounds extra."

Claude's eyes bulged.

"You will take the message I shall write to M. Wharton, the same gentleman to whom you have taken all the others. If he is not at his office, find him. Ask at his house. If he is not there, find out from his servant where you may locate him. You must find him with the least possible delay. Do you understand?"

"*Oui, Monsieur.*"

"Do you know where you can buy a good, fast horse?"

"My uncle keeps a stable, Monsieur. He has some excellent horses. They are used by the couriers."

"How much would he charge for the best one?"

"Forty livres, Monsieur, if he could get it back."

"Since he is your uncle, he will accept thirty, I am sure," Edward said dryly. "Get that horse, and leave at once. I shall take you to the stable in my coach. While you are preparing your things, I will write a note."

The proprietor brought writing materials and wax to Edward, who scratched a quick note to Wharton:

> Sam:
>   No more need for patience. British army defeated and taken prisoner at Saratoga. This is what we have waited for. Use every pound of capital we have and whip the bear.
>
>   Edward

He scrawled instructions for paying Claude on the outside of the paper and then, after folding it carefully, sealed it.

For a moment he sat there, weighing the letter in his hand. He rubbed a finger over one of the wax seals and smiled to himself. Such a flimsy bit of paper, yet fraught with such consequences. He would be rich because of it; but first, before he could enjoy his wealth, he would have to play the hare to the others' hounds. Well, let them come. He had the start he wanted, and he had no intention of losing his advantage.

Claude returned, and they proceeded a short way to his uncle's stable, where Edward left him after discovering that the horse he mentioned was ready to be ridden.

Edward was humming as he walked into the Hotel d'Hambourg. Carmichael, seated at his desk, raised his head swiftly when he saw who it was.

"Good afternoon, Carmichael," Edward said cheerily.

"Well, good afternoon, Dr. Bancroft," the secretary stammered. "You surprised me. I'm delighted to see you so happy."

Edward smiled and walked into his office, his humming a trifle louder. He closed the door behind him and leaned back against it, sighing with relief. It had worked. Lee had not stopped here first before he set out for Passy. It made things infinitely easier, for Carmichael was a large and strong young man.

He opened the compartment in his desk and removed everything in it. Making a bundle of the papers, he stepped out into the office and informed Carmichael that he would return later in the afternoon.

He stopped next at his banks and withdrew most of the money he had on deposit, leaving only enough for Ellen's expenses. This money he placed with the papers he had taken from his desk and ordered Philippe to drive him home.

Ellen was not at home when he arrived and Bertram informed him that she was not expected to return until supper. She had gone to an auction with Mme. de Treymes, Bertram explained, and hoped to buy a larger dining room table, which, he added in a solemn voice, had been needed for a very long time.

"Since it would please you so much," Edward said with a smile, "I hope Miss Vaughn is able to obtain it."

"That is most generous of you, sir," Bertram replied happily. "You and Miss Vaughn will be able to have even more guests at your table, whom it will be my pleasure to serve."

"I sincerely hope so, Bertram."

Edward packed a portmanteau with the clothes he would need for the next few days and placed the packet of papers and the money in a small leather bag. How much should he tell Ellen?

Nothing now, he decided. He would send word later.

After leaving a note telling her that he had been called away on business, he stepped into his coach again and drove off toward the center of Paris.

In a few minutes he had found what he was seeking: an empty coach. He leaned out of his window and called for Philippe to halt. Transferring his luggage, he sent his coach back to the stable and then ordered the new driver to proceed. When they had gone about ten blocks to the north, he stopped the coach and paid the driver.

He waited on the corner until the coach was out of sight, then walked swiftly down the street to a small, red brick house. Putting down his luggage, he opened the little leather case which contained his papers and drew out one that was liberally sealed. Ripping it open, he took the key which it contained and unlocked the door of the house. As he walked inside, he smiled when he saw the name beside the door: E. du Pont.

CHAPTER XIX

EARLY THE NEXT MORNING, while women emptied buckets in the street and swept dust from the steps before their houses, Edward walked into the Cafe Dijon. An old drudge, shapeless in a spotted, gray dress, was muttering to herself as she scrubbed the dirty floor.

She looked suspiciously up as he entered. Then, as if reassured by what she saw, she grunted an almost inaudible *"Bonjour, Monsieur"* and sloshed more water on the floor.

Edward asked her where he could find the proprietress, but before she could answer, there was a sound of footsteps behind him. He turned and saw Mme. Hartouque leaning against her counter, staring at him.

"You are back again, Monsieur? Was Jean's work not satisfactory? He has not been here to tell me how it went."

"It was more than satisfactory, Madame. I brought the two hundred francs and another hundred as a reward for the excellence of his work. But I have come today about another matter."

"So? Well, it is early in the morning, you realize. Before we can discuss such affairs, we must arrange the cafe. You do not mind waiting, Monsieur?"

"I do," Edward said bluntly. "I cannot afford to waste a single minute. That is why I came so early."

He drew out his wallet and placed some money on the bar.

"I would be grateful, Madame, if you would bring cognac and some glasses. Perhaps we could discuss the matter more privately elsewhere."

"But of course, Monsieur," Madame agreed with a shrug. Her eyes brightened as her fingers scooped up the money.

When they were seated at the table in the little room where the previous interview had been held, Madame looked at Edward with frank curiosity.

"I hope, Monsieur, that you are not allowing our first success to affect your judgment. You must realize that such enterprises as these are dangerous, always very dangerous, which is why they are so expensive. One must wait for the dust to settle, so to speak, before repeating them. That is why Jean has not returned. He waits, like a cautious man, until the authorities have forgotten the fire. Otherwise . . . "

As Edward sipped at his brandy, he calculated that he would have just time enough to complete the last phase of his plan before Mme. Hartoque learned what had happened to Jean.

"Don't worry, Madame. I quite realize the danger, and I have not returned to arrange another fire. This is a completely different matter, a much different matter than the last. All I want from you is two of your men. They must be strong, capable with the knife, and silent, as Jean is. I would prefer to have him, but as I am pressed for time, I shall leave it to your discretion to select two others as capable as he."

Madame poured herself another glass of cognac.

She sipped it slowly, peering into the bottom of her glass as if she might discover there the reason for Edward's request.

"I think I can arrange that, Monsieur. Is it a killing?"

"Yes."

"That will come high, Monsieur. Who is the person?"

"I don't know yet."

Madame set her glass down on the table. She stared at him with new interest.

"You don't know?"

"No, Madame, I have no idea who it will be."

"*Tiens,*" she exclaimed, "I like your frankness, Monsieur. I admire it. In fact, never before has a patron of mine proposed such an affair to me. Questions have no place in my business, Monsieur, but I cannot help asking you—"

"I am sorry I cannot answer, Madame," Edward interrupted. "I have told you all I can. I do not know who this person will be. I am aware that the more important he is, the higher your charge will be. I am prepared to pay."

"Such a strange request," she murmured, picking up her glass again. "Very well, Monsieur, it shall be as you wish. I will charge you two thousand francs now. That will provide for anyone up to a cafe owner. Higher than that, and you must send one of my men back to me; I shall raise the price to correspond with the importance of the unknown."

"That is satisfactory," Edward replied. He counted out two thousand francs and placed them on the table.

"How soon can you send the men?"

"This afternoon?"

"Excellent. The address is 23 Rue Nancy. The word to use is *Dijon*."

Edward waited impatiently all afternoon. Finally, as the shadows began to lengthen and night fell over the city, there was a knock at the door. Edward peered out cautiously from one of the front windows and saw two figures standing close together beside the door. He watched them for a moment, noting their clothes and the way they pressed themselves against the door for concealment. Then he moved quickly to the door.

"Who's there?"

Very softly came the answer: "Dijon."

He unbolted the door and opened it. The two men entered, and he closed the door behind them. He led them into the living room and lit candles, then had an opportunity to observe them closely while they blinked in the sudden brightness.

They were dressed in such ragged clothes that the only difference he could see between them was that one man was taller than the other. As they became accustomed to the light, however, he saw that the smaller man was the more alert; he was scrutinizing Edward with obvious curiosity, while his companion still blinked and shook his head slightly as if to clear the brightness from his eyes.

"I have been expecting you. I hoped you would arrive before this," Edward said as he sat down. "Mme. Hartouque told you what I wanted?"

There was no answer, but the smaller man grinned and drew a gleaming knife from inside his jacket.

"She has told you all you need to know, I see," Edward said. "This is the plan. Don't ask any questions until I have finished. Listen carefully. If you plan. Don't ask any questions until I have finished. Listen carefully. If you do not understand something I say, raise your hand and I shall repeat it, or, if necessary, I shall explain it further."

Both men nodded.

"We will start tonight. Time is precious to me . . . ."

The taller man raised his hand uncertainly.

"I cannot waste any time," Edward said more distinctly. "I must find a man in Paris who looks so much like me that people will believe he is me."

Edward paused to scrutinize their faces. No expression had appeared on the face of either man; he felt as if he were talking to statues. Sighing, he shook his head and continued, hoping that the men really did understand his words.

"When we find this man, I will give you a signal. From that moment on, we must never let him out of our sight. As soon as we can make certain that we are unobserved . . . "

Edward made a motion with his fist toward his heart. The faces of his listeners brightened instantly; they both nodded their understanding.

"After we have killed him, we will bring him back here, in a coach. We must bring him back here, do you understand?"

They nodded, but there was doubt in the smaller man's eyes, as if he wondered why anyone wanted to bother with a corpse.

"I shall change his clothing and put certain papers in his pockets. When I have finished, we shall drive to Ablon and dump the body into the Seine."

Edward paused while his visitors nodded.

"When we return to Paris, after we have disposed of the corpse . . . "

The taller man raised his hand.

"After we have thrown the body into the river," Edward amended, "your work for me will be finished. If you do well, better than Mme. Hartouque has led me to expect, I shall leave a reward for you with her."

The smaller man frowned and shook his head vigorously; Edward was forced to smile.

"Very well then. I shall give it to you myself, when we return."

They nodded in unison, both of them smiling broadly.

"I may speak now, Monsieur?" the smaller man asked.

"Yes, certainly," Edward nodded.

"We understand your plan, Monsieur," the man said, "but we do not know if it will succeed. It is difficult to find a man who looks just like another. Cristophe, my companion, does not think you will have success."

"How do you know he feels that way?" Edward asked, puzzled. "He has not said a word since he first arrived."

"He cannot, Monsieur. He has no tongue," the man explained. "I, Sebastian, am his companion and his tongue as well. I can tell how he feels from the way he looks at me."

"I see." A shiver ran down Edward's spine. He had heard of this particularly brutal punishment, but he had never encountered a man whose tongue had been torn out. "He may feel that way, but I believe you and I will be able to find this man."

"I think we will, Monsieur. The strength of Cristophe lies more in his hands than in his head. You and I will discover the man, Monsieur; Cristophe will deal with him."

They set out about nine o'clock that evening, Cristophe leading the way. They walked for many blocks, coming closer and closer to the river. The night was overcast, and rain was imminent on the cold, wet wind.

Finally, Cristophe turned into an alleyway and knocked on a door that was hidden by the darkness from all strangers. It opened, and a wave of warm air, heavy with perspiration and smoke, billowed out over them. Edward frowned as they entered. He doubted whether he could find the man he was seeking in this wretched little cafe, but he silently led the way to the bar.

The three of them surveyed the crowd while sipping their drinks to allay suspicion. Edward turned to Sebastian and shook his head. Sebastian shrugged with eloquent shoulders. Cristophe shrugged, too, and Edward led them out of the cafe.

"No one there to interest us. Try another cafe, Sebastian, perhaps a little better than this one."

Sebastian nodded. He led them back the way they had come and then west, parallel to the river. The rain was even closer now than when they had started out; beads of moisture gathered on Edward's brow as he followed Sebastian's tattered coat down the darkened streets. He brushed away the moisture nervously, but it returned again as soon as his hand dropped to his side.

Edward's spirits brightened considerably when they entered the next cafe. There was a better class of people here, although they had not reached the cafe-owner status to which Mme. Hartouque had referred. Perhaps the hunting would prove more successful.

People went in and out of the cafe in a veritable stream. The three men spent nearly two hours there, watching and waiting, but found no one who resembled Edward in the slightest.

During the course of the evening, they visited several more cafes, with no success. Finally Edward gave the signal and the three of them walked back to the little house at 23 Rue Nancy. After he arranged for them to meet him at eight o'clock the next morning, he hurried inside and went to bed.

As he lay there in the dark, his mind whirled with plans for tomorrow. Time—how precious it had suddenly become after this fruitless evening! Six hours wasted already, and he knew there could be no more than a day or two for him to find his double. By that time, Lee or Wentworth would be close on his trail—or worse. Mme. Hartouque, Bertram, the coachman he had taken as far as the head of the street—any one of them might provide his pursuers with the small bit of information they needed. They would descend on him like vultures. If Wentworth should find him first, Edward would be the one floating in the Seine and not his double. He steeled his mind to sleep.

The next day, all morning and all afternoon, the three men coursed through markets and cafes, up and down the streets, searching, peering, glancing sideways at passersby, and staring at faces across smoke-filled rooms. Now and then one of them would halt with an oath—a jubilant oath—but would return glumly to the hunt after a more careful second glance.

Late that afternoon, they stopped at a small cafe for a glass of wine and a brief rest from the strain of searching. As they sat there, Edward noticed a man at the bar who, every few minutes, would turn around and survey the other customers in the cafe. More than once his glance had paused at their table. As Edward observed this, he noticed also that their table was always the first to receive the glance. Edward grew suddenly nervous. He rose and threw some money on the table; his agitation alone was enough to alert the other two.

As soon as they were outside, Edward looked up and down the street, but seeing no coach, he hurried them through an alley to a main thoroughfare. There he spied an empty coach. Hopping into it, he gave directions to the driver to proceed at once to Rue d'Angouleme, the intersection nearest his house.

Sebastian had climbed in directly behind Edward, but Cristophe barely had time to put his foot inside when they started. The mute lurched in wildly and sprawled at Sebastian's feet. This amused Sebastian, who laughed until he noticed that Edward was staring to the rear. He became alarmed, and his anxiety communicated itself to Cristophe, from whose tongueless mouth issued a series of animal grunts.

"A king's man," Edward explained, still peering back. "That man at the bar of the cafe was an agent, I'm sure. We can't afford to be followed. I don't see him now; but when this coach stops, we will all separate. Meet me at my house at six o'clock tonight. Be careful. Make certain there is no one watching you when you arrive. Come in one by one. Is that clear?"

Edward turned to see if they understood. Cristophe's mouth still trembled from the unaccustomed effort he had made to speak, but the swift nodding of the two men told him what he wanted to know.

As the coach stopped, Cristophe and Sebastian scrambled out the door and in a moment were lost on the crowded street. Edward hurriedly thrust some money into the coachman's hand and walked toward the corner. He stopped in front of a shop window just before he turned down Rue Nancy. He could feel his heart beating furiously as he took out a handkerchief to mop his perspiring face. There seemed to be no one following him; he stared into the window for another minute, then went around the corner. Striding rapidly down the street, he turned in abruptly at Number 21. Pausing a few feet inside the gate, he noted that the street was still empty. Swiftly he made his way inside.

He walked immediately to a window in the front room and scrutinized the street. People passed by occasionally, but they passed only once; best of all, no one loitered there, standing in a doorway or leaning casually against a wall or a gate. He sighed with relief, walked into the living room, and poured out a large glass of cognac.

It had been unfortunate, this encounter with the king's man. Would Cristophe and Sebastian return tonight, now that they had scented danger? Would he be forced to finish the work alone? There was no profit in worrying, he told himself; only the night could answer his questions. With the brandy warming him, his determination to carry out his plan became stronger than ever. He did not court danger, but when it came to him, he was always surprised by the exhilaration he felt and the certainty that he would succeed.

Once he had reached England, he would no longer have Wentworth to fear; Paul was ruthless in his own territory, here in Paris, but complacent about activities elsewhere. As if to reassure himself, Edward opened the small leather bag and looked inside. There was enough here for him to live most comfortably as long as he had to keep out of sight. When he reappeared, recovered from the supposed beating he had been given by cutpurses in Paris, he would reestablish himself. The money he would make on the news of Saratoga would be an impenetrable shield for the future.

The feeble sun seemed to stop in the sky that afternoon. While Edward watched and waited, time ran out so slowly that he had to pace incessantly to keep himself from becoming too nervous. When he heard the church bells toll six o'clock, he waited breathlessly. Slowly the minutes passed and a feeling of frustration came over him. Cristophe and Sebastian would not return; they had been frightened away, and he would have to finish the work alone.

He could do it alone, he was certain; but it would prove far more difficult, far more dangerous. Putting the body into the river would be a superhuman task for one man. He did not wish to return to Mme. Hartouque. There was no need to face her questions about Jean. Despairingly, he looked at his watch again. Six-thirty; the last half hour had been a week.

Seven o'clock came, and Edward still paced restlessly up and down the front room, stopping every other minute to peer out into the street. At seven-thirty, as he was looking out the window, he saw the watch pass by. He drew back instinctively, but realizing that he could not be seen at the darkened window, he stared out again until the men had passed and the street had lapsed back into silence.

He was standing by the window when eight o'clock sounded. He counted the bells carefully. Just as their music was dying away, his eyes detected a sudden movement to the left of his house. He gave a long sigh, and a smile of relief smoothed his face. At least there would be one to help him, even if it were the more stupid Cristophe, whose tall figure he had recognized. He hurried to the door, and when he heard the swift patter of footsteps outside, he swung it open. Cristophe stood close beside him as he closed the door, pointing toward the right while those animal sounds seeped up in his throat. Edward looked out and noticed another figure approaching from the right.

Cristophe motioned toward the rear of the house.

Edward, with sudden comprehension, led him swiftly through the darkened rooms and carefully opened a back door. The tall, ragged man disappeared toward the side yard.

Edward hurried back to the front door and looked outside. A man was standing just inside the gate, peering cautiously around him and then scrutinizing the house. Slowly he began to move toward the door. Edward could not see any sign of Cristophe, but he knew he could not be far away, waiting, perhaps, for some distraction which would enable him to move closer to the man.

Edward opened the door slightly. Through a small pane of glass he saw the unknown man stop short and raise his head. The man turned and began to walk toward the street. Through the open door came a curious, whistling noise. The bushes separated, and Cristophe jumped to the stranger's side just as he fell to the ground.

When Edward stepped outside, he heard Cristophe grunt savagely and saw him pull his knife from the man's body. The stranger groaned, rolled over, and lay still. Cristophe leaned down and, picking up the man's body, carried it quickly inside the house. It was the king's man Edward had seen during the afternoon.

"Good work, Cristophe," he whispered.

Just then footsteps sounded again outside the door. Cristophe peered out, nodded, and Edward opened the door for Sebastian. Before they could warn him, Sebastian took a step forward, tripped over the body on the floor, and fell to his knees. He scrambled to his feet and was about to rub his hands on his pants when Cristophe reached out and caught hold of his wrists. The little man looked down at his hands and with sudden comprehension snatched a rag from his pocket and scrubbed them furiously.

When he recognized the figure on the floor, he drew his foot back and kicked the body angrily.

Edward led them into the living room after they had deposited the body of the agent in a small room at the back of the house. Cristophe had searched the man's pockets, and now handed the papers he had found to Edward.

While they waited for Edward to finish reading the papers, they gulped at the cognac he had poured for them. Edward looked up with a slow smile.

"We did well tonight. He was a king's man, as I suspected, but he was alone. He was to report to his superiors tomorrow night, so we still have time."

The two nodded their understanding, but they shifted about uneasily. Edward reached into his pocket and brought out a few gold coins. Their faces brightened as they scrutinized the bright louis in their hands.

"That is a reward for what you did tonight," Edward explained. "The reward I promised you earlier will be much larger than that. We must finish our work quickly; but before we leave here tonight, I want to know if you are both willing to do what I have asked."

Cristophe nodded vigorously; the louis or the pleasure of dispatching the king's man—one of them had convinced him. Sebastian stood unmoved, his face betraying no evidence of either willingness or aversion.

"If you are wondering how long you will be working for me," Edward continued, addressing himself to the smaller man, "I can say that tonight will be our last night together. I must find the man I am searching for tonight—tomorrow will be too late."

Sebastian raised his eyes to Edward's and nodded his willingness.

They started out immediately, Sebastian in the lead, with Edward following and Cristophe in the rear.

On Rue Nancy they moved out of sight of each other, for Edward was still uncertain whether the dead agent had had an assistant. They passed down the street successfully, however; apparently the papers had told the truth. They moved closer to each other once they had left Rue Nancy, yet kept far enough apart to disappear should one be stopped.

They had walked nearly a mile when Edward saw the lights of a cafe. He had just noticed Sebastian stop before the doorway, when a man suddenly walked out.

The man drew abreast of Edward and squinted at him in the faint light reflected from the window of the cafe.

"Bon soir, M. Gallet," the man called out to Edward's amazement. "I missed you tonight. I had hoped we might have a cognac together."

Edward had started violently when the man spoke to him. Recovering his presence of mind, he muffled his voice and his face as best he could before replying.

"I am sorry also, Monsieur. Perhaps tomorrow night. *Bon soir.*" As the other man walked on into the darkness, Edward stared after him, his face wreathed in a smile. Cristophe came up beside him, and Edward reached out and patted his back with sudden jubilation. Cristophe jumped away as if Edward had beaten a sword on his back and looked warily and wonderingly at him from a safe distance.

"Come along," he said to Cristophe. "I must talk to you and Sebastian."

Just beyond the cafe, there was a small alley into which Edward led the others. He told them of his encounter with the man on the street.

"He mistook me for another," he said slowly.

"This means that the man we have been seeking is almost within our grasp. He comes here, to this cafe, regularly. He was expected tonight, but has not yet come, so we shall watch for him."

Cristophe raised his hand. Sebastian turned on his companion in sudden fury.

"The man we have been looking for," he explained rapidly, his excitement increasing as he talked, "comes to this cafe. He looks just like Monsieur. We shall wait for him to come here. Then . . . "

Cristophe nodded with sudden comprehension. Edward led them out of the alley and across the street to a spot where they had a good view of the cafe and the surrounding buildings.

"You wait over there," he said to Sebastian, pointing to a dark corner beyond the cafe. "I saw a small space there between two buildings. Wait until this man approaches. When you see that he is the one who looks so much like me, go up to him and beg for alms. He will give you nothing, probably, or tell you to be off, but Cristophe will be beside him then."

"You, Cristophe, stand in that little alleyway where we were talking. When you see Sebastian stop the man, run up to him quickly, but silently. You know what to do then. Be certain you are neat, so there will be little blood. Above all, don't let him cry out. As soon as it is finished, carry him back into the alleyway and wait there."

"Sebastian, when Cristophe has carried the man into the alleyway, open the door of the cafe and look inside. That will be the signal I shall be waiting for. As soon as I come out, we obtain a coach. Then we take our drunken friend home. Now, do you both understand what you are to do?"

They nodded, but to make certain, Edward went through it once again. He could not risk an error now. Edward watched Cristophe and Sebastian move to the places he had designated. When they had stationed themselves to his satisfaction, he walked into the cafe.

It was not crowded. As Edward moved toward the bar, he saw a gleam of recognition spring up in the proprietor's eyes and a smile brighten his face. But as Edward approached, the smile faded. He ordered a glass of cognac, and the man served him with a puzzled look, which forced a smile from Edward.

"Pardon, Monsieur," the man apologized when he noticed the smile on Edward's face. "It was most impolite of me to stare at you, but I thought when you first entered that you were someone else. The resemblance between you and another of my customers is most remarkable."

"Indeed? I should like to meet this customer of yours. Perhaps he is a relation of mine."

"Ah, Monsieur jests." The proprietor beamed, happy to have his embarrassment ignored. "No, you are English, Monsieur, and he but a poor French clerk. I doubt very much that he is a relation of yours, unless certain of your ancestors remained in France. But there is a remarkable resemblance, though he is not quite so tall as you, Monsieur."

Edward and the proprietor proceeded to other topics. As they talked together, the bottle of ordinary cognac on the bar was unobtrusively changed by the proprietor for a better bottle. Edward had scarcely tested this new cognac when Sebastian's head appeared for a moment in the doorway and then disappeared like a puppet brought on in the wrong scene. Edward pulled out his watch and whistled softly.

"What a pity! I must leave you now; I am late."

"To your health, Monsieur, and a long and happy life," the proprietor said, lifting his glass.

Edward bowed and placed some money on the counter.

Outside he found Sebastian waiting for him. The little man nodded toward the alleyway, and they hurried toward it. Edward could barely distinguish Cristophe and the crumpled figure at his feet.

"Good. I'll get the coach at once. Any trouble?"

Cristophe shook his head slowly and smiled. Edward hurried toward a main thoroughfare where he might be able to find a coach. It was late, and he knew that coachmen were not fond of cruising about these streets without a fare. He finally managed to find one and gave the driver the address of the cafe.

"We must stop for my friends," he said as he climbed in. "One of them is not feeling too well. Too much cognac."

The coachman clucked sympathetically and flicked his whip over his horses. When they reached the cafe, Edward sighed with relief when he saw the street was empty. Cristophe and Sebastian moved forward as soon as they saw the door of the coach open and Edward's head appear. The coachman watched with amusement as the two men approached with their burden supported between them. The man's head had fallen forward and was bobbing from side to side. When they reached the coach, Edward reached out, seized an arm, and with the aid of Cristophe's mighty heave, placed the body on the seat of the coach. Edward called out the address on Rue Nancy, and they began to move up the street.

Edward tried to peer through the blackness inside the coach. He felt an overwhelming desire to study the features of the dead man. He could barely make out the position of the man's body, slumped as it was in one corner of the seat where Cristophe had pushed it. The face, turned toward the far side of the coach, remained a mystery. He had to restrain himself from asking Cristophe to turn the dead man's face toward him.

"We must think now about this coachman," he said quietly. Sebastian nodded and pulled out his knife. Edward shook his head, and Sebastian put the knife back inside his jacket again.

"Not unless it is absolutely necessary," Edward warned. "I have a better plan. As soon as we reach the house, you and Cristophe carry this man inside.

"Put him in the back room, where we placed the body of the king's man. Change his clothes to the ones I showed you. While you are doing that, I will take care of this coachman. As soon as I have finished with him, I shall come into the room and let you know. Wait there—don't come out into the living room."

Sebastian nodded a reluctant understanding. It was obvious he would much prefer to use his knife, which was far simpler and required no planning. He shrugged as if to say this was a waste of time.

The coach pulled up in front of the house, and Edward jumped out. After opening the front door, he hurried back to assist Sebastian and Cristophe; but they had already removed their burden from the coach and were dragging the body rapidly up the steps.

"We shall try and sober him before we take him home to his wife," Edward said, gazing up at the coachman. "It may take us a little time, but I shall pay you well for waiting."

"Very good, Monsieur," the coachman replied. Slumping down on his box, he turned his coat collar up over his ears to keep off the damp air and stared fixedly forward at his horses.

"It is close to rain," Edward said after a moment of silence.

All that came from the coachman in answer to this statement was a grunt and a more pronounced slump on the rickety box. The coachman's face had disappeared somewhere inside his coat collar.

"In fact, it has begun to rain," Edward continued.

He paused, then added, "I think I shall go inside and have a glass of cognac to warm me."

The coat collar quivered, and the tip of the coachman's nose thrust out as if sniffing the air.

"If you would care to come inside, I should be pleased to offer you a glass," Edward remarked. "It might make this period of waiting pass more quickly."

The nose protruded farther from the collar. The coachman's face appeared, pleased but puzzled by this unexpected invitation.

After a polite though cautious stare which seemed to satisfy him, he struggled laboriously to the ground, groaning and wheezing with the sudden effort that taxed his stiff muscles.

"Monsieur is most kind," he said after he was safely down on the ground. "This is a foul night, but a little cognac would improve it."

Edward led the way into the house. While the coachman stood uncertainly in the living room, Edward disappeared into another room and returned a moment later with a bottle of cognac and two glasses.

The candlelight danced over the glasses as he set them down on a small table, the sparkle of them matching the appreciative gleam in the coachman's eyes. The soft, throaty gurgle of the cognac as it was poured into the glasses was more than the coachman's conscience could bear; he shifted nervously on his feet and walked to the window to stare out at his horses and make certain that they were all right.

Edward turned his back to him. Reaching into his pocket, he took out a packet which he emptied into one of the glasses.

A second later he lifted the glasses from the table. He held one toward the coachman and raised his own glass in a mocking toast toward the foul weather outside.

The coachman downed his cognac in a single gulp. Edward took a small sip of his and then hastened to refill his guest's glass.

"Ha! That is excellent cognac, Monsieur," the coachman exclaimed. "It drives out all the wet I took inside me."

"I am glad," Edward said with a smile. "It should not be too long before we are ready to leave."

Edward started to walk toward a comfortable chair. Before he reached it, he dropped his glass into the seat and turned to catch the groaning coachman just before he struck the floor. He dragged the unconscious man to the chair, stretched him out in it, and removed the glass from beneath him. He looked down at him for a moment, then walked quickly to the room at the rear of the house.

The two men were standing beside the bed when Edward entered the room. They stood aside.

As he glanced down at the bed, Edward started violently at the face of the man who was lying there. It was an excellent likeness. After a day or so in the Seine, this dead man dressed in Edward's clothes would be indistinguishable from Dr. Edward Bancroft.

There were slight differences, to be sure, Edward noted as he studied the man's face. The eyes were set closer together, and the nose was slightly broader; but few would recognize such minor discrepancies.

The physique was nearly the same. Whatever differences did exist would disappear after the river had done its work.

"You have done well, Sebastian. As soon as I have put the necessary papers in his pockets, you and Cristophe can take him to the coach and drive him to Ablon."

They nodded and watched as Edward carefully inserted various papers in the pockets of the dead man.

He paused at the identification paper signed by Deane and Franklin. Sighing, he folded it into his wallet, which he then placed in the man's jacket. When all was finished, Edward took off his ring and twisted it onto the man's finger. It was a tight fit; but Cristophe, seeing Edward's difficulty, stepped forward and jammed the ring down on the dead man's finger.

"You had better take him along, too," Edward said, pointing to the body of the king's man. "Put heavy stones in his clothing, and take him farther down river. I don't want him found at the same time as this other."

They carried the king's man to the coach first.

When they had returned for their second burden, Edward turned to Sebastian.

"I shall wait here with the coachman, in case he should wake up and wonder where his coach is. Hurry back as quickly as you can. But do a good job at the river, and be especially careful that you are not observed."

"*Oui, Monsieur*," Sebastian agreed. "We will return shortly."

After they had carried the second man outside, Edward closed the door behind them. He walked back to the table.

"*Bon voyage,* Dr. Bancroft," he said, raising his glass toward the street.

Edward settled in to wait for the return of Sebastian and Cristophe. He passed the time watching the fitful sleep of the drugged man. The coachman stirred from time to time, muttering and turning from side to side. His breathing was irregular, alternating from snores to wheezing gasps. Edward had not used this particular drug for some time, and he was fascinated to watch the effects change from hour to hour. He had discovered the drug in Surinam, where the natives used it during certain festivals.

He noticed that the drug affected the user's color strangely. The coachman's face, when Edward had saved him from falling on the floor, had been a glazed white. Since then it had reddened increasingly until it was now an ominous purple. Edward thought of apoplexy, but soon he was relieved to see the natural color returning and to hear his breath assume a more normal rhythm.

It was almost dawn when Edward heard the noise of a coach coming down the street. He sprang from his chair and rushed to the window. It was the coach; he recognized it even before it had pulled to an awkward stop in front of the house. Edward opened the door for the weary men and closed it swiftly behind them.

"It was all right?" he asked nervously. "No trouble, no difficulty?"

Sebastian shook his head. His pants were still wet, as were Cristophe's, from his work at the river.

"No one saw you? No one stopped you?"

"No, no trouble," Sebastian replied.

"Good. The coachman is our last chore, then. We must put him back on his coach and turn him loose.

"That will be your last work for me, and I shall leave it to you where you take him. Be certain that he's at least twenty blocks from this house, however. He may remember the address when he awakens, but that will not be for some time."

They nodded their understanding. Edward reached into his jacket and pulled out two bundles of notes.

Giving one to each of them, he waited while they counted the money.

"You have done well, both of you," he said. "That is why I have given you a larger reward. If I should need assistance again, I shall ask Mme. Hartouque to send both of you."

The men beamed with pleasure as they stuffed their money inside their jackets. They picked up the coachman and staggered out under the heavy weight.

Edward followed them to the door and stood there watching until the coach had disappeared from sight. It was lighter in the street now; dawn was approaching. Low clouds scudded past, so low that they seemed to be just over the tops of the buildings. It will be an unpleasant day for travel, he thought.

After removing the nameplate by the front door, he changed his clothes and made a small bundle of the clothes still left in the house. He started toward Rue d'Angouleme. At the first alley he reached, he walked down several doors and deposited the bundle of clothes beside one of the shuttered houses. He turned back and walked quickly to Rue d'Angouleme, carrying only the small leather bag which contained his papers and his money. There was still an hour till sunrise; by the time that hour was over, he would be in a coach, moving toward Calais.

CHAPTER XX

THE DISCOMFORT OF THE COACH TRIP to Calais kept Edward's mind from dwelling too much on what might be happening in Paris. His fellow passengers laid the blame for their discomfort, with some justification, squarely on the shoulders of their coachman. At each stop, all would alight, grateful for a few moments of rest, to gather in small, spiteful groups and make loud and increasingly rude comments about the obvious defects in the coach and the failing sight of their driver.

At Boulogne sur Mer, where the coach made its second overnight stop, he could not sleep. All night he paced anxiously up and down his small bedroom, wondering whether Lee and Wentworth were on his trail, visualizing couriers riding to the ports to alert the authorities.

When morning at last brought the welcome voice of the innkeeper calling his guests to breakfast, Edward found he was too nervous and too tense to eat.

When the coach reached Calais, Edward washed at the inn and then left in search of Captain Hynson.

He stopped first at the Cafe des Anglais, as Hynson had recommended, but Mme. Perret was unable to tell him where Hynson was. He had been expected earlier in the week, she informed him, but he had not yet come back from England; surely he would arrive soon, perhaps today. The woman was as eager to find Hynson as Edward, she explained, for she, too, had work for the captain. Her shrug implied that perhaps it was the authorities that delayed him, or a girl, or several girls. The captain, she leered, was an impetuous man.

Several times that day, Edward stopped to see if Hynson had appeared. He did not want to delay crossing to England any longer than was necessary, but it would be far easier and safer to cross with Hynson than to risk apprehension aboard the regular packet.

He was returning to the Cafe des Anglais for a final inquiry before deciding what course to follow when he heard a familiar voice. He smiled. That voice, which he had often heard raised in anger, was now raised in song. It tumbled out of a little cafe farther down the street and ran along the buildings like a bawdy urchin. The song was a familiar one to Edward; it dealt in a rude fashion with the more salient characteristics of George the Third's anatomy. He had heard it last aboard the *Reprisal*, when one of the sailors had burst forth as Wickes gave chase to the British corvette.

Hynson's scrawny figure was bent over the bar as Edward entered the cafe. He was surrounded by admiring listeners and a tight-lipped proprietor, who clearly liked neither the song nor the singer but was too outnumbered to make an effectual protest. The captain's left hand held tight to the bar while his right waved a bottle of cognac.

Edward took a seat in the corner and watched with amusement as the captain's cognac diminished noticeably after each stanza. He noticed that the puckered face of the unamused proprietor was beginning to annoy Hynson and that every time he lifted the bottle, a few drops spilled on the bar. Finally, the audience grew tired of hearing the same stanzas and returned to their seats. Edward moved closer to Hynson.

"Now put it down, my friend," he heard the proprietor say, "and pay up. We've all enjoyed your little song, but it's time you paid for the cognac."

"You haven't enjoyed it a bit, you lying buzzard," Hynson bellowed, leaning belligerently over the bar, "but don't worry, I'll pay. If that's all that's troublin' you, mate, don't pucker your pretty face any longer. I can pay for a dozen bottles of this filthy stuff, if I was fool enough to rot my belly with it."

"Captain Hynson."

Hynson straightened and turned quickly about.

More cognac slopped out of the bottle and splashed on Edward's sleeve.

Hynson flushed and thundered an order to the proprietor to find a cloth to wipe his friend's coat before the cloth was eaten away.

"Dr. Bancroft! Damn me, sir, I'm sorry for wettin' you with this foul stuff. Here, you, give us a bottle that's fit for my friend here."

Hynson led Edward to a table and gulped a glass from the fresh bottle of cognac before he spoke.

"It's a long time since I've seen you, Doctor. Have you found some work for me?"

"Yes, Captain, I have. I want you to take me to England—at once."

Hynson grunted with surprise and then stared mournfully into his glass. As if the sight of the cognac made him sadder than he wanted to be, he reached out and with a single, practiced motion, emptied the glass in one swallow.

"At once, eh? I'm not one who usually lets work interfere with pleasure, Doctor. I had a good tipple planned for tonight, too, but you never can be certain, can you? It's short notice, Doctor. I still have a job to do here for a friend of mine. He told me he'd pay me well for it, and I hate to lose the money."

"Look here, Hynson, don't worry about money," Edward exclaimed. "You know how well I've always paid you. I'll give you whatever you ask for this trip, providing it's below a pirate's price. Take me to England tonight, and I'll pay you whatever you think your friend's bit of work is worth as well."

"You know, Doctor," Hynson chuckled as he refilled his glass, "it's a pity you're not a sea captain. You'd make a great trader—you could talk the Indians out of their beads. You can't talk old Joe Hynson out of his word, though, not that easy. No one ever said I wasn't a man of my word, whatever the size of the bribe. I don't want them to start talking tomorrow."

Edward shrugged and filled their glasses again.

They sat at the table for some time, talking in a desultory way about conditions on the channel, the weather, and the personal deficiencies of the other patrons in the cafe. Finally, Edward noticed, Hynson was beginning to nod.

"I must say good night, Captain," he said, leaning toward the drowsing captain and phrasing his words carefully. "I shall have to find someone else with enough courage to take me to England tonight."

Hynson squinted and focused his eyes with difficulty. An angry red crept over his cheeks.

"Courage? What do you mean 'courage,' Doctor? You won't find no one in this port with more courage than me. No one, d'you hear?"

"Perhaps not, perhaps so," Edward answered.

He picked up his hat and his small leather bag and started for the door. Hynson staggered to his feet and caught him by the arm.

"My friend said he'd pay me twenty pounds, Doctor. Are you willin' to match that?"

Edward reached into his wallet and pulled out several notes, then placed them on Hynson's clenched fist. The sailor looked down, opened his fist, and closed his fingers around the notes. He followed Edward meekly to the door.

They walked down to the waterfront, and, after several false starts, Hynson found his boat. He readied her speedily for the voyage, Edward giving him what help he could. There was a fair breeze blowing from the southwest; Edward figured that, with luck in clearing Calais and entering Dover, he might find himself on his way toward London on the morning coach.

They moved out of Calais in pitch blackness. Edward's eyes were slow in accustoming themselves to the undulant darkness of the water. Occasionally he was able to discern the outline of a large ship that had been anchored just off the channel; but Hynson, however unsteady he had seemed in the cafe, now had the night vision of a cat. He saw everything Edward never saw until they were almost upon it—small boats which passed so close to them that Edward had only to reach out to touch them; floating hazards of barrels and logs that moved past them harmlessly, although any one of them might have bashed in a side of Hynson's small boat.

The air was warm, and Edward sniffed at the strange odors that wafted past them. Above all was the briny tang of the sea, the salty smell which left a wet trace on his face and hands. The smell of fish was strong, too; and from time to time, the sickly sweet stench of Calais sewage filled the air about them and made it nauseating to breathe.

Gradually, as they cleared the harbor and the few visible lights faded to soft, orangy dots, the sea breeze freshened and the odors of the land and the scents of man were driven off. Beyond the circle of that filthy harbor, there was no smell save that of the sea, the clean sea, freshened by the wind and the tossing, air-spun salt waves.

Edward sniffed gratefully at the fresh air. Stretching out, he gazed up at the bright stars. He was free now; France lay behind him in the darkness. Out of sight were Wentworth and Lee and the king's men.

The strain he had undergone these last few days had vanished; the pursuit was ended, and in his heart he felt an unaccustomed peace. He knew that for the first time in weeks he would be able to sleep through the night.

While Edward thought and meditated, Hynson was busy with the sails and the rudder. He moved about so frequently that he no longer claimed Edward's attention each time he went past. He had become a part of his boat, as much a part as the creaking ropes and the steady thump of water against the bow and the occasional roll of the little craft as she labored through the channel waves.

It was not a rough sea, but the wind was steady and seemed to increase as they moved closer to England. Several hours out of Calais, Edward sat up and went to where Hynson was sitting beside the rudder, the bowl of his pipe glowing like an eye in the night.

"Think we'll make it before long, Captain?"

"Aye, Doctor, we will. The way this little beauty's running, we'll make it an hour before I thought we would."

"Fine. I need to land as soon as I can."

"You sound like someone's chasin' you, Doctor," Hynson chuckled.

"No," Edward shook his head and laughed, "it's not quite that bad, Captain. Let's say I have a few more enemies than I had when you last saw me."

"I shouldn't be surprised by that. You're in a fine position to make enemies, Doctor. You've got money, for one thing—that always sets people against you. And you must be lucky, too—you're here, and whoever's after you is still in France."

"No one can count on luck, Hynson," Edward disagreed. "You have to be more clever than the others. That's why you make enemies."

"Couldn't say about that, Doctor. I've had enemies in my day, too, but they was ones that was jealous of my boat or my clothes or the way the girls chased me. If they was captains, I didn't worry. I never saw a captain yet I couldn't give as good as I got. The mates, now, Doctor—they're another piece of the pig. Dangerous fellows they are, always with their eye on the captain's cabin, and not bashful about how they get there."

"You have to expect that, don't you, Hynson? Doesn't every good mate want to be a captain some day?"

"Yes, they do. Maybe there ain't enough room for all of them. It's like your business, Doctor. There ain't enough room in it, either, is there? Can't think of no other reason why you'd come roarin' out of France with a satchel in your hand, lookin' as though the Devil himself was chasin' you."

Edward shifted uncomfortably and gazed out over the water.

"I don't know rightly what your business is, Doctor, but I'd say you had a mighty broad back—an easy target for a knife."

Hynson fell silent and tended to the sails before rejoining his passenger.

"Perhaps I should take up some safer occupation," Edward mused when the captain returned, "something like sailing or fishing."

"You could do worse, Doctor. As I said tonight, you'd make a fine trader. You might even make a good captain, Doctor; you learn fast, and you can drink along with me, for a short distance, that is."

"A very short distance, Hynson," Edward laughed. "I am not blessed with your capacity."

"A pity it is, too. But then, I always was a great one for cognac and rum," Hynson said proudly. "When I was in the Colonies, things weren't easy for me, what with those religious people and their laws against the few remaining pleasures of the poor. Whenever I finished what I was doin', I'd trot around to the tavern and wash down the dust that was caught in my throat. I built up quite a tolerance for rum that way."

"I can see how you might have. It must be a valuable asset."

"It is, Doctor, it is. Sailors respect that, and so do other captains. I've seen some of them come into a tavern, just after they finished unloadin' a fine cargo and signin' on a new crew. Their wives and their supper would be waitin' for them, but I've seen them sit down to their rum and not move for two or three days. They'd stay there perfectly happy, three or four of them, swappin' yarns, tradin' lies, drinkin' rum, and cursin'. The lads around the taverns begged to be the ones who carried the thundermugs in and out, so they could hear the stories that were told. But then, that was Philadelphia."

"It's not the same here, in England and France?"

"Nothing like the same. Over here you worry—you worry about what you say, about who you're talkin' to, about the king and the king's men and the bloody government officials. You didn't have worries like that in the Colonies. There was always more of you than there was officials. It's killed the stories here for sure, Doctor, and it's also taken a lot of pleasure out of life."

Hynson stood up, and Edward relaxed. He watched the captain make his way carefully about the small craft, checking and tightening ropes and sails with total assurance.

He wondered what it would be like to be caught in a storm in a boat as small as this. He knew about the sudden storms that flashed through the channel, piling waves to enormous heights and hurling strong ships upon the rocks of the coast. Would Hynson be as calm as he was now? Probably. Edward had never seen him otherwise when he was at sea.

"We should make Dover in another hour, Doctor," Hynson said when he came aft again. "At least we will if this wind don't change."

"That's splendid. Where do you plan to land?"

"Don't know exactly," Hynson replied, scratching his head and peering through the darkness toward the English coast. "To me, it makes no difference. This little beauty will go wherever I want her to. I thought I'd let you choose the spot."

"What about the place where you were tied up when I first met you? That wasn't a spot that would require the attention of the watch."

"You sound like all your troubles weren't left behind in France, Doctor."

"The French king has a long arm, Captain."

"You're right, I guess. I don't know much about him, but then I don't want to," Hynson muttered. He leaned back against the rail, one hand loose on the rudder, and looked out across the water again.

Edward felt a sudden urge to stretch and move about. He went forward to the bow where he stared at the restless, whitecapped water. The boat was running swiftly in the stronger wind, but he could feel her quiver more and more as the minutes passed.

Spray from the waves soon forced him back beside Hynson again. In the distance, tiny lights suddenly spoke to them through the blackness.

"That must be the Calais packet," Hynson murmured.

Edward watched the lights until they flickered out. Hynson's words had brought back uneasy recollections to him. He felt as if he had gone through this dark voyage before, as if he were reliving one of his dreams. His surroundings, his companion, even the words he spoke fell into a half-remembered pattern. They evoked a tenuous recollection that stayed just beyond his grasp.

Hynson sniffed suddenly, then began to lower sail. When he sat down again, he pushed the rudder sharply. The little craft shuddered and eased slowly into her new course.

They were nearing Dover. The captain picked his way by instinct into the harbor; Edward was just able to discern the indistinct mass of shipping and shoreline before them. Hynson maneuvered more rapidly the closer they came; he was like a hare covering its tracks, shifting and changing about at the slightest hint of danger. Boats and ships and hazards of all kinds surrounded them, and Hynson's little craft turned and twisted with such agility that Edward soon lost all sense of direction. When Hynson finally brought the little craft up alongside a looming pier, Edward felt as if he were in a completely strange place.

After the boat had been tied up and they had climbed the swinging ladder to the secure footing of the wharf, Edward recognized certain landmarks. The front of one darkened cafe was the one from which he had pulled Hynson many months ago. They continued on up the empty street, their footsteps loud in the quiet, until they had reached the central part of the city.

Edward paid Hynson and bade him farewell, then made his way quickly to the coaching station. An hour later, he was on his way to London.

It was afternoon when he descended from his coach in Cavendish Square. Sam Wharton's house stood shuttered.

As he gazed at it, listening to the fading clop-clop of the horses' hooves as they moved away, he drew a deep breath. This was the haven he had planned to reach, and this was the day he had planned to reach it. His plan had succeeded—he was safe from Wentworth, beyond the revenge of Lee.

He lifted the knocker on the door and banged it sharply against the metal plate. He listened for several minutes, but no sound disturbed the quiet of the house.

Again he knocked, and this time he heard the shuffling of feet inside.

A shutter above him creaked, and a voice demanded, "Who's there? This is no tavern!"

Edward smiled as he recognized the voice of Wharton's servant. He moved back from the door and gazed up at the partly opened window.

"It's me, John—Dr. Bancroft. Is Mr. Wharton here?"

"Who did you say it was?"

"Dr. Bancroft."

"Oh, it's ye, is it, Doctor? Mr. Wharton isn't home, sir. He's to the country."

"I see. Well, let me in, John. I've come a long way. I'll stay until he returns."

"As ye say, sir. I'll be down at once."

The heavy door opened a moment later and jerked to a stop at the end of a chain. John's face peered out through the crack, surveying Edward as a final precaution. At last the door swung open all the way.

"I imagine if ye've come a long distance, sir, ye'd like to rest," the servant offered. "Mr. Wharton's room is ready, if ye'd care to use that."

"I'll do that, John," Edward replied with relief. "Did Mr. Wharton say when he expected to return?"

"He went to the country for a few days, sir. Said he was coming back to his office late in the week. I judge it'll be Thursday or Friday before he arrives."

John led the way to Wharton's room. After he had set down Edward's bag, he bowed and departed.

Edward slipped out of his clothes and pulled on one of Sam's enormous nightshirts. He smiled to himself as he stretched out on the comfortable bed— the only person he could think of, besides Sam, who could properly fill out the nightshirt he was wearing was Mrs. Earnshaw.

For the next few days, Edward stayed in Sam's house, sleeping, reading, and recovering from the excitement of the past week.

On Thursday morning, he woke to an insistent shaking. "Edward! Edward! Wake up!" Wharton kept repeating.

Edward grunted and started to turn over on his side, but Sam pulled hard on his arm, straightening him up in bed.

"Damn, man, wake up," Wharton bellowed. "I have to talk to you."

Edward sat up in bed lazily and smiled. "Hello, Sam."

Sunlight filtered through the windows. Edward squinted at the brightness and tried to judge the hour. It must be noon or perhaps even later than that.

"I'm glad to see you, Sam. I have news for you. But first, what about the word I sent regarding Saratoga?"

"I got it," Wharton boomed. "And I got it just when we wanted it most, Edward. I beat the others by a whole day. We've had so much to do at the office that except for the last few days I've practically slept there."

"I knew you'd be happy when you received that news," Edward laughed. "It's what we've been waiting for all this time. How much did we make? Have you figured that out?"

"I hardly dare tell you, Edward. The last time I checked we had cleared more than two hundred thousand, but we've been blacklisted."

"What? Didn't you spread the orders around so they couldn't tell who was doing the selling?"

Wharton raised his hands and grunted sorrowfully.

"I did the best I could, Edward. I took as much profit in the first sale as I thought was wise, but it was too much, apparently. They checked the orders and found they were all in Peabody's name. He's been dodging the writ server ever since. I had to send him to Scotland to keep him out of danger."

"Well," Edward sighed, "at least they can't connect my name with this."

"This time they can't," Wharton agreed with a laugh, "but they're trying; they don't even respect the dead."

Edward peered curiously at Wharton, who seemed to be enjoying a private joke.

"What do you mean?" he asked.

"I was going to ask you, before we started talking about the trading, how you'd like to go to your own funeral."

"Funeral? Go to my own funeral? Oh! You don't mean they sent that body all the way from Paris?"

"Indeed, they did. The news is out—at least two journals have printed what they can discover. Walpole came in to see me last night with a copy of a journal he had obtained from Paris. It seems that you were killed, robbed, and thrown into the Seine. Your body has been returned to London, and your dear wife is prostrated with grief."

"How are my obituaries?" Edward asked with a smile.

"I think you will be pleased." Wharton paused while Edward stretched comfortably and sat up in bed.

"You know, Edward," Wharton continued admiringly, "you're an ingenious devil. You fooled everybody with this scheme of yours. You had me fooled, too. Tell me something—who was the man you threw into the Seine?"

"I didn't throw anyone in the Seine."

"You know what I mean. Who was he?"

"I really don't know, Sam. A clerk, I was told."

"How did you ever find him?"

"By looking. He was the last piece in my puzzle. I had to find him—so I did."

Wharton shook his head, bewildered.

"I can't understand it," he sighed after a moment. "I've never known a luckier man than you in my life. But I hope you'll be careful now, for a while at least. Why don't you go away somewhere, until all this dies down?"

"I intend to. First, though, what about this funeral of mine? When is it to be held?"

"That was the first thing Walpole spoke about when he showed me your obituary last night. He said I should come to the funeral at five o'clock tomorrow afternoon, at the church just below your house."

"St. Mark's. Ah, that's Olivia's revenge, I suspect. She knows how much I dislike the man there. I think I shall attend it." Edward glanced up at Wharton with a speculative smile.

"Good God, Edward," Sam protested, "don't take a risk like that. You aren't safe here yet. You ought to go to the country. Better still, go to Scotland where Peabody is. Let this affair quiet down first. You don't want to lose everything you've gained because of some silly whim. Be sensible."

"Nonsense, Sam. I'm perfectly safe now. I don't intend to take any unnecessary risks, but I'll be damned if I'm not going to my own funeral."

"I think you're mad," Wharton groaned, shaking his head. "However, if you've made up your mind, I know I can't change it."

"I can't go in my own clothes," Edward mused. "I'll need a disguise of some sort."

"If you want any of my clothes ... " Wharton began.

Edward laughed quietly. Taking hold of the nightshirt, he held it out in front of him.

"Thank you, Sam," he chuckled, "but I think I need more disguise and less material. I can't be a mourner very well, but I could be a spectator. I know—a scavenger. Do you suppose John could find a costume for me?"

"Possibly." Wharton rose. "I'll see to it now."

Edward leaned back against the headboard of the bed, his head cradled in his hands. There was a broad smile on his face as he imagined the scene at the funeral tomorrow.

Wharton returned a few minutes later.

"These will barely cover you, Edward," he said, holding up a bundle of rags in one arm, "but they will have to do. They're cast-offs—clean, fortunately for you. It would be otherwise if we had to get them from a real scavenger."

"They'll do nicely, I'm certain. Thank you, Sam. What time is it now?"

"Just after eleven. I think I shall go back out to the country to relax. I'll let someone else run the firm until this Saratoga news dies down. Another surprise like the one you've given me, and I won't be fit to do it."

"You'll recover quickly, Sam, especially if there's enough port near you," Edward chuckled. "I think I'll stay here until after the funeral and then go north, as you suggested. I'll let you know where as soon as I'm settled. There's one matter I want to take up with you before you go. Open that little leather bag there, will you?"

Wharton picked up the bag and opened it. He reached inside and pulled out a package, then stripped the wrapper from it. His eyes widened as he gazed at the fat bundle of bills.

"That bag has about twenty thousand pounds in it, Sam," Edward said before his partner had recovered from his astonishment, "mostly in notes, although there are some jewels as well."

"Where did you get it, Edward? You never made that much working for the Americans."

"That was just how I got it, Sam—working for the Americans. I didn't get it in salary, however, if that's what you mean."

"It must have been blackmail," Wharton gasped, sinking into a chair, "or robbery. What else would pay so well?"

"No, Sam, neither one. The money came from hard work and a little luck. There were a few honest commissions to start with, and after that quite a few prize sales. I have an understanding with several of the agents. The last sale netted me almost two thousand, but I had to give back some of it in order to persuade the captain to sell at my price. As you can see, it was an effective system."

"It certainly must have been," Sam whispered with respect. He started to put the money back in the bag. "Do you want me to add this to your other funds?"

"Only half of it. I don't know how long I'll be up north, and I want to live comfortably. I think I'll take half of it with me."

Wharton divided the money, then turned his gaze from the bag.

"I'll be going now, Edward. Don't forget to write me your address."

"I won't. Good-bye, Sam, and thank you for all your help. Keep after the market—don't let that blacklisting stop you. Remember that the Exchange will forget all about this soon."

Edward spent the rest of the day reading. He rose late the next morning and waited impatiently for the hour set for his funeral. When it was time for him to dress, he called in John for assistance.

The ragged clothes fit him fairly well, though a bit loosely around the waist. When he had finished putting them on, he stepped in front of the glass and surveyed himself.

"What do you think, John?"

The old servant stepped forward, chuntering to himself over this inexplicable whim of the doctor's. He pulled sharply on one sleeve of the jacket. There was a slight ripping of cloth, and the jacket now gave Edward a much more disreputable appearance.

"Why should ye ever want to wear such rags as these when ye have such fine clothes, Doctor?" John muttered despairingly. "I suppose it's a masquerade where all the quality's to be scavengers?"

"Something of the sort, John. How do I look?"

John stood back and surveyed him carefully, his eyes checking every detail of face, hair, and clothes. He made a few more changes—a comb destroyed all semblance of order in Edward's hair—and then nodded his approval.

"That's it, Doctor. A fine scavenger ye are now, begging your pardon, sir. That was a good idea of yours not to shave."

When Edward turned to the glass again, he could not suppress a start of astonishment. John's last few, deft touches had effected a major change in his appearance.

"You've done a superb job," Edward told him. "I'm grateful. You might give those clothes of mine a good brushing, and please put one of Mr. Wharton's heavy sweaters in my case, will you? I'll be back in a little while."

Edward threw the sack which John had brought for him over his shoulder. Bashing a filthy hat onto his head, he walked out of the house just as four o'clock was striking.

He had allowed himself sufficient time to walk the distance from Wharton's house to his own and still be there in time to watch the procession of mourners.

That was one ceremony he did not want to miss; he would never have such an opportunity again, he told himself with a wry smile. He wanted to take in the whole macabre spectacle, to observe those who were present, to chide those who were absent, and to amuse himself by noting the semblances of grief and sorrow displayed.

His excitement mounted as he walked through the streets. He found it easy to play the part of a scavenger after dodging a few blows from the attendants of the well dressed pedestrians. At every appearance of authority, he hunched lower and slunk across the street or down an alley, as if his sack contained the spoils of a robbery. How simple, really, the transition from one class to another—a change of clothes, an absence of lace, an abundance of rags, and one's entire viewpoint could change.

The opprobrium in the glances flung at him made him rebel. He found that respectability and property acquired a cold, disdainful aspect. The dirty alleys became friendly and helpful; they were asylums from the contempt of the self-righteous. Shop windows were no longer invitations to buy but challenges to steal; shop doors not entrances but barriers.

Edward moved as unobtrusively as possible. Here, where the buildings were familiar and where he could see at some distance the bulk of his own house, his caution warned him that he must be prepared for any emergency, that he must have a path of retreat ready in case he should be surprised by a caretaker or spotted by one of the runners.

Looking for a safe place from which to observe the funeral procession, his eyes quickly scanned the houses opposite his own and selected Number 10. That house, bleak and shuttered, was still unoccupied, he noticed. There was a yard beside the house, he remembered from the many times he had walked past it. The yard was not enclosed, and a small alleyway connected it to the street in the rear.

He crossed the street as he drew closer to his own house. He slowed his pace, scanning the houses ahead of him to detect anyone who might be observing his approach. Satisfied with his inspection, he turned off the street at Number 10 and walked swiftly out of sight down the secluded alleyway.

From the alleyway, his view of the street and especially his own house was excellent. As he moved forward to gain the best vantage point, his eyes stopped on his front door. A wreath was hanging there, stark and huge and ominously black against the door. That must be Olivia's idea, he told himself with a grimace. Knowing what it had probably cost, he smiled as he thought how furious she would be if she knew that he was across the street, deprecating it.

Edward scrutinized the scene carefully. No one approached from either direction, but several coaches stood between his house and the church which was some five hundred yards away. The coachmen had gathered into a small, garrulous group not far from the gate which led into the church. Edward could see them talking to one another; occasionally, their voices carried as far as his hiding place.

He had just turned his gaze from the coachmen when he froze to attention: the door of his house was opening. People began coming out singly and in pairs, making their way toward the church. At this distance, and with the added distraction of sunlight reflected from the windows, identification was difficult. He did recognize Mrs. Walpole, however, and Thomas at her side.

The main portion of the procession was filing into the church when a carriage rolled swiftly down the street. It stopped before Edward's house. A woman stepped out, simply but elegantly dressed. She looked first at the house and then at the church; seeing the end of the procession, she waved her coachman forward and stood against the wall as if waiting to be the last one inside the church.

It was Ellen, he knew at a glance. She looked so fragile, standing there in her dark costume outlined by the sunlight. A sudden remorse assailed him. As he watched her, he was painfully conscious of how attractive she was and how much he would like to step out of this ridiculous costume and take her away with him. He reassured himself that there would be time for that later; just then the door of his house opened again.

Down the steps, followed closely by his servant Richards and his wife's companion Mrs. Goodson, came Olivia, in bright blue silk. She was not smiling, but she was definitely not mourning—she looks positively triumphant, he thought. That frump! Wearing a dress like that to a funeral, to my funeral. Whatever has gotten into her?

He saw Ellen cover her face and press herself close to the wall until Olivia had passed. As she rearranged her scarf and started after this last group, he noticed something bright sparkle, fall, and roll into the gutter.

Edward realized that he could not hope to speak to Ellen now, but he was determined to recover whatever it was she had dropped. He would present it to her as a surprise when she came to join him in the north. Once she had passed through the churchyard gate, Edward crept cautiously toward the place where she had been standing. It was not until he had reached the street that he caught sight of a real scavenger moving rapidly in the same direction. Realizing that the other man must have seen what happened, Edward began to run toward the bright object.

He reached it first and seized what Ellen had dropped; it was the emerald brooch he had given her so long ago in France. He stuffed it into his pocket. As he turned, he felt a violent pain in his side. With the breath knocked out of him, in an instant of helpless but brilliant clarity, he watched the other man's foot draw back, ready to deal him another blow. His vision clouded, and he was barely able to jerk himself to one side as the scavenger kicked again.

Edward drew his breath in shuddering gasps and lashed out at the man with a sudden rain of blows.

They might as well have fallen on stone. The scavenger, although thin, was tough and strong and cunning; he circled warily around Edward, looking for an unprotected spot to gouge or kick again. Edward realized that he was fighting for his life against this man who would kill for such a treasure.

The scavenger caught Edward's fist on an upraised arm, and kicked out viciously. The blow caught Edward on the shin, and, as Edward bent forward in agony, the scavenger brought his clasped hands down on Edward's neck, knocking him flat on the cobblestones.

With his last bit of strength, Edward clutched blindly at the man's hands as they tore his pocket. Holding on grimly, he twisted and rolled over on his side, pulling the scavenger off his feet. The man snarled and pulled back his knee to deliver another blow.

Just then a hand reached down, took the scavenger by the collar, and shook him so hard that Edward could hear his neck crack. The hand loosened, and the scavenger dropped on the cobblestones and lay still.

"So, my dearies, fighting in the streets, are you?" asked the constable. "Usually you've got more sense than to brawl about where quality lives. What is it this time?"

He looked enormous looming over them; his shoes were almost as wide as the span of Edward's hand. When both men on the ground remained silent, a hand like a beam end descended.

The burly man picked up the scavenger and cuffed him until he blubbered and squeaked in helpless terror.

"What's this all about?" the burly man repeated.

"I'll tell you," sobbed the scavenger, twisting from side to side, trying to relieve the fierce pressure on his throat. "I found a pin, but he knocked me down and stole if from me just when you came up. I was going to turn it in and get a reward."

"Get a nice reward, eh? Turn it in like a little gentleman, eh? You lyin' whoreson, you wouldn't give a shoe back to a blind beggar."

The man cuffed the scavenger again and dropped him to the street. He turned his attention to Edward, his hands opening and closing like the gills of a fish.

"Give it 'ere, you."

Edward had risen to his feet. He moved back slightly, trying to keep a safe distance from those formidable paws.

"I haven't got anything," he said.

"Ha!" grunted the man. "That's a fat lie. Give it to me."

"Look," Edward said desperately, "it's mine. I can even tell you what's written on the back. It says, 'Ellen, from Edward.' "

After Edward finished speaking, the man uttered a low, disbelieving whistle. He reached out with a lunge and grasped Edward by the jacket.

"Give it to me, before I make a proper mess of you!"

Edward squirmed in the man's relentless grasp and kicked fiercely at his shin. His foot connected, and he jerked himself free as he felt the grip on his coat weaken.

"Balmy, that's what," the huge man hissed. His hand slid inside his jacket and reappeared with a short, heavy club. "Give it 'ere, you crazy bastard, or I'll bash you about wi' this till you've only a hole for a head."

Edward turned to run, but before he could take more than a step, the man brought the club down on Edward's arm.

The blow struck a nerve, and Edward gasped with the sudden shock. In the next moment, the man had jumped on him and battered him to the street. Blows rained on his head and face and neck and body in swift succession. Edward tried desperately to crawl free, but the huge man was merciless; he kept one great knee on Edward's back while his club beat on him relentlessly.

"Balmy," Edward could hear the man muttering to himself as he began a new series of blows. "The streets'll be safer with this one gone."

With one agonizing effort, Edward kicked out, and his foot caught the man in the side. As the other's head bent toward him, Edward twisted and lashed up with every particle of strength he had left. His fist caught the man on the jaw, and the burly man grunted and rolled over onto the cobblestones. Edward stumbled to his feet. He saw the scavenger disappear into an alley. Just as Edward broke into a stumbling run to follow him, the club bit savagely into his shoulder.

Edward's eyes closed, and a great wave of blood and sickness rose inside him. The cobblestones pressed against his face as he sagged down on them. He felt a hand tearing at his pocket. When he tried to reach out, the pain welled up inside him again and spilled over into his eyes; his hand trembled, but he could not move it. Slowly his fingers relaxed until they were quite flat against the cobblestones. His eyes closed, and a sigh stirred his body for a moment; then he was quiet, motionless on the cobblestones.

The huge man's eyes brightened when they saw the brooch. He placed it in his pocket after a quick inspection and then looked up and down the street.

He saw a wagon approaching, waited until it had reached him, then put up his hand to halt it. He loaded Edward's unconscious body into the back, then seated himself beside the nervous driver.

After a twisting ride through the streets, the wagon passed beneath an arch and pulled up in front of a long, two-storied building. The driver sat rigidly in his place until the huge man had pulled Edward's body off the back and motioned him forward.

As soon as he had been released, the driver whipped his horses; and when he had passed under the arch again, he wiped his face nervously with his sleeve.

Slinging Edward over one shoulder, the burly man walked inside the building and stopped at the desk inside the door. He dumped his burden down on the floor before the startled clerk and wiped his forehead, grinning.

"This one's quality, Jack. That would make him worth more than the ten shillings you give for the ordinary kind. This one gives fine jewels to ladies, he does. Strong as a bull, too. He gave me a bad time."

The clerk reached into his drawer and pulled out a purse, from which he carefully extracted ten shillings.

"There," he said. "Don't bring any more today. We can't take care of the ones we've got already."

"All right, Jack, all right. It's me duty as constable to pick these balmies off the streets when I find them; but if you say so, I'll bring no more today. Be certain you tell the doctors that this one's strong." The man flicked Edward over onto his face with his toe.

"They're all the same here, weak or strong," the sad-faced clerk answered. "Once they're chained up, they're all alike, gentle as babies."

The burly man shrugged, pocketed his shillings, and walked out. The clerk called out, and several shabbily dressed men shuffled into the room. Without a word, they seized Edward's arms and shoulders and dragged him like a sack of grain, disappearing down a long corridor.

The clerk picked up a quill and in the ledger before him wrote carefully:

December 14, 1777. Man, about 35, black haired, fair complected. No papers. Scavenger. Committed as insane. Corridor 3, No. 321064, Bedlam.

EPILOGUE

St. MARTIN'S CHAPEL, LONDON

Dear Brother Francis,

Our Lord works in most mysterious ways! Alleluia!

I cannot yet believe the wonder of it.

Last week, on my usual visit to those poor suffering creatures of His who are herded together in Bedlam, one of them, filthy and bloody of face, suddenly rose to his knees and seized my hand. The guards who accompany me on my round surged forward with their clubs raised, but I waved them back as I closed my hand around the paper he had put in it.

Leaning down to comfort him, I heard him whisper, "Wharton, 6 Cavendish Square," a phrase he repeated and repeated till it seemed like a prayer.

When I left Bedlam I went to Cavendish Square and did meet a Mr. Wharton to whom I gave the paper the Bedlamite had given me. Most affected was this gentleman, suddenly all aquiver with tears in his eyes. He did question me briefly, asked me to return in a week, and pressed money upon me to further the work of the Church.

Since he had asked me to do so, I returned to Mr. Wharton's. He received me most kindly and, as I left, handed me an envelope with words of thanks and gratitude.

In my study, I opened the envelope and sat at my desk, too amazed to count what it contained.

So, dear Brother Francis, we can now have the new roof we need for the chapel.

The Lord surely works in mysterious ways!

—Brother Richard